CLIFFHAVEN

A. M. GRIMM

LILAC LAKE PRESS

CHAPTER 1

hen Elizabeth Watson came face to face with a rusty shotgun, she had no one to turn to. There was no musclebound hero swooping in to save her, no fairy godmother waving her wand to make the danger disappear. There was only Elizabeth. But in all her twenty-six years, she'd never had a hero by her side, so she'd learned to go without.

"I've got you now, you son-of-a-bitch!" The angry, grating voice pierced the night.

Her hands flew into the air in a sign of surrender as her heart stuttered in her chest. The man with the shotgun was on the other side of a tall iron gate, and the barrel of the gun poked through the bars, pointing directly at her chest. Before the arrival of the man and the gun, she'd debated climbing the gate to reach the other side. Now that seemed like a profoundly insane idea.

Typically, she sought to reason with people, to find middle ground and make peace. With her soft brown eyes and round, kind face, she was usually successful. Then again, she'd never tried to reason with a gun.

Rain pounded onto her, dripping from the ends of her hair

and plastering her jeans to her thighs. It was the darkest part of night, and the only light came from a lantern swinging from the crook of the man's skinny elbow. They were surrounded by forest, a dense wilderness so wild, so far from safety. The only civilization for miles was behind that iron gate, past the shotgun.

"You're trespassing!" The man was old, bent, and disheveled, but he held the shotgun as if he slept with it cradled in his arms.

Her eyes riveted on that steel barrel. If she ran, would he pull the trigger?

"I'm supposed to be here. At least, I think—"

The old man sneered, his eyes sweeping from her sodden trainers to her bedraggled, unruly curls. "You don't belong here." He shoved the barrel forward, jabbing her shoulder, rocking her back.

Her eyes narrowed, and her jaw clenched. An electric rush of adrenaline pumped through her veins, fueling her body to answer the ancient question—fight or flight? She'd spent years fleeing, running from place to place, trying to make a home wherever she found herself and never quite succeeding. She'd never fought, not once, so the anger surging through her took her completely by surprise.

Really, what did she have to lose?

"Get that gun out of my face." She swept her arm under the barrel, directing it into the night sky. The man's beady eyes widened in surprise, and his fingers tightened on the stock. "Is this Cliffhaven?"

"Yeah." The man leaned closer, exposing a gaunt face that was grizzled, unshaven, and scored with deep lines. Rain dripped off his dirty cap, and he scowled as if the expression was a permanent fixture on his face. "What's your business here?"

"I'm Elizabeth Watson." He only glared at her, so she added, "The conservator? Caroline Arrington hired me."

2

"You that fancy art restorer?"

She nodded, and after a tense silence, he swung the shotgun onto his shoulder. With the barrel facing the opposite direction, she could breathe again.

"You were supposed to be here this afternoon." His voice rasped like he'd spent a lifetime smoking and yelling at women in the rain.

"I got lost. My phone doesn't get a signal up here."

"Heard they was hiring an art restorer. Never thought they'd get a woman for the job."

Her hands balled into fists. "I'm not sure what my gender has to do with it."

"No offense meant." He raked his eyes up and down her length, over her strong build and generous curves. "Just wasn't what I was expecting."

She folded her arms across her breasts. "And who are you, if I may ask?"

"Caretaker. Name's Meeks."

"Will you please open the gate?"

His black-eyed glare fixed on her for a long moment. "Gates are closed after dark. Come back tomorrow."

"I can't. My car's stuck in the mud on this godforsaken track. Everything I own is in that car." She rubbed her forehead. After driving nineteen hours with only a brief nap in the backseat of her car, the last thing she needed was to convince a man with a gun that she belonged there. "Please, just let me through the gate. Caroline's expecting me."

"If I was you, I'd go back to your car. Wait 'til morning."

"But it's midnight! I can't spend the night in the middle of the woods."

"Safer than wandering around Cliffhaven at night."

"Safer?" She peered past Meeks to where the driveway disappeared into darkness. "But I'm supposed to be staying at the house for a few weeks while I work." She needed free room and board, was counting on it.

His bushy, gray eyebrows raised, and he snorted skeptically. "Staying in the house? Alone with Mr. Arrington?"

"Look, I was supposed to meet Caroline here earlier today. I'm already late." She wrapped her fingers around the cold iron bars of the gate, bringing her face close to his. "I can't lose this job."

He spit onto the gravel drive. "Come back tomorrow. It's for your own good." Then he turned and stepped away from the gate.

"Please," she said, her voice breaking on the word. She closed her eyes, willing away the tears that threatened. In the wake of their confrontation, the ferocity that fueled her defiance drained away. She was just a young woman, friendless in a foreign place, with exhaustion weighing on her limbs like lead. "I don't have anywhere else to go."

He turned back and eyed her. For a moment, it looked as if he might leave her there, soaking wet and shivering in the dark forest. But then he shuffled back to the gate, pulling a massive iron keyring from his pocket. He rejected several heavy keys before selecting one and fitting it in the lock.

Her whole body sagged in relief. She could still make it to the house, apologize profusely for her late arrival, and, if she were lucky, keep this job.

"Some folks don't know what's good for them," Meeks grunted. The colossal gate swung open, the hinges creaking like something from a horror movie.

Elizabeth stepped through the opening, giving the scowling man a wide berth, then ran a shaking hand through her tangled curls. She'd never faced a gun before. Had she really just knocked it away like it was a fly and not a lethal weapon? What an insanely stupid thing to do.

"Do you always point guns at strangers?"

"Just doing my job. Someone was sneaking around here last night. Thought they might be back." He gave her a sharp, sidelong look. "Didn't expect an art restorer to show up in the middle of the night, and without a car."

"I told you, it's stuck in the mud."

Meeks shuffled away with a gait that was surprisingly quick for a man of his apparent age, leading the way down a narrow, overgrown path that might once have been a driveway. The gravel was thin and sparse on the sandy soil. She peered down the lane, but it disappeared into darkness, swallowed by the surrounding forest.

"Stay close," he barked over his shoulder. "I don't want no trouble if you get lost in the forest, or the wolves get you."

Her hands fluttered to her mouth. "There are wolves?"

Her gaze swept the black forest, and her body curled inward, as if to make a smaller target. She'd never known the profound isolation of being alone in the wilderness, so far from any safe haven. The wilderness was alien to her, its sights and smells and creatures unknown, and she had a vivid imagination. After the noise and bustle of New Orleans, this profound silence, the complete darkness, made her want to bolt in the opposite direction.

She'd left New Orleans the same way she always left her current residence—in a hurry. Though she was used to moving from place to place, accustomed to packing her meager possessions in whatever receptacle was available and leaving (sometimes in the dead of night), it had been a while since she'd left amid such turmoil, leaving so much chaos behind her.

There was no denying it. She'd messed up in New Orleans. Spectacularly. And her life had just . . . imploded. There'd been scandal. Ruin.

She'd run from New Orleans so far, so fast, and now it all threatened to catch up with her at once—the exhaustion, the shame. That's what happened when you stayed in one place too long, got too attached to people and places that weren't permanent. She should've learned that lesson long ago. Getting close to people wasn't worth the cost, the pain it caused when they hurt you.

This job would be exactly what she needed—a new place, new people, new work she could lose herself in. The perfect escape. And this isolated island off Michigan's upper peninsula was about as far from sunny New Orleans as she could imagine.

She'd been hired by Caroline, a woman she'd never met, after an online interview. Only now, as she hiked through the freezing rain contemplating Meeks's shotgun, did she question the wisdom of accepting a job offered by a stranger.

In truth, she'd had little choice. She had no income, but that didn't stop the interest on her student loans from compounding in a way that was, to her, obscene. She'd had to take the first job she could find.

She hadn't realized the island that would be her home for the coming weeks was so isolated. As she'd driven further north, the towns became smaller and farther apart, separated by vast swaths of forest, giving the impression she'd left civilization behind. A ferry carrying cars and passengers across Lake Superior was the only way to the island, the dockworkers had assured her, at least until the waters froze.

"You coming or not?" Meeks threw the words over his shoulder, not bothering to stop and wait.

Wrapping her sodden cardigan around her shoulders, she shivered and quickened her step. Blackberry bushes and tree limbs invaded the narrow gravel drive on either side, where forest threatened to overtake what man had carved out of the wilderness. The air smelled of rain-soaked earth, of the evergreen needles that littered the forest floor—the scent of the wild.

At the edge of the forest the trees parted, revealing a long stretch of lawn. Looking down the sloping hill at the view before her, Elizabeth stumbled, her eyes widening as she stared.

At the base of the hill, the lawn ended at a sprawling mansion, at first only an immense shadow on the landscape. She blinked rapidly, then gave a slow, disbelieving shake of her head. Caroline had said the house was large, but this was the size of Buckingham Palace. Most of the massive building lay in shadow, the details obscured by the dark and driving rain.

Meeks continued down the sloping hill toward the house, his lantern bobbing from the crook of his elbow, shotgun tucked into his armpit, barrel facing the ground.

As she approached the mansion, signs of its neglect became obvious. The roof sagged, and overgrown grass brushed the stone facade. An elaborate fountain that might once have been grand stood in the center of the driveway, crumbling to ruin, filled with muck. The estate had been utterly abandoned, and for some reason she couldn't fathom, the sight of it caused her throat to thicken.

Every window was dark. She was late, hours late, but was no one there to greet her? "It doesn't seem like anyone's home."

"He's home all right."

"He?"

Meeks glanced at her. "Miss Caroline must've warned you about Mr. Arrington."

"Do you mean Caroline's brother?"

Then, as if their conversation had conjured it, a light appeared in a first-floor window at the western end of the house. Elizabeth blew out a relieved breath and followed Meeks up the stone steps to the entryway, flanked by massive pillars. Meeks thrust a gnarled hand deep into the pocket of his dirty raincoat and produced the heavy iron keyring.

She eyed the sculptural iron knocker on the gargantuan door. "Shouldn't we knock?"

Meeks's scowl deepened. "He won't answer."

As his arthritic fingers fumbled through the keys, she rubbed her arms against the cold, trying to squash the doubts and fears that sprang up like weeds. She couldn't shake the feeling someone watched her, silent and malevolent in the darkness. She folded her arms across her chest protectively, scanning the grounds around the house for signs of life. The shadows cast by overgrown trees lining the drive provided so many places a man could hide.

Meeks fitted a key into the lock, and the metal hinges creaked as the front door swung open. He gestured toward the open door. "In you go, if you're so hell-bent on getting in tonight."

She peered into the house, but the light from Meeks's lantern barely penetrated the gloom.

"Come on, come on," he grumbled. "Haven't got all night."

As she crossed the threshold of Cliffhaven, Elizabeth shivered, as if cold hands danced across her bare flesh. She'd entered a great hall, and it was like stepping into a cave—dark, damp, and sonorous.

"Miss Caroline will be back in the morning," Meeks said, still standing outside.

Her breath caught. "She's not here?"

"Nope." He held the lantern aloft with a scowl. "I'd say good night, but I can't imagine that's what you'll have in there." He nodded toward the house then turned away.

"Wait!" She clutched the door frame. *Don't leave me.* "Would you mind showing me to my room?"

"I'm not going in there." His voice was shrill, and he shrank away from the doorway. "Your room's on the first floor. Behind the staircase, corridor to the right, at the end of the hall." Rather than meet her eye, his gaze shifted over the stone facade of the mansion as if he expected it to spring to life and attack. "Go to your room. Stay there."

8

"What about Caroline's brother?" She looked back into the house, searching for some sign of habitation, finding none.

Meeks nodded, his squinty eyes peering through the rain at the darkened house. "He's in there somewhere. And I'd stay out of his way if I was you." He frowned. "Don't know what Miss Caroline was thinking, having you stay here alone with Mr. Arrington. Well, that isn't my business. Not my responsibility." He shook his head, as if eternally disappointed by the stupidity of others, and grasped the doorknob.

"At least leave me your—" The door slammed shut, plunging her into complete darkness. "Light," she finished, her voice weak.

She pulled her phone from the pocket of her messenger bag, turned on the flashlight, and aimed the tiny beam of white light around the room. The cavernous hall was empty except for broken furniture littering the stone floor. The smell of damp, rot, and something foul permeated the air.

Why hadn't Meeks wanted to enter the house? Did the fear that flashed across his face have anything to do with Caroline's brother?

As she took small, tentative steps across the stone floor, she recalled the strange way Caroline had ended their interview. *One last thing. During your stay at Cliffhaven, please don't seek out my brother. I know that sounds strange, but he's lived alone at Cliffhaven for years, and he's become . . . a little odd.*

At the time, Elizabeth hadn't given it a second thought. She'd assumed Caroline's brother was one of those harmless hermitic men—too occupied with their own lives to tolerate interruptions from others—and had reassured Caroline she would stay out of his way. Now, as she crept through the dark mansion, alternatives occurred to her, each darker than the last. Maybe he was . . . disturbed. Or a murderer, preying upon innocent young women who blunder through his house at night.

Her throat dry as dust, she inched forward into the center of the vast hall, hearing only the creaking of the old house and the wind whistling outside. She crept forward, her body tense and tight, ready to run at the slightest provocation.

Just find your room and stay there until morning.

At the back of the hall, a grand double staircase wound its way up, both ends disappearing into the gloom. What had Meeks said? Her room was behind the staircase, at the end of the corridor.

She crept past the magnificent stairs, where a black corridor stretched out on either side. Was it right or left? She held her breath, turned left, and made her way down the hallway.

As she moved through the silent house, anxiety settled upon her like a cloak. The mansion was empty and desolate, like a grand mausoleum.

The corridor was just as neglected and ruined as the hall. Cobwebs hung from the corners. Everything was coated with a thin layer of black residue—it covered the dusty carpet, the walls, even the wooden doorframes. She reached one tentative finger to touch the wallpaper, which was peeling off in large strips, and her finger came away smudged with the dark substance. Was it ash?

She aimed her light down the hallway, illuminating an open door. It was an enormous bedchamber, complete with a massive four-poster bed and a sagging mattress, but the room was in complete disarray. Furniture lay broken in fragments, as if destroyed in some violent frenzy. In one dark corner, a cheval mirror stood elegantly on an antique frame, but the glass was shattered. The room wasn't fit for human habitation, but when her light fell on the bed, it illuminated a set of man's clothes laid out neatly, waiting for someone to return.

She recoiled, then retreated to the corridor, shutting the door behind her. What kind of man would live in this dark and dismal place?

She pulled her keys from her pocket, selected a travel-sized vial of pepper spray that dangled from her keyring, and removed its cap. Taking a deep breath, she continued down the passageway with soft, silent steps.

At the end of the corridor was a set of wooden doors, intricately carved, depicting the lives of wolves in every aspect— howling at a wooden moon, banded together on rocky cliffs, sleeping in tall grass. *Incredible.* The doors were damaged, the wood cracked and covered with the same dark residue as the walls of the corridor. She reached into her messenger bag for her magnifiers, then pulled back, shaking her head. Work would have to wait.

Hadn't Meeks said her room was at the end of the corridor? This had to be it.

When she knocked on the door, it opened under her touch. She peered inside, where dim light glowed from the far corner of the vast room.

"Hello?" Her voice was small and unsure.

She slid into the room, and the feeling of being watched, being unwelcome, overcame her. Only the gentlest flickers of light glowed between the shadows. Several tattered armchairs covered in blood-red velvet sat in front of the largest fireplace she'd ever seen. The remnants of a fire still burned there, but the edges of the room remained hidden in a circle of darkness where nothing stirred.

"Caroline? Mr. Arrington?"

She was drawn to a small circle of golden light provided by three tapered candles burning in a brass candelabrum. The candlelight illuminated the walls on either side, revealing floor-to-ceiling shelves containing thousands of books.

Though it wasn't the bedroom she'd sought, the tension in Elizabeth's shoulders melted away as her eyes fell on familiar titles. *Janson's History of Art, Classical Art From Greece to Rome.* It was a treasure trove of books about art, and their presence was as reassuring as old friends. She stood quietly, a small smile curving her lips, and then she spied an intriguing title: *Women, Art, and Society.*

As she reached high above her head, straining to grasp the book that was just out of reach, a sound filled the darkness. The telltale creak of a floorboard turned her body to stone. She stood, frozen in this vulnerable position—stretching beyond her capacity, straining her ears to hear any sound. The floor creaked again, suffering from what could only be the weight of another person.

"Who's there?" Her voice sounded tremulous even to her own ears.

There was only silence. A deep, vast silence in which her fear seemed to echo and multiply. Then the shadows just beyond the candlelight shifted, revealing a human form.

And Elizabeth knew.

Caroline's brother was here—hiding in the shadows, watching from the dark.

CHAPTER 2

The shadow in the darkness took shape as the man stepped into the edges of the dim candlelight. He was built like a gladiator—towering and powerful—surely capable of snapping her like a twig. She must have made a sound, some involuntary expression of the awe that burned inside her like a brand, because he drew back.

Then he stood, half-visible in the candlelight, silent and staring.

"What are you doing here?" His voice was deep, the sound of it staccato and strangely quiet for all the suspicion it conveyed.

"I'm Elizabeth." She pulled her hands back to her chest, where they curled around each other. "The art restorer. Caroline hired me."

"I know who you are. Why are you in *here?*"

He paced, his body tense and wary, like a prowling wolf caught in a spotlight. He kept to the shadows at the edge of the candlelight, where she could barely make out his features.

"Meeks let me in. I was looking for my room, but I must have gone the wrong way."

She struggled to school her expression, to mask the fear this man inspired.

He watched her, his frown deepening. "You don't belong here." His voice, quiet and cold, cut through the air.

Pain, old and familiar, tightened her throat. No matter how many times she heard those words, they always hurt.

"You're right, I'm sorry. I was just admiring your books." She gestured toward the shelves, and her flailing hand knocked over the candelabrum, sending it hurtling off the desk.

As the candles fell toward the edge of a velvet curtain, she gasped, but the flames bounced harmlessly against the wooden floor and were extinguished. Letting out a sigh of relief, she looked up, ready to apologize again for her clumsiness, and saw that the man before her was completely undone.

He dove toward the fallen candles on his knees, his body taut with anxiety as he frantically searched for any sign of flame. When he found none, he glared up at her accusingly, and his entire face was finally visible in the dim light.

She drew in a quick, startled breath. His face was made up of two parts, each shockingly different. On one side, the skin was flawless—perfectly sculpted, undeniably handsome. But on the other, the skin was scarred and discolored, as if someone had painted a wine-colored phantom's mask across his upper cheek and forehead. The damaged skin was textured, like melted candle wax. His face was a juxtaposition of texture, color, and emotion—a face made to be sketched, to be painted. Raven-black hair framed that face, brushing his collar. His eyes were green—emerald-bright and shining with fury.

She stepped backward, away from his anger, and tried to suppress the shock and fear she knew was written all over her face.

Still kneeling, he picked up the lifeless candles with shaking hands. "Get out."

Her mouth opened to speak words of reconciliation, but no

sound escaped. He looked up at her, emotions flickering across his features in quick succession—anger, desperation, and shame. He brandished a candle toward the door and roared, "Get out!"

Her heart stuttered in her chest. This man's powerful voice, raised in anger, banished all logical thought, triggering flight. *Calm down,* she told herself, fighting the panic. *You're not a child. You're safe.*

But her traitorous body had a life of its own, divorced from her reasoning mind, and it was fleeing, running from the library, through the dark house, and out the front door.

Outside, the rain and wind slapped at her face, mocking her cowardice. She might have kept running down the drive and through the forest, except that she ran headlong into an immovable object.

The soft figure grunted as it slammed against a marble pillar. In her panic, Elizabeth slipped on the wet stone, tumbling onto her back. Pain jolted through her, and she lay on the cold stone, rain beating down upon her face, fresh and cool against her burning skin.

"Are you okay?" A pale, heart-shaped face floated above her, the sea-green eyes familiar.

"Caroline?" Relief flooded through her. It didn't matter that she barely knew her employer, that they'd never met in person. In that moment, just seeing a friendly face was everything.

"I'm so sorry! Are you all right?" Caroline said, reaching out her hand.

Elizabeth used it to scramble to her feet. "No harm done."

Caroline stepped back, her lips curving up in a tentative smile. She was an attractive woman a few years older, probably in her mid-thirties, and tall—several inches above her own five foot seven. Her strawberry-blonde hair fell loose in a sharp bob at her shoulders. Her body was toned, sleek, and athletic—exactly the type that usually made Elizabeth self-conscious of her well-rounded frame. But when Caroline smiled, Elizabeth felt warm and welcome.

"You made it. I'd almost given up on you," Caroline said. Her trench coat gaped, revealing pink pajamas with kittens gamboling across the flannel, the legs tucked into sturdy rain boots.

"I'm sorry I'm late. I tried to text you, but my phone doesn't get service this far north."

"That's all right. It's so nice to finally meet you!" Caroline swept her into a hug. Elizabeth stiffened, her arms pressed against her sides, her face frozen in surprise, until Caroline let go. The embrace intensified the urge to run that still pumped through her limbs.

"Sorry," Caroline said, her smile sheepish. "I guess you're not a hugger. I'll try to remember that."

"That's okay. I'm just not used to it."

"I called Meeks to check in, and he said he'd let you in the house. I pictured you wandering around Cliffhaven in the dark, and I thought I'd better come up." Caroline's smile faltered. "Are you all right?"

Elizabeth closed her eyes, swallowing hard, as if she could force the urge to run down her throat. "I'm fine."

But the worried look hadn't left Caroline's eyes. "You ran into Adam, didn't you?"

Yeah. He caught me poking through his room, touching his books. And I almost set the house on fire.

Elizabeth ran her hand through her thick, russet curls, still wet with rain. "I tried to find my room, but I must have gone the wrong way."

Caroline's shoulders slumped. "What did he do?"

"Just asked me to leave. But he was angry."

"Well, you had to meet him at some point. Adam can be difficult, but that's because he hasn't spent much time around people lately. He just needs to get used to sharing his space, and he'll be fine." Caroline sounded confident, but as she looked up at the mansion's crumbling facade, worry marred her pretty face.

Doubt opened a black hole in Elizabeth's stomach. "He doesn't want me here."

"To be honest, he was never on board with hiring a restoration expert. But we need to know if this house is worth saving." Caroline tightened the belt on her rose-colored trench coat with nervous fingers. "Anyway, you must be exhausted. Let me show you to your room, and we can reassess in the morning."

Reassess? What did that mean? Had she driven nineteen hours with everything she owned packed in her car, only to be told there was no job?

Caroline ushered her back into the great hall, where the smell of rot and abandonment was suffocating. Did she even want this job? Was she that desperate?

Yes. Yes, she was.

That's what happened when your career was in shambles, when you let your personal life interfere with your professional life. Now she needed to redeem herself, needed to succeed on one big project to make everyone forget her failure. If she could succeed at work, surely that would plug the hole in her heart, stabilize her life that seemed so precarious.

Caroline opened the drawer on a marble-topped side table and rummaged through it. "Where do they keep the damn candles? Aha!" She held up a white taper and a brass holder. After fishing out a box of matches, she lit the wick.

"You guys must really like candles."

"There's no electricity in this part of the house." Caroline's eyes were apologetic before they flicked down to stare at the stone floor. "There's a generator for the necessary functions, the kitchen and all that, but I'm afraid we use candles and lamps for most rooms."

Elizabeth stifled a groan. No electricity would make her job that much harder—examining art by the light of the sun, only during the day? But the candlelight was soft as it illuminated Caroline's kind, nervous face, and she didn't want to add to the worry wrinkling the corners of her eyes. "It's romantic."

"Or gloomy, depending on your point of view." Caroline gestured to the grand double staircase. "Your room is on the second floor."

Elizabeth drew a deep, steadying breath and followed Caroline up the stairs. Their feet thumped on the bare wood, throwing up dust.

"The house is in rough condition." Caroline's fingers left a trail in the dust on the banister as they climbed. "But I didn't want to spend more money on it until we know if it's worth saving. The truth is, we've had an offer of sale for Cliffhaven. They want to knock down the house, build a luxury resort or something. And I just don't know what to do."

The stairs creaked under Elizabeth's feet, and she wondered if they were structurally sound. "I'm not really an expert in the restoration of buildings."

"I know." Caroline ran a hand through her strawberry-blonde bob, looking lost. "I thought it would help to bring an expert in—someone to help me figure out what to do with all this. And after the interview, I knew you were the one."

Again, Elizabeth found herself wanting to help Caroline, to banish the haunted look from her eyes. "After I've examined the art, I can estimate its value, tell you what it would cost to restore. Maybe that will help you make your decision."

"That's the plan. But it isn't just about the numbers. There are . . . other considerations." Caroline lifted a hand to her lips as if afraid something might escape them.

They reached the second floor, stepping onto a gallery that wrapped around the grand foyer. The light from Caroline's candle flickered as she turned to face a corridor shrouded in gloom.

"God, this is dismal." Caroline's face was ashen as she pressed closer to Elizabeth. Together, they walked down the dim hallway, past a child's broken rocking horse. Dust covered the floor like a carpet.

Rows of lamps lined the corridor, affixed to the wall—sculptural sconces with varying metal tones. Elizabeth approached them, squinting in the dim light.

Caroline paused, the candlelight casting shadows on her face. "Are those sconces anything special?"

"It's damascene." At Caroline's quizzical look, she added, "That's where they inlay metal into metal to create these intricate designs. That scrolling pattern was cut into the steel, then the copper was hammered into the carved areas."

She ran her finger over the fine metalwork. The pattern cut into the substrate metal was intricate, very fine. The carving of such a hard metal must have been laborious, but the result was sharp, clean—a masterful example of the technique. "These could be valuable." *Very* valuable.

"Really? I had no idea." Caroline held her candle higher, inspecting the lamps as if for the first time. "When my great-grandfather built the house, he wanted every piece to be a work of art."

Elizabeth gave the sconce one last caress. "I've never seen copper used quite like that."

Caroline frowned, and sadness colored her light green eyes. "Copper was important to my family." Then she opened a heavy oak door and gestured for Elizabeth to lead the way.

It was like stepping into the eighteenth century. The chamber was large, dominated by an oversized four-poster, canopied bed. The furniture was Jacobean—heavy, dark wood carved with intricate geometric motifs. An enormous fireplace was set with logs and tinder, but nothing burned in the hearth. A bookshelf covered the rest of the wall by the fireplace, filled with leather-bound tomes and a selection of crystal vases, and a crimson velvet chaise lounged beneath. The jacquard wallpaper was intricate, with swirling flowers that looked like faces, complete with eyes staring back at her.

Her gaze fell to the carpet, and an electric thrill travelled up her spine. She knelt, hardly daring to touch the threads. "This carpet. Is it Savonnerie?"

Caroline tilted her head, looking baffled. "I don't know. Is that a brand?"

"It was a manufactory in Europe during the seventeenth century. Very prestigious." She stroked the intricate knotting. It was surely made in the Savonnerie style, with multiple borders and the wool and silk knotted into a French design—framed medallions and bouquets of flowers against a deep blue ground. Was this another example of a priceless work of art, casually decorating the floor of this dusty chamber? Or simply a flawless fake?

She folded back the corner, examining the weave. Hadn't a Savonnerie sold for millions at an auction at Christie's last year?

Caroline laid the candleholder and box of matches on the dresser. "I know it's dreary, but you should have seen it before Mrs. Hodges—she's the housekeeper—cleaned."

"It's lovely. Elegant." Definitely grander than any place she'd ever called home. And there'd been more of those than she could count.

"And dilapidated. Thanks for being a good sport." Caroline smiled hesitantly. "I'll be back tomorrow morning. We're having a staff meeting at nine o'clock; you can meet everyone."

"You're not . . ." Elizabeth froze, her feet rooted to the floor by the dawning realization. "You don't live here."

"Not yet. I just returned to Cliffhaven a few days ago. I took one look around, then rented a furnished room in town." Caroline tilted her chin down, looking up at Elizabeth through her eyelashes, her kind face apologetic. "This is the first time I've been home in over ten years. When I offered you room and board, I had no idea the house was in such terrible condition. There's an inn in the village, if you prefer."

That would have been great, if it weren't for her mountain of student debt and miniscule bank account. *It's only for a week or two.*

"I'll be fine here." She leaned against one of the bed's thick posters.

"Well, you'll mostly have the house to yourself, anyway. Mrs. Hodges lives in the village, and Meeks is the only other help. He lives in the groundskeeper's cottage on the edge of the estate."

"So it will just be your brother and I, here in the house."

"I guess so." Caroline turned back to Elizabeth, a concerned look wrinkling her brow. "Look, I can tell you're uncomfortable. Maybe this was a mistake. Why don't you come back to my apartment with me, crash on my couch, and we'll reevaluate in the morning?"

"No," she said quickly. "This is fine. Posh, even. You should see some of the dumps I've lived in."

"I'll be back tomorrow for the staff meeting, then I can show you around." Now that the time had come, Caroline seemed hesitant to leave. "Goodnight, Elizabeth. Take care."

As Caroline stepped through the doorway, her eyes grazed the dark corners of the chamber as if afraid of what they might find there. Then she closed the door gently and was gone.

Alone in the vast bedchamber, Elizabeth's shoulders tightened. The air was colder here, and goosebumps rose on her skin. *Get a grip. You've stayed in worse places than this.*

She crossed to the heavy drapes, pulled them back to reveal large, leaded windows. The rain had stopped, and the moon's light shone on the back of the estate, where rolling lawn ended abruptly at an immense body of water. Was it Lake Superior, the largest of the Great Lakes that wrapped around the island? She stood at the window for a long moment, admiring the water stretching out as far as the eye could see—a dark blue horizon just visible in the moonlight.

The view of the lake tugged at her memory. Had her childhood home been near water? Her first foster home had been near Oregon's coast, and she remembered, so distantly, sitting in the sand on a beach, watching her foster siblings splash in the water, longing to join them. But it was like a wall stood between her and other children. Her side of the wall was safer, but so lonely.

She dropped the curtain and shuffled to the bed, letting her messenger bag slump to the floor. She flopped backward onto the mattress, not bothering to burrow into the soft duvet. The last few days had been exhausting, and she needed a minute's rest before trekking back to her car to get her suitcase. Just one moment to rest and try to make sense of the last twenty-four hours.

She pressed her palms to her eyes. Everything was a blur. First her flight from New Orleans, then the long, frantic drive north, then Meeks's shotgun. Knocking over the candles in the library. Caroline's brother watching from the dark.

He'd been in the library the entire time she'd been there. What kind of person kept to the shadows, spying on someone without making their presence known?

In any case, she'd blown her first impression. *We'll reevaluate in the morning.* Caroline had been nice about it, but after she talked to her brother, heard how the art conservator had almost burned the house down then run from the room like a frightened rabbit, she probably wouldn't have a job.

Tears stung her eyes. This work was supposed to be her escape, her redemption. But she hadn't really thought this through, had she? She'd just run, as fast and as far from her problems as she could get. And now here she was, at the northern edge of the world. There was nowhere left to run.

Wiping at her eyes, she fished her phone from the pocket of

her jeans. Still no signal. Without it, she was completely cut off from the outside world. Her chest constricted at the thought of being so vulnerable, so alone.

Not that there was anyone to call. But that was fine. Good, even. She didn't need the heartache of pining after someone when she was forced to move again, didn't need the misery of relationships falling apart. Sure, it might be nice to have a friend or lover listen as she poured out her heart, someone to embrace her and tell her it would be all right. But it wasn't worth the pain when the relationship fell apart, the misery of missing someone who was no longer there.

Her lips began to tremble. *No. Get a grip, Elizabeth.*

She didn't need friends. She didn't need family.

But the tears came in earnest, then—huge sobs that shook her body as she pressed her forehead into the pillow. She cried, alone in the dark room, until her tears were spent and she gave in to exhaustion.

Her last thought before sleep took her was of a solitary light burning in the window of the desolate mansion. Then she slept and dreamed of shadows and darkness.

CHAPTER 3

$\mathcal{I}$n the light of day, Cliffhaven's ominous aura of
desolation was gone—cleansed, perhaps, by the
sunlight streaming through broken stained-glass windows.
Elizabeth stepped through the grand foyer, a vast space dominated by the curving, elegant lines of the double staircase, and
marveled at the majestic marble columns supporting the
second-floor gallery.

There was beauty everywhere, but decay had left its mark.
The vaulted ceiling soared high above, marred by gaping holes
in the roof. The floor was cream-colored marble shot through
with the palest pink, but it was littered with layers of dirt and
debris. Cracks snaked through the walls, destroying plaster
medallions created by master craftsmen.

She sniffed at the subtle smell of rot that permeated the air,
shaking her head. Here was a place full of beauty and artistic
value, and it had been completely neglected. How could Caroline's brother live amidst it all and not do anything to protect it?
Perhaps the man cared nothing for beauty or art.

She glanced at her phone. Time for the staff meeting. Time
to find out if she still had a job. Following the smoky scent of

burnt coffee and the low sound of murmuring voices, she stepped through an open door behind the grand staircase.

Dim light filtered through dirty windows, illuminating an enormous kitchen built to feed a large household. One wall was lined with stoves and burners, all woefully out of date. In the center of the kitchen ran a long wooden island that might have been beautiful had it not been covered with a thick layer of dust and grime. Shelves and cabinets lined the walls, but more than one door hung askew, broken off its hinges. The countertops were filthy, and Elizabeth's sneakers were glued to the sticky floor.

"Elizabeth." Caroline, wearing sea-green scrubs that brought out her eyes, greeted her warmly. She looked tired, her eyes rimmed with red, as if she hadn't slept. "We're just waiting for Adam, then we can begin."

He was coming? A terrible fluttering bloomed in her stomach as she thought of the man who'd hidden in the shadows.

Meeks also occupied the kitchen, sitting at a farmhouse-style table on the edge of his chair, as if he might bolt any second. His features were clearer now, in the morning light— the grizzled beginnings of an unkept beard, the arthritic hands fisted around a wooly hat, the bushy eyebrows drawn low in a scowl. He shifted, clearly uncomfortable, and his eyes darted to the door.

"Can we get this started, Miss?" he said.

"If I can stand to be in this house day after day, you can take it for fifteen minutes."

This sharp voice came from a woman leaning against the stove, arms crossed over her chest. She was either middle-aged or life had marked her prematurely, gouging worry lines into her forehead and around her narrow lips. She was thin with a face that was all sharp angles and stress. Dull gray hair formed a frizzy halo around her pallid face, and she wore a stained apron over a limp sack of a dress that hung to the ground.

This was a cold woman. Not aggressive or hostile, just insular, protective, private. Qualities Elizabeth could understand, even approve of, though she noted how it kept the other occupants of the kitchen at a distance.

Caroline appeared at her elbow. "Elizabeth, this is Mrs. Hodges."

"The housekeeper." Elizabeth smiled. "Nice to meet you."

Hodges nodded once, her face somber.

"Mrs. Hodges has breakfast for you." Caroline's smile was too bright, as if she were trying to make up for the gloom that hung in the air. "She makes all Adam's meals, so one more person shouldn't be too difficult."

Hodges's mouth pressed into a thin line, so Elizabeth said, "Please don't go to any trouble."

"It's my job." Hodges dug around in the dirty refrigerator, which looked to be at least fifty years old, before pulling out an enormous tin can with a peeled-off label. She lifted the sharp edge of the can, which was already open, and scooped a foul-looking substance into a ceramic bowl. The one piece of modern equipment in the kitchen was a small microwave, which Hodges used to heat the bowl. For sixty seconds, she clicked her ragged fingernails against the soiled countertop until the microwave beeped in finality.

Elizabeth accepted the bowl, which held a porridge-like substance of a dubious brown color. The smell was revolting, but she managed a hesitant smile. "I really appreciate that, Mrs. Hodges. Thank you."

She took a seat next to Meeks at the farmhouse table. He massaged his knee, looking at her from under eyebrows that were gray and overgrown. "Towed your car out of the mud with the plow truck. It's out front."

"That was kind of you. Thanks."

He grunted. "You'll need better tires on that old heap before winter."

"I don't plan to be here this winter, Mr. Meeks."

As she moved her spoon through the gooey contents of her bowl, she contemplated the dirty, outdated kitchen. What kind of man was Caroline's brother, living in a place like this, tolerating the disorder and filth?

"I told Adam nine o'clock," Caroline said, frustration pinching her features. "We'll wait a few minutes. I'm sure he'll turn up."

Hodges dragged the chair next to Elizabeth across the floor and sat down, studying her. *Geez. Stare much?*

Meeks shifted in his seat and muttered, "Let's get this over with. Some of us have work to do."

"You just can't stand to be in here, can you?" Hodges sniffed, leaning toward her. "Old goat thinks the house is haunted."

"I wouldn't be surprised if it is," she said. If any place truly was haunted, it was surely this mansion, with its crumbling walls and abandoned corridors. They felt alive, watchful.

Hodges was looking at her again, an odd expression on her face. Heat flooded Elizabeth's cheeks, and she tried to smile, but Hodges kept staring, all frozen and silent, like Elizabeth was a particularly difficult calculus problem she was determined to solve.

Great. Now your coworkers think you're crazy, and it's only the first day.

The long pause became awkward, then Hodges leaned over, her face deadly serious, and raised one eyebrow. "You believe in ghosts?"

Elizabeth tried to laugh, but it came out weak and uncertain.

She had believed in ghosts, as a child. There had been a time when it was the only belief that kept her clinging to life—the idea that the ones we love go on after death. But that had been the desperate need of an orphaned child. She didn't *really* believe in ghosts. Though sometimes, in the dead of night, the child inside her wondered, doubted, feared.

She bent her head, her face flushed. "I don't know what I believe."

Hodges leaned forward, eyes fever-bright, and opened her mouth, but whatever she was going to say was lost when Caroline cleared her throat.

"I'm not waiting for Adam any longer." Caroline threw her hands in the air then took a deep breath. "Well, it's no secret that Cliffhaven has been neglected for some time. And now we're faced with the decision of what to do with it. We've been told that saving Cliffhaven is a lost cause, that it isn't worth the time and expense. But I just couldn't give up on it. So we've brought Ms. Watson—Elizabeth," Caroline shot her a quick smile, "to inspect the art in the house and give us her professional opinion about whether it's worth the time and money involved to restore. We hope you'll help her in this effort."

"I can save you some time, Miss Caroline," Meeks said, clutching his cap tighter in his fist, "and you can send this young lady back where she came from. This house should come down, and the sooner the better."

Caroline shook her head. "Really, Mr. Meeks, now is not the time."

Meeks pounded his fist on the table. "This place is cursed. First the fire, and now—"

"That's enough," Caroline said, her eyes darting to Elizabeth. "If you'll excuse us for a moment." She grabbed Meeks's thin arm and guided him toward the back of the kitchen. She cast a quick glance over her shoulder, gave a forced smile, and began a whispered, heated conversation with the defiant man.

Elizabeth turned back to Hodges, who was still staring at her, brow furrowed, lips pursed.

Then the screen door slammed, and she jumped. Meeks had

stormed out of the kitchen, marking the end of their whispered conversation.

Caroline placed her fingertips to her forehead, lips trembling, before returning to the farmhouse table. "Sorry for the interruption. Where were we? Hodges, we want to assure you that your service to our household won't go unrewarded. No matter what we decide to do with Cliffhaven, we promise you'll be taken care of."

"Well, you don't have to worry about me, Ma'am." Hodges's voice was hoarse. She seemed nervous, rubbing her palms across her soiled skirt over and over. "It's past time I retired."

Caroline sagged against the stove. "You're leaving us?"

"Honestly, I don't have another winter left in me." Hodges didn't meet Caroline's gaze. "I've already packed. I'm leaving today."

"Can't you give us two weeks' notice?"

"I won't spend another night in this house." Hodges's fingers clutched at a pendant hanging around her neck, a golden cross, as if the religious icon gave her comfort.

"You're leaving us shorthanded, Mrs. Hodges."

"Can't be helped." Hodges cleared her throat. "And I'm owed three weeks' wages."

Caroline nodded, sliding into the chair next to Elizabeth and pulling out her phone. "Give me a second to pull up my account."

While Caroline tapped and swiped at her device, Elizabeth crossed the room and sniffed at the pot of burnt coffee on the stove. If the disgusting food and grimy kitchen were any indication of the quality of Hodges's service, maybe her departure wouldn't be such a loss to the household. And she was odd, with that strange intensity. Maybe she'd spent too long in this dark and dreary house, so isolated from the rest of the world.

She turned away from the stove and recoiled. Hodges stood

very near, staring at her with those serious eyes. The woman was quiet on her feet.

Hodges rubbed her palms again on the dirty apron. "I . . . I don't think you'll like it here."

"I already do. The house is incredible. But I'm glad I won't be here by the time winter rolls around. You made it sound so difficult."

Hodges leaned forward, her voice low. "That's not the reason I'm retiring. Don't get me wrong, the winters are hard enough." She cast her eyes around the room, shrinking back, looking smaller, fearful. "It's this house."

Elizabeth froze, fingers wrapped around an empty coffee mug. "What about the house?"

"It *is* haunted."

Elizabeth tilted her head, a half-smile playing on her lips. Was Hodges making fun of her? No, her face was deadly serious, her eyes burning with intensity. A thrill shot through her blood, a frisson of excitement. "What have you seen?"

"Things that would make you run away screaming." A muscle twitched under Hodges's eye. "There've been so many deaths here. Those souls aren't resting easy. And I don't know if they'll like a stranger coming here and changing things."

The first pang of unease prickled over her skin.

"You'll see," Hodges said. "And when you do, if you're as smart as you look, you won't wait around to see what happens. If you know what's good for you, you'll leave, too."

"Mrs. Hodges?" Caroline said from across the room, holding up her phone. "I'm transferring the wages to your account. Do we owe you anything else?"

Elizabeth backed away, but Hodges grabbed her arm hard enough to make her wince as jagged fingernails dug into her skin. "Take my advice," Hodges said, her voice a harsh whisper. "If it starts getting worse, if you see things . . . just leave."

CHAPTER 4

*E*lizabeth staggered, reaching one hand to brace against
the rusted metal frame of her car. "Incredible," she
whispered.

She and Caroline stood in the gravel drive, and the view of
Cliffhaven's grand facade had her breath catching in her throat.
The morning sun shone on the magnificent house, illuminating
details that were hidden the night before by the dark and
driving rain.

The mansion was four stories of dark, weathered stone, with
a facade that stretched hundreds of feet across the overgrown
lawn. Countless chimneys jutted from the steeply gabled roofs,
and tall pointed-arch windows and doorways soared upward,
reaching for the heavens.

She drew in an awed breath. Cliffhaven was the finest
example of a Gothic mansion she'd ever seen. Some found the
Gothic style imposing, but to Elizabeth, it was solidity and
strength. It embodied having the courage to be fixed, steadfast—
boldly occupying a place for all eternity.

"Just incredible," she said, turning to Caroline. "I've studied the finest examples of architecture in North America. How is it I've never heard of this place?"

Caroline's brow furrowed, and she glanced toward the western wing. "Our family is . . . private."

The two women stood next to each other, their shoulders almost touching as her hungry eyes swept the length of the building. The magnificence of the manor house was a strange contrast to its current state of disrepair—broken windows littered the facade, turrets leaned alarmingly, and sculptures crumbled. But the mansion was beautifully situated high on a cliff overlooking the vast lake with no end on the horizon. The coastal wind carried the sound of waves crashing against rock, filled the air with the scent of the lake. Evergreens towered protectively over the lawn, marking the border of a dense forest.

Caroline's gaze travelled over the broken windows and crumbling stone, and her shoulders sagged. "This was my home. I spent my childhood here, and it's heartbreaking to see it like this."

Elizabeth couldn't fathom growing up in a place like Cliffhaven. Her memories of the home she'd shared with her mother—the only home she'd ever known—were vague, but she knew it had been small and cozy, so unlike this cavernous mansion.

"You said you haven't been here in ten years?"

"Something like that. I left when I married my husband." Caroline fidgeted with the ring finger of her left hand and seemed surprised to find it bare. "Ex-husband. When we divorced, I knew it was time to come home. But I didn't know my brother had so completely neglected the estate."

Anger colored Caroline's voice. "Adam and I own Cliffhaven together, and he's been living here all this time. I don't know what he was thinking, letting it fall down around him like this.

He hasn't even fixed the damage done by the fire, and that was years ago!"

At that moment, as if they'd summoned him, Caroline's brother appeared, making his way across the grounds. Even from a distance he looked large and powerful, and his jet-black hair shone in the sunlight. He gave no sign he was aware of the women watching him, simply followed a gravel path away from the house.

Suddenly, Caroline's shoulders slumped in defeat. "I can't do this." She cupped her face with her palm, hiding her trembling lips, and a tear slid down her cheek.

Oh, God. Elizabeth froze, unsure. She'd had so little practice with friendship, so few opportunities to console. She reached toward Caroline's shoulder, then drew her hand back.

Glancing at her with embarrassment, Caroline wiped the tears from her cheeks. "I'm sorry. I shouldn't have come back to Cliffhaven. I was wrong, thinking all this could be fixed. Maybe Adam is right, and we should just let the house rot."

Elizabeth recognized the despair and doubt in Caroline's eyes, could feel it herself. She, too, was intimidated by this dark, dismal place. Part of her wanted to run away to some bright, safe haven that was all her own, but that place didn't exist.

She turned back to Cliffhaven's opulent, decaying facade and felt an unfamiliar pull, something drawing her in. What fine art might be hidden in the house, decaying slowly after being forgotten by the world? If the Savonnerie carpet and damascene sconces were any indication, the house could be full of priceless pieces, neglected and needful.

"Don't make your decision now," she said, turning back to Caroline. "Let me go through the house, evaluate the art, and let you know what it would cost to restore. If money's an issue, there might be pieces you can sell that could pay for the house renovation."

"Money isn't the issue. It's complicated."

"Please, at least let me look. And if you decide not to save the house, I can help you figure out how to save what we can." She caught Caroline's gaze, willing her to trust, to believe in her. "Let me help. I know I can help."

The sorrow in Caroline's eyes seemed to lighten. "All right. If you can bear to be inside this dismal place."

Elizabeth's heart beat faster as excitement rose within her. "I'll start by making an inventory of Cliffhaven's art, noting any damage and the steps required to restore each piece."

"That's going to be a big job. There's more art in the house than I even know." Caroline ran a hand through her strawberry-blonde bob and gave her a crooked smile. "I could show you the portrait gallery. That seems like a good place to start."

She followed Caroline to the gallery that wrapped around the second floor, where sunlight streamed through stained-glass windows. Dozens of paintings decorated the gallery walls—portraits and landscapes and still lifes.

Caroline walked toward a painting prominently displayed at the center of the wall, above a black marble fireplace. The portrait was life-sized, a striking portrayal of a couple on their wedding day. The woman was young and lovely, with long, black curls cascading over delicate shoulders. She wore a floor-length gown the color of the finest pearls that shimmered, luminous in the rich light. She was angelic, with delicate features and a kind smile.

If the woman in the painting was an angel, the man standing next to her, his hand resting possessively on her shoulder, was something much darker. He stood rigidly by her side, jaw tense, eyes cold. He was broad-shouldered with a proud forehead and arrogant chin, and he towered above his bride.

"That's my mother, Audrey," Caroline said, her voice full of reverence and sorrow. "And my father, Stephen."

"She's beautiful." Elizabeth walked to Caroline's side. "And the painting itself is stunning."

"Adam painted this," Caroline said proudly. "From a photograph of their wedding day. My brother's a talented artist. At least, he used to be. I don't know if he even paints anymore."

Intrigued, she stepped closer to the portrait. The artistry of the painting was remarkable, full of rich color, fine detail, and nuanced light. *That hulking brute painted this?*

"My parents died not long after Adam finished it," Caroline said, her eyes on the painting. "In the fire, here at Cliffhaven."

There was a moment of silence, then Elizabeth bit her lip and leaned towards Caroline. "My parents died, too. When I was seven."

Caroline looked at Elizabeth as if seeing her anew. "Then you know how it feels—to be suddenly so alone in the world. Where did you live after they were gone?"

"Nowhere. I mean, nowhere for long. I was sent to live with an estranged aunt in Oregon. But she was young, barely an adult, not ready to care for a child." And Elizabeth certainly hadn't made it easy for her, crying for her lost mother every day, nightmares filling every night. "When my aunt decided she didn't want me, there was no other family, so I went into foster care. I bounced around a few families at first, but when it was clear nobody wanted me, into different group homes." The last resort for troubled teens.

She was surprised how easily the words spilled out of her. It was more than she'd told anyone on first acquaintance, ever. Was she that starved for human connection? Or was there something about Caroline that inspired confidence?

"I was seventeen when my parents died," Caroline said, "just finishing my senior year of high school. I couldn't stand to be in this house, so I ran away." She smiled ruefully, as if amused by her foolishness. "I'd only been dating Brad—that's my ex—for a few months, but I convinced him to get married and start a new life in Seattle. Stupid, really, thinking I could outrun my grief."

"I don't know." Elizabeth thought of all the times as a child she'd been forced to pack up, start a new life in a new place with strangers. As an adult, she'd continued the habit, staying no more than a few months in any one location. "Moving can make everything easier—leaving everything behind, starting over in a place where there are no memories."

"But now I want those memories. I need them."

Frowning, Elizabeth turned back to the portrait. "How old was your brother when it happened?"

"Adam must have been fifteen." Caroline put her hand to her forehead and shook her head. "That's so young. I told myself he was better off at home, that I didn't know how to raise a teenager. But I just left him behind, didn't I? In this empty, rotting house. I guess one reason I came back is to try to make up for that."

"That's admirable."

"I'm just trying to fix my mistakes. But now that I'm here, I find I don't know him at all. Maybe he isn't the man I thought he'd be."

Elizabeth turned back to the beautiful portrait. Audrey Arrington's smile was gentle and loving. She looked like the mother Elizabeth had longed for, someone who made you feel loved and wanted. As the familiar ache grew in her chest, she turned away from the painting.

"At least you have someone," she said. "A brother. You aren't alone in the world."

"You're right. But I can't believe he's let this happen," Caroline said, gesturing to the decrepit house around her. "He was always so strong and capable, even as a child."

Caroline looked back at the portrait, her face reflecting loneliness and loss that Elizabeth knew too well. "So many terrible things happened here. So many memories. So many ghosts." Her eyes swept the room, lips trembling, and there was fear, there, on her face.

"I've got to go." Caroline stepped back, toward the staircase. "Can you find your way around without me?"

"Absolutely. I'll start inventorying the art today." But her confident words didn't seem to lighten the burden Caroline carried, so she said, "Please don't worry. We can make all of this right."

Caroline's sorrowful gaze rested on her, and she paused, her hand on the banister. "Thank you, Elizabeth. I'm so glad I hired you."

Then she walked with quick, nervous steps down the grand staircase and straight to the front door, as if eager to be gone. With one hand on the doorknob, she suddenly turned back.

"Elizabeth, please be careful." Caroline put one hand to her lips. "I mean, parts of the house could be dangerous, after having been neglected for so long. Just . . . take care."

Elizabeth stood on the gallery, bewildered by Caroline's sudden urgency. "I will." Caroline nodded, as if to reassure herself, then disappeared out the front door.

Elizabeth had to stop herself from following. Without Caroline's company, the house seemed bleak and full of shadows.

ELIZABETH WALKED along the cliff's edge with a reckless disregard for the two-hundred-foot drop. Her long strides ate the ground while her gaze fixed on the horizon. The golden sun hung low in the sky, almost touching the dark blue water. Soon it would set.

Her pace was too fast for the rocky edge, but she was determined to burn through the energy coursing through her. The sound of the surf crashing against rock filled the air, the perfect soundtrack to her mounting excitement.

After Caroline had left, she'd wandered the sprawling mansion for hours, exploring room after room, all stunning in their elegance but marred by decay. Every chamber she'd visited held works of art, even the bedrooms she'd wandered through on the second floor. There were countless paintings, priceless antiques, and marble statues, but all was dusty, disheveled, and in some cases broken beyond repair. The entire house probably contained hundreds, if not thousands, of pieces.

What a strange, glorious place she found herself in. The house was a labyrinth, an architectural wonder, housing priceless antiques any museum would be desperate to acquire.

She lifted her nose, scenting the fresh, coastal breeze. The wild landscape was so different from the heat of New Orleans, the crush of people on the city sidewalks, the smell of hot pavement and rotting trash.

She stopped abruptly at the cliff's edge. Before her was an outcropping of rock—a precipice surrounded by the endless lake with a panoramic view of sunset. She faced the fiery sun as it kissed the edge of the water, the surrounding sky painted with vivid pinks, reds, and oranges. She swallowed thickly, as if the magnificence of that moment was caught in her throat.

She crept to the very edge of the precipice, staring down at the deadly drop to the rocks and sea below. It was a long way down.

Stones crunched behind her, footsteps that were barely audible over the crashing waves. She whirled around, had a brief glimpse of a tall, burly body behind her. They locked eyes, and her feet slipped on the loose stones.

She gasped, her eyes widening, arms pinwheeling. Panic gripped her, and as he reached toward her, she lost her footing at the cliff's edge.

CHAPTER 5

*E*lizabeth's feet scrambled for purchase against the loose stones, and she fell to her knee with one foot dangling off the edge of the cliff. Adrenalin spiked through her blood as she lunged forward on her hands and knees. Adam was by her side in an instant, gripping her elbow and pulling her upright, into his arms, away from danger.

Her breath came in shallow gasps, and her eyes, wide with fear, darted back to the precipice. The waves crashed against the rocks below, but now the sound was threatening.

"Are you hurt?" The wind whipped Adam's dark, unruly hair, and his emerald eyes were sharp with concern. The golden light of sunset softened his sculpted features, and his arms were strong and secure around her, flooding her body with warmth.

Her instant attraction to the man before her came as a surprise. But the pleasure pooling in her stomach was unwelcome, and she pulled her arm from his grasp and took a step back—away from him, away from the cliff's edge. "I'm fine."

He glanced down at his hands that had, only a moment before, been cradling her arm, her waist. "You're bleeding." He gestured to her skinned knee as blood seeped through her torn jeans.

"It's nothing."

"You were very close to the edge," he said, frowning with disapproval.

She took a ragged breath. "A bad habit of mine."

He didn't take his eyes from her face, regarding her with a frank intensity that made her shift uncomfortably. "I . . . I wanted to apologize for the way I behaved in the library last night." His words were unhurried, as if he weighed and measured them carefully before doling them out.

A blush burned across her cheeks, and she shook her head. "That's not necessary."

"Yes, it is. I was rude." He kept the scarred side of his face turned away. Did he make a conscious effort to hide the discolored, textured skin? "I'm unaccustomed to having strangers here."

"I understand," she said, tucking a curl behind her ear. "I shouldn't have been in your rooms."

"But I was wrong to speak to you that way. I was taken by surprise, but that's no excuse. When you knocked the candle over . . ." He looked up to the sky, as if seeing something haunting there, then closed his eyes and took a deep breath. "Fire unnerves me."

She thought of the portrait of Adam's mother, imagined her likeness on the canvas devoured by flames. "Thanks for the apology. But I respect your privacy, and now that I know where your rooms are, I'll avoid them."

He looked at her with eyes so full of vulnerability, it stopped her breath. Then he ran his long fingers savagely through his hair, and the moment was gone.

Silence stretched between them. To fill it, she gestured to the rugged cliffs and dark water. "How big, exactly, is Cliffhaven?"

"Thousands of acres. There's the house and cliffs, of course, but there's also old-growth forest, sand dunes, and beaches. The estate covers most of the island."

"It's a beautiful place."

He nodded, gazing toward the sun-streaked horizon. "I come here often at sunset."

"I can see why. It's breathtaking."

"Yes," he said, though his gaze shifted back to her. "Breathtaking."

The heat in his eyes was unmistakable, as was her response. Her lips parted, and her breath quickened. Suddenly, it was all too overwhelming—the spectacular sunset, the stress of the last days, and the intriguing man who looked at her with passion in his eyes.

"If you'll excuse me," she said, moving tentatively toward the path.

He stepped back with surprising grace. "You should go straight back to the house. It'll be dark soon, and it's dangerous here at night."

Though his tone held only concern, her back stiffened. "Dangerous?"

"Wolves, bears. They don't often attack, but it happens. Southerners don't seem to understand what precautions are necessary."

She tilted her head and said lightly, "Mr. Arrington, are you implying I don't know how to take care of myself?"

He looked at her again with that frank, serious gaze, as if his penetrating eyes could see every part of her. "On the contrary, something tells me you're quite good at caring for yourself, Miss Watson."

She walked past him quickly, giving his body a wide berth, her face flushed and hot. She took long, purposeful strides, eager to reach the protective hedges that would block his view of her. Just before she turned the corner at the hedge, she braved a quick look behind her.

He was silhouetted against the blazing sun just as it sank into the water. He stood, tall and strong, at the cliff's edge, but he wasn't looking at the sunset. He was looking at her.

She turned away, disappearing behind the hedges, the image of Adam standing on the cliff burned into her mind. Why did he seem less intimidating in this wild setting? It was as if he were part of the untamed beauty—more at home in it than the grand, decrepit house.

With the coming of evening the air turned colder, and she shivered as it kissed her bare arms. When the mansion came into view, she stopped, facing the house with her hands on her hips. The windows were dark and impenetrable, capable of hiding anything.

Nothing was cared for. The grass grew long, and fallen trees marred what was left of the lawn. But the place had a wild, windswept beauty that tugged at her heart. As she stood looking at the house, an uncomfortable feeling blossomed in her stomach—an alarming ache she didn't understand, something that felt like longing.

She walked quickly, fighting the urge to run, though she was no longer sure what she was running from.

OLD HOUSES HAD their own language—the creaks of ancient wood settling, the sighs of air squeezing through crevices. At least, that's what Elizabeth told herself as she listened to the strange sounds slithering through Cliffhaven's corridors.

She threw open the window of her bedroom, embracing the cold, fresh air flooding the room. The darkness of the northern night was complete, other than the dazzling display of stars glittering in the sky.

Candlelight flickered, casting shadows over the sinister faces hidden in the damask wallpaper. In this house, anxiety followed her like an unwanted companion.

Was she alone in the mansion, or had Adam returned? Was he pacing the wooden floor of his library, as she'd seen him last night?

She gathered the hem of her nightdress and knelt in front of her battered suitcase, scanning its contents, making sure everything was in place. *See? Everything's okay.* She exhaled a breath, and tension drained from her shoulders and jaw. *You're ready to go, when the time comes.*

It was a silly habit, making sure her belongings were arranged neatly in her suitcase. She knew this idiosyncrasy for what it was —a coping mechanism leftover from childhood, when she'd been forced to move at a moment's notice. There'd been so many times she'd had to leave her temporary homes, sometimes in the dark of night. So many treasured belongings left behind, so much grief and fear of the unknown—where would she go? Who would she live with? Would she be safe? At a time when her life had spun out of control, her suitcase became her world, her home. And sometimes, even that had been left behind.

Not anymore. It soothed her to know her things were safe, that she could be gone with a moment's notice and leave nothing behind.

She reached under the sweaters and jeans, pulled out the parcel wrapped in a green silk scarf. She carefully unwrapped the silk, revealing the beloved picture frame, and sighed. It was a simple drawing, really—an amateur's best attempt at sketching a mother and daughter, side by side. But her mother had had some talent; it was there in the complexity of Elizabeth's chestnut curls, the life given to the clasped hands. She touched her fingertip to the glass over the heart signature, the x's and o's repeated like binary code—the language of love.

She ran her finger over the drawing's cheap frame. When

she'd arrived at her first temporary home, ravaged by grief, the frame had been broken—a remnant of violence and death. Every time she'd looked at the splintered frame and her mother's damaged sketch, her grief had compounded, like interest she could never repay. She'd laid on her new, unfamiliar bed for weeks, refusing to speak to anyone.

Elizabeth shuddered as she remembered that raw, unrelenting grief—like a massive black hole that had sucked her in. Until one morning she woke gripped by determination to fix the shattered frame. She'd fitted the frame back into place, glued and sanded the wood, mixed cheap acrylic paints until the color matched perfectly, fitted new glass over the sketch. It had been the first thing she'd ever restored, and when it was complete, when every sign of violence had been eradicated, she'd felt something like triumph. *This*, she'd thought. *This I can make right.*

Kneeling on the cold Savonnerie carpet, Elizabeth wrapped the framed sketch in the silk scarf and tucked it back into the corner of her suitcase. She zipped the battered suitcase closed and slid it underneath her bed.

Elizabeth dove into her bed and burrowed underneath the thick down comforter. She gazed at the stars outside her opened window, listened to the faint sound of the crashing surf, then drifted into that unsettled sleep where she was convinced she lay awake, tossing and turning, slipping in and out of dark dreams.

Until she jolted awake, her eyes popping open. She sat up quickly, as if some threatening noise had woken her. But there was no sound, no light except the moon's rays that shone through her open window. Her breathing was shallow and uneven as she tried to get her bearings in the unfamiliar room.

"Who's there?"

Her words were met with nothing but silence. And the feel

of unseen eyes watching her, their unwelcome gaze slithering over her skin like a snake.

Her nostrils quivered. Was that smoke, lingering in the air? She followed the scent to the edge of her bed. There, on the floor, something glowed red, curving upwards—a demonic smile in the darkness. Something was burning. As she watched, the smoldering embers disappeared, leaving charred paper crumpled on the floor.

Her heart thumping in her chest, she bent over with trembling fingers and picked up the blackened paper. Her breath came hard and fast as she turned the paper over in her hands. It was the sketch. Her mother's sketch. Some of the writing was still visible, but half the picture had burned away, including the daughter's face. *Her* face, half burned, her tremulous smile distorted into a grimace. Grief gripped her like a punch to the gut, stealing her breath.

She jumped off the mattress, falling to her knees and yanking her suitcase from under the bed. Rifling through the contents, she found the green silk scarf and, hands shaking, unwrapped it.

The frame she'd restored was there. But it was empty, with nothing behind the glass but old cardboard.

Her mouth went dry, and she shook her head. *No. This can't happen.* The picture didn't slip from its frame, jump from the suitcase, and light itself on fire.

Hodges's words returned to her, echoing through her mind: *The house is haunted.*

Elizabeth narrowed her eyes at the dark corners of the room, half expecting to see wispy figures floating across the corridor.

Calm down, she thought. *There's a rational explanation.* But rational thought found no purchase in the dark, in the creaking, cavernous house that seemed alive in the night.

Her gaze darted to the candle on her nightstand, but the wick was black and unmoving, long dead.

Then she heard it. A low sound, barely audible above the coastal wind whistling outside her window. A strange slithering behind the walls, as if the house itself were alive. Breathing. Watching.

She stood, clutching the burned drawing to her chest, her eyes flitting around the room. Old houses never seemed empty, lifeless. It was as if they had a life of their own, borrowed from the lives of others, long dead.

Hodges's eyes had been so wide, so full of fear. *I've seen things that would make you run away screaming.*

Then the floorboards creaked in the corridor outside her room.

"Who's there?" She swiped her keyring from the nightstand and flicked open the pepper spray, aiming it toward her chamber's open door. She hadn't left the door open, had she?

"It's me." The deep voice was tentative, uncertain. "Adam."

Then he was there, standing in her doorway, holding a golden gilt candelabrum, three candles casting light and shadow over his chiseled face. "I heard a scream."

Her eyes narrowed. "I didn't scream."

The man was enormous—as tall as the doorframe and thick with muscle. She was keenly aware of her vulnerability, trapped in this bedroom, him blocking the only exit.

His eyes were wary, guarded. "Maybe you had a nightmare." Then his gaze swooped around the room, searching. "You're all right, then?"

"I'm fine." *Other than ghosts burning my precious personal belongings.* Her hand tightened around her mother's blackened sketch. His brows drew together, as if he didn't quite believe her.

He was dressed in fine clothing, but all of it was threadbare. He wore a black smoking jacket that was faded and worn, as if it were decades old. Under the jacket, his cream-colored shirt appeared to be made of fine linen, but the cuffs were tattered. He looked like something from another age—a well-dressed man trapped under glass, walking the floors of his library in solitude as his clothes faded and his hair grew long.

His face was unique, with that discolored, textured skin ranging across his forehead, surrounding one eye. But much more noticeable was the beauty of his features, like something Michelangelo might have carved from marble—strong, smooth, and charismatic.

He nodded, turning the scarred side of his face away as he moved back toward the corridor.

"Wait," she said.

He paused, the flawless side of his face turned toward her, eyebrow raised.

"Is . . . is Cliffhaven haunted?"

"Haunted?" He was still for a moment. "You believe in ghosts, Miss Watson?"

She dropped her eyes to her hands. "I did, as a child. But what child doesn't dream of ghosts and monsters?"

It had been more than dreams, though, hadn't it? It had been shortly after the accident. She'd been seven, still struggling with the idea that her mother would never return. She'd woken in the night from a terrible dream, slick with sweat and fear. Half-asleep, she'd felt a cool, soothing hand on her brow. She'd opened her eyes, and there she was—the figure of her mother, sitting next to her on the bed, smiling benevolently.

As a child, she'd believed wholeheartedly that the ghost of her mother had visited her that night. And when she was sad or lonely, when the laughter or tears of her foster family had driven her to her room and she felt particularly alone, she would imagine her mother returned—that she would caress her face, hold her close.

As an adult, she knew that childhood vision of her mother

had been her own invention. She'd been an overwrought child, one that had suffered a terrible trauma. It made sense that her childish psyche would invent the comforting presence of her mother. She'd been half-asleep, dreaming. But another part of her, the part that tossed salt over her shoulder after a spill, the part that balked when she saw a black cat, wondered. Were ghosts real? Could loved ones visit us after death, warning us of danger, keeping us safe?

Her gaze fell to the charred paper still clutched in her hand. Yearning overtook her—a desperate longing for the veil between life and death to be so thin.

But if the souls of loved ones remained after death, that meant other souls surrounded us—darker, antagonistic. Ones that lived in the dark spaces of houses, remembering, haunting. Meaning harm.

Adam shifted, drawing her gaze. He stared into the lit candle he held, seemingly entranced by the flame, lips curved into a half-smile that was both bittersweet and melancholic. "We're all of us haunted, aren't we?"

And then he was gone, melting into the shadowy corridor, leaving a void in his wake.

She pressed a hand to her heart. Who *was* he? This handsome, tortured man living in a desolate mansion—a gothic fantasy come to life.

Clutching what remained of her mother's drawing to her chest, she slipped back into bed, shivering. But the pounding of her heart didn't slow, and her eyes wouldn't close. So she imagined, as she'd done a thousand times, her mother, sitting on the edge of her bed, reaching out to smooth back her hair.

Adam was right, she thought as she drifted toward sleep.

We are, all of us, haunted.

CHAPTER 6

"You didn't . . . see Adam last night, did you?"

Caroline's brow was furrowed, one hand resting on her stomach, picking at the sky-blue scrubs she wore. She'd returned early that morning, bringing coffee and breakfast sandwiches that they'd consumed huddled over a broken table in the great hall.

Elizabeth thought of Adam standing at the cliff's edge, of the heat in his eyes as he gazed at her. Then the candlelight flickering over his face as he stood in the doorway of her room. "We bumped into each other."

She'd never met anyone like him—as tall and powerfully built as a prizefighter, but with a surprisingly gentle manner. He was the oddest mixture of refinement and wildness, as if a patina of gentility concealed a passionate nature.

"I guess you're going to run into each other, even in a house this size." Caroline's gaze roved over her face. "Did you sleep okay?"

"Yeah, fine."

Which wasn't exactly true. After the mysterious events of the previous evening, she'd tossed and turned through the darkest part of night, when every creak and groan of the old house took on a supernatural sound. When she'd finally dragged herself out of bed, the acrid smell of smoke still lingered in the air.

But with the morning light streaming through her bedroom window and the sound of the surf crashing outside, it had been easier for her mind to settle on rational explanations. Maybe she hadn't put her mother's sketch away after looking at it, and it had fallen to the floor where a spark from the fireplace had caught. It was possible.

Or maybe it *was* a ghost. Maybe Cliffhaven was haunted. She could live with that.

"There are a few parts of the house I'd like to show you myself," Caroline said, leaving her unfinished sandwich and crossing the hall to stop in front of mammoth double doors. They were impressive, with rounded edges and intricate geometric carvings. Caroline pulled on the doors, rattling their hinges as if they weren't valuable pieces of art, and Elizabeth bit back a request for her to handle them carefully.

"Damn. Why would Adam lock these doors?" Caroline stepped back, hands on her hips, frowning. "What could he possibly be keeping in there?"

Elizabeth ran her finger over the carving, and a shiver passed through her. The heavy, locked doors reminded her of the story of Bluebeard, that fairy-tale of the rich, powerful man who took a new wife. How he'd kept just one door locked from his innocent bride, and the horrors she discovered when she turned the key.

Caroline threw her hands into the air. "I guess you'll have to start without me. I'll find Adam and be back with the keys."

"No problem."

Caroline regarded her for a moment, slowly recovering her sweet smile, then pointed to a smaller set of doors across the hall. "Check out the parlor. You'll like it." Then she marched across the stone floor, disappearing behind the double staircase.

She gulped down the dregs of her coffee, eager to discover more of Cliffhaven's secrets, and slipped through the door Caroline had indicated.

The curtains were drawn in the high-ceilinged room, but small slivers of sunlight peeked through gaps in the cloth. In the dim light, the white sheets covering furniture looked like ghosts, silent and watchful.

The walls were covered with wooden paneling, cream-colored and intricately carved, and a soaring vaulted ceiling was cris-crossed with wooden beams. The room was inviting. Sumptuous, even.

Then her gaze fell on the floor-to-ceiling fresco running the length of the eastern wall. She stared, mouth open, hand to her heart.

It was a mythological scene—centaurs surrounding a Rubenesque maiden draped over a rock. She moved closer, excitement jittering through her limbs. There was the basic color palette of the eighteenth century. The subtle, sophisticated use of color. That noble simplicity, the reliance on Prussian blue. It was neoclassical, surely, but was it authentic?

She leaned closer to the fresco until her face was an inch from the wall. The paint and plaster had been torn from its original location and transferred to a canvas. She frowned. Detachment of a fresco and its transfer were dangerous, irreversible procedures that usually damaged the original work. But the tearing appeared to have been professionally done, and they'd only removed the topmost layer of plaster. More damaging, perhaps, was that the fresco had been left untended for perhaps a century.

Could this be an authentic piece, torn from a villa in Europe? Or a fantastic reproduction, forged by a master and sold to an eager, if ignorant, buyer? She wouldn't know until she examined it further, but the pigments appeared to be hundreds of years old.

A wide grin lit her face as she lifted her tablet and pulled up the spreadsheet she'd created—a master list of Cliffhaven's art. She added the fresco, recording its location in the house and notes about its restoration. It was in desperate need of cleaning, but other than that, it was in excellent condition.

With an eager spring in her step, she returned to the great hall, where a set of French doors caught her eye. After a sharp rap on the door and a moment's wait, she entered.

The room was large and bright, with one wall made entirely of glass. The sun sparkled through the windows, setting the entire room aglow. The smells of paint and canvas permeated the room, and empty easels stood at the base of the windows. Clean paintbrushes lay next to a utility sink, drying in the sun. Shelves of paint and supplies lined the walls, all neat and organized.

She clapped her hands in delight. Cliffhaven had an art studio. Caroline had mentioned Adam was a painter. She meandered to the center of the room, where an easel displayed a half-finished canvas.

When her eyes fell on the painting, she recoiled, her hand covering her mouth. On the canvas, dark clouds swirled around a ruined wasteland. The foreground was filled with body parts —twisted torsos, bent limbs, and agonized faces. The subjects seemed to reach out of the canvas, pleading with the viewer for help.

She couldn't tear her eyes away, and she involuntarily pressed her clenching hand to her stomach, as if touching a wound. She stood there, contemplating the portrait of pain before turning away with a shudder.

A row of canvases leaned against one wall, their backs facing the room. She glanced at the door nervously then pulled a canvas away from the wall to see the picture it held.

It was death. Broken bodies littered the landscape of what looked to be Hell. In the center of the picture, a man without a face was tortured by demons and fire. His body twisted in agony as flames leaped out of the canvas.

Elizabeth closed her eyes, trying to rid her mind of the despair the painting evoked. She returned the canvas to its place, her stomach churning with guilt and revulsion—the price of voyeurism.

She leaned against the wall and pressed the back of one hand to her hot cheek. The paintings shouldn't disturb her. The subjects were macabre, but surely it was only an artistic representation—a metaphor. She'd seen unsettling art before, and it had never made her ache as these paintings did.

Adam had painted those canvases. What had driven him to create those images of torture and death?

A feminine voice floated through the air, coming from the next room, and she sighed in relief. *Caroline.* She followed the sound to the door, but when she heard a male voice, her hand froze on the doorknob. The voices grew closer, raised in anger.

Her heart tripped, a small stumble in her chest. She wanted nothing to do with an argument between Adam and Caroline, but the voices were almost upon her. The doorknob turned under her hand, and without thinking, she flattened herself against the wall behind the door.

What am I doing? But there was no time to reevaluate her decision as Caroline and Adam burst into the room and the door pressed against her chest.

"The trust documents are very clear, Adam." Caroline's voice was tight and tense. "Mom and Dad left Cliffhaven to both of us."

"I know what the trust says, Caroline. Of course, this house is yours as well as mine. But you can't just march in here, giving orders and making demands!"

Elizabeth squeezed her eyes shut in mortification. *Oh, go away, please. I want nothing to do with this.* But their footsteps stopped in the middle of the room, and their voices grew louder.

"Well, *somebody* has to do something!" Caroline said. "You've let everything fall apart. This house is rotting, falling down around you, and you're too lazy or foolish to do anything about it."

"Lazy? And where have you been all these years?" Adam's voice was rough and raw. "At least I stayed! You *left*, Caroline. You left me to rot."

A sudden silence descended, and Adam's words hung in the air.

"I meant," he said, in a much quieter tone, "that you left the *house* to rot."

"I think you meant exactly what you said." Caroline's voice was no longer angry, but sorrowful. "You're right. I did leave you. And I'm so sorry." Her words ended in a sob.

"Caroline." Adam's voice softened. "Please don't cry. I don't blame you for leaving."

Caroline took a deep breath and continued with a shaking voice. "Adam, I was only seventeen when the fire took Mom and Dad. I was lost and scared, and I ran away. I thought you would be okay. You were always so strong and self-possessed, I thought you didn't need me.

"But I'm back." Caroline's voice grew stronger. "And you need me now, whether you know it or not. We have to decide whether this house is worth saving. And we don't have much time."

"Would you ever really want to live here?" Adam's voice turned bitter. "In this horrible place?"

"I don't know. But I need a home now, and this is all I've got." There was a pause. "I'm hoping Elizabeth can give us some answers."

"That's the other thing. Did you really have to hire that woman?"

"What's wrong with Elizabeth?" Caroline's voice sharpened. "I think she's wonderful."

"I'm sure she is. But is it absolutely necessary for her to stay here?"

"What's wrong with her staying here, for heaven's sake?" Caroline sounded both frustrated and amused. "There's plenty of room. And it's only for a few weeks."

When there was only silence from Adam, Caroline continued, her voice gentle. "You've got to let the outside world in. You can't just lock yourself away from everything."

"Fine," he said, sounding defeated. "She can stay. And sell any of the damned art you want. But I'm still not agreeing to restore Cliffhaven."

"It's a start, I guess." Caroline paused. "Thank you, Adam."

Footsteps led away, followed by the sound of a distant door closing. *Thank God.* Elizabeth closed her eyes and slumped against the wall. But as her weight shifted, the floorboards under her feet creaked—the smallest sound, but it filled the silent room like a tell-tale heart. She froze, her eyes widening in horror.

No, she thought, even as heavy footsteps sounded on the wooden floor, growing nearer. *This can't be happening.*

Then the door swung aside, and Adam's towering figure loomed before her.

CHAPTER 7

*E*lizabeth pressed against the wall, wishing she could disappear into it. As her heart pounded in her ears, images from his paintings flashed through her mind—torture, death. Who *was* this man? How would he react?

Adam's face was inscrutable as he stared down at her. Her cheeks heated under his gaze, and he cocked his head to the side, raising one dark eyebrow.

"I know this looks bad," she said, inching sideways, away from his hulking figure. "I swear to you, I wasn't trying to eavesdrop."

"What *were* you trying to do?" His narrowed eyes followed her as she slid across the wall. He was so enigmatic, she couldn't tell if he was furious or amused.

"I was looking for Caroline when I heard . . . well, you sounded angry, and I didn't want to . . ." She bit her lip, trying to stop the guilty words spilling out.

"Didn't want to see me?" A muscle twitched in his jaw, and he turned the scarred side of his face away. "I don't blame you. I wouldn't want to see me, either."

And suddenly, her fear and mortification drained away. The

56

sight of his face in profile, the sculpted cheekbones, the brow wrinkled as if he were in pain, seized her. Despite his obvious physical power, despite his brusque and standoffish manner, she instinctively knew Adam would never hurt her.

"I've grown into a monster of a man." His voice was low, resigned. "Even if people can overlook my monstrous proportions, there's still the matter of my face."

She pushed away from the wall. "You don't frighten me."

He captured her gaze with his own, his eyes full of gentle accusation, a self-deprecating smile turning up one corner of his mouth. "Liar."

She crossed her arms over her chest. "If I am frightened, it isn't of your face."

The half-smile that had played on his face fled, and his voice turned to iron. "Don't pity me. That's so much worse." Then he turned on his heel and left the room.

She slumped against the wall, cursing under her breath. What had come over her? Yes, the man intimidated her, but that was no reason to hide behind a door like a fearful child. What would he think of her now, after she'd so obviously hurt his feelings?

That's none of your business. She raked one shaky hand through her curls, took a deep breath, and pushed away from the wall. *Get the job done, then get the hell out of here.*

WHEN ELIZABETH ENTERED THE KITCHEN, searching for Caroline, she found it occupied by a man, bent double, his head hidden inside the open refrigerator. Her heart tripped in her chest, one unsteady beat.

"Hello."

He straightened, towering above her. He was a burly man of late middle age, exuding the vitality of someone much younger.

57

His craggy face was like something carved from granite until his lips lifted into an easy smile. "Hi. Just grabbing a bottle of water."

He wore a suit that might once have been elegant, but the cuffs were threadbare, the knees of his trousers faded. His dark hair was liberally streaked with gray, slicked back over a high, proud forehead. He was built like a linebacker, full of strength that hadn't faded with age.

"Jack Arrington. Adam and Caroline's uncle. And their attorney, by the way."

She shook his outstretched hand, and his meaty hand engulfed hers. "I see the family resemblance. I'm—"

"The art specialist, I know." His intelligent gray eyes appraised her from head to foot. "Well, don't leave me in suspense. What's your verdict?"

"My what?"

"The house, of course. Do you recommend restoring it?"

"Uncle Jack, she can't possibly have formed an opinion." Caroline entered the kitchen carrying a paper bag of groceries. "She's only been here a couple of days."

"Seems like one night would be enough." His gaze wandered around the decrepit kitchen, disapproval curling his lip. "I still can't believe you hired someone without consulting me."

Caroline set the bag on the counter with too much force. "Someone had to do something."

Jack shook his head. "This house is rotten to the core, from the crumbling foundation to the moldy roof."

"And whose fault is that?" Caroline snapped.

Jack was still for a moment, regarding her. Then he folded his arms across his chest and said, "If you've got something to say to me, Caroline, just say it."

"Fine." She spun to face him. "How could you let this happen?"

"What, exactly?"

"The house, for a start. It's falling apart around us, and nothing's been done to protect it."

Jack's lips pinched together, and he threw his hands into the air. "I did my best. Adam refused to make any improvements."

"And what about Adam? He's become a hermit!"

Jack leaned against the kitchen counter, looking weary and regretful. "I did anything I could think of to get him to leave this place. I brought him brochures for tours around the world, even filled out college applications for him. But he was determined to hide away here." Then his shoulders sagged, and he gave a frustrated shake of his head. "It's been hard to watch him make these choices. But I tried."

Caroline bit her lip. "But he was just a teenager, and you—"

"Enough." Jack's voice lowered, and his gray eyes hardened. "At least I was here, Caroline. You're the one who left. Maybe you could find some forgiveness in your heart for those of us who stayed." A heavy silence followed his words, in which Caroline's mouth hung open as if she'd been slapped.

"I've got business with Adam. You and I can have another conversation when you're feeling less emotional." Jack grabbed his briefcase roughly and swept out the door.

"Less emotional?" Elizabeth said, placing her hands on her hips. "Is he for real?"

"Jack's ideas about women are a little old-fashioned." Caroline's chin dropped to her chest, and she seemed to shrink inward. "But he's been good to Adam. Better than I've been." She took a deep, pained breath and closed her eyes.

Elizabeth twisted her fingers together. She couldn't bear seeing Caroline look so sad, so defeated. "Well, you're here now," she said bracingly. "That's what counts, isn't it?"

Caroline looked down at her clasped hands, where her pink manicure was starting to chip. "I'm not so sure."

Determined to change the subject, Elizabeth peeked into the

paper bag Caroline had brought. "I don't suppose some of these groceries are for me?"

"Of course. I'd planned to cook dinner for us, but you should know I'm hopeless in the kitchen."

Elizabeth blew out a breath. She was tired, particularly after her emotional exchange with Adam, but Caroline's hopeless expression tugged at her. "Can I help?"

Caroline picked up a rag and started scrubbing the counter. "That absolutely isn't in your job description."

"I don't mind." She pulled her thick curls into a haphazard ponytail.

"Can you cook?" Caroline asked hopefully.

"Not very well. Though I adore food, obviously." She glanced down at her body. Its generous curves had plagued her teenage years, but no amount of dieting or exercise diminished her lush hips or prominent backside. She'd had to accept that she was strong and sturdily built, with a penchant for the sweets denied her in her youth.

"Why is that obvious?" Caroline's pretty face scrunched up in confusion.

"Well, my . . ." She gestured vaguely at her body, but Caroline's penetrating stare caused a blush to rise to her cheeks. "Never mind. I can cook a few things. I've been fending for myself a long time."

Caroline opened the refrigerator and pulled out a paper grocery bag. "I just bought what I like—whitefish, pasta, some veggies. And a Sauvignon Blanc, of course."

"That sounds better than anything I've eaten in days. I can cook the pasta."

"Great. I'll see what I can do with these fillets. How hard can it be?" Caroline took the whitefish out of its wrapping, giving it a dubious look.

"I had a boyfriend who said if you don't know how to cook

something, just put it in a pan with butter and see what happens."

"Wise words." Caroline picked up a fish fillet, eyeing it as if it had insulted her. "I've been so overwhelmed these last few days. I'm beginning to think I've taken too much on, opening a clinic here on the island."

"You're a doctor! I should have known, with the scrubs." Elizabeth rummaged through a cupboard and pulled out a stock pot. "You're opening a clinic? That seems like a big project."

"It is, but it will help the community. There isn't so much as a doctor's office on the island."

As Elizabeth filled the stock pot with water, Caroline turned to her and said, "I'm really glad you're here." She looked out the kitchen window and let out a deep breath. "I'm glad I'm here. I wasn't sure I would be."

Elizabeth fiddled with the burners on the stove until she found one that worked, then watched the flame rise under the pot of water.

Caroline pulled lemon and garlic out of her market bag. "You know, if you'd like to have visitors, they'd be welcome to stay at the house."

"I won't have visitors. I usually don't stay in one place long enough to form deep attachments."

Caroline squinted at her as if she found that explanation inadequate, and Elizabeth turned away. Surely Caroline, so recently divorced, understood that the brief happiness love bestowed wasn't worth the inevitable pain when the relationship fell apart.

Caroline filled a sauté pan with pre-cut veggies, then glanced back at her. "Are you all settled into your room?"

She thought of her belongings, still packed in her suitcase. "As settled as I ever get. It's been a whirlwind since I left New Orleans. I left town pretty quickly."

"I'm sure you were glad to leave that mess behind." Caroline froze, eyes widening, and her fingers fluttered to her lips.

Her stomach dropped. How did Caroline know? "You called my references."

Caroline nodded, her face contorting into a grimace. "I spoke with your boss at the museum. He told me your work was outstanding, that you were an expert with restoration. And he told me not to hire you."

She closed her eyes, took a deep breath. "He told you what happened."

"He did, but it was quite wrong of him. Your personal life is none of your employer's business." Caroline's lips pursed in disapproval. "I decided he was a chauvinist asshole and hired you, anyway. Besides, it doesn't sound like you did anything wrong."

"I was stupid. But I'm not ashamed of what happened. I made a mistake, that's all. Got personally involved with a coworker, and it blew up in my face."

Caroline shrugged as she added fish fillets to the sauté pan. "It happens."

"Not to me."

She knew better. But he'd been so charming, so handsome, and he'd seemed willing to keep their work and relationship separate. She'd thought they'd had a connection, so she'd bent her rules about spending too much time with one person, too much time in one place. And it had almost cost her career. "I was an idiot. I let a relationship get in the way of my work."

"He must have been worth it."

"Not really, as it turns out. He slept with my intern."

"No!" Caroline's mouth opened in shock. "That bastard."

Elizabeth let out a shaky breath. The truth was, it still hurt. He'd toyed with her, but ultimately didn't want her. He'd chosen someone else—someone beautiful, blonde, and perfect. Her childhood all over again.

"The worst part was that my job just fell apart. I had taken a chance and accepted my first steady job—ever—in a museum." And she'd loved that place—the air heavy with the weight of history, of beauty, of art. The smell of paint and canvas. That feeling of accomplishment when she took a work of art that was damaged and restored it to its former glory.

But then she'd lost it all. No, she'd *ruined* it all.

"After everyone found out, work just fell apart." The whole situation had been so ugly, so embarrassing. Her boss giving her the side-eye, snide comments from coworkers at the watercooler, sexist jokes in the break room meant to be overheard. "It was awful. So I left."

She'd run away, given her two-week notice by e-mail and cashed in the vacation days owed to her. It had been instinct— get as far away from the problem as possible, and it usually resolved itself. Or it didn't, but she'd never know, because she wouldn't be around to be bothered by it.

Caroline shot her an empathetic look. "That sounds so painful."

"I didn't love him, so it didn't hurt as much as it might have."

But she'd lost everything. And for what? A few orgasms and a month of daring to dream someone could actually want her? She'd been a complete idiot, and she'd had to learn the lessons of her youth all over again—loving people hurt too much. It was that simple. And if she was stupid enough to stay in one place too long, she'd pay the price.

Caroline's pert nose wrinkled in confusion. "So you left a job you loved . . . because of some guy?"

"I just had no idea how to handle the situation. But when you put it that way, it sounds pretty pathetic."

"I'm not trying to minimize your feelings. Break-ups are brutal, as I so recently found out. But to give up something you love seems extreme."

"It turned out okay. Starting a new life in a new place is good for me. It keeps me strong."

"But you left behind something you loved—your job."

"Life is full of sacrifices."

"True. But maybe one day you'll find the sacrifice is too much, too high a price to pay. One day, you might want to stay somewhere for good." Caroline cast her a hopeful glance.

She gave Caroline a wan smile. "Maybe."

Elizabeth pulled a colander from one of the cabinets and dumped the cooked pasta inside. "So my boss said not to hire me. Guess he thought you wouldn't want someone entangled in a love triangle with coworkers."

Caroline shook her head, setting her strawberry-blonde bob swinging. "That wasn't it. He thought I shouldn't hire you because you just left, took off with no notice. He thought you should have stayed to fix the problem."

Elizabeth blinked. It hadn't occurred to her that her former employer wanted her to stay, that the worst of her crimes had been leaving.

"This is kind of like a sauce, right?" Caroline asked, gesturing at the liquid bubbling in the sauté pan. She poured the sauce over the pasta, brought out three dishes, and plated the food.

"Might as well save some for Adam," Caroline said, placing a serving on a silver tray and covering it with a domed lid. She slid the other two plates onto the farmhouse-style table. "Let's eat."

But after a few bites, Caroline seemed to lose interest, and her green eyes turned serious and somber. "It's weird to be back, to be in a place with so many memories of my parents. I feel like they're still here, you know? Still walking the corridors of Cliffhaven, reaching out to me."

An involuntary shiver danced across her flesh. "I know what you mean."

"About my brother." Caroline swirled pasta around her fork, then glanced at her. "You've seen Adam's face."

"I have." That chiseled face, with textured skin and guarded eyes, intrigued her. It was so rich with detail, so interesting.

"He got those scars trying to save my parents from the fire." Caroline's mouth trembled. "It started in the middle of the night. Adam woke, and instead of running to safety, he came to my room and took me outside. Then he went back for my parents." Caroline shook her head, and a single tear trailed down her cheek. "It must have been an inferno. Burning rubble fell on him, and firefighters had to drag him out of the house. That's how he got the scars."

Caroline wiped the tear away and took a deep breath. "I want you to know that about Adam. If he does things now that are strange or unkind, remember that he saved my life because he was willing to risk his own."

Elizabeth's throat was tight as she nodded. "I'll remember."

When they finished their meal, Caroline took the dishes to the sink and eyed the plate that remained under the warming lid. "Adam didn't come down for dinner." She looked at Elizabeth, her eyes hopeful and apologetic. "Would you mind taking his tray to the library?"

"Me? Don't you think he'd be more comfortable if you took it?"

Caroline grimaced. "Jack might still be there, and I don't need to hear more about how I'm a failure as a sister. But I didn't hire you to do stuff like this, so I'll just—"

"That's okay," Elizabeth said, taking the tray from Caroline. "I'm happy to do this for you."

The relief in Caroline's eyes was worth the fluttering in her stomach as she contemplated going back to the west wing. She would be alone with Adam for the first time since the eaves-dropping fiasco. She was determined to make up for her unprofessionalism, to show Adam she didn't find his scars repulsive or frightening.

She made her way through the shadowed, dusty corridors, hugging the silver tray to her chest. Her eyes swept the corners where cobwebs swayed gently against blackened walls. It smelled of dust and decay.

She stopped in front of the carved oak doors and swallowed, her pulse swift and staccato. Then she rapped on the door three times and waited in the dim light, unable to shake the feeling that entering Adam's rooms was like walking into a lion's den.

CHAPTER 8

"Come in." The muffled voice on the other side of the door was deep and calm.

The library was much the same as before—lit by fire and candlelight that illuminated the floor-to-ceiling shelves of books. Adam sat behind a large mahogany desk, his head bent over papers.

He finished writing with a flourish then looked up. At the sight of her, he stiffened, his eyes widening in surprise even as his face grew guarded.

She lifted the silver tray. "I've brought your dinner."

"Surely that isn't in your job description." His voice was tense and wary.

"I didn't mind."

"Then thank you. You can set it on the table by the fire."

She could feel his eyes on her as she walked to the hearth, and her face flushed with heat. Bending to set the tray on an antique table, she was grateful for the curls cascading across her face, shielding it from his view.

Her eyes were drawn to a mirror decorating the wall above the fireplace. It was the frame that caught her eye, the black inner frieze bordered by raised, gilded mouldings. Both the frame and the mirror had been subjected to violence; the glass was broken, with cracks snaking out from the center, and the corner of the frame hung askew. She cast a sidelong look at Adam, then reached one finger out to caress the wood. "I can fix this." And suddenly she didn't just *want* to fix the broken frame, she *needed* to—to see it restored, to prove nothing was beyond repair.

Adam rose, as if intending to move toward her, then seemed to think better of it, crossing his arms over his muscular chest and leaning against the desk. Only the rigid line of his jaw gave away his tension. "I don't want it fixed."

That was the problem right there. She planted her fists on her hips, frowning as she considered the man before her. His cream button-down shirt was folded to the elbows, exposing powerful forearms. Guarded green eyes peered out from underneath tousled black hair.

She'd never seen a man so captivating. There was something about him that was intense even in silence, even in stillness. Heat flooded her body, followed immediately by an overwhelming need to bolt from the room.

"I . . ." She swallowed, steeling herself. "I wanted to apologize for my behavior earlier. I was unprofessional, and it won't happen again. But I need you to know that I had no intention of eavesdropping."

"I know." His bright green eyes sharpened, and one corner of his mouth turned up. "But hiding behind the door was an interesting choice. Why would you do that?"

"Panic, I suppose." *And I'd just seen your secret paintings of fire and death.*

He seemed to contemplate her words, and it struck her how everything he did was unhurried, as if time moved more slowly for him. "Fear can make us act irrationally," he said, glancing at her before looking away. "I don't blame you for avoiding me.

My behavior has been . . . eccentric. I'm out of practice with civility, as if my polite parts have rusted from disuse. A consequence of my self-imposed isolation."

Then he crossed the room, his strides long and unhurried, and stopped in front of the small table, just a step away. This close, he towered over her, and it was as if he was daring her to react.

Maybe he thought she'd run away again. Maybe she should.

She was keenly aware of the presence of his powerful body, its energy and heat. What would he feel like, pressed against her?

Don't get too close. Be professional.

Hadn't it been exactly this, an attraction for what amounted to a coworker, that had caused her latest disaster in New Orleans? If there was a silver lining to that fiasco, it was that she'd finally learned her lesson—keep the people you work with at arm's length. Hell, keep *people* at arm's length. It was just professionalism and good sense.

Hadn't life been trying to teach her this lesson over and over, and she refused to learn? Since the death of her mother, she'd been in a constant state of motion—always moving from place to place, never finding a home. Every time she'd been forced to move, it meant leaving people behind, experiencing the grief of loss all over again. Until she'd learned a simple solution—don't care too much about anyone.

Adam lifted the domed lid from the silver tray. "Did you make this?"

"Caroline and I made it together."

He contemplated the meal before him as if it were alien. "It smells delicious. Would you join me?"

"I just ate. But don't let me stop you." She stepped closer to the gleaming gilt frame hanging above the hearth. "Do you mind if I take a moment to examine this piece? For the catalogue of Cliffhaven's art?"

His jaw clenched, but he nodded graciously. "Be my guest."

As she examined the frame, the gilded arabesque, the patinaed wood, his voice sounded behind her. "Hodges wasn't the best cook, so I'm in the habit of eating thoughtlessly, tasting as little as possible. Alone."

She turned back, saw him take a mouthful and close his eyes with pleasure. He murmured, as if to himself, "How can a simple plate of food make my life seem so lacking?" Then he ate with relish, seeming to savor every bite.

She tore her gaze away from him. *Work, work. Focus on work.*

"Do you know anything about this frame?" she asked, pulling out her phone and snapping a photo.

"It's old."

She shot him a look. Was he toying with her? He was an artist, but how much did he know about antiques?

"Have you ever heard of the Italian Cassetta frames?" she asked. He raised his eyebrows, which was no answer at all. "Fifteenth century. They have these distinctive mouldings around a central frieze. This one's adorned with an arabesque pattern, which wasn't uncommon. This simple, minimalistic style would fool the casual observer into thinking it isn't valuable. But they're highly sought after . . . when authentic."

"You doubt its authenticity."

"I just wonder how so many incredible pieces could be stashed in one house then left to rot." More likely, one of Adam's ancestors had a predilection for fine antiques and had either knowingly purchased fakes or been taken advantage of by an unscrupulous dealer.

"So you're an art appraiser."

"Not really. My education is in art conservation."

"A restorer, then."

"Technically, I'm a conservator, but yes."

"What's the difference?"

"Restorers focus on repairing art so it looks exactly like

the original artist intended. Conservators concentrate on stabilizing the piece and halting any further degradation. Like with this broken frame, a restorer might use something permanent, like glue, and try to make it look exactly as it originally did. A conservator would repair the frame in a way that makes you see the breaks, in a way that's reversible."

"You work on paintings?"

"I specialize in frescoes, but yes."

He leaned back in his chair, regarding her. "So the decision whether to restore Cliffhaven is in your hands."

"I don't know why people keep saying that. I'm just making an inventory of the art and calculating what it would cost to restore, maybe giving my opinion on whether it's worth it. The final decision of whether to restore the house is yours and Caroline's."

"But the reality is that your recommendation will determine whether Cliffhaven is restored." He rose and took a deep breath, as if steeling himself for something unpleasant. "I can save you time. Cliffhaven can't be restored. It shouldn't be."

"Why not?"

He pressed his lips together, eyes full of unspoken words. So that's how it was. This man had secrets, and he didn't trust her with them.

"You don't want me here," she said. "Don't bother denying it. But since I *am* here, I'll make my own determinations about the art. And the house."

His back stiffened. "If it pleases you."

"It does. But I'll do my work quickly and be gone before I've caused you too much trouble." She slipped her phone into the back pocket of her jeans and cleared her throat. "Well . . . good night, Mr. Arrington."

"Please, call me Adam." He met her gaze briefly, as if gauging her reaction, then looked away.

"Good night, Adam." The intimacy of saying his name felt strange on her tongue.

"Good night, Miss Watson. And thank you for the meal."

She left the room, closed the door behind her, and leaned against the wall to steady her breathing.

His manner was so strange, as if he were out of practice with human interaction. She couldn't account for his lightning-quick shifts between interest and apathy, between discourtesy and oddly formal etiquette. But she couldn't deny that her heart beat faster when he was near.

She frowned as she pushed away from the wall. Why was he opposed to Cliffhaven's restoration? Did he know something about the house he wasn't willing to disclose?

The vague sense of unease that was her frequent companion since she arrived at Cliffhaven returned. She took a step down the corridor, then stopped abruptly, cocking her head to listen. What was that sound? A scuttling, furtive noise. She slid closer to the wall and pressed her ear against the blackened damask wallpaper. There it was—a faint sound, but there. Something moving behind the walls.

Recoiling, she took several steps backward. *Mice, or other vermin. Something that makes its home in the darker places.*

But other images passed through her mind, each more sinister than the last.

CHAPTER 9

The next day dawned crisp and clear, an undeniable invitation to search Cliffhaven's grounds for art to add to the inventory. The unseasonably warm weather felt like the last gift of summer, and Elizabeth was determined to enjoy it before autumn returned. So she stood in the waist-high grass, overlooking the wild, untended grounds, snapping a picture of a stone sculpture decorating the house's facade—a grotesque waterspout, a vaguely canine gargoyle with a wolfish grin, its tongue jutting between pointed teeth. She added the photo to her inventory, noting that while the piece wasn't too degraded, it would need a good cleaning.

Towering evergreens and the lake provided a breathtaking view, and the soothing sound of waves crashing against rock filled the air. The water was alive with shades of blue—azure and cerulean in the bright sunlight, looking like an advertisement for a tropical holiday.

The neglected mansion stood in sharp contrast to the picturesque scenery. The house, all dark stone and vaulted arches with ivy snaking up the masonry, rambled across the lawn. Its graceful lines were marred by broken glass and crumbling stone, but it was still majestic—a wonder of architecture and art.

The smooth sound of a powerful engine cut through the morning birdsong, and she lifted her head. A sporty, red coupe sped up the driveway, performed a tight turn, and skidded to a stop, spraying gravel. As the dust cleared, a blonde woman stepped out from behind the wheel. She was long and lean, clad in sharp, fashionable lines.

The woman gave no indication that she saw Elizabeth, but her eyes roved over the house from behind designer sunglasses that hid her expression. She scanned the horizon quickly, assessing everything around her before turning back to the car and gesturing to someone inside.

A man stepped out, and he was a masculine reflection of the woman—long, lean, and blonde. Elizabeth's eyes stayed on the woman, who walked up the marble steps to the front door and entered the house without knocking. As Elizabeth contemplated that familiarity, she noted with surprise that the man had turned toward the side of the house and was walking toward her. He wore a white polo shirt and perfectly tailored trousers. His face was open and friendly, his smile easy-going as he reached out a hand to shake hers.

"Hi. I'm Christopher Vails." His hand was warm and soft. His white teeth shone against his late-summer tan, and she had the fleeting thought she'd seen him in an advertisement featuring polo or yachting.

"Elizabeth." She returned a smaller version of his welcoming smile.

"You must be the art expert Adam's been grumbling about." She raised her eyebrows, and he quickly added, "Not grumbling about you, personally. Just about the changes to Cliffhaven."

"I am well aware of Mr. Arrington's grumblings." She put her hands on her hips and cast a frustrated look toward the west wing.

"I'm sure you are. He can be a lot, right?" Christopher chuckled. "My sister Vanessa and I grew up with Adam and Caroline. Our house is right down the road, so we're neighbors." He crossed his arms and leaned back, appraising her with a smile. "I have to say, you aren't really what I expected."

Was there a flirtatious curve to his smile? It couldn't be. She rarely got attention from men, certainly not men that looked like they'd stepped out of a magazine ad. "Do I want to know what you expected?"

"Certainly not someone so young and attractive." He leaned toward her with the casual confidence of a handsome man accustomed to attention from women. "I heard you were an art restorer, and I pictured an underfed academic with a nervous tic."

"I'm not that young."

Christopher stuffed his hands into his pockets, as if he sensed her disapproval, and regarded her. "So what do you think of Cliffhaven?"

She set her hand on the stone wall of the house and looked up at the towering turrets. "It's incredible. I've never seen anything like it."

"Forgive me, but when you smile, you're absolutely stunning."

She shook her head. "You're flattering me, Mr. Vails."

"Modest, too. Call me Christopher."

She stepped back, away from his gaze that was too self-satisfied, too intimate.

He stared at her with a bemused expression. "Why don't you come inside and meet my sister, Vanessa?"

"I suppose I could take a coffee break."

He gestured for her to lead the way, flashing blindingly white teeth in an affable smile, and they followed the sound of feminine voices into the great hall. Elizabeth was surprised to find Caroline, her fingers drumming impatiently against her thigh, in quiet conversation with the woman who'd entered the house.

Vanessa. The physical resemblance between the siblings was obvious; they were blonde, lean, and tall with the same angular features. But one look at Vanessa's face revealed their differences. Where Christopher was charming and friendly, Vanessa's gaze was cool and condescending. Standing next to her, Christopher seemed to fade a bit, as if he stood in her shadow.

Her beauty was striking, from her flawless features to her luxurious hair. She seemed entirely self-possessed, as if every movement of her body was choreographed to present the woman to her best advantage. Even her fingernails gleamed, painted scarlet in a perfect match to her fine jacquard jacket.

She appraised Elizabeth, lifting one perfectly sculpted brow in contempt. The condescension on her face was obvious, as if she wanted Elizabeth to see it. Her face transformed into a smirk, and the smile, like the rest of her, seemed carefully curated.

Christopher set his hand gently on the small of Elizabeth's back, and Vanessa's eyes narrowed. "Elizabeth, this is my sister."

"Vanessa Vails," the woman purred. She used her fine leather handbag like a flag, waving it subtly to communicate her status. Then she turned back to Caroline, as if she'd given Elizabeth all the attention she deserved. "It's wonderful to see you, Caroline. I swear, it's been ages since we've been together at Cliffhaven."

"It has been a while," Caroline agreed. Her face had a closed expression Elizabeth had never seen her wear.

"I'm so glad you're home," Christopher said, wrapping one arm around Caroline's shoulders and kissing the top of her head.

Some of the tension left Caroline's face as she smiled at him. "It's been too long, Chris. Thank you for everything you've done while I've been away."

"I haven't done nearly enough."

"Truly, he hasn't," Vanessa said, placing one hand on her hip and looking down her nose at Christopher. "You only see Adam when you can fit him into your schedule. Usually between each failed romance." She turned to Caroline. "Chris has worked his way through every available woman on the island. It's embarrassing, really."

"*Vanessa*," Christopher said, his voice tight and pleading. He thrust his hands into his pockets, shaking his head and looking defeated. "If you ladies will excuse me, I'm going to go find Adam. Elizabeth, it was wonderful to meet you." He gave them a strained smile and disappeared into the west wing.

"He's such a child." Vanessa's lip curled. "Christopher is used to being the golden boy, but now that our parents are gone, I'm calling him on his bullshit."

Caroline's face fell. "I heard about the death of your father, Vanessa. I'm so sorry. He was a kind man."

"It's been hard." Vanessa sighed. "Particularly with Christopher's penchant for failed investments. But we're doing quite well, I assure you. So how long will you be on the island, Caroline? Enough time for us to get together for lunch, I hope."

"I've moved back to the island permanently," Caroline said. "I'm opening up a clinic in the village."

"Surely you don't intend to live at Cliffhaven?" Vanessa looked around the dilapidated hall, looking like she tasted something sour.

"We haven't decided whether to restore the house. Elizabeth is here to help with that, and I know her input will be invaluable." Caroline gave Elizabeth a warm smile.

Vanessa leaned away from Caroline, her beautiful brow crinkling, a frown marring her face. "If I were you, I wouldn't want to live in this drafty old relic. And it's so expensive to renovate. Last year we redid our kitchen, and the cost was outrageous!"

Caroline's gaze, as it swept the hall, was full of sorrow. "It's just hard to give up something that's been in the family so long."

"And there really are some incredible works of art," Elizabeth said, hoping to return the smile to Caroline's face. "I'm finding more pieces each day, each more impressive than the last. Even the house itself is a work of art."

Vanessa arched one sculpted eyebrow, and her voice turned cold. "You get paid either way, right?" Then she turned to Caroline and said, "Why don't the two of us go out and get a drink? I'd love to catch up. In private."

An electronic trilling sound filled the air, and Caroline pulled her phone out of her purse, something like relief on her face. "That's the nurse I've hired for the clinic. I should take this."

"Of course," Vanessa said coolly. "I'd heard about your new clinic, though I didn't believe you'd be working there. It's hard to understand why people work when they don't have to."

"And I've never understood how people could be idle when there's so much work to be done. It's funny how people can be so different." Caroline's fingers tightened around her phone. "Now you really must excuse me."

As Caroline walked away, Vanessa called after her, "Call me so we can catch up. I mean it!" Caroline didn't answer, just waved vaguely and disappeared into the dining room.

Vanessa removed her jacket and turned her cool gaze back to Elizabeth. "Where's Adam?"

"I'm not sure. Maybe in the western—"

"Take this," Vanessa interrupted, dropping her jacket into Elizabeth's arms.

Elizabeth's mouth opened in surprise. She started to tell Vanessa there was nowhere clean to put the fine jacquard coat, but she was walking away, her heels clicking harshly on the stone floor as she sashayed out of sight.

Ugh. Elizabeth rolled her eyes. She'd known women like Vanessa before—those who pretended to be polite while subtly cutting you apart. She went out of her way to distance herself from that type of person, but their words still cut and slashed at her feelings like knives. Still, Vanessa was intimidating, with her impossible beauty, perfect grooming, and fine clothes.

She ran her hands over the lush curves of her hips and frowned. She'd purchased her simple sweater and jeans at a second-hand store.

There was no denying that Vanessa, with her obvious wealth and sophistication, belonged to the world of Cliffhaven more than she ever would. She could study fine art, even save it from destruction, but that art would hang in the hallowed halls of houses like Cliffhaven, in places she would never belong.

Vanessa obviously knew her place in the world, was secure in it, belonged to it. Where did *she* belong?

Longing surged within her, ballooning inside her chest, and she closed her eyes. Her fingers flexed into fists, the muscles jumping under her skin. She had to move, had to go.

She threw Vanessa's scarlet jacket on a broken side table and burst out Cliffhaven's front door. If she could just keep going, keep moving, she could leave all those feelings behind.

CHAPTER 10

*E*lizabeth slipped off her jeans and let them drop to the sand. Naked, she ran to the lake and dived under the surface. The frigid water was a shock, and she came to the surface sputtering and laughing. But it felt incredible against her bare skin, like a caress.

The placid water was deep blue, reflecting the sun's light and twinkling like millions of gems scattered on the surface. Gulls circled the sky, their cries filling the air.

After leaving the unpleasant interaction with Vanessa, she'd walked along the cliff's edge, then followed a steep, rocky path down to a sandy beach. The sun's heat on her skin and the sound of the surf soothed her, smoothing out all her rough edges.

Cliffhaven's beach was a secluded cove of fine, golden sand bordered on three sides by rugged cliffs. And it was completely deserted.

A joyful laugh escaped her as she looked back at the shore. The rocky cliffs were shot through with brightly colored stripes of red, orange, and green. From this vantage point, there was nothing to indicate the presence of humanity—it was all cedar trees, craggy cliffs, and sapphire lake. All of it called to her, like a place she'd known before.

She was so tired of moving, changing homes every few months. It was a bone-deep weariness. If she could have a home, if there was a place she could belong to, she'd want it to be like this.

Her gaze flickered to the top of the cliff, drawn to movement. A lone figure stood at the edge of the rocks, watching her. At that distance, she couldn't tell who it was, or even if it was a man or woman. The figure stood still, watching her openly.

The hairs on her neck stood on end, and she stepped back into deeper water. Who was it? Had they seen her undress?

Elizabeth shivered as cold water seeped into her core. She glanced longingly at her pile of clothes lying in the sand, but there was no way to get to them without exposing herself to the spying figure.

A splash sounded behind her, and she whirled around. Someone was swimming toward her, coming around the western edge of the secluded cove. The swimmer moved fast, their strong strokes propelling them through the water like a torpedo.

Elizabeth looked back to the cliffs, but the mysterious figure had disappeared. She glanced down at her breasts, just visible under the crystal-clear water, then toward shore. The swimmer would be upon her before she reached her clothes. *Please don't let it be . . .*

As the powerful swimmer neared her, Adam's raven-colored hair and muscular arms were unmistakable. She groaned, crossing her arms over her chest and sinking into the water up to her chin. Just one more mortifying moment in which her unprofessionalism was on display.

When he'd swum to within a few yards of her, he stopped, standing abruptly. His eyebrows raised in surprise as water dripped from his broad shoulders. "Miss Watson."

He breathed deeply from exertion, and his heaving chest was sparkling wet in the sunlight. His eyes roved down to her tightly crossed arms beneath the water, but if he noticed her nudity, he gave no sign.

"Good afternoon, Mr. Arrington." She forced nonchalance into her voice, as if skinny-dipping were a daily, dignified occurrence. "Nice day for a swim."

The corners of his mouth turned upward in amusement. "Actually, you look rather cold. Your lips are blue."

"I just . . ." Her mind was a jumble of excuses and explanations, all bouncing around her head so she couldn't make sense of them. He waited patiently for her to continue, a bemused expression on his face. What was it about this man that made her want to confide in him? His patience? The way he looked at her as if she held all his attention, as if whatever she said enthralled him?

"I'm freezing," she admitted. "I'm also naked, as I'm sure you're aware." Yes, the amusement in his eyes was unmistakable.

"But I couldn't go back to shore because someone was watching me from the cliffs. Now they're gone, but you're here, and I'm still stuck in this frigid water."

Adam's smile melted away, and his gaze swept the cliffs. "Someone was watching you?"

"Up there." She pointed. "They left when you came."

"It was probably just Meeks. Or maybe Christopher's looking for me."

"You know the neighbors are here?"

"Why do you think I'm not up there? It appears that both of us hide from people."

She wrapped her arms tighter around her chest. "I don't hide. I just prefer . . . a little distance."

"Is that it?" He cocked his head, taking one step toward her. "It doesn't seem to matter how far I go to hide from you. You find me, anyway. Or is it me that finds you?"

Heat coursed through her, pooling in the most pleasurable of places. Of its own accord, her body gravitated toward him, hands tingling with the desire to reach for him, to fold herself into his strong arms.

Oh, no. Nope. Absolutely not. *For heaven's sake, be professional! Arm's length, Elizabeth.*

He looked at her with concern. "You're freezing. Why don't you go back to shore? You can use my towel. It's behind that fallen tree at the edge of the sand."

Now that he mentioned it, she was freezing. How could her body be so traitorously heated while her teeth chattered so hard they might break? She nodded, and Adam turned to face the horizon, offering her a view of his broad shoulders and muscular back. Grudgingly, she peeled her eyes away and turned toward the shore.

Would he turn to catch sight of her naked body? She wanted him to, wanted to catch him staring at her with hungry eyes. Then she'd walk to him, confident and devastatingly seductive, wrap her arms around his neck, and . . . *That's quite enough!*

She shook herself out of the reverie, ran to shore, and wrapped his towel around her torso before glancing back at him. He stood patiently in the water, his back to her, and she sighed in disappointment. "You can turn around."

He moved through the water toward her and stepped onto the sand. He wore a skin-tight black suit that covered him from hip to thigh, exposing the powerful muscles of his legs. Water dripped from his chest and hair, and he looked like a god— Poseidon emerging from his kingdom, vigorous and impossibly powerful. Or Hades, all dark and mysterious.

"I can hold the towel so you can put your clothes on, if you like," he said.

"All right."

She unwrapped the towel and held it up so it obscured his view of her body. As he took the towel from her and stretched it wide, he held her gaze, as if proving to her he could be trusted not to peek.

Would it kill you to take a peek? Just a little one?

He obviously had no desire to catch a glimpse of her, and the corners of her mouth turned down in disappointment. Was she the only one feeling the thrum of energy coursing between them?

When she was dressed, he lowered the towel and they fell into step together, walking toward the trail.

She spied a wooden staircase leading from the beach to the top of the cliffs. "It would be quicker to take those stairs back to Cliffhaven."

Adam eyed the staircase dubiously. "It's not safe. It was built in my grandfather's age, and we haven't kept it up. The whole structure should come down."

"Let me see." She quickened her step, approaching the gray wood clinging precariously to the rock.

The staircase was past its prime. Black mold spread across the wood, and there were gaps in the railing where it had broken and fallen away. Nails jutted from the rails with rusty, jagged edges.

She placed her foot on the first step, tested it, and found the wood soft with rot. "You're right. It needs to be torn down."

"I keep telling you, some things aren't worth saving." His unkempt hair blew in the wind, curling into his emerald eyes. "The first November wind will probably bring it down, save us the trouble. Until then, you shouldn't use it."

His advice doused her libido like a bucket of cold water. Her eyes narrowed as she placed her hands on her hips. "You keep warning me away from things as if I'm a child. I'm not stupid, Mr. Arrington."

He leaned back as if she'd struck him. "I'm just concerned for your safety, as you should be."

"I can take care of myself, thanks."

"I'm sure you can, better than most. But many outsiders underestimate the dangers here." His eyes grew guarded, and it was like a barrier had fallen between them. He retreated, taking one step away from her. "I'm sorry to have offended you, Miss Watson. My concern was kindly meant."

She watched him walk away, cursing under her breath. The man was intriguing, but he had a way of touching the parts of her that were raw and vulnerable. Did he do it deliberately? Either way, it would be best to keep her distance from this man who triggered her emotions so easily.

She waited until Adam was out of sight, then made her way across the sand alone. Movement stirred at the top of the cliff, drawing her eye. The dark figure was back, watching her openly. Maybe they'd never left.

She stared back, her anger building. Putting her head down, she ran toward the trail, adrenalin fueling her quick climb. She pushed herself hard until her breath came in gasps and her calves ached. But by the time she reached the top of the cliff, the figure was gone.

IT WAS AT NIGHT, when all was still, that she felt the weight of Cliffhaven—it's emptiness and solitude. It felt cavernous and dark, full of unknown secrets.

Sleeping in an unfamiliar room was normal for Elizabeth, so why, since coming to Cliffhaven, did she toss and turn, lying awake staring at the ornate plaster ceiling of her bedroom, her eyes tracing the geometric pattern endlessly, imagining she could feel unseen eyes watching her?

One moment, the fire lay dying in the hearth as freezing November rain pounding against the windowpanes. The next, she was suddenly alert—ears straining to catch the slightest sound, skin prickling on the back of her neck, overcome by a primal awareness: *danger.*

She threw back the duvet and leapt from her bed. Grabbing her phone from the nightstand, she cast its cold white light around her room, onto the weighty bookshelves, the fireplace, over the velvet settee.

All was as it should be. Then what could explain the pounding of her heart? Her complete conviction that she wasn't alone?

She tilted her head, listening. Had the floorboards creaked, just outside her room?

She threw open her chamber door and burst into the corridor. But it was silent and still, the dark corners of the hallway full of shadows.

If ghosts did exist, and they chose somewhere to haunt, it would surely be this desolate mansion straight out of a gothic movie. Were the souls of Cliffhaven resting, as Hodges said, uneasily?

Or was it Adam that wandered the deserted halls of Cliffhaven at night, candlelight glowing in his raven-black hair, flickering in his guarded green eyes? A thought came to her, unbidden: *he's the one that's haunted.*

Then something moved in the darkness, just outside the realm of her phone's light. Something wispy and white, like the fluttering of fabric.

A thrill shot across her skin. Breathless, she crept down the corridor to the gallery that wrapped around the second floor. Gripping the wooden banister, she leaned over it, staring at the long drop to the stone floor of the great hall below.

There was nothing. No ghosts, no brooding man wandering the lonely halls of his house. Nothing but the silent emptiness of Cliffhaven, a barren fortress around her. Her shoulders drooped, and she turned back toward her room.

Then the massive front door opened. The sound of creaking

hinges tore the silence, rooting her to the floor. The door opened slowly, inexorably, as if pulled by some unearthly hand. She gaped, her mouth open in shock, as freezing rain and cold air pounded into the hall, fluttering the hem of her nightgown.

Wiping her clammy hands on the skirt of her nightgown, she stepped onto the staircase. Her shoulders tense and tight, she crept down the stairs, wishing the hall wasn't a pool of blackness, a darkness so impenetrable, it could be hiding anything.

The door stood open, a silent invitation. Her stomach quivering, she stepped outside, the stone portico cold on her bare feet, and the darkness of the northern night enveloped her.

Again, there was nothing. Just the scent of wilderness and rain in the air, the wind lashing the evergreen trees, and her car parked in the drive.

She squinted into the darkness, then lifted her phone to cast its light. The bitter night breeze cut through the thin cotton of her nightgown, and she shivered, so that the small beam of light shook as it illuminated her car.

She froze, shock and dismay rooting her to the spot. Then she ran down the portico steps, only vaguely aware of rain soaking her, the biting wind raising bumps on her flesh, and stopped in front of her car.

It was destroyed. The windows were smashed, with fragments of glass hanging from the frame like broken teeth. The paint was gouged in long streaks, as if sliced by metal claws. The tires slashed. Blood-red words, jagged and angry-looking, were painted across the hood of her car:

GET OUT

Her breath caught in her throat. It was heart-wrenchingly familiar—the smashed car, the jagged metal, the broken glass— and she was plunged back in time to another car, twisted and broken.

Run, Lizzie!

Her heartbeat was thunder in her ears, and she was choking, smothering, couldn't get enough air into her chest that was tight as a drum. She took two frantic steps back and ran into something solid.

She lashed out blindly, thrusting her elbows into the mass of flesh behind her. Two powerful arms wrapped around her chest, twin bands of iron holding her in place.

She was trapped.

CHAPTER 11

"Jesus, Lizzie! It's me!"

But the words were just sounds to her, with no more meaning than grunts. Images flashed through her mind—broken glass, twisted metal, dripping blood —and her body fought to free itself.

"Lizzie." It was Adam's voice in her ear, quiet and calm. "It's okay."

And his voice grounded her firmly to that place, that time. She wasn't a child watching her mother's life ebb away. She was at Cliffhaven, in his arms.

"Let me go!" He released her, and her muscles tensed for flight.

Then he was before her, emerald eyes holding hers. "Lizzie, take a second. Breathe."

She closed her eyes, willing herself to relax, to fight the instinct to flee that still pounded through her.

"Are you hurt?"

She shook her head.

"What happened?"

"I don't know. I followed . . ." *A ghost. A fucking ghost.* "The front door was open, so I came outside and found this." She gestured to her car, her eyes fixing on the crimson droplets dripping from the hood. They looked like blood.

"Get out." The words were dirty in her mouth, appalling. Tears stung her eyes, and she dashed them away before they could fall.

She was unwanted. Again. Always.

His hands slid over her arms, a soothing gesture, and she looked up at him. "Why did you call me that?"

"What?"

"Lizzie. My mother called me Lizzie." Her eyes roamed back to the battered car, the dripping scarlet paint. "Run, Lizzie," she whispered, lost in memory. Then she shuddered, her entire body convulsing as if it could rid itself of pain.

"You don't need to run."

Didn't she? She'd forgotten, for a moment, that she wasn't alone. He was there, standing by her side, ready and willing to face whatever darkness fell beyond their circle of light. Warmth spread through her chest, and she wanted to lean into it, lean into him.

Her fists tightened as she waged a silent war within herself. Then she whispered, "My mother died in a car accident. She was trapped inside." The scent of gasoline. The blood dripping down her mother's face. "She told me to run, so I did. Then the car caught fire."

Adam's face paled. "That's . . . horrific."

Horrific. Yes. The perfect word.

"I guess we have that in common," he said, and she looked at him questioningly. "Fire stole our families, robbed us both of our lives. Didn't it?"

She hadn't thought of that—the two of them, bonded by flame. A tragic connection.

"So running away saved your life, then." His bright gaze

penetrated her. He made her feel exposed, as if there were nothing his eyes didn't see.

"It was a long time ago."

"That doesn't matter, does it? Not for me. The fire that took my parents might as well have been yesterday."

Their eyes met, and it was as if her insides began to melt, to soften.

"So the damage to your car . . . that really triggered you."

The first seed of embarrassment took root. "I'm fine." She collected the parts of her that were melting, gathered them up, and gave them a good shake. They needed to be strong enough to hold up her life, not gooey and pining for this handsome man. "You can go back to bed. I don't need help."

His head flinched back. "I know you don't. But I'm offering it, all the same."

She crossed her arms over her chest and glanced around the grounds. There was no sign of anyone else in the darkness, but the long shadows of trees and bushes were perfect places to hide.

She approached her car warily. Angry gashes had been scratched into the car's paint, and she traced the deep gouges with her finger, following them all the way around the car. Her little sedan hadn't been new in a decade, but it had been with her for years—more permanent than the apartments she leased month-to-month or the friends she left behind when it was time to move. With a pang, she realized it was the most constant thing in her life.

And now it was broken, ravaged, violated. A sick feeling infested her stomach as she opened the trunk and took inventory of her restoration supplies. There were the solvents, gels, and sponges. The brushes, gauze, and alcohol. The putty and resin. It was all there, undamaged. *Thank God.*

"Do you know who might have done this?" Adam's voice was calm.

She recalled the front door opening of its own accord, the sounds slithering behind Cliffhaven's walls. Her arms fell to her sides, her mind skipping from thought to thought like a pebble thrown on a lake. Ghosts don't smash car windows and use spray paint. Whoever vandalized her car was human. But maybe *something* had wanted to show her the damage. A benevolent spirit, looking out for her, warning of her of danger in the night.

"I have absolutely no idea who would do this to me."

She closed the trunk lid carefully, her body humming with anger. Whoever it was, if they thought they could frighten and intimidate her by vandalizing her car, they were wrong. She was used to being unwanted, being on the outside. And she didn't frighten easily.

Adam walked around the car, surveying the damage, his face inscrutable. "Maybe it was just teenagers looking for trouble."

"But these scratches in the metal, and the angry message—it feels personal." She recalled the groundskeeper she'd met on her first night at Cliffhaven, his strangeness and hostility. "Would Meeks do something like this?"

"Absolutely not." He shook his head. "Maybe it was someone you knew before you came here. Did you leave anyone behind who might be angry with you?"

"Nobody who would follow me all the way to this island."

"Perhaps . . . a man? A lover?" His face was blank, perhaps carefully so.

"Give me a little credit. You think I would date someone who would do something like this?"

Adam appraised her. "We don't always see our lovers clearly."

Her fingers tapped a beat on the skirt of her nightdress. "There was someone in New Orleans. But he wouldn't do this."

His eyes narrowed. "How can you be sure?"

"Because I didn't mean that much to him, okay? I was nothing to him. He didn't want me." She pressed a shaky hand to her forehead. "This was done in anger. I've never had a relationship that would inspire that kind of passion."

"That's very hard to believe."

"Well, it's true. I guess I should call the police."

Adam frowned and began pacing, hands clasped behind his back. "Is that necessary?"

She stared at him. "Why *wouldn't* I call the police?"

He huffed out a breath and looked away. "Do what you must. But I hope this incident proves to you that remaining at Cliffhaven isn't a good idea."

She threw her hands into the air. "What does that even mean? Do your guests often have their cars vandalized? Is that a common occurrence?"

"Bad things happen here," he said, and she was brought up short by the raw emotion in his voice. "You need to know that, to understand it. Now, for God's sake, keep yourself safe and leave."

He doesn't want me here, either. Well, that shouldn't be a surprise. Nobody had ever wanted her.

Memories flashed through her, all her failed attempts to find a home—her aunt depositing her at child protective services as if she were an article of clothing that didn't fit right; her foster parents refusing to meet her eyes as she packed her few belongings into a garbage bag; her caseworker dropping her off at the orphanage after so many failed attempts at rehoming, explaining that some kids just didn't fit in with families.

Her throat constricted, fighting the emotions rising within her. And goddammit, hot tears were streaking down her cheeks, but that didn't matter nearly as much as making him understand. "It's easy for you to say that, sitting here in your gorgeous mansion overlooking the sea, but not all of us have a home. I have nowhere to go, nowhere to run to." She dashed angrily at the wetness on her cheeks. "I've only had myself to rely on for the last couple of decades, and you know what? I've done just fine at keeping myself safe. So save your advice and your lectures. You don't know anything about me." Ignoring his stunned expression, she looked down to her feet, bare and numb against the sharp gravel driveway.

"I want to," he said.

"Want to what?"

"To know you."

She lifted her head, and he stepped toward her, his careful eyes searching hers. He was offering something, but she didn't know what it was, exactly, or how to accept it.

She stood unmoving, her lips slightly parted, contemplating the effect he had on her body. She wanted him to move closer, wanted to feel that energy that pulsed between them. He looked down at her, his bright green eyes alive with heat, and she swallowed the lump in her throat.

She wanted his comfort. She ached for it. And giving in, going to his arms and allowing herself to be held would be so easy, would feel so damn good it was scary.

"Let me at least pay to have your car fixed." His words—so practical, so unromantic—jolted her out of whatever spell she'd been under. "This happened on my property, so I'm responsible, in a way."

"That's not necessary."

"Please, it's nothing."

"*No.*" Her voice sounded too angry, too strident, so she took a deep breath. She folded her arms across her chest, striving to make her voice strong, but it came out hard and cold. "Your help isn't needed. Or wanted."

He absorbed her words like they were blows, then inclined his head. "I understand." Then he turned on his heel and strode away, his spine stiff and straight, and disappeared around the corner of the house.

Alone again. Remorse flooded her. She turned back to her vandalized car, trying to recapture the anger that had fueled her only moments before, but the sharp edge of her fury had dulled.

As the darkness of the night began to fade into early morning, fear creeped into her, bringing a barrage of questions. Who mutilated her car? Was she in danger? And what if her unrequited desire for Adam morphed into something she couldn't control?

This was exactly the kind of complicated situation—fraught with emotion and desire and mystery—that she always avoided. She'd spent years building walls around her heart, shielding it from the pain of loved ones lost. She'd fortified that wall until it was strong and solid, but now she began to see that something so hard was also brittle, and its destruction could begin with one small crack.

WHEN ELIZABETH finally dragged herself up the staircase in the great hall, fatigue and concern weighed on her, as heavy as her broken car. The sun was beginning to peek through the leaded windows, casting burnt pink and orange beams across the portrait gallery, illuminating swirls of dust.

At the top of the stairs, she stopped short. Meeks stood in front of the portrait of Adam's parents, a cap clenched in his gnarled fingers. He clearly hadn't heard her approach; his lips were moving, whispering words as he looked adoringly at the painting of Adam's mother. Then he froze, cocking his head at a sharp angle, and his eyes darted to Elizabeth. They were red-rimmed, swimming with tears.

"I . . . I'm sorry," she said, backing away, ready to run from this emotionally fraught encounter. But Meeks beat her to it, shuffling away without a word, dashing the tears from his cheeks as he disappeared down the staircase.

She turned back to Audrey Arrington's portrait, searching

for an explanation for Meeks's tears. Had the woman truly been that beautiful, or had Adam painted his mother kindly, inventing that beatific smile? If so, he hadn't treated his father so benevolently, hadn't bothered to hide the haughty tilt to his chin, the domineering hand gripping Audrey's shoulder possessively, almost digging into her flesh.

Meeks had been talking to Audrey, hadn't he? As if she were present, still walking this world.

She could understand the impulse. Even now, she sometimes whispered to her mother when the world seemed dark and lonely. Believing her mother could hear made the world easier to face.

Her mother had been everything. What had Audrey meant to Meeks?

CHAPTER 12

*A*fter snapping a few photos of her vandalized car, Elizabeth set out on foot, following the winding road through the forest, down to the village. The town was tidy and well-tended, with flowerpots bursting with autumnal color in every doorway. In a marina off the main street in the village, sailboats swayed gently on the waves.

As she walked down Main Street, the strangers she passed acknowledged her with a nod, smile, or greeting. Children rode their bikes down the middle of the sleepy street with beach towels slung around their necks and paper sack lunches swinging from the handlebars.

She stopped in front of a stately brick building boasting a sign emblazoned with the word "POLICE". She needed to report the damage to her car, had to have a police report to file an insurance claim. But she couldn't force her feet down the little sidewalk toward the station. Flashes of memories stung her—uniformed officers escorting her out of the foster home; sitting in the backseat of a patrol car behind the metal cage, feeling like a criminal, knowing she must have done something very wrong; a black garbage bag on the seat next to her containing everything she owned.

With those memories burning away her contentment, her feet, seemingly of their own accord, turned away from the police station. She would file the report, she *had* to, but a cup of coffee first might bolster her resolve.

She entered a little café with a red-checked awning, and every face in the full restaurant turned to look at her with frank curiosity. She smiled self-consciously and took a seat at the long counter.

"Hey there." A young woman stood behind the counter, pad and pencil in hand. Her hair stuck out in short, blonde spikes, and her face reminded Elizabeth of a pixie—all pointed lines and elfin delight. She wore torn denim and a t-shirt touting a punk rock band, and her smile was huge and genuine. "You must be that art restorer they hired up at Cliffhaven."

"How did you know?"

"It's a small town, and everybody's been talking about you." The waitress put her hand on her hip and looked Elizabeth up and down. "It's the hair that gives you away. Those movie-star curls live up to the hype."

Heat tingled across her cheeks. But it pleased her to be recognized, like she was a temporary member of the small community.

"I'm Elizabeth."

"Jenna. Welcome to Arrington Island. What'll you have?"

She picked up the laminated menu. "What's good?"

"Everything. My brother Tony's cooking today. You've got to try one of his pasties."

"What's a pasty?"

Jenna cocked her head, as if she couldn't believe her ears. She placed both hands on the counter and leaned toward her. "Trust me."

"Okay, I'll give it a try. And coffee, please."

It wasn't long before Jenna returned, placing a steaming pastry on the counter and watching as she took a tentative bite.

"It's good." Elizabeth nodded her appreciation. "Amazing, actually. Thanks for the tip."

Jenna leaned over the counter conspiratorially. "So what's it like working up at Cliffhaven?"

"It's interesting. The house is incredible, like nothing I've ever seen."

"I've always wanted to go inside that mansion. Ever since I was a kid I would see it there, high on the cliffs, and wonder what it was like. My brother Tony used to scare the hell out of me with stories of Cliffhaven's ghost. You haven't seen anything paranormal up there, have you?"

Elizabeth thought of fires that started themselves, of doors opening in empty rooms. The feeling of unseen eyes upon her. "No," she shook her head, "of course not."

"Yeah, I guess it's silly."

She lifted another forkful of the delicious pasty. "Is everything your brother makes this delicious?"

"Yeah, but don't tell him I said that." Jenna wiggled her eyebrows playfully. "It's kind of a bummer the restaurant's closing. Owner's moving to Arizona. It's no big deal for me, I can find work anywhere. But it's going to be hard for Tony. He just moved back to the island after going to culinary school. His food is amazing, but nobody will hire him to cook like that around here. He might have to leave the island, which would totally suck."

Elizabeth's eyes widened as inspiration struck, and she leaned forward eagerly. "Could I meet your brother?"

"You betcha." Without moving away from the counter, Jenna yelled, "Tony! Come meet a satisfied customer!"

A moment later the kitchen door swung open, and a man appeared. He was in his mid-thirties, tall and lean with a cheerful crop of red hair. Freckles splashed across his face, and he wore the same wide grin as his sister—genuine and a bit mischievous. His immaculate chef whites seemed out of place in the casual café. He reached for Elizabeth's hand with long, clever fingers.

"You the satisfied customer?"

"That's me." Looking into his cheerful blue eyes, she couldn't help smiling back. "Elizabeth Watson. I'm working up at Cliffhaven."

"You liked your meal?"

"I loved it. You know, they're looking for a chef at Cliffhaven. Would you be interested?"

"Seriously?" Tony's eyebrows raised and his grin widened. "Jenna, is this some kind of prank?"

"As if I don't have better things to do." Jenna slapped a hand-written bill on the counter in front of Elizabeth, grabbed a coffee pot, and pranced away.

"It's not up to me who they hire, but I can tell the Arringtons you're available," Elizabeth said. "Want to give me your number?"

He drummed his fingers on the counter, eyes bright and eager. "Would it be weird if I came up there tonight? Maybe cooked a few things the Arringtons can taste?"

She cocked her head to one side, considering. Caroline had said she could have guests. And Tony's cheerful face in the gloomy kitchen would be like a light in the dark.

"Yeah, that might work. I'll tell Caroline to come over for dinner, maybe around seven?"

Tony's sky-blue eyes lit up. "Awesome. Let me run to the market and I'll meet you there."

Elizabeth placed cash on top of the bill. "Perfect."

"Thanks! Have a good day, eh?" Tony said as Elizabeth slung her messenger bag across her body and made her way toward the door.

"You're not going to believe this!" Tony's cheerful voice

carried across the restaurant, making Elizabeth laugh as she swung out the door into the bright sunlight.

~

WHEN TONY ARRIVED LATE that afternoon, Elizabeth was there to welcome him. His red hair stuck out at every angle, and he carried two large paper sacks overflowing with groceries. The smattering of freckles across his nose and his delighted smile made him look youthful, like a boy ready to make mischief. But his smile faltered when he looked around the depressing kitchen.

"The kitchen is kind of bare bones at the moment," she said apologetically. "I'm not even sure if all the appliances work."

Tony clapped his hands together and rubbed them in anticipation. "That's okay. If I can cook a bouillabaisse on a hot plate in a dorm room, I can work with this."

As he began unpacking food from grocery bags, she said, "I've got the Arringtons coming in for dinner at seven. What did you decide to make?"

"I've planned a four-course meal. I really want to show them what I can do." Tony ran one freckled hand through his red hair, demonstrating why it stuck out at odd angles. "We'll start with a fig and goat cheese salad, then gazpacho. I'll have some homemade rosemary focaccia on the table, too. For their entrée, I'll roast lamb chops and pair them with grilled tomatoes and parsnip puree. Then we'll end with a simple crème brûlée."

"It sounds wonderful. I'll check back in a while to see if you need anything."

She wandered into the dark and dismal dining room just off the kitchen. The vast chamber was dominated by a heavy dining table she guessed could accommodate at least fifty guests. She threw back the heavy curtains hanging across one wall, disturbing enough dust to make her sneeze. The drawn curtains revealed a wall of windows overlooking the lake—a breath-taking view that would be awash with pinks and oranges at sunset. With a little effort, the room would be stunning.

After discovering delicate china and heavy flatware in a buffet, she set the massive table for two. She took one of several tarnished silver candelabra, filled it with white candles, and placed it on the table.

As she stepped back, appraising her work, the dining room door swung open, and Caroline swept into the room wearing pink scrubs and a stressed expression.

"Oh, Elizabeth! Adam told me what happened to your car. It's just awful!"

"It'll be fine. I filed a police report after lunch. They'll handle it."

Caroline's eyes swept the dining room, and they were apologetic when they turned back to her. "I'm so sorry, but I can't stay for dinner. One of my new patients just went into labor."

Elizabeth's shoulders sagged. "Really? I met this chef in the village who's looking for work, and I thought he might be good for Cliffhaven."

"So you invented this dinner party so we could try his food?"

"Yeah. I hope you don't mind."

"Of course not. It was kind of you to go to the trouble." Caroline looked at the table set for two. "Why don't you take my place at the table tonight with Adam? You two can decide whether to hire the chef."

Elizabeth bit her lip. An intimate dinner was pretty much the opposite of maintaining distance and professionalism, but how could she refuse?

"I can do that, I suppose. But before you go, why don't you come to the kitchen and meet the chef? Maybe he'll have something for you to sample, and you can tell me what you think about hiring him."

Caroline glanced at her watch. "Actually, I wouldn't mind grabbing something to eat. It could be a long night."

In the kitchen, Tony was hard at work in front of the stove. There seemed to be a lot going on, with several pots on the range and dishes of ingredients on every surface, but all was tidy and organized.

"Tony!" Caroline's green eyes widened in surprise.

"Hello, Caroline." A broad smile stretched across Tony's face as he wiped his hands on his apron.

"You two know each other?" Elizabeth asked.

"We went to school together." Caroline's gaze was fixed on Tony's face. "You were a few years younger than me, I think?"

"Not too many years younger."

Inexplicably, Caroline blushed. Elizabeth looked back and forth between Caroline and Tony, feeling as though she'd missed something.

"Tony, Caroline can't stay for dinner. Do you have anything she could taste before she leaves?"

"You betcha." Tony aimed a flirtatious smile at Caroline then darted between the stove and counter, gathering samples and plating them artistically.

Caroline ran her fingers self-consciously over her strawberry blonde chignon, uncharacteristically quiet as she watched Tony work. He laid several small plates of food on the table before her, and she gave him a shy smile before taking a bite. Making a small sound of pleasure, she tried a bite from the next plate. "Tony, everything tastes so good. Where did you learn to cook like this?"

"Culinary school." Tony's grin somehow got even bigger, and his chest puffed out. "It's really good to see you again, Caroline. I'm glad you came home."

"Me, too." Caroline gazed at him, her food forgotten. Then she started, as if waking from a dream, and checked her watch anxiously. "Darn! I really need to get to the clinic. It was nice to see you, Tony."

Caroline waved to Elizabeth and sent her a meaningful smile before she slipped out the kitchen door.

"Is she incredible, or what?" Tony shook his head in awe. "I had the biggest crush on her in high school. But I was a lowly freshman and she a senior, so I didn't have a chance. Is she still married?"

"Freshly divorced."

"Hot damn." Tony rubbed his hands together. "Her ex-husband was such an idiot—all foam and no beer, know what I mean? She could do so much better."

She laughed and leaned her hip on the counter. "Well, she loved your food. And you'd be such a happy addition to this house."

They were interrupted by the sound of heavy footfalls in the dining room. She swiveled her head toward the sound, then looked back to Tony, all playfulness gone.

"Now we just have to convince Adam."

CHAPTER 13

*E*lizabeth wasn't prepared for the unexpected intimacy of dinner by candlelight with Adam. It didn't help that he looked just as flustered as she felt. They faced each other across the ornate wooden table, candles flickering between them.

He'd dressed for dinner in a dark blue jacket the color of the lake after sunset and matching trousers. He was clean-shaven, and even his normally windswept hair looked as if he'd tamed it, but his powerful body appeared even larger seated at the dinner table. She had the unsettling idea that he was like a wild animal —no less dangerous for being cleaned up and dressed in fine clothing.

His gaze was direct and unwavering, as if he drank in every detail of her, and her breath quickened in response. The room seemed too warm, and she didn't know what to do with her hands.

"What do you think of the salad?"

Adam looked down at his plate as if he'd forgotten it was there. "It's delightful. I've had nothing like it in years."

"I think Tony would be a good addition to the household. His food is amazing, and he's honest and cheerful."

"Does this Tony have red hair? Always grinning like he's just pranked someone?" She nodded, and a ghost of a smile flitted over his face. "I went to school with him. He was gregarious, always had lots of friends."

"That doesn't surprise me."

As they ate, she was acutely aware of Adam's every move—how his long fingers tore bread and lifted morsels to his lips, how he drank wine as if taking immense pleasure in it. The only sound was the clinking of silverware against china, and the silence between them was heavy and intense.

"Since we're a bit understaffed, I'll clear." Elizabeth rose, gathered their salad plates, and deposited them on a serving cart. She retrieved two bowls of gazpacho from the buffet before crossing to Adam's side of the table.

When she bent and placed the soup in front of him, she found herself mere inches from his body. He stiffened and drew in a quick breath. Only when she had moved back to her side of the table did he seem to relax.

"You don't have to serve me."

"I don't mind. While it isn't exactly in my job description, it seems appropriate."

"It makes me uncomfortable," Adam said as he lifted his spoon.

"You didn't mind Mrs. Hodges serving you."

Adam put his spoon down. "That is entirely different. Hodges worked for me."

She shrugged. "I'm here, in this house, as an employee."

His jaw tightened, and he leaned forward. "You work for Caroline, not me. That's a distinction I'd prefer you internalize."

She blinked, and her body heat seemed to rise several degrees. After bolting a few bites of the gazpacho, she escaped to the kitchen, where Tony was putting the finishing touches on the entrée plates. He looked nervous, so she gave him a thumbs-up and an encouraging smile.

When she returned to the dining room with the lamb, Adam stood by her chair. He reached out, taking both plates from her, and said, "Please, sit down." She sank into her chair slowly, unsure, and he laid a plate before her. While he was still bent in front of her, inches from her face, he locked his green-eyed gaze on hers. "You are not my servant." His words were heavy with weight and sincerity, so much that she was speechless. Then he moved back to his seat with surprising grace.

She took a bite from her plate and closed her eyes. "This lamb is incredible. What do you think?"

"Delicious. If Tony is willing to stay and work in this dismal place, it's fine with me."

She eyed the crystal chandelier that hung uselessly from the ceiling. "It might be less dismal if we had more light. How long has the electricity been out?"

"Years. It never worked well to begin with." Adam paused, his fork halfway to his mouth. "I suppose that if you had your way, we'd have workers crawling around my house like insects, fixing the electricity and God knows what else."

"Light would be nice. And internet. You object to people working on Cliffhaven?"

"I don't expect you to understand." His gaze travelled to the candle, where flames danced, casting flickering shadows across his scarred face. "You've already turned my world upside down. Must you disrupt it further?"

She put her fork down and took a deep breath. "Do see that plaster work?" She gestured to a medallion on the ceiling decorated with a fleur-de-lis. "It's so intricate, so fine, it must have been done by a master craftsman. But it's been damaged, probably by a leaking pipe. We can save some of it."

"Why would you want to save any of it?"

"You mean, just knock it out and start over? Some people

would do that, I guess. But I like to save whatever I can. There's so much here worth saving."

Adam glanced around the neglected room, looking unconvinced. She leaned closer, her voice pitched low with intensity. "This house is incredible. There might not be anything like it on this continent. I don't understand how someone could let it fall to ruin. Doesn't it make you sad?"

"Of course. It breaks my heart to see this crumbling stone, these broken windows. But the slow destruction of Cliffhaven is right. More than right, it's *just*." He seemed to catch himself, pressing his lips together and meeting her gaze with guarded eyes.

"Why?" Her fingers clenched around the napkin in her lap. "Tell me why."

"Let's just say all this," he gestured around the room, "is what I deserve."

"You've been neglecting Cliffhaven . . . because it's what you deserve?" He nodded, and she leaned back in her chair, crossing her arms over her chest. "You're going to have to do better than that."

He raked a hand through his dark hair. "The house used to symbolize everything my family accomplished. It was grand, beautiful, and shared its success with the entire island. Now it embodies my mistakes. My failures." Shame darkened his face, and she knew there was more to this story, that Adam had secrets he guarded. "So let the house crumble to ruin, like my family name, like me. I deserve nothing less."

"This house isn't just about you," she said. "People put their lives into this home for hundreds of years before we were born, and it will be here long after we're gone. Master artisans spent years building this house, and now it's home to priceless art that has value to all of humanity." She gestured around the room. "The care of all this has been entrusted to you. It's your responsibility, even if you don't understand it. Even if you don't deserve it."

Adam blinked, leaning back in his chair as if he had no idea how to respond.

She lifted her glass of wine to her lips, hoping it would cool her boiling blood. "If you were so opposed to restoration, why did you agree to hire me?"

"For Caroline," he said simply. "Now that she's returned, I'll give her whatever she asks for, whatever she needs. She needs a home, and she thinks this is it. I know better." He looked down at his uneaten lamb. "Caroline won't stay long. She'll realize her plans to restore Cliffhaven are doomed, and she'll leave. Again."

"Why do you keep saying the restorations are impossible?"

Adam gazed out the window at the setting sun. "If I was a superstitious man, I'd say this house is cursed."

Unease danced across her skin. "But you're not a superstitious man."

"Either way, this place will never be a happy home. Some things deserve to be ruined."

She shook her head. "I just can't agree with you. If we have the power to save something, something beautiful or useful, it's irresponsible to let it go to waste." Her eyes flashed with purpose. "Broken things still have value."

He scowled. "You can't possibly know what you're undertaking here."

"I do this for a living," she said sharply.

"Do what, exactly? Invade other people's houses, evaluate their possessions with a cold eye, reduce art to dollars and cents?"

"Is that what you think I'm doing here?" She could feel heat spreading across her cheeks, hot anger taking hold. "For your information, my job is to *save* art. To restore it. I'm the one who comes in and cleans up the mess and degradation people like you allow to infect your art, to save the pieces you so callously disregarded. This place means so much more than dollars and cents, can't you see that?"

He raised a single eyebrow. "Then just leave me out of it as much as possible, if you don't mind." He threw his napkin down on the table. "We're finished here, aren't we?"

She looked at his untouched plate. "Tony made dessert."

"I've lost my appetite. Please excuse me, Miss Watson." He rose and walked toward the door, his back rigid.

"Just for the record," she said, and he paused, though he didn't turn to face her. "I'm going to do everything in my power to convince Caroline to save whatever we can."

"And I wish you luck, Miss Watson," he said quietly, all the anger gone from his voice. Then he slipped out the door.

She gathered the dishes, setting them in the cart with too much force, and returned to the kitchen wearing a frown. The counters and stove were clean, and sparkling dishes sat in the drainer while Tony paced the floor.

He stopped, took in Elizabeth's scowl, and his face fell. "He didn't like it."

"No, Tony, that's not it. Everyone loved your food. You can probably expect a call from Caroline."

"Yes!" Tony pumped both his fists in the air in triumph.

She couldn't help returning his smile, allowing his enthusiasm to wash away her anger. "I hope you and Caroline can negotiate something that suits you both."

"Honestly, I'd take whatever she's offering," Tony said happily. "I can't wait to get started!"

"You know, the Arringtons might be able to offer you housing. There's plenty of room, and I've heard there are cottages for servants on the edge of the forest."

"No, I've got a house on the river I could never leave." Tony leaned casually against the wall, apparently deep in thought. "Have you ever felt like, all of the sudden, everything in your life is working out perfectly?"

"I'm not sure I have." She tried to mask the sorrow in her voice with a smile but failed, and Tony looked at her with concern. "Don't mind me. I'm just tired. I think I'll go to my room, if you can show yourself out?"

They said good night, and she slunk out of the kitchen, using the light of her phone to guide her through the dark, lonely house.

She'd told Tony the truth—she didn't remember ever feeling like her life was working out perfectly. She certainly hadn't felt it after her mother died, or when she'd bounced around different foster homes.

But she'd pulled herself out of that system, had educated herself and become a professional. She was on the path she'd always wanted for herself, and she'd done it on her own, without needing anyone. Why, then, did it feel like it wasn't enough?

She knew that by moving from place to place, never staying long enough to forge lasting relationships, she was living a lonely life. Her transitory existence suddenly seemed inadequate, like a pair of old shoes she'd outgrown, now too tight for comfort. Something about Cliffhaven made her feel as if her life, and the pattern that had forged it up to that point, was lacking.

Walking through the dark corridors, she yearned to feel what Tony described—that sense of certainty that the path she was on was the right one, that everything was falling into place and would lead to her inevitable happiness.

In her lonely little room, she pulled her suitcase from under the bed and let out a breath when she saw her belongings arranged inside.

See? Everything's okay. Even if you're living in a haunted house. Even if your car's been vandalized, and you're battling an inappropriate attraction to an infuriating man who opposes your work at every turn.

Maybe it was time to give up this old habit of keeping her

possessions together. She wasn't a child anymore, bouncing between foster homes, where the need to move could come with only hours' notice.

She pulled a nightgown from the battered suitcase and contemplated the armoire that stood empty against the wall. It would be easier to access her clothes if they were hung in the armoire, and they'd get less wrinkled.

Then she bit her lip, sighed, and pushed the suitcase back underneath her bed.

CHAPTER 14

*W*hen Adam painted, he was on fire. Eyes burning with a passion that was finally unbridled, his powerful body moving with grace as the paintbrush cast bold strokes on canvas. With all his energy focused on the work, he looked unencumbered by those emotions that normally constrained him—the brooding intensity, the constant guarding of his words. The black t-shirt he wore hugged his chest and biceps, and it struck Elizabeth again that his upper body looked like it was sculpted by Michelangelo—perfect proportions and flawless grace.

She'd come upon him in the art studio, and seeing him this way—so passionate, so free—stole her breath. She had to force her gaze away, pressing one hand to her chest, because something was swelling inside her, something alarming and bitter-sweet and seductive.

She'd been avoiding him these last few days. Losing herself in her work, in the exploration of Cliffhaven. Each day she discovered small things that gave her immense pleasure, like the frescoes adorning a second-floor bedroom, or the Louis XV furniture with gilded bronze ornamentation in the music room.

With every new day, she fell more in love with the house, and when she pressed her hands against the damask wallpaper, she could feel it, begging to be brought back to life.

Adam lifted his head, as if sensing her presence, and smiled. Apparently, the anger he'd displayed during their intimate dinner was forgotten. The corners of her mouth lifted in response.

"Elizabeth. Do you need something?"

"Actually, yes." Her fingers tapped a nervous beat against her jeans. "I'm almost done with my inventory of Cliffhaven's art."

His smile faltered, and he turned his gaze back to the canvas. "You move quickly."

"I enjoy the work." She hugged her tablet to her chest. "But there's part of Cliffhaven I haven't been able to access—those locked doors off the great hall?"

He stiffened, and a muscle twitched in his jaw.

When he didn't answer, she added, "I can't finish my report until I've gotten in there."

"Can't you just leave it?" His voice was low, almost a whisper. "Finish your report, leave some stones unturned."

"But the inventory would be incomplete. I couldn't possibly."

A mirthless smile turned up one corner of his mouth. "No, that isn't in your nature, is it?" He turned his gaze to her, and his emerald eyes were hot, intense. Then he threw down his brush and palette carelessly. "Come on, then." And he marched past her, out of the studio.

She followed, struggling to keep up with his long strides, suddenly overcome with nerves. "It doesn't have to be now."

"We both know you won't stop until you've seen it all, until you've unearthed every secret." Then he muttered under his breath, "And what sick part of me *wants* to show you, though it will do me no good?"

What the hell is in that room? Secrets from his past? A pile of dead bodies? A sex dungeon?

By the time she reached the large set of sculpted double doors, he had a key in the lock. "Let's get it over with," he said, opening the door, then gesturing for her to go before him.

She swallowed, anxious and eager, then stepped into the cavernous room. Windows lined one wall of the immense space, and dim light filtered through the dirty glass. The stone floor stretched an impossible distance, open and empty except where a grand piano sat uncovered, collecting dust, at the foot of a small dais.

"It's . . . a ballroom."

He arched one eyebrow. "What did you expect?"

A sex dungeon.

The ballroom was a showpiece, obviously designed to highlight the family's collection of fine art. Paintings of every size and shape decorated the walls, which were paneled with cream-colored wood and decorated with gilded ornamentations. Statues carved from truly exquisite marble adorned the corners of the room.

But the most stunning detail was the domed ceiling. The fresco painted on its surface was magnificent, running the entire length of the massive room. It depicted brawny Greek gods, satin-draped goddesses, and dozens of *putti*—chubby angels with silver wings—all resting on clouds, gazing at the mortal realm below.

Her mouth fell open as she spun in a slow circle. "Where did your family get this?"

Adam frowned at the wall of paintings. "Which piece?"

"The ceiling. The fresco. Is it genuine?" Her gaze roved over the masterpiece on the plaster above. "This is either a fantastic reproduction of an Italian Renaissance-era fresco, or it's authentic."

"Do you mean the ceiling could actually be from the sixteenth century?"

"Or the seventeenth." Her heart beat faster as excitement

coursed through her. "It would have been quite an undertaking to get one of this size across the ocean."

"My great-grandfather was a collector, so I suppose it's possible." Adam clasped his hands behind his back and gazed up at the ceiling as if he hadn't seen it in years. "My grandfather used to tell me stories about Cliffhaven—how it was made, the people that lived here. He said entire rooms were shipped from Europe."

"I don't doubt it." She crossed the marble floor with quick strides, then crouched at the base of the wall, touching the delicately carved golden wood with the tip of her finger. "This paneling is from France. Definitely eighteenth century. So is that gilt."

"Gilt?" Adam asked, leaning next to her.

"It's when you cover a surface with gold leaf or powder. This is an impressive example of the technique used in the 1700s."

She turned her gaze back to Adam. Their eyes met, and he drew in a quick breath.

"You're an artist," she said. "You know what goes into creating something like this. Don't you think it's worth protecting?"

He stood abruptly, his face stony and defensive. Though his giant frame towered near her, he seemed to deliberately keep himself several steps away, out of arm's reach. "It's not that simple."

"You knew this was here." She stood and gestured around the room, a mix of anger and confusion bubbling within her. "You knew what it would mean to me, to the entire estate, and you kept it locked up."

He ran one dinner-plate sized hand through his thick black hair. "I knew if you saw this, you'd recommend restoring the house."

She tilted her head and appraised him. "Why don't you want Cliffhaven restored? Tell me the truth."

He pulled away from her, his eyes shuttering, his chin jutting out in defiance. "My reasons are my own," he snapped. Emotions passed over his face like clouds in a storm—there was pain, indecision, guilt, shame. He ran a hand over his face, avoiding her eyes. "I'm sorry. I'm not fit company."

Then he turned on his heel and left. The desire to go after him was so strong, denying it gave her whiplash.

She gazed up at the fresco. What were the odds that an unknown Renaissance-era fresco had been removed from a villa in Europe and shipped across the ocean? It could be a reproduction, a masterful one. But some instinct, some burst of intuition, was whispering that this fresco was authentic. That would make it priceless.

She aimed her phone's camera at the ceiling, zooming in on the image. Incredible. A masterpiece, hidden in the northern wilderness. Her eyes narrowed at a corner of the fresco, where daylight poured through a hole in the roof the size of her fist. Water damage had destroyed the paint and plaster, distorting a cherub's face into something grotesque.

Pain and indignation roiled within her. How could anyone allow the slow destruction of something so precious?

Like Adam said, his reasons were his own. They had nothing to do with her. And if she ached when she saw the pain in his eyes, if she wanted to soothe him, that just meant it was time for her to get the hell out of there.

She would have to examine the fresco, look for clues indicating whether it was authentic. Then finish the report and leave this place that aroused so many inappropriate feelings with her. The fresco would need to be stabilized, immediately. But she would never see it restored.

Her belly knotted. What would it be like to restore something so masterful, so precious?

She closed her eyes, and an image burned there—Cliffhaven as it should be, whole and glorious. This desolate house, with its crumbling statues and waterlogged frescoes, needed to be restored.

She could convince Caroline, she knew she could. But Adam, with his dark moods and mysterious secrets, was another matter entirely.

IN CLIFFHAVEN'S ATTIC, it was easy to believe in ghosts. The dusty, dim interior was perfectly suited to housing a poltergeist or two. The attic held what most attics did—old furniture, possessions prized by others for unfathomable reasons. Some larger items were covered by drop-cloths, looking like motionless ghosts drooped in every corner, too lazy to get up and haunt.

Cobwebs and dust marred Caroline's strawberry-blonde bob, and the sleeves of her scrubs were rolled to the elbows as she dug through an ancient steamer trunk. She held up a stack of papers, her face glowing with excitement. "I knew we kept the paperwork."

Elizabeth plucked a receipt from the top of the pile emblazoned with "Sotheby's" in gold lettering. The next document was brown with age, crispy around the edges, but it made her heart stutter. "This is a certificate of authenticity. For an Italian landscape."

Caroline tapped a teetering stack of papers. "And there are tons of them!"

Tamping down the excitement that tingled through her, Elizabeth said, "That doesn't mean anything. Anyone can fake a certificate."

"But these receipts!" Caroline plucked one from the stack. "This one is from Christie's. Doesn't that mean anything?"

Her heart pounding, she took the receipt. "We can check.

Cross-reference their records, if we can get online. But it's a good sign." *A very good sign.*

She pulled the completed inventory from her messenger bag. "Either way, it doesn't really change my report. Or my conclusions."

Caroline's face fell. "You've finished the inventory?"

"Here's a copy." She held out the pages. "I'll email you a digital file once I get somewhere with internet."

Caroline didn't take the document, so Elizabeth let it fall to her side. "I guess my work here is done." Ignoring the tiny crack that pierced her heart, she set the inventory on top of the pile of papers.

Caroline's eyes were wide and worried. "But I still don't know what to do."

"It's all there, in my report. I can't authenticate your pieces, technically. But it's my opinion that they *should* be authenticated, that it wouldn't be too expensive or difficult—especially now that you have that paperwork—before selling anything."

"So you think we should sell?"

"No, Caroline." The words slipped out before she could stop them. "I mean, it's up to you. But Cliffhaven is worth more than the sum of its parts. This house is a work of art in itself. There's nothing like it in the northern part of the U.S.; it's rivaled only by the Biltmore Estate, or Hearst Castle in California. And its condition really isn't too bad. It's certainly has more value than a luxury resort."

"Adam still doesn't want to restore the house." Doubt turned down the corners of Caroline's mouth. "He's almost convinced me to give up."

"If money's an issue, you could sell a few pieces to pay for the restorations."

Caroline let out a humorless laugh. "It isn't that."

"You can't just abandon this art." She reached out, touching Caroline's wrist tentatively. "If your frescos are as old as I think they are, they're important. Priceless. They have value to all of humanity, part of our shared human history. They need to be stabilized and protected."

Caroline threw her hands into the air. "What can I do if Adam won't agree?"

"At least stabilize the frescoes, as soon as possible. Then, if you don't restore the house, an expert can remove the frescoes and you can sell them. You could get a ton of money at auction."

"They can be removed from the house?"

"Absolutely." But the thought of removing them made her stomach churn. They were part of the house now. "But first they have to be stabilized, to stop any further harm or degradation. I can recommend some experts who'll do a great job."

"That would at least buy us some time to convince Adam to restore the entire house." Caroline's green eyes lit. "Will *you* stay? Stabilize, or whatever the word is, the art yourself?"

She leaned back, surprised. "Me?"

"Why not? You're an expert. I studied your C.V. and called your references. Wasn't this the work you did at the museum?"

"Yes." She'd worked on frescoes there, but those pieces hadn't been nearly as old, nearly as valuable. "I don't think that's the best idea. But I can give you names of some experts who—"

"Adam will never agree to let someone else in. Besides, I want someone like you." Caroline's voice trembled as she looked around the decrepit attic. "Someone who can restore everything here that's broken."

Caroline's eyes were wide and hopeful. "Stay. Stay and help me make this right."

God, she wanted to. Desire, seductive and impossible to ignore, pulled at her. To work on those masterpieces with her own two hands would be the pinnacle of her career, a once in a lifetime opportunity.

But it was time to move on. In New Orleans, she'd broken all her rules—she'd taken a semi-permanent job at the museum, stayed in one place longer than she should, got too attached to people that would let her down—and everything had gone wrong. She'd fled with her professional career in shambles, her heart bloodied and bruised.

If she were honest with herself, she was already forming attachments to Cliffhaven, to the house and the people who called it home. Those attachments would only make it more difficult to leave when the job was over. Better, easier, to say goodbye now and start somewhere new.

All her belongings were still in her suitcase. It would be so easy to leave, to extricate herself from the entanglements that would only get more complicated if she stayed. But when she thought of packing her suitcase into her car and driving away from Cliffhaven, a sadness ate away at the edges of her, and sorrow held her in its grip.

She was an expert at leaving. Why, then, was it so difficult?

The house intrigued her, of course, with its treasures and mysteries. She was burning to get her hands on the frescoes, to watch some part of Cliffhaven returned to glory. And Caroline, who'd been so kind, was relying on her. But it was the thought of Adam—of saying goodbye, leaving him alone in the cold halls of this desolate mansion—that tied her stomach in knots.

She thought of how he'd looked that first night in the library —his powerful body kneeling before her, his piercing green eyes. The pull toward him was strong, undeniable. Terrifying, actually. And staying longer would only make it harder to keep him at arm's length.

"Don't say no," Caroline said, interrupting her circling thoughts. "Just think about it. We'll talk tomorrow, and if you still want to leave, I won't try to stop you."

CHAPTER 15

*W*hen Elizabeth tiptoed to the kitchen early the next morning, she was greeted by the homey scent of baking bread. Tony, wearing a black half apron over jeans and a maroon t-shirt that clashed wildly with his red hair, pulled a tray from the oven and shot her a cheerful grin.

"Caroline offered you the job!"

"Yep. I was so freaking excited to get started, I hit the grocery store, and here I am."

"Something smells amazing."

Tony pointed to golden pastries resting on a silver tray. "Apple tarts. There are oats in the crust, so it counts as breakfast. But didn't you already have one?"

Her hand froze, hovering over the pastries as she looked up at him. "Not yet."

His face scrunched up in confusion, then he shrugged. "Maybe it was Adam. But yeah, have as many as you want."

He stared at the silver tray of pastries, his smile fading. "I used to scare my sister with stories of Cliffhaven's ghost. I always thought I was just messing with her." His blue eyes, usually so alive with humor, were somber. "But it feels strange here, doesn't it?"

She stilled. "What do you mean?"

Tony looked at her sharply, then his ears turned pink, and his lips broke into a sheepish grin. "Never mind. I stayed up last night binging *Ghost Hunters*. Guess it took a toll."

She bit her lip, evaluating Tony as he turned back to the oven. Should she confide in him what she'd seen—fires that started in empty chambers, doors that opened themselves, the strange sounds she heard at night?

Yeah, great plan. If you want him to think you're crazy.

Just as Tony slid a pastry onto a small plate and handed it to her, the kitchen door opened. It was Adam, wearing an inscrutable expression and a jet-black sweater the exact color of his hair. He saw Tony, and his hand twitched toward the textured skin on his cheek, then fell to his side.

Tony's mouth dropped open in surprise, then he recovered his characteristic grin. "Adam! By God, you've gotten enormous since I last saw you. What have they been feeding you, growth hormone?"

A surprised laugh escaped Adam's large chest, dissolving the tension in the room, and he clasped Tony's outstretched hand. "It's been a long time, Tony."

"Too long." Tony clapped his hands together, and his eyebrows wiggled playfully. "I hope you're hungry because, boy, do I have a breakfast for you. Let me just poach the eggs really quick."

As Tony turned toward the stove, Elizabeth's eyes met Adam's then skittered away. The kitchen that had only a moment before felt large and roomy was now too small, too close.

Adam pulled three plates from a broken cupboard and laid them on the farmhouse table. "I was thinking you might want an office. Somewhere to put your restoration supplies."

"That's a good idea, if it isn't too much trouble."

"You could use the parlor off the great hall."

"I could never use that fancy room."

"What about that old butler's pantry?" Tony said, gesturing with a spatula toward a doorway.

She poked her head into the small room. It was windowless and cramped, but it held a small desk, and empty shelves lined one wall. "This is perfect. Thanks."

Tony put his hands on his hips. "Damn! Another broken burner. Now there's only one working on this stove. Good thing I thrive on challenges."

Tony left the room, and Elizabeth turned back to Adam, who was frowning as he looked around the derelict kitchen.

"I've gotten used to Cliffhaven as it is now, run-down and broken. It was fine when I was here alone." Adam turned his emerald eyes to hers. "But now you and Tony are here, and it doesn't seem right."

His gaze swept over the cabinets with broken hinges before darting back to her. "Someone like you really doesn't belong here."

Her mouth dropped open, but he'd already pushed through the door into the dining room, leaving without looking back.

Ouch. His careless words were efficient, stabbing her directly where it hurt most. Did she have a bullseye painted on her insecurities?

Her stomach knotted, and the thought of food was suddenly revolting. She yanked open the kitchen door and burst outside. The clouds had darkened to flint gray, perfectly matching her mood, and the wind blew urgently. She stomped along the gravel path toward the cliffs, her fists clenched at her sides.

The nerve of him, saying she didn't belong at Cliffhaven. As if she didn't know. What an insufferable man, plaguing her with his mercurial moods.

She stopped at the cliff's edge, where a wall of rain was

visible in the distance over the lake. Ten-foot waves pounded the rocks below mercilessly. She took a deep breath, letting the feel of the wind in her hair and the scent of the lake calm her. She closed her eyes, allowing herself a brief moment of peace, and found in it forbearance.

She had no right to be angry at Adam. The most he was guilty of was brutal honesty. And if he was a bit anti-social, that was probably natural, given the events of his life that must have formed him. He'd suffered a terrible tragedy while still a child. He'd reached adulthood locked away, alone, in this ruined place. There'd been no family to guide him, no friends to help share the pain. She, more than most, knew what that did to a person.

She sighed and shook her head, determined to banish all thoughts of Adam and any feelings he might inspire.

ELIZABETH FROZE, one hand on the crystal doorknob to her room, listening. The second-floor corridor was deserted, but still a sound filled the air. A scuffling noise, coming from behind a door a few feet away.

It was almost midnight, the end of a long, exhausting day. Tony had left hours ago, and the house was empty.

She'd *thought* the house was empty.

Noises absolutely shouldn't be coming from behind the heavy oak door at the end of the corridor. Her chest rising and falling with shallow breaths, she stepped toward the sounds, now clearly identifiable as footsteps.

She threw open the door, stifling a scream when confronted with a shadowed figure. "Adam! God, I thought . . ."

He was dressed all in black, so that his outline blended into the shadows. He held a single candle in a brass holder, and it cast flickering light across his chiseled features. Raising one dark eyebrow, he said, "What did you think?"

That you were a ghost.

She swallowed, shaking her head. "It doesn't matter."

They stood on the landing of a circular staircase. The narrow stone steps coiled down in a tight spiral, looking treacherous. The stone walls were rough-hewn, cold to the touch, and frigid air brought goosebumps to her skin. It smelled of cold, damp stone.

"Another staircase," she said. "I'm not sure I'll ever learn my way around here."

"These are the servants' stairs. They're hardly ever used."

No surprise there. The tight spiral staircase was cavernous—a secret, solitary place that reminded her of a tomb. And the landing was small, forcing her close to Adam, so his scent enveloped her.

"Caroline says you're leaving." His green eyes held hers. "She said I should convince you to stay and restore the frescoes yourself."

"Actually, the best thing for these frescoes would be to remove them and restore them off-site."

"That's not going to happen." His voice was flat, his eyes shrouded.

She blinked. "I don't think you understand. Trying to restore the frescoes here could seriously degrade—"

"Not one piece of art is going to be removed from this house. Under any circumstances."

She gritted her teeth. Couldn't he see these frescoes were important? That they had value beyond being the possessions of one stubborn, hermitic man? But one look at the muscular arms folded at his chest and his clenched jaw, and she knew he wouldn't change his mind.

"If Caroline wants the frescoes restored, it can be done here," he said. "If she can find an expert willing to stay and do the work." He looked at her, then, with eyes that had softened. If she didn't know better, she'd think he looked . . . hopeful.

126

She let out a breath. "Restoring the frescoes—or at the very least stabilizing them—is a good idea, from a financial perspective. Even if you don't restore the house, you'll make a nice profit from any art you sell."

"I've had enough profit. It doesn't interest me."

"What about the art, then? You know these pieces should be saved."

His face hardened, turning to sculpted stone. "My father's possessions. They can burn, for all I care."

She gasped. "You don't mean that."

There was a savage glint in his eyes, but pain marred the lines of his mouth. What had happened between Adam and his father that created so much bitterness, so much anger?

"If the art is so important, why aren't you staying to stabilize it yourself?" he said. "Because deep down, you know staying is a bad idea."

Ignoring the sting of his words, she said, "Why is it such a bad idea?"

"There are things people like you don't know, dangers you've never dreamed of." His emerald eyes looked haunted. "The damage to your car isn't the worst thing that could happen to you here."

"People like me?" Her back stiffened. "You're always trying to get rid of me, using safety as an excuse. Just say you don't want me here."

"It isn't an excuse." His eyebrows drew together. "Accidents happen. Tragedies occur. You should know that better than anyone."

Anger blazed inside her. "My safety is none of your business. And I don't think you're being honest."

He froze, eyes narrowed. "About what?"

"The reason you don't want Cliffhaven restored. The truth is, you don't want people here, invading this world you've created for yourself."

His lip curled into a sneer of self-disgust. "Of course I don't. You think I like showing my scars to strangers? Watching their faces twist with horror and repugnance? Seeing their fear?"

His words reached into her chest, touching her heart, erasing her anger. Her fingers stretched toward his arm, but she pulled them back. "You . . . I mean, the *house* has been so neglected, and it's such an incredible place. It could thrive again, I know it could."

Watching her, his face lost its bitter edge, and he slumped against the stone wall. "If you don't restore the frescoes, no one will. Caroline won't call those experts you recommended. She'll give up, maybe leave the island, and the house and I will continue as we did before you came."

The thought brought a heaviness to her chest. How could she walk away knowing that this place, this person, existed, and they were wasting away, alone and forgotten? "Now that I've gotten to know Cliffhaven, I don't think I could bear letting it fall to ruin."

She leaned against the staircase's iron railing, biting the inside of her cheek. She *could* stay. It was possible. Just to stabilize the frescoes, make sure they were protected. The work was important, and it had nothing, absolutely nothing to do with the handsome man looking at her with hope and passion and longing in his eyes.

He stepped toward her, closing the distance between them. His wide shoulders blocked out the world, creating a space that was only the two of them—only his leather and cedar scent, only the heat between them. And again she felt that pull to him, like if she moved into his arms, they would fit together perfectly.

"But could you really stay?" He raised one eyebrow. "Commit to this project, remain here until the frescoes have been restored?"

Unease skittered through her. "Why would you doubt me?"

His emerald eyes searched her face. "Because there are times, like now, when you look as if you'll run away at any moment. Like a deer about to bolt."

He dipped his head toward her, his lips inches away, and his voice lowered to a whisper. "Are you going to run away, Lizzie?" An ache flooded her, and suddenly she was hollow, carved out by need. And madness took hold, the words leaping from her before she could rein them in. "I'm staying. I'll stabilize the frescos myself." *And damn the consequences.*

For a moment, she thought he would sweep her into an embrace. His face was a storm of conflicting emotions—hope and despair, longing and fear—a man at war with himself.

It took all her willpower to wrench away from his gravitational pull. She stepped back, placing a hand over her racing heart. There was no room here for desire or longing; those feelings would only get in the way of her work. And her work was suddenly more important than it had ever been. It wasn't just restoring her career and reputation—these frescoes were precious. Priceless. More important, even, than her life.

"Caroline will be pleased you're staying." The heat in his eyes had cooled to resignation. "You'll need the roof fixed to protect that fresco. I'll hire a contractor, but I'm not sure we can get it done before the snow falls."

Her smile slipped. A sinking feeling in her stomach accompanied the dawning realization: winter was coming. A northern Michigan winter.

Winter was anxiety, it was freezing temperatures and barren wastelands. Winter was ice slicking over roads, snow blinding drivers, her mother's car skidding sideways off the road, tumbling into a ditch. Winter was the wind that tore at her exposed skin, carrying the stench of gasoline and smoke. But, most of all, winter was the cold that infected her on the day of her mother's funeral, a cold that seemed to settle into her chest and reside there.

No, winter didn't bear thinking about. And now she was confronted with it, the reality of it coming closer each day. Trepidation settled in her stomach as the enormity of her decision rested there.

"It's late," he murmured. "I guess I should wish you good night."

"Good night, Adam."

He stepped down the spiral staircase, and when the flickering light from his candle disappeared, the darkness was complete. Alone in the gloomy stairwell, she shivered and reached for the light of her phone. *Damn.* It was dead again. She'd forgotten to charge it in the kitchen, which was, it seemed, the only room powered by a generator.

Her hands brushed the cold stone walls, searching for the door. They fumbled in the dark, her heart beginning to race, but the door seemed to have disappeared.

I'm trapped. The thought was ridiculous, but logic couldn't calm her shaking hands or loosen the breath locked in her chest. Then her fingers closed around the doorknob, and her shoulders sagged in relief.

The second-floor corridor was pitch-black. Cool air brushed her skin, raising the hairs on her arm, sending a shiver through her. She stood in the empty hallway, her skin prickling, her breath coming fast and uneven.

Then, on the wall in front of her, the mounted gas lamp suddenly burst into life. With a popping sound, it lit, spurting flames and flicking golden light into the dark corridor.

Her breath caught in her throat as she stared at the hissing flame. It was impossible. The damascene lamps she'd admired on her first night at Cliffhaven, the ones Caroline said were broken, were now hissing like a coiled snake. And there was no one there to turn the switch.

Before she could exhale, the next mounted lamp lit, a few feet from the first. Her eyes bulged as slowly, one by one, the lamps lining the corridor sputtered to life, their flickering flames leading down the empty hallway.

She sucked in a breath, her trembling hand covering her mouth, heart pounding in her chest. Spellbound, she stood in the deserted corridor, staring at the long-dead lamps brought to life in this haunted house.

CHAPTER 16

*E*lizabeth pressed her hand against her heart and said, "Is someone there?"

And she wanted there to be, wanted to hear a soft, feminine voice answer in the stillness.

Beyond the lit lamps, the corridor faded into darkness—a yawning abyss where anything could hide. And the flames called to her, beckoning her forward. She crept down the corridor, her footfalls soft on the crimson velvet carpet, knowing she was being led to somewhere or something, and it was stupid, *stupid* to follow. But some desperate desire that she was afraid to name overshadowed her fear.

So she followed the lit lamps to the second-floor gallery, where the faces in the portraits glared down at her. She lifted her nose, scenting the strange odor that filled the air—sulfurous and metallic. The scent of Hell.

More lamps burst to life, one by one, along the wall of the gallery. Past paintings of Adam's ancestors, of pastoral landscapes. Until, finally, the last lamp lit next to the life-size portrait of Audrey and Stephen Arrington that hung above the cold fireplace. Then all was still, but for the hissing, flickering lamps.

Her heart pounding with every step, she approached the portrait of Adam's parents. Audrey Arrington, life-sized, in her bridal veil and luminous dress the color of the finest pearl, smiled down on her like a benevolent mother. And her husband, Stephen, glowering with displeasure. His stare was hypnotic, unescapable. As she stared at his cold, dark eyes—black as night—the hairs on her arms raised. She froze, breath held, ears straining for any sound.

She wasn't alone. She knew it with unshakable certainty. The very air was heavy with the presence of another. And she could *hear* something, couldn't she? Scratches, whispers, slithers in the dark.

"Audrey?" Her voice was a whisper, forced out of her tense throat. She leaned closer to the portrait, silent. Listening.

Then fire leaped in the hearth—flames soaring four feet high where only an instant before there'd been nothing. She gasped, staggering back even as the flames shrank, catching and feeding off the dry wood on the grate.

A small trail of flame creeped out of the grate, crawling across the stone floor of the hearth toward her bare feet. She stared at the fire, her eyes bulging.

Put it out! Her mind screamed, but she was frozen in horror.

This was no earthly fire. No natural flame travelled in that thin line across stone, slithering *up the wall* like a snake from hell. When the flames reached wallpaper, they seemed to be extinguished, but, inexplicably, a thin black line appeared in its place. It snaked across the wallpaper, the edges glowing red in the darkness, smoke wisping.

The wallpaper was burning, but not naturally; thin black streaks curved across the wall, from left to right. And the snaking black line was forming shapes. Letters.

She gasped, and the breath caught in her chest, lodging there.

It was a message. A message written in fire. When the black snake stopped its progress across the wall, two words were burned into the damask wallpaper in ghostly writing:

Run Lizzie!

Adrenalin rushed through her bloodstream. The words echoed in her head, taking on the timbre of her mother's voice —the terror and desperation of her last words.

Panic consumed her. Her hands clutched the sides of her head, pressing against her temples. Then she ran—through the portrait gallery, down the grand staircase, her feet flying across the stone floor of the grand foyer. She threw open the front door and ran into the dark night with no coherent thought of where she was headed.

A dark figure hulked at the bottom of the portico steps.

"Adam!" Without thinking, she launched herself into the shelter of his arms.

"What's wrong?" His hands wrapped around her shoulders protectively.

She shook her head, mouth open, but no words could describe her horror. "Upstairs."

He pulled her behind him, his body tensing like a coiled spring. "What's upstairs?" His voice was a growl.

She could only shake her head, her body trembling. Her mother's voice, urgent and terrified, echoed through her mind. *Run, Lizzie!* It was the accident all over again—the twisted metal, the smell of burning flesh.

But Adam's eyes were before her, calm and steady, bringing her back to the here and now. "Show me."

She shook her head. *I can't go back up there.*

But he clasped her hand, and she looked down at their

entwined fingers. Her heart slowed its pounding, her breath steadied. Giving in to the intense need coursing through her, she laid her forehead against his chest. He drew in a sharp, surprised breath, then his arms came around her. Carefully, gingerly, as if she were a ghost that might turn to a wisp of smoke in his arms.

"Are you hurt?" His voice was gruff, and the sound of it reverberated in his chest, under her cheek.

"No."

What was it about this man that was so reassuring? It wasn't just his physical strength, his calm amidst chaos. There was something about him that was solid and steadfast, that communicated he could be relied on.

She took a deep breath and leaned back, lifting her chin to look into his eyes. "You need to see for yourself." And she led him back into the house, up the grand staircase, knowing he would stay by her side.

In the second-floor gallery, the gas lamps that had blazed so brightly were now extinguished. The only light came from the smoldering logs in the hearth, and the letters on the wall were barely visible. The smell of sulfur lingered in the air.

Adam looked expectantly at her, and she took a steadying breath. "Those lamps were lit. They started in the corridor by my room, lighting one by one. Lighting *by themselves*, leading me down the hallway. They led here, to the portrait of your parents."

Adam's eyes fixed on the painting, his throat working with emotion. Then his gaze flicked to the damascene lamps. "These lights haven't worked in years."

She stepped to the closest one. "How would I turn them on?"

"That knob, there."

She fumbled, and he stepped close to her, placing his fingers over hers so they turned the knob together. The lamp spurted to life, and golden light spilled across the portrait gallery.

Adam's eyes widened. "I'll be damned."

"Don't say that." Not while the smell of sulfur lingered in the air.

"Look at the wallpaper," she said, for the light of the single lamp illuminated the message written in fire.

Adam blinked, his mouth falling open. Then he tilted his head, stepping toward the wall and examining it. He ran his fingers over the black edges where the wallpaper had burned away, exposing the pale white plaster beneath in long, linked letters.

"The fire just . . . started in the hearth. By itself. Then it spread from the fireplace across the floor and up the wall, forming those words."

He cast a quick, appraising glance at her, and tension tightened her shoulders. "I didn't do this," she snapped. He wouldn't believe her; who would? It was all too insane.

After a moment, he said, "Okay." And that simple word had her shoulders sagging with relief.

He stepped away from the wall, casting his eyes over the wallpaper. "It's damned strange."

Her fingers tapped against her lower lip, then she blurted, "It's a warning. Something telling me there's danger here, that I should leave."

"Something?"

She began pacing across the wide gallery. "Adam, you must know this house is haunted."

"Like . . . ghosts? You don't really believe that, surely."

"After something like this? Of course I do." She bit her lip, struggling with warring emotions, then shrugged. "When I'm alone at night, facing the dark, it's easier to believe. This isn't the first thing I've experienced that I can't explain."

"Like what?" His voice was soft, his expression earnest as he approached her.

"After my mother died, I . . . I saw her."

"Her ghost?"

"Maybe. I don't know." She looked down, away from the scorched message on the wall, away from his scrutiny. "I had nightmares after she died. Terrible dreams, and I would wake up sweating and shaking. One night, when I woke, she was there. She sat next to me on the bed, smiling, and caressed my face. I could feel her hand."

She looked up, and he was watching her with no trace of judgment, no disdain. "I know I might have imagined it. But sometimes it feels good to believe she was there, that she watches over me."

"I know what you mean," he said, glancing around the gallery. "My parents seem to be everywhere in this house. But I think it feels that way because I carry them in here." He tapped his chest.

An involuntary shiver shook her. Or maybe his parents *were* still here.

"Maybe there's something special about Cliffhaven," she said slowly. "Something that makes it a place ghosts can inhabit."

"It wasn't built on an ancient burial ground or anything like that."

"How do you know?" She pointed at the jagged letters on the wallpaper. "Those are my mother's words. The last words she ever said to me. Nobody else even knows about them."

"I knew about them. You told me after we discovered the damage to your car."

His gaze fixed on the portrait of his parents, and his smile faded. "If they were still here, somehow, watching over me . . . I hate to imagine what they'd think."

"Would they be disappointed that the house is so neglected?" That *he* was so neglected?

The muscles in his jaw jumped. "We'll never know, will we?" His voice was hard, harsh. "They're gone. And I don't believe in ghosts."

She ran one tentative finger down the blackened wallpaper. It didn't matter if he believed. It was possible, wasn't it, that some spirit was watching over her, warning her of danger?

Someone had vandalized her car, had left the hateful message written in paint. It wasn't a stretch to think there was someone outside Cliffhaven's walls who meant her harm.

Adam gestured to the ruined damask wallpaper. "This looks more like a threat to me." His gaze shifted to her, then, with something possessive and dangerous glinting in his green eyes.

"Why would a ghost threaten me?"

"Lizzie." He shook his head, his face somber. "Most monsters are human."

Then he crossed to the fireplace, gazing down at the glowing red coals. "You were leaving."

"What?"

"After this happened, you were headed out the front door. You weren't even going to tell me about it." His eyes didn't meet hers as he toyed with the banister railing, tracing patterns into the dust. "You find me that terrifying? Scarier than threats burned into wallpaper?"

"You aren't . . ." She shook her head, pressing her hand to her forehead. "I can handle this by myself."

"But you don't have to. I'm here." He opened his arms, palms facing up—an invitation.

Her stomach fluttered, and her knees weakened. It was as if his words went right to the heart of her. Then she was leaning toward him, and he was watching her with something like hope in his eyes.

God, she wanted him. She wanted to fall into those steady arms, to taste the steadfast promise on his lips, nestle into the comfort of his sturdy body.

But if she did, what then? How would it feel when his embrace was withdrawn, when she was alone again? It would weaken her, and she'd be all the colder and lonelier in the absence of his comfort.

"Withdrawing again?" he whispered, his lips curved in a rueful smile. "What a safe little space you've made for yourself— alone, where nobody can touch you, nobody can hurt you."

She stepped back, looking at him reproachfully, and he said, "I'm not judging. Who would I be to judge you? We've both built our own little worlds, far away from others."

He saw her. Really saw her. "Getting close to people only hurts, in the long run."

"I know what it's like to think you're better off alone," he said. "Seclusion can be comfortable, in an odd way. Mine has been. There was no one to judge me, no one to recoil with disgust after seeing my scars. But sometimes it feels like loneliness echoes through my days like sound bouncing around a canyon. My isolation is thick even in the air I breathe. I can feel it resting upon me—a weight that's never relieved." He looked at her, his eyes full of emotions she couldn't name. "Do you ever feel so profoundly alone you can barely breathe?"

Yes. A million times yes.

But his words awakened a fear that slumbered inside her, a confused, complex anxiety. She backed away from him, folding her arms across her chest like they were armor.

He watched her silently for a moment, then turned back to the message written in fire. "Maybe this will seem clearer in the morning light."

"Do whatever you think is best." Because she would be leaving when the frescoes were finished, and whatever was happening here would go on without her. Or it wouldn't, but she'd never know, either way. That was for the best, so why did her chest feel hollow?

He eyed her. "You have a stake in this, too. It's your name on that wall."

"It's only a few weeks, then I'll be gone." So there was no

need to turn it over in her mind, obsess about it. She would finish the work and be on her way, leaving the problems of haunted mansions and devastatingly attractive men behind. And if anxiety scraped at her, she could just add that to the rest of the emotions buried so messily inside her.

What if Adam was right, and the message written in fire wasn't a warning, but a threat? What if something dark occupied the house, some spirit residing in Cliffhaven that didn't want her there, didn't want the house restored?

Maybe she *should* leave. It was just a job, after all, no matter how much she might need the paycheck, need the redemption. What kind of fool would ignore the warning signs, the desperate plea for her to leave?

Her eyes flitted to Adam, then across the gallery, to her mother's last words. Something squeezed in her chest. Apparently, she was that kind of fool.

CHAPTER 17

*W*atching her car disappear down Cliffhaven's drive, bumping along behind a tow truck, felt like seeing another piece of her past abandon her. There was no doubt her little sedan needed to be repaired, but without her car, she was even more vulnerable. Even more cut off from the outside world.

She stood in the drive, gripping her keyring tightly, her fingers closing around the small vial of pepper spray as if it might protect her from all manner of unseen horrors. Her eyes were drawn to the scarlet stain where paint had dripped off her car onto the gravel. She stared at it for a moment, anger growing within her, before stomping off to Meeks's shed. She retrieved a shovel and wheelbarrow, then attacked the problem herself.

As she shoveled scarlet gravel into the rusty wheelbarrow, her mind returned to the scorched wallpaper, to the words burned there. *Run, Lizzie.*

Maybe there *was* something special about Cliffhaven, making it a place where the veil between worlds was thin. There, in those lonely corridors where the shadows were long, it was almost as if she could *feel* her mother. Memories surfaced, fresh and vivid—the touch of her hand caressing her hair, the knowledge that she was safe and loved, secure in the place that was home.

But if Cliffhaven was a place spirits could inhabit, that meant there were dark spirits, too. And sometimes she could feel antagonism as if it were a palpable thing, a malevolent force wishing her ill.

Elizabeth leaned against the shovel, and Cliffhaven's front door opened. Adam appeared, dressed for the outdoors in dark denim and a green, cable-knit sweater exactly the color of his eyes. When he saw her, he ran one hand through his unruly black hair and straightened to his full height.

"Good afternoon." His brow furrowed as he took in the wheelbarrow and shovel. "I should have done that."

"No, I feel better having done it myself."

Adam's head snapped up, and his eyes squinted at a spot in the distance. She followed his gaze across the horizon, where a lone rider approached on horseback.

"Vanessa," Adam murmured.

His neighbor. The one full of wealth and condescension. She rides horses, because of course she does.

Elizabeth had never seen anything like Vanessa on horseback. She rode as if she bent the horse to her will, exercising perfect control over the animal. She slapped her mount fiercely with a crop, though the horse already ran like the wind at full gallop. Vanessa didn't slow as they approached a fallen tree, and Elizabeth gasped as she and her mount jumped effortlessly over the hurdle. They approached the house at full speed, stopping at the last possible second mere feet from Elizabeth and Adam.

Vanessa sat astride her mount like a queen on a throne. Her long blonde hair spilled over one shoulder in a flawless braid. Her riding helmet and jacket were matching crimson velvet, and her leather boots came to her knee. She glanced at Elizabeth, at her faded leggings, at the shovel still gripped in her hand, and her vermillion lips curled up in a small, satisfied smirk.

"Vanessa, you'll overwork your mount," Adam said, frowning. "He's exhausted." He reached out to the horse and ran his large hand down its length as if looking for an injury.

"He'll be fine." Vanessa brushed away his comment with a flick of her delicate wrist, and her voice lowered intimately. "It's true I demand a lot from my mount, Adam. But when he satisfies me, I reward him as he deserves." She gave Adam a suggestive look.

Ugh. Elizabeth had to fight not to roll her eyes. But the double meaning of Vanessa's words seemed lost on Adam as he continued to assess the quivering horse.

"Why don't you take him to our stables?" he said. "We'll give him water and rest before you ride out again."

"What a wonderful idea!" Vanessa beamed at him as if he'd suggested a romantic rendezvous. "You and I can spend some time together."

She slid off the horse gracefully, landing on her feet next to Adam. She took one step towards him and gazed up through her eyelashes. "It's so good to see you."

Adam took a small step away from Vanessa, but she caught him by the sleeve. "I've left messages with Caroline, but you haven't returned my calls, you naughty boy."

"I, uh, don't enjoy talking on the phone."

Vanessa pouted prettily. "Let's not play games, Adam. After all, I know every part of you." She moved her slim body within inches of Adam's.

He tensed, then glanced at Elizabeth. "Let's get your horse some water."

Vanessa appraised Elizabeth, cocking one perfectly sculpted eyebrow and resting her hand on her thigh. It was a cutting assessment, designed to demean her. Her pale blue eyes were cold and sharp as ice.

Adam frowned, then cast another concerned glance at the sweaty, overworked horse. His eyes softened as he turned back to Elizabeth and said, "Please excuse us, Miss Watson."

"Of course," she said. Why did her voice sound so stiff, so formal?

Adam's brow furrowed, and he seemed about to speak, but Vanessa threaded one arm through his and pulled him toward a stone bench. When her mount didn't immediately respond, she jerked the reins severely, causing the horse to flinch and fall into step behind her. She led the horse and man away, sparing Elizabeth one triumphant backward glance.

Heat flooded her body, and her hands tightened to fists as she watched the two of them sit on a stone bench directly in her line of sight. Together, they looked like something out of a magazine—wealthy, beautiful, and so perfect you wondered if it could be real.

She hefted the shovel and returned to filling the wheelbarrow with broken glass and blood-red gravel. *Don't mind me. I'm just the help.*

"It's that ridiculous restaurant of his." Vanessa's sharp voice carried on the coastal wind.

"Honestly, Vanessa, how much is he losing?" Adam asked, inching away from her on the bench.

"Everything," she spat, contempt curling her crimson lips. "He's sunk everything into this absurd venture. And you've enabled him, supported him with your investment. The idiot's losing everything."

"Let me help."

Her chin lifted. "We don't need charity. I can handle it. I'll look after him." Her voice warmed, and she slid closer to him. "I'm good at that—looking after men."

She placed her manicured hand on Adam's forearm. "It can be like before. It was so good between us."

"What are you doing, Vanessa?" Adam looked down at her scarlet nails resting on his skin. "You don't want me."

She reached toward his face but stopped with her hand inches away. Adam's discolored, textured skin obviously unnerved her, and Elizabeth's fingers tightened on the shovel. *She's going to hurt his feelings.*

"My scars still repulse you, don't they?" Adam turned the marred skin toward her, and she flinched. "I remember when you came to see me after the fire. You saw my scars for the first time, and you ran away in horror. It taught me a valuable lesson —nobody wants to see my face."

Vanessa's mouth contorted. "There's always plastic surgery. Honestly, I don't know why you haven't done it already, with all your money."

"It wouldn't make a difference. My scars are on the inside now, too."

After a moment's awkward silence, Vanessa said, "Nonsense. You're just being gloomy, which has always been a bad habit of yours. If you're going to be so depressing, I'll be off. I have a date, anyway." Vanessa waited, as if hoping he'd react. His expression was impassive, and her face tightened in annoyance.

Adam stood and patted her horse affectionately. "Take it easy on this guy on your ride home, okay?"

"If it pleases you." Vanessa gathered the reins and climbed effortlessly into the saddle. "I'd do anything to please you." After one last coy smile, she dug her heels cruelly into the horse's flank and was off.

As Elizabeth watched her ride away, Adam approached her. "Sorry she was rude. She's a lot, but her heart's in the right place."

He shoved his hands in his pockets. "Do you think I need plastic surgery? Turn this nightmare of a face into something less terrifying?"

She examined his face the way she might a statue or work of art, and she smiled. "No. It's part of you, isn't it?"

He stared at her smile as if hypnotized, then he blinked. "I'll never have the scars removed."

"Why not?"

"They're a reminder of my failures, of who I'm not." He looked at her wistfully, as if she possessed something he wanted desperately, but had resigned himself to living without. "And sometimes I need reminding."

"WHAT IN GOD'S name are you doing?"

Elizabeth looked up from her work, her brown eyes magnified through the lenses of her restorer's visor. She'd been examining the fresco in the parlor, her heart thumping with excitement, when the booming voice startled her.

It was Jack, Adam's uncle, his colossal frame taking up the entire doorway. His fine wool suit, starched and pressed and tailored, was every inch the uniform of an upstanding lawyer. But with his wide, muscular shoulders straining the seams, and his ham-sized hands clutching a briefcase, he could just as easily have been an aging football player appearing before a judge to account for his misdeeds. His forehead was furrowed, his lips pressed into a thin line of disapproval, marring his otherwise handsome face.

She pushed the visor up to rest on her forehead. "I'm starting work on this fresco."

She'd already identified pigments commonly used in the Renaissance period, including indigo, malachite, and red ochre. The discovery was exciting, and she was convinced the fresco had been taken from its original home, probably a villa in Italy, and shipped to America.

His craggy face was disappointed, even frustrated, as he let out a heavy sigh. "So you've decided to restore the house."

She took off the visor and placed it carefully next to her other tools. "Not necessarily. Once the frescoes are stabilized, they could be moved, sold." She paused, unsure. "But you should really talk to Adam or Caroline. It's their decision, not mine."

He appraised her for a moment, his captivating gray eyes thoughtful as he tapped one finger against his briefcase. "I'd like to think Caroline hired an intelligent woman, and you see that any cash the Arringtons throw at this money pit of a house would be a complete waste."

She tilted her head, unease spreading through her. "I can't say I agree with you."

"Then I'll have to rely on Adam and Caroline to have more sense." He waved dismissively and lowered his chin, looking down at her. "Why don't we go talk to Adam together? He's usually in the library at this time of day."

Regretfully, she left her tools and the fresco, following Jack through the house in a cloud of his expensive aftershave. When they reached the library, he opened the carved double doors without knocking.

"Jack." Adam's deep voice sounded from within the room. "Good to see you."

When she walked through the door, Adam jumped to his feet, running one hand through his hair. "Elizabeth."

The two men shook hands, and seeing them together, the family resemblance was obvious. They had the same dark hair, the same broad, muscular build, the same extraordinary strength. But while Adam exuded an aura of gentleness—like he went to great pains not to cause harm—Jack seemed careless with his strength, as if he were in the habit of breaking things.

Adam looked between her and his uncle, seeming to take in her discomfort, Jack's self-assurance. "Something tells me this isn't a social visit."

"Not completely, though I don't need a reason to see my favorite nephew. I thought the three of us should discuss the decision to restore Cliffhaven." Jack was energized, excited. She could picture him in front of a jury just like this—poised to argue, eager for the fight, confident he would win.

She straightened, her chin jutting into the air. If he meant to convince Adam to abandon the restorations, she wouldn't make it easy for him.

Jack crossed his burly arms over his chest. "You've started work on the house? Without consulting me?"

Adam held up his hand. "We haven't decided to restore the house yet. Miss Watson is preparing certain pieces of art to be moved—those pieces that can either be stripped from the house and sold or protected during renovations. A minor expense, I'm told, compared to the value of the art in question."

"Really?" Jack said skeptically. "Are there such valuable pieces?"

Adam turned to her with an apologetic smile. "Jack knows nothing about art."

"Not a subject valued highly at law school, I'm afraid. But how valuable can these pieces be if they're old and damaged?"

"I don't know," Adam said. "And to be honest, I don't care."

"Well, she should know." Jack turned to her, stuffing his hands in his pockets. His eyes narrowed. "How much is the art worth?"

She hesitated. "That's a very complicated question without an easy answer."

"You don't know. But that's because you haven't authenticated the art, right? Basically, you don't know if it's worth *anything*."

"Technically, I'm not an appraiser, so I can't authenticate the pieces, but I have enough experience to—"

"So you're going to start restoring art, and you don't even know it's worth? Do you know how ludicrous that sounds?"

Her hands balled into fists. "Adam refused to allow the pieces to be moved, so we can't—"

"And you aren't really an expert, are you? I looked into your background, and you left your last job under quite murky circumstances, didn't you?"

Heat blossomed in her cheeks, and she dropped her gaze to her worn out sneakers.

"Stop cross-examining her." Adam's voice, deep and commanding, echoed across the vaulted ceiling. Jack turned to him, and for a moment, the two men faced off—two alpha males at odds.

Then Jack laughed and held up his hands. "Sorry. Bad habit." He turned back to Elizabeth, his face repentant. "I'm just looking out for my family. I can't let people take advantage of their ignorance.

"But maybe all this arguing is irrelevant." Jack smiled and puffed out his chest. "The development company that wants to purchase Cliffhaven has increased their offer by twenty percent."

"Have they?" Adam toyed with a pen on his desk, looking disinterested.

The smile melted from Jack's face, replaced by a look of concern. "That offer won't last forever. Sell the art, if you must. Then take my advice and sell this property." When Adam didn't respond, Jack threw up his hands. "I've brought you an amazing offer, and you're throwing it away."

"There's no rush with real estate."

"Come on, Adam." Jack sat on the corner of Adam's desk, looking down on him with concern. "I'm worried about you, stuck here in this dilapidated house, wasting away."

"If that's the only reason you've come—"

Jack growled in frustration. "At least think about it. Think about what's best for you. For Caroline."

"Fine. I will. And in the meantime, Miss Watson will restore the frescoes." Adam's voice rang with finality, and Jack shook his head, disappointed.

Then Jack's eyes fixed on a framed document hanging with pride of place above Adam's desk, and he frowned. "I wish you'd take that damned thing down."

She squinted at the document. "What is it?"

"A survey," Adam said. "Commissioned by my father to determine whether Cliffhaven's land had enough copper to make mining worthwhile."

She moved closer to the document, inspecting it. "There's copper here?"

"No, as it turns out. Though copper runs through a lot of Michigan's upper peninsula." Adam stepped closer to her, his shoulder brushing hers as his eyes traced the survey. "My great-great-grandfather made his money mining copper on the mainland, enough to build Cliffhaven and fund the family's art collection for generations. But the family mines eventually stopped producing, and my father sold them off, one by one." His face tightened, shadowed. "When Cliffhaven was all my family had left, my father hoped to mine the land here. He and Jack commissioned that survey. But there was nothing, not a trace of copper."

Jack grunted disapprovingly. "It's disrespectful to your father, hanging a reminder of his biggest failure for all the world to see."

Adam whirled around with a face like thunder, and the anger in his eyes seemed out of all proportion. "My father mismanaged the estate, and you know it. We almost lost everything."

She examined the innocuous-looking document. It was dated 2012, the year her last foster family had given her up, the year she'd entered her first orphanage. The year she'd given up hope of ever finding a home.

"Why do you keep the survey where you'll see it constantly?" she asked.

Adam turned to her, and the tension drained from his shoulders. "It grounds me. It reminds me to base my decisions on the realities of life, not on what I wish was true."

"And with that philosophy, you've brought the estate back from the brink with your expert investments." With a charming smile, Jack gestured widely. "You have the money and resources to go anywhere, live a lavish lifestyle. You've earned it."

An alarm sounded from Jack's pocket, and he pulled out his phone. "I'm due in court—another contentious divorce. The glamorous life of a small-town attorney." Jack rolled his eyes then clapped Adam's shoulder. "Good to see you, Adam. I'll be in touch."

After the door shut behind him, Elizabeth let out a breath. "Your uncle is a force of nature."

"Yeah. He and my dad were close. He was my guardian after . . . the fire. He ran Cliffhaven until I was of age."

Nerves had her tapping her foot against the plush carpet. "Are you considering the offer to purchase Cliffhaven?"

"Of course not. The last thing I want to do is tear down the house so a developer can build condos." Adam plunged his hands into his pockets. "Jack's been trying to get me to sell the house for years. I know he only wants what's best for me, but it's getting tiresome."

Elizabeth examined his face, looking for any signs he wasn't being honest, and found none.

So many people had conflicting ideas about Cliffhaven's future. Jack would tear the house down, sell the land to a developer. Adam would let the house, and all its precious contents, rot. And Caroline was paralyzed with indecision.

But Cliffhaven could be so much more—a place celebrating art and beauty, a light for the world. A home.

It was a battle for the soul of Cliffhaven. And it wasn't just the mansion or the art that was at stake; it was the lives of people she was beginning to care deeply about.

Maybe that was why she was ready, eager even, to fight.

A HIGH-PITCHED SCREAM broke the afternoon stillness, causing Elizabeth to jump out of her office chair and run to the kitchen. There was Tony, standing on a chair, clutching his red hair in his fists, eyes bulging, mouth twisted in horror.

"What's happened?" She glanced around the room. "Was that . . . did you just scream?"

"Uh, yeah, that was me." His voice was unnaturally high, his eyes scanning the ground like the kitchen was filling with lava. "I just saw a mouse. Or a rat. It ran under the oven."

Her shoulders relaxed, and she fought the smile that tempted her lips. "Just one?"

"One's enough. We seem to have a pest problem."

"You can't solve it up there."

"True." He crouched, lowering the toe of his sneaker to the floor as if expecting it to bite. "I suppose it would look bad if I ran out the door screaming and took the rest of the week off. God, I'm a total wuss. Caroline said there are mousetraps in Meeks's shed."

"I'll run out there and see what we have." She grabbed the jacket hanging on the back of her office chair.

"Great. In the meantime, I'll be disinfecting the kitchen like a maniac. And don't feel like you have to mention this little scene to Caroline."

Elizabeth laughed as she put on her coat. She'd been sitting in her office for at least an hour, and the idea of getting out into the fresh air energized her. She wrapped herself into a cozy blanket scarf, said goodbye to Tony, who was still perched on top of the chair, and stepped into the brisk, autumnal air. The fresh scent of pine and brilliant sunshine were her companions on the short walk to Meeks's shed.

When she arrived at the rickety structure, she had to force open the ill-fitting door. Inside, it was dark and dirty, with broken flowerpots piled in the corners and rusty gardening implements hanging from a pegboard. Everything was disorganized and haphazard, covered in a thick layer of dust.

Elizabeth swept aside grease-soaked rags and turpentine, scanning the shelves for anything that might get rid of mice. She pushed aside an old oil lantern, and when she saw what was hidden behind it, her mouth fell open. She reached out with shaking fingers and grasped the object, pulling it closer. Inspecting it. Heat rushed to the surface of her skin as anger surged within her.

It was a can of spray paint, almost-new and scarlet—the exact shade as the words that had been painted onto her car.

CHAPTER 18

$\mathcal{E}$lizabeth charged across the overgrown lawn, fingers tight around the can of spray paint. Her gaze narrowed on two men standing just outside a large outbuilding, between the edge of Cliffhaven's forest and a paddock. Her blood pounded in her ears, dulling her senses, so she barely noted the scent of autumn leaves filling the air, the coastal wind fresh on her cheeks.

The two men appeared to be repairing the paddock fence. Adam, his shirtsleeves bulging against muscle, lifted a fencepost with one hand and dropped it into a hole. As he held the pole in place, Meeks poured a dry mixture into the pit.

Two horses stood in the paddock, watching the men work as if supervising, and the sight of the enormous beasts almost brought her up short. But nothing could interrupt her single-minded focus, and it was concentrated now on confrontation.

Meeks's grizzled face looked sour in the afternoon light. He saw her approach, and his mouth set into a grim line. "Bloody hell."

Marching straight up to the two men, she thrust the can of

spray paint under Meeks's nose as if it were a smoking gun. "I found this in your shed."

The old man leaned his bent body against the fence, his arthritic hands tipping up his gray woolen cap to get a better look. He squinted and scowled at her. "So what?"

Her pulse accelerated, a staccato beat beneath her skin. "This is the paint that was used to vandalize my car."

He spit skillfully into the grass near her shoes. His eyes shifted away, and he shrugged. "Maybe. You say it was in my shed?"

"Are you telling me you didn't know it was there?"

His eyes narrowed. "You think I messed up your car."

Adam leaned forward, draping his forearms across the fence. "May I see the paint?"

"I can handle this," she snapped.

"I'm sure you can. But tempers are running high, and—"

"She's trying to blame me for the paint on her car!" Meeks rasped angrily, spittle flying from his lips.

"I found it in *your* shed!"

"I've never seen that paint before in my life," Meeks said defiantly, thrusting his bony chin in the air. "And why would I bother messing with your car?"

"How should I know? To frighten me, or get rid of me, or maybe you just think it's fun." She dropped the paint into Adam's hands. "Do you know how this got into the shed?"

"Keep your temper, woman," Meeks sputtered, his face red. "Remember who you're talking to."

"Meeks, for God's sake." Adam had the grace to look sheepish before examining the can. "It does look like a similar color."

"It's the *exact* color. I tested it."

"I've never seen it before," Adam admitted. "I certainly didn't put it in the shed."

She whirled back to Meeks, and the old man growled, "Don't look at me! I told you, I've never seen it."

Adam held up both hands. "Meeks says he's never seen it before, and I believe him."

She set her hands on her hips. "Then how did it wind up in his shed?"

"Maybe the person who painted your car put it in the shed to make it look like Meeks or I had done it."

His expression was so sincere, so earnest, so clearly wanting to avoid a confrontation. Her gaze slid back to Meeks, taking in his defiant stance, his thin lips curled with contempt as he glared back at her, the smug smile as he basked in his employer's protection.

Adam clearly believed Meeks was innocent. How well did he know his caretaker?

"I'm giving this to the police," she said, snatching the paint from Adam. With a sharp look at both men, she turned and marched back to the house without looking back.

Meeks's parting words carried to her on the wind. "I told you she'd be nothing but trouble. Get rid of her before she causes even more."

～

"Am I disturbing you?"

Elizabeth stood in the doorway of the ballroom, hesitant. She'd expected the room to be empty, but Adam sat beneath the glass wall overlooking the lake, an easel before him, a sketchpad in hand. He wore black trousers and a sweater with a rolled collar, his broad shoulders and muscular biceps stretching the seams.

"No." He brushed his ebony hair away from his eyes and gestured to the domed ceiling. "I'm sketching the fresco. I'd forgotten how incredible it is."

"I can't wait to get up there and inspect it. Caroline hired a contractor to bring in scaffolding." She held up the plastic sheet. "So I need to drape this over the gilded paneling. To protect it. But I can come back later—"

"No. Stay." His eyes, soft and warm upon her, were like a caress. He looked at her as if he were drinking her in. Then he ripped the top paper from his sketchpad, letting it fall to the floor. The charcoal in his hand moved across the fresh paper as his gaze darted between her and the sketchpad.

Keenly aware of his scrutiny, she began hanging the plastic over the priceless gilded paneling.

"Adam!" The booming voice echoed across the ballroom, and she whirled around. It was Christopher, an affable smile well at home on his face, his hands deep in the pockets of his neatly pressed trousers. "I've been looking for you all over this damned place."

Christopher gave her a friendly nod then crossed the ballroom to Adam. "What are you doing inside on this beautiful day?"

Adam glared at the sketch he'd been working on. "Just wasting my time."

She went back to work, securing the edge of the plastic to the paneling, but couldn't stop her eyes from darting to the two men.

Christopher ran one hand over his blonde hair in a habitual gesture, as if making sure every strand was in place. Then he leaned over the easel. "What are you working on?"

"Nothing." Adam grabbed at the paper, but Christopher reached it first, pulling it from the easel and examining it.

"Wow. Sometimes I forget how talented you are." Christopher looked up at her. "It's you."

"It's nothing," Adam said, snatching the sketch from Christopher and laying it face down on the easel.

Curiosity led her across the room, made her lean over the

easel to view the paper. It was her face. He'd captured the round curve of her cheek, had drawn her with one delicately arched brow, looking at him with distrustful eyes. He'd made her look impossibly beautiful.

"You've been too kind with your charcoal."

"I don't think so." He leaned forward, examining the drawing with a furrowed brow, then looked up at her. "You must not see yourself as I do."

Her body was suddenly impossibly heated, like she was standing too close to the sun. She tore her eyes away from his and stepped back to the gleaming gilt. Kneeling, her face flushed, she picked up the plastic and began fixing it to the wall.

"So," Christopher said, "have you two decided whether to restore the house?"

"Not yet."

Christopher wrinkled his nose. "If I were you, I'd ditch this moldy old relic. Sell to those developers, take the money and build something new and modern. Maybe in the south of France, or somewhere tropical."

"The tropics don't suit me."

"Too true. I can't see you lounging next to a pool with an umbrella in your drink." Christopher wiggled his eyebrows playfully. "But if you sold Cliffhaven, you'd have even more money to invest in my winning ventures."

"And how goes our latest venture?"

"Funny you should ask." Christopher cleared his throat and flashed a winning smile. "The restaurant's going great, full steam ahead. There're just a few extra operating costs I hadn't anticipated."

"How much?"

"Forty thousand should easily get us through to next quarter. And that'll buy you another five percent."

Elizabeth's mouth fell open, and she turned swiftly toward the wall to hide her shock. That would value the business at something around two million dollars. Could a bistro in the northern wilderness really be worth that?

"I'll write you a check," Adam said, then he lowered his voice. "But honestly, Christopher, is this for the restaurant or for you and Vanessa? Because if you two ever needed anything, you just have to ask."

"It's for the restaurant, of course." Christopher's voice tightened. "This isn't a handout. It's an investment. You're going to get all your money back, and then some."

"Did you ever read the business plan I wrote up for you?"

Christopher recovered his winning smile. "Of course. How stupid would I be to disregard free advice from a financial guru like you?"

He clapped his hands together. "Well, that's settled." Christopher took a step toward her, resting his arm on the wall above her and leaning close. "What do you say, Elizabeth? Want to go out tonight and help me celebrate? Have dinner with me."

Adam froze, and she fumbled the plastic sheeting, dropping it to the floor. Was he teasing her? "Uh, thanks, but work keeps me pretty busy."

"Come on, you must take a night off now and then."

She knew her smile was crooked but couldn't straighten it. "You don't really want to have dinner with me."

Christopher cocked his head. "Why wouldn't I want to have dinner with you? You're smart. And pretty." Heat rose to her cheeks.

"All right." Christopher chuckled, holding up his hands in surrender. "I know when I'm not wanted."

"Amazing, since it's such a rare occurrence." Adam rose from his seat, the whisper of a smile on his face. "Let's go get that check."

Elizabeth shook her head as they sauntered toward the door. Christopher was too smooth by a mile. He probably wooed every woman who crossed his path—the type to dazzle his dates with flowers, fine restaurants, and moonlit kisses. But, like a honeybee, he would soon flit off to find other flowers to enjoy.

How different he was from Adam. Where Christopher was genteel and smooth, Adam was unpolished, unfashionably honest. They made an interesting pair—one seeming to skim over the surface of life, the other exploring its depths. Adam was more interesting, more compelling in every way.

"You're not pretty."

She started, looking up. Adam hadn't left. He was standing in the doorway, his hand on the frame, looking back at her.

She laughed. "I'm not?"

"I mean, pretty doesn't describe you at all." He regarded her, and his voice deepened, lowered. "Your beauty is like something painted by Rubens. You're alabaster-skinned, strong and soft at once. Venus come to life."

He moved toward her, eyes tracing her face, her shoulders, and she could feel her skin heat in the wake of his gaze. "But your face is like something sculpted by Da Vinci. Strong, soulful, with a vulnerability that makes me ache."

A flush of warmth spread from her center, bathing her in a pleasurable ache. And a craving so intense, so delicious, welled inside her.

He stepped closer and whispered, "What makes you vulnerable, Lizzie?"

She was feverish now, heat ripping through her like a wildfire. His emerald eyes held her, and she couldn't tear her gaze away.

"You coming, Adam?" Chris's voice sounded from the hall, breaking whatever spell they were under. With one final, intense glance back at her, Adam left the ballroom.

She pressed a hand to her heart, but it didn't slow the fierce pounding. She'd never been called beautiful. Not once.

She shook her head to clear it. He was an artist, that's what they did—see the beauty in everything, even things overlooked by others. He didn't mean anything by it. Not the way she wanted him to.

Anyway, Adam kept telling her to leave. How much plainer could he be that he didn't want her there? And he belonged to a completely different world—a world of wealth and status, a place surrounded by beauty and priceless art. She was a visitor in that world, a tourist come to gape at its magnificence, and she would never truly belong.

Setting her hands on her hips, she surveyed the empty ballroom, satisfied that the gilt would be protected from all manner of construction detritus. The precious art was protected, and Cliffhaven was ready for the real work to begin. It was finally time to do what she did best—restoration.

She eyed the priceless, masterful ceiling fresco, and anxiety built within her. The task before her was monumental, beyond anything she'd ever attempted. Would her best be good enough? She simply didn't know. But she would give it everything she had, even if it took sleepless nights, sweat, and blood.

As she cast her eyes over the beautiful, damaged house, she only hoped she had enough to give.

CHAPTER 19

s Elizabeth hiked through the forest that lay to the east of Cliffhaven, the canopy of brightly colored leaves swaying gently in the breeze was as beautiful as the most masterful fresco. The trees looked as if they were on fire, colored in vivid reds and oranges, and the air was fresh and sweet in her lungs.

The forest was deserted, other than the wild creatures that made this place their home. An enormous porcupine waddled across the trail, paying no mind to Elizabeth, and she watched, delighted, as it climbed a tree.

The northern wilderness was familiar, like a childhood friend grown almost out of recognition. She had distant memories of hiking with her mother, wandering the forests near their home, her mother hugging an enormous birch tree, laughing.

She'd avoided the north her entire adult life, believing it would dredge up painful memories. But now that she was there, it felt right. The crisp air was at home in her lungs, the bulky sweaters were a cozy refuge from the cold world. Surrounded by nature, she felt at home in it. It was a wild place—more dangerous, surely, but it inspired you to *live*. Even her body, so accustomed to feeling oversized and out of place at dinner parties and crowded nightclubs, felt natural. The weight of her, her solidity and strength, suited the wild environment.

She hiked until the trail opened before her, sunlight illuminating where forest ended and beach began. Following a sharp bend in the trail, she suddenly came upon an enormous animal standing alert at the edge of the forest, staring at her.

She froze, her heart thudding powerfully in her ears. Even when she recognized the large, black horse from the paddock at Cliffhaven, she remained paralyzed. The horse's powerful body, so much larger than her own, inspired a primal fear.

"Don't touch him." Adam's voice was calm in her ear, and she turned to find him one small step away. How had he moved so quietly on the autumn leaves?

He wore dark denim and a wine-colored sweater that perfectly matched the vibrant leaves overhead. This close to him, she could smell his skin—like leather and cedar—an intoxicating scent.

She glanced at the horse. "Is he dangerous?"

"He could be, with someone he doesn't know." Adam reached out to soothe the great beast. "Heathcliff doesn't trust many people."

"Heathcliff?" Her lips curled upward, despite her anxiety. "Like from Wuthering Heights?"

"He's hot-tempered and wild, so the name seemed appropriate." Adam smiled self-consciously and ran a hand through his jet-black hair. "You're a long way from the house."

"I like walking in the woods. It's so wild here, like the dark forest of a fairy tale."

Adam kept his eyes on her as he ran one calming hand down Heathcliff's neck. She watched his palm slide over the smooth coat and wondered how his caress would feel on her own skin.

"Tony insisted on packing lunch for me." He tapped a leather saddlebag. "I'm not sure what's in here, but it weighs a ton. Hungry?"

"Sure," she said, tearing her eyes away from his hands.

"I know a great spot for a picnic. Follow me."

"What about Heathcliff?"

"He'll be fine. Even the wolves leave him alone."

They left the horse at the edge of the forest and walked to where the packed earth gave way to sand. Before them was an immense dune—a towering mound of pristine, golden sand. A trail led up the hill, a thin ribbon of yellow through the tall grass that grew in the silt. The dune was so high, the trail appeared to lead straight up to the blue sky.

It took effort to move through the sand up the steep hill, but she kept up with Adam's long strides. When they finally reached the top of the dune, the view opened before her. The lake dominated the horizon—there was nothing but sapphire water as far as the eye could see, so the lake looked massive and endless.

"It's breathtaking." She crept to the edge of the dune, where the slope down to the water's edge was incredibly steep. Hundreds of feet below them, sunlight glittered on white-capped waves crashing against the shore.

Adam spread a woolen blanket over the sand and knelt upon it. As he unpacked the leather satchel with a seemingly unending supply of food, he said, "I can't believe Tony packed all this. Does he really think I eat this much for lunch?"

She settled herself across from him. "Everything looks so delicious and elegant." She spooned tapenade onto a toast point and nibbled the corner. "Tony's idea of a picnic is much different than mine."

"What's yours?"

"A peanut butter and jelly sandwich, maybe an apple. Should that embarrass me?"

"There's nothing wrong with simplicity."

"No, but this tastes better. Try some." She handed her toast point to Adam, who devoured it with one bite.

"Are you enjoying your work at Cliffhaven?"

"Of course. It's an incredible place." She gestured to the panorama of golden dunes, sapphire sea, and blue sky. "You're lucky to call it home."

Adam leaned back on his strong hands, looking relaxed. "Where's your home, then?"

And, just like that, she felt the familiar ache—the longing for something she would never possess. She looked down at the blanket, where her fingers worried the woolen edging. She usually had a quick comeback when someone asked about her nonexistent family, a funny quip that would make the questioner smile and allow her to change the subject. Why was it that with this man, she had no words—no desire or ability to camouflage her feelings?

She shrugged and tried to smile. "I don't have one."

His eyes softened. "I'm sorry, that was callous of me. I assumed that after your parents died, you'd lived with family."

"I started with my aunt, but that didn't last long. Then I bounced around different foster homes, never staying too long in one place."

"Why not? Were the homes awful?"

"Some of them." She took a blackberry from a small container and rolled it between her fingers. "But there was one family, the Millers. They were good people, even had a daughter around my age that was nice. But after a while, I . . . well, I messed it up."

"How?"

"Deliberately. I was cruel to them, broke the rules. And when that didn't work, I stole the family car and crashed it into a neighbor's living room. I was twelve."

"You didn't want to stay with them?"

"It wasn't that, exactly. I just knew it wouldn't work out, that eventually I'd have to find a new home. And the longer I was there, the more I cared for them, the harder it would be to leave."

Adam frowned, as if trying to understand. "Why was it a foregone conclusion that you'd have to leave that family?"

Her throat thickened, as if sorrow could lodge there. *Nobody's ever wanted me, not for forever.*

"It turned out okay." She sat straighter, and the cheer in her voice was only slightly forced. "I emancipated myself at sixteen, and I've been making my own way since then. I have a good life."

"And you still move from place to place. Doesn't that get old?"

"It's starting to, I guess."

She turned her gaze away from his appraisal, toward the lake. Maybe it was the beauty of this place that aroused feelings in her that had been dormant for so long, feelings she barely recognized and didn't know how to deal with. It was a place that made her want to belong.

She picked up a petite squash tart. "You know what it's like to be alone. It makes you stronger."

"I wasn't always so isolated here. When I was young, Cliffhaven was filled with people." Adam looked down at his empty hands. "After my parents died, everything changed."

"Caroline told me you were just a teenager."

He nodded. "I was fifteen."

"Why didn't you go back to school?"

"My face." Adam smiled ruefully. "I couldn't stand people looking at me with pity or disgust. It was as though my scars reminded everyone my parents had died while I lived."

"You know, your scars aren't that noticeable."

"You're the first person who's thought that."

"Maybe I'm not. Maybe you just weren't around people enough after the fire to see what they really thought." She took another bite of tart, watching him react. "So after Caroline left, you were alone in the house?"

"Pretty much, after Uncle Jack let the staff go."

"Jack fired the staff?"

"He was trustee for the estate, and he thought Cliffhaven didn't need a large staff, since I was the only one living there."

"He let everyone go? That's a horrible thing to do to a child who's just lost his parents. You must have been lonely."

"Chris kept coming around." Adam smiled at the memory, then shrugged. "Meeks was here, and Jack hired Mrs. Hodges. Caroline got a tutor when I refused to go back to high school. But after he left, I was alone."

The way he looked at her made her want to lean into him, to bury her face in his chest and feel his strong arms around her. She wanted to run her hands through his thick hair, to press her lips against his. Her breath quickened and her lips parted as she thought of the possibilities.

She closed her eyes, willing herself to get control, and stood up. "I should get back to the house."

He gestured across the lake, where dark clouds gathered. "We both should. It smells like rain."

He packed the satchel quickly and lifted the blanket, shaking sand into the wind. Together, they walked down the trail.

At the bottom of the dune, the edge of the forest was lined with thick slabs of sedimentary rock. A hole had been carved into the rocky hillside, like the entrance to a cave, supported by rotten wood beams. An iron gate was mounted to the rocky walls, blocking the entrance, but it hung askew, as if it had been forced open.

Adam frowned. "This old mine is supposed to be blocked off."

Copper. "Does your family still rely on income from mining?"

"No, those days are over. I've made other investments that turned out to be lucrative. The money doesn't matter to me, but

I like knowing Caroline has enough for whatever she might want." His brows pulled in as he looked down at the sandy soil. "Who would have thought she'd want things that can't be bought? Things much harder for me to provide."

"She just wants family," she said, struggling to keep her voice light. "A home. Surely those things aren't too much to ask?"

He looked at her, eyes shining with curiosity, as if he would open her heart and examine it, if he could. "No. Those things aren't too much to ask." Then his face darkened, and he shook his head. "But they aren't things I can give."

"But she only wants you. And Cliffhaven. Isn't that all within your power to give?"

"But what kind of man am I?" Suddenly his voice was frayed, full of loathing. "And what kind of home is Cliffhaven? A dark, damp, desolate wreck, haunted by its past."

Even as her heart squeezed for him, a bittersweet smile spread across her lips.

He watched her, some of the tension draining from his face. "Am I amusing you?"

"A little. I wish you could see Cliffhaven through my eyes. It's magnificent. Sure, it's had tough times, but with a little work, it could be incredible." She looked around at the pristine dunes, the wild forest. "To have this amazing place be your home? It's beyond anything most people dream of."

Then her words came out fast and fierce. "And Caroline is proud to have you as a brother. She loves you. You don't know how lucky you are to have that."

He looked stunned. Then rain dropped from the sky, breaking the haze of solemnity that hovered over them. In the time they had taken to examine the abandoned mine, flint-colored clouds had rolled across the sky, blotting out the sun, and the wind was insistent as it blew her hair back.

"It's getting colder." Adam looked at her with concern. "And you just have that light jacket. You'd get back much faster if Heathcliff and I give you a ride."

As they neared the enormous beast, he pawed at the ground and made a sound of impatience. How did people approach such a powerful animal, let alone ride it?

"Sorry, but there's no way I'm getting on a horse. I kind of have a fear of large animals."

"Are you talking about me or the horse?"

A laugh bubbled out of her. Then the rain became sharp needles, pricking her skin and sliding down her neck. Thunder rumbled in the distance, echoing across the lake.

Adam cast his eyes across the sky. "Autumn storms can be deadly up here. The temperature drops quickly, and wind sweeps across the lake, giving us thirty-foot waves. I wouldn't feel right leaving you alone."

She bit her lip and eyed Heathcliff. "Are you sure he can take our weight? Neither of us is exactly petite."

"He's a Belgian. He can handle it."

She hung back, twisting her hands together. But Adam stood before her looking wild and tempting, his expression hopeful.

"All right," she said.

"You'll get up first and sit in front." He knelt before her and linked his fingers together. When she put her foot in his hands, he boosted her into the saddle like she weighed nothing. "Now hold on tight, and I'll sit behind you."

She gripped the saddle tightly, but Adam swung up behind her before she could blink. He wrapped his powerful arms around her and grasped the reins.

The wind blew harder, propelling icy shafts of rain that stung the skin. Adam settled the woolen picnic blanket around his shoulders then draped it over her, so they were cocooned inside together. The warmth was immediate and welcome.

She swallowed, acutely aware of Adam's thighs pressed

against her, his muscular arms around her. His strong chest against her back.

"You're trembling." His voice was husky, pitched low as he spoke into her ear.

"I'm a little afraid." She swallowed the lump in her throat. "Of the riding, I mean."

"We're just going to take it at an easy walk. Heathcliff, we've got a lady aboard." As if the horse understood, he set off at a gentle pace.

She relaxed into the movement, hardly aware of the rain dripping off autumn leaves, so focused was she on the pleasurable ache flooding through her body. Was it her imagination, or had he lowered his head to her hair, inhaling her scent?

A tidal wave of desire crashed over her, and she longed to give herself up to this wilderness, to behave like a wild thing— to beg him to touch her, to taste her.

She closed her eyes. *I'm lost. Lost to this man, this place.*

For the first time, she wondered if it might be worth it. If, instead of being lost, she might be found.

CHAPTER 20

"What a downpour!" Caroline took in the sight of Elizabeth, the sodden blanket still draped over her shoulders, and Adam, his clothes dripping onto the stone floor. She'd met them in the hall, dressed for dinner in tan trousers and an ivory blouse that set off her porcelain skin. "I didn't know you two were together."

"We weren't." Elizabeth took a step away from Adam, biting her lip. "I got caught in the rain, and Adam gave me a ride home."

Caroline looked back and forth between the two of them, a satisfied smile spreading over her face. "Tony has dinner ready. I thought the four of us could eat together."

"I'll go change," Adam said, smiling tentatively before disappearing into the west wing.

"Let me take this for you," Caroline said, unwrapping the blanket from around her shoulders. "I've got a bottle of cabernet breathing in the dining room. Would you like a glass?"

"I'd love one. But I need to get out of these wet clothes."

"I'll bring the bottle to your room, and we can chat while you dress."

After retrieving the wine and two crystal glasses, Caroline made herself at home in Elizabeth's room, curling up on the velvet chaise by the fireplace. She poured a glass of the plum-colored wine and handed it to her.

"Have you heard from the police about who might have vandalized your car?"

"I called the station yesterday, spoke to an Officer Ogie, but he said there are no suspects."

Caroline tucked her strawberry-blonde hair behind one ear. "It was probably just teenagers. But let me know if you have any other trouble."

"I will."

She pulled her suitcase from under her bed, and Caroline gasped. "You haven't even unpacked yet! Oh, I've kept you so busy, you haven't had a chance. Let me help."

Before she could stop her, Caroline opened the Jacobean armoire and began hanging her blouses and pants. Anxiety prickled over her skin, but she said nothing as Caroline systematically unpacked her clothes.

"Oh, this sweater is gorgeous! Want to wear this for dinner?"

She took the proffered sweater and turned her back to Caroline before peeling off her wet shirt. To combat the churning in her stomach, she turned her gaze to the bedroom window. The sky had cleared, and the setting sun was a ball of orange fire sinking slowly into dark blue waters. "I could look at this view forever."

Caroline frowned. "Don't the cliffs make you feel . . . exposed?"

"That's part of what makes it seem so wild here, like nothing is protecting you from the elements."

"You seem to enjoy it in a way I never have."

"You never loved it here?"

"I did, as a child. But Cliffhaven doesn't feel like my home anymore. I don't think it ever will." Caroline sipped her wine, looking wistful. "But maybe that's not a bad thing. I'd like to believe it means we haven't figured out the perfect use for Cliffhaven yet."

Elizabeth pressed her lips together. She was starting to have definite ideas about the perfect use for Cliffhaven. But was Caroline ready to hear them?

Caroline pulled Elizabeth's toiletry bag from the suitcase and set it on the nightstand. "I've decided to hire a housekeeper. Maybe if we tidy things up around here, it will help convince Adam that Cliffhaven should be restored."

Then her face turned pensive. "It's funny, isn't it, the twists and turns life takes? I always thought that by the time I was this age, I'd have two or three kids running around the estate." She glanced up, her eyes full of pained resignation. "I used to want children desperately."

"Now you don't?"

Caroline tilted her head with a sardonic smile. "I'm not as young as you."

"Oh, please. Plenty of women your age have children. You're not senile yet."

Caroline snorted. "I suppose not. I guess we never know what the future holds."

She leaned over, refilling Elizabeth's glass. "I know we're doing the right thing, restoring these frescoes. I was thinking that if you want to stay longer, you could restore more of our art."

"I still plan on leaving when I'm finished with the frescoes." But as she pulled on fleece-lined leggings, she was surprised to find her resolve wavering.

"Isn't it exhausting moving so much? My move here really took it out of me, emotionally." Caroline looked down at Elizabeth's empty suitcase. "Haven't you ever wanted to find a place, stay there, and make it your own?"

Longing pulled at her. "If I ever find a place that feels like home. But I'm not sure I know what that feels like."

"It's the people," Caroline said. "People make a place feel like home." The two women's eyes met, and they shared a smile.

"I'll go tell Tony we're ready for dinner." Caroline turned to leave then seemed to think better of it, placing a gentle hand on Elizabeth's forearm. "I'm really glad you're here."

She looked into Caroline's smiling green eyes, realizing they were just one shade lighter than Adam's. "There's nowhere I'd rather be."

～

AT NIGHT CLIFFHAVEN SEEMED DESOLATE, more like a mausoleum than a home. Elizabeth could feel the emptiness of the mansion as if it were a tangible thing, echoing around her.

As she walked down the second-floor corridor, she drew her robe tighter across her chest. The bathroom was just down the hall, but at night, the trip was full of shadows. She eyed the damascene lamps, now cold and dark, wondering when they might burst to life again.

They'd had a lovely dinner. She'd sat next to Caroline, and they'd been easy together, like it took no effort to slip into friendship. Adam seemed to have enjoyed himself, laughing at Tony's jokes and debating the merits of modern art. He'd even opened a bottle of Macallan after dinner, as if he'd wanted to prolong the camaraderie.

She swayed into the wall of the corridor, catching herself with one hand braced on the damask wallpaper. Maybe she'd had a little too much whiskey.

But she felt good. Better than she had in a long time.

Then a floorboard creaked, and she froze. Dim light glowed through a crack at the bottom of a door at the end of the hall. Someone was in the bathroom.

She swallowed the lump that rose in her throat. Nobody ever came to the second floor.

Before she could turn back, the door was thrown open and an immense figure emerged, surrounded by steam that billowed into the corridor.

"Adam!"

He was fresh from the shower, gripping a towel loosely around his hips with one hand as water dripped from his dark hair onto his shoulders.

"Lizzie!" He fumbled the towel, catching it just before exposing himself.

"You scared me half to death." She placed her hand on her heart, her eyes roving down to the towel slung around his hips. Her mouth went dry.

Don't stare. Don't stare. You're staring.

"I just came for a bath," she said, acutely aware of her nakedness beneath the robe, and the heat of a blush spread across her cheeks.

What was wrong with her? She wasn't an innocent teenager who'd never seen a man before. Though, to be fair, she'd never encountered a wet, mostly naked man in a candle-lit corridor.

He ran one hand through his damp hair. "My shower isn't working."

"I'm not surprised, given the state of the plumbing." She began to move past him toward the bathroom.

"I enjoyed our picnic today."

His words halted her movement, so that she stood before him, looking up into his eyes. "I did, too."

They stood in the darkened corridor, almost touching, a silence stretching out between them. A silence so full of unsaid words and desires, it was almost unbearable.

Then he took her hand gently in his own, and she drew in a surprised breath. With that simple gesture—the first between them that indicated anything more than friendship—her heart began to race. Hope kindled inside her like a small, fragile flame.

He examined her hand. "You're so strong, so solid. The kind of woman who won't break if I touched you." His voice lowered to a whisper. "Can I touch you?"

Even as a small part of her whispered that this was a terrible idea, her body leaned toward him. Maybe it was the alcohol buzzing in her blood, or maybe she'd just denied her desires for far too long. She took one step forward, closing the distance between them.

He dipped his head down slowly, letting her know his intention, giving her the opportunity to move away. She lifted her lips to meet his in a sweet, searching kiss.

An electric thrill charged through her body, and the delicate kiss transformed, deepened, as desire took hold. She wrapped her arms around his neck, he plunged his free hand into her curls, and the kiss turned fierce and fast.

Desire engulfed her, and she was suddenly burning, burning to have him. She thrust both hands into his hair, pulling him closer, because she could bear no distance between them. His arms tightened around her, bearing her weight as he dipped her back, devouring her mouth.

Then the kiss changed, grew soft. His lips brushed hers once, twice, so tenderly it made her ache. He lifted his head, and she opened her eyes to find him looking at her with wonder. She could feel him, hard as iron against her thigh, leaving her flushed and breathless.

God, were her hands shaking? What the hell was she doing? She pulled her arms from around his neck, taking one step back.

He released her at once, his brow furrowing. "I'm sorry," he said, searching her eyes.

"Please don't apologize." She could hear the odd formality in her voice, the distant civility she always took refuge in when she needed to push someone away.

"I . . . I just don't want you to think I'm taking advantage of you, or the situation."

"You don't have to voice your regrets." She bowed her head. "Let's just forget it happened and say good night."

Forget it happened? How was she supposed to do that when she could still taste him, when she wanted him more than she'd ever wanted anything? When just his kiss could shift something profound inside her?

And, dammit, *that* had been the wrong thing to say, because he arched one eyebrow, and his eyes grew distant. "I am sorry, though."

"Yeah, I get that." She was still reeling, still searching her brain for the right words when he took two steps down the corridor, away from her.

He turned back, giving her a sad half-smile that made her heart race. "Good night." Then he disappeared into the darkness, and her shoulders sagged.

A bath now sounded unbearable—to be in the space still humid from Adam's shower, to be thinking of what it would be like to share the claw-footed tub with his powerful body.

Just put on your nightgown and go to bed. Where she could toss and turn, punishing her traitorous body.

Back in her room, she eyed the cedar armoire. She hadn't been able to stop Caroline unpacking her clothes, but maybe it wasn't such a bad thing. Maybe they could belong there, for now.

She opened the armoire, searching for her nightgown, and blinked in confusion. Then she froze, her mouth falling open, eyes widening with shock. Her face contorted with repugnance and horror, and she clamped a hand across her mouth.

There was an animal—a dead animal—hanging among her blouses and pants. A rat, dangling limply from a wire hanger wrapped around its neck. Its eyes bulged grotesquely, and blood matted its fur. Its long tail was limp and lifeless, brushing against her favorite sweater.

She jumped back, her feet skidding across the wooden floor, and she fell, hard, onto her backside. The room closed in around her, and she put her hands on her knees, fighting the nausea that rose within her.

A dead rat. Hung so neatly among her shirts and scarves, the wire hanger bent and wrapped so carefully around its neck.

Someone had killed the poor creature and left it hanging in her armoire.

Then she heard it. That familiar slithering, scraping sound.

Every muscle in her body froze as her breath caught and held. The hairs on the back of her neck lifted.

Then a slamming noise filled the air, and she watched in horror as a vase from the bookshelf flew into the air. It crashed to the floor, the crystal shattering into a thousand shards.

She scrambled to her feet and bolted, flinging open her bedroom door and racing down the hallway. In the dark, Cliffhaven was all yawning corridors and darkened doorways. Heart racing, she ran down the grand staircase.

Adam. I have to get to Adam.

As she flew through the western wing, she realized she wasn't simply running *away*. She was, for the first time in her life, running *toward* something. Someone. Because Adam was what she wanted, what she needed. There was no time to examine this urge, to take it apart and bury it deep. Because she was there, banging on the door to his room.

"Adam! Are you there?"

The door flew open, and he was there, his face full of concern. "What's wrong?"

"Upstairs, in my room. It's . . ." She shook her head, her eyes filling with tears.

He pulled her close, wrapping his arms around her. With her

face pressed against his chest, she took a series of gulping, gasping breaths. Why was the truth easier to face from the safety of his embrace?

"Someone was in the house. Adam, someone was in my room."

CHAPTER 21

$\mathcal{E}$lizabeth stood in her room, arms folded across her chest, refusing to look at the dead rat hanging in the armoire. Adam stood next to her, offering a wastebasket to the policeman, who looked as if he was about to be sick.

"No thanks, I'm fine." Officer Ogie's face was pallid, tinged with embarrassment and a light green color. "Tell me again what you think this rat has to do with you, Miss Watson."

Her fingers clenched into fists. "It's obvious this is meant to be a threat. It's in my room, for heaven's sake!"

"Elizabeth does seem to be the target," Adam said, "particularly if the same person is responsible for the vandalism to her car."

Officer Ogie tipped his cap up and eyed her suspiciously. He was a thick man whose neck bulged over the navy collar of his uniform, and his pasty skin spoke of too much time indoors. "Mr. Arrington, let's shoot straight with each other. Has it occurred to you there might be some other explanation for this little . . . incident?"

Adam's brow furrowed. "What other explanation? The rat obviously didn't hang itself."

Officer Ogie took off his hat, rolled it between his fingers. "Well, now. We get along on this island nice as you please, without a peep of trouble." He gave her a side-eyed, condescending glance. "Then this young lady popped up out of nowhere, and all of the sudden we've got vandalism. Dead animals."

Adam's jaw tightened. "What are you suggesting?"

Officer Ogie pulled him aside, turning his back to her, lowering his voice to a stage whisper. "Well, now, in my experience, some girls do things like this for attention." He nodded sagely and scratched the five o'clock shadow spreading over his neck.

"What kind of woman would kill a rat for attention?"

"Could be that girl wants to get noticed. You know, by a rich fella like yourself."

Adam's voice turned to ice. "I can assure you Miss Watson isn't that kind of woman."

"Now, you can't know that for sure. You've only known her a few weeks."

"I've gotten to know Miss Watson quite well in the short time she's been here."

Officer Ogie looked at Adam slyly, his black eyes shining with prurient interest. "Oh, it's like that? The two of you know each other very well, eh?"

Adam glared at the policeman with such silent intensity that the man took a step back, the smug smile slipping off his face.

Heat and humiliation spread through her. "I can't stand here and listen to you talk about me like I'm not here. I didn't do this. The sooner you realize that, the sooner you'll find whoever did it, whoever vandalized my car."

"Someone's clearly targeting Elizabeth," Adam said. "And I can prove it. Come with me."

Adam strode from her bedroom. Baffled, she followed him and Officer Ogie to the portrait gallery, where the fire-damaged wallpaper was clearly visible by the light of Adam's lamp. The blackened wallpaper, the scorched words of warning, made her stomach churn. How was it that the acrid scent of old smoke still lingered in the air?

Ogie stared at the words on the wall for a long moment, blinking.

"Someone's been targeting Elizabeth, threatening her." Adam's voice was low and intense. "First the vandalism to her car, then this message on the wall, now the dead rat."

"Interesting." Officer Ogie's eyes flicked first to Elizabeth, then to Adam. He removed his hat and scratched at his thinning gray crewcut. "You remember old Fire Chief Baldwin? Course you do. He worked the case of Cliffhaven's fire all those years ago."

Adam nodded. "He was a good man."

"Yep, he was. Before he died, he said something strange." Ogie extended one thick finger to the edge of the scorched wallpaper, examining it. "He knew the cancer was coming for him, see, knew he was passing. And he told me that if there was ever another fire at Cliffhaven, to investigate whether it was arson. Funny thing for a man to say." He looked at Adam, his eyes narrowed. "Unless he knows something. Maybe he thought Cliffhaven's fire was set on purpose, just couldn't prove it."

Adam's face hardened. "I'm not sure what that could possibly have to do with the current situation."

"Looks like fire damage to me." Officer Ogie glanced at the blackened wallpaper. "You sure do have a lot of fires up here, Mr. Arrington. Could be someone likes setting them."

Adam's fists clenched. "I'm not the one threatening Miss Watson. I expect you to do your job and find out who is."

Officer Ogie fondled his hat and looked pointedly at Adam. "You've been alone up here a long time, Mr. Arrington. A lot of folks on the island think that's pretty strange. If there's any more trouble, I might take a harder look at what's going on up here, maybe crack open some old case files."

Adam's eyes blazed with anger and contempt for the man before him. "Old case files? I know of some old cases, *Ogie,* that were never opened at all. Even though people *begged* for your help. Where was your concern then?" Adam was furious, incandescent with rage. He looked dangerous, and Ogie seemed to know it, because he backed away, hands held up.

"Now, calm down, Mr. Arrington."

"Oh, *mister* Arrington, is it? Now that my father's dead? Or is it that I'm not a scrawny kid you can bully anymore?"

The policeman hitched up his belt and backed toward the staircase. "Well, I'll file a report with those pictures you sent me."

"Aren't you going to take the rat?" she asked. "Check it for fingerprints or something?"

"I don't want that thing in my office. You'd better bury it before the ground freezes." With a final shrewd glance at the two of them, he said, "I'll be in touch, Mr. Arrington. You can be sure of that."

~

"THAT WAS A COMPLETE WASTE OF TIME," Adam growled as he paced her room.

"He thinks it was *me*. Or you."

Adam glared at her. "You don't think I did this, do you?"

"Of course not. But what did he mean by saying he might open old case files?" And when had Adam begged for the policeman's help?

A muscle tightened in Adam's jaw, and he didn't meet her eyes. "I have no idea."

He had *some* idea, of course he did. His anger had so obviously burned away, leaving his features etched with barely disguised pain. But there was no use going over it now, not when he was pacing the floor like a caged animal and there was a dead rat dangling in her closet.

"Adam, whoever did this was in my room."

"I'm hiring a security specialist. Tomorrow."

She shook her head. "What kind of sick person does something like this?" Steeling herself, she took a deep breath and reached inside the armoire.

"What are you doing?"

Her lips trembled. "Someone has to bury this poor creature."

Adam caught her hand and held it to his chest. "Let me take care of this. Gather the things you'll need for tonight, and we'll find you a different room."

He stood before her, calm and strong, and she was reminded of a boulder at the lake's edge—impervious to the battering waves crashing all around. She nodded, wiped the tears from her eyes, and gathered her pajamas and toiletries.

It felt good to lean on someone, to let him help. The feeling was new and strange, but undoubtedly a relief.

"I'll take you downstairs," he said, "then take care of . . . the rest."

As they moved through the house, Adam hovered protectively, but Cliffhaven was silent as they made their way to the west wing.

He stopped in front of the door to his chamber. "Take my room tonight."

"No, I couldn't possibly."

"There aren't any other beds with clean linen."

"You need sleep, too."

"Please. I want you to." He led her into his bedroom and performed a quick search. "I don't think anyone's been here."

Elizabeth opened her mouth to ask him to stay. She wanted

his strong arms wrapped around her, wanted to fall into bed with him and forget her fears. But the words wouldn't come.

He stood in the doorway, ran his hand through his dark hair. "If you need anything, I'll be right across the hall with my door open, all night."

"Thank you, Adam."

For a moment, he looked as if he might move toward her, but then he shook his head, and the door closed softly behind him.

Alone in the dark room, a shiver shook her body. Surely a ghost wasn't capable of killing a rat and hanging it in her closet, any more than they could smash up her car. This was a human action . . . wasn't it?

She could still hear the crystal vase crashing to the floor, smell the burning wallpaper from the message written in fire. *Run, Lizzie!*

Something was trying to warn her. But warn her of what— of the person who had vandalized her car, left a dead animal in her closet?

Was she in danger?

She slipped into Adam's enormous bed, inhaling the scent of him that clung to the sheets. The scent soothed her and, exhausted, she fell into a fitful sleep tarnished by nightmares and shadows.

ELIZABETH WOKE EARLY the next morning groggy and exhausted, as if she hadn't slept at all. Dim light filtered through the torn curtains of Adam's room, illuminating the fire-damaged space.

It was grim. Blackened walls and broken furniture littered the chamber. The room had to be a constant reminder of the death of Adam's parents. She couldn't understand why he would choose to sleep here when there were plenty of undamaged bedrooms in the house.

He's punishing himself. But for what?

She dressed in the only outfit she'd brought with her—jeans and an amethyst-colored sweater. She would have to go back to her room eventually, but before she forced herself to return to the chamber tainted by death, she would allow herself coffee.

When Elizabeth entered the kitchen, she found it already occupied. Caroline, Adam, and Tony sat together at the farm-house-style table, their heads close together, their faces wearing identical looks of concern.

"Elizabeth." Caroline crossed the room and wrapped her in a hug—an embrace that was becoming familiar, even welcome. "I can't believe someone left a dead animal in your room. First your car, now this."

"Sit down." Tony gestured to the seat he'd just vacated. "Let me get you breakfast."

"You don't have to do that," she said, slipping into the chair.

"Yes, I do. If I don't do something, I'm going to march into the police station and ask to be deputized just to make my search for the asshole who's messing with you legitimate. And it would be embarrassing when the cops laugh in my face. So I'll stick with what I'm good at—breakfast."

"Thanks, Tony." She took a deep breath, and her shoulders relaxed.

Adam sat at the table looking pensive, his eyes scanning her like they were searching for something.

Caroline's pretty face scrunched up in concern. "What did Officer Ogie say?"

"Nothing," Adam said bitterly. "We won't get any help from him."

"Ogie's an asshole," Tony said. "I've got nothing against cops, but this guy gives them a bad name. When Pete Johnson beat up his wife—left her with two black eyes and a split lip—Ogie convinced her not to press charges."

A smashing sound broke the silence, and Elizabeth whirled around in her chair. Caroline had dropped her teacup, but she wasn't looking at the pieces of shattered china spread across the kitchen floor. Her eyes were locked on Adam's, her lower lip trembling.

Adam shot from his seat and wrapped an arm around Caroline's shoulder. "It's all right. No harm done." His voice was low, soothing. "It's over."

What's over? What prompted the silent, private conversation that passed between Caroline and Adam? What put those shadows into her eyes?

Elizabeth looked at Tony, but he only shrugged and pulled a broom from the pantry. "Elizabeth, maybe someone just wants to frighten you."

"Nobody even knows me. Why would anyone on this island want to scare me?"

Caroline settled into the seat next to her and let out a shuddering breath. "Have you offended anyone?"

She shrugged. "Only Meeks. And I did that by existing."

"I don't know Meeks well," Tony said, bending to help Adam remove the broken china. "Would he have any reason to do this?"

"That's ridiculous." Adam shook his head. "The man is in his seventies."

"He doesn't want me here," Elizabeth said. "He's made that clear. And I found the paint in his shed."

"I've known Meeks my entire life," Adam said, "and I'm absolutely certain he did not hang a dead rat in your closet."

"He's worked here that long?"

"He's lived here his entire life. His mom was a maid, and he was born in one of the staff cottages at the edge of the forest. He started working in the gardens when he was just a teenager. And he absolutely did not do this." Adam dropped the broken china into a wastebasket. "We all need to recognize that the house simply isn't safe until we figure out what's going on."

"The lease on my apartment is up next week," Caroline said, her fingers drumming nervously on the table. "I was planning on moving back to Cliffhaven."

"You could all stay at my house," Tony offered. "It's no Cliffhaven, but it's big enough, and I'd love to have you."

"That's a lovely offer," Caroline said, and as she looked at Tony, some of the sadness left her eyes.

"A great idea," Adam agreed. "Can Caroline and Elizabeth stay with you tonight?"

"Wait," Elizabeth said. "You wouldn't be coming?"

"Someone has to stay and make the house secure. I can install locks, get a security system."

"Well, I don't want to leave Cliffhaven." She crossed her arms over her chest. They all gaped at her, and the incredulous looks on their faces made her want to bolt. "I can't leave the art until it's stabilized."

"Of course you can," Caroline urged. "Nothing in the house is worth your safety."

"No one is asking you to stop working," Adam said. "Just take a break for a few days while we improve security."

"I don't want to take a break."

"Listen, if someone is willing to do that to a rat," Tony said, "they're crazy. Sick. They could be capable of anything."

"I'm not going to stop working on the most important project of my life just because some coward tries to intimidate me. I'm not letting them run me off, and I'm absolutely not leaving Cliffhaven unprotected while some lunatic sneaks around." Elizabeth followed Adam's gaze to her fingers, which were clamped onto the table and turning red. She slid her hands into her lap and took a breath.

Tony laid a platter of frittata and fruit on the table then touched Caroline's forearm. "You'll stay at my house, won't you? Until we know it's safe."

Caroline nodded. "But I wish you'd come, too, Elizabeth. Or I could pay for you to stay at the hotel in the village."

"This isn't about money."

Adam's brows drew together. "Is it that important to you?"

"I don't expect you to understand." She shut her eyes, hating the tears that threatened to fall, hating the trembling of her lips that meant she was about to lose control. "Work is all I have right now."

Caroline leaned over and clasped her hand. "That's not true. You have us."

Her lips curved in a rueful smile. It was a nice sentiment. But she knew that when her work was finished and she left Cliffhaven, she wouldn't have any of the people who were becoming so important to her.

"I'll be fine." Ignoring the tension that radiated from Adam, she slid a piece of frittata onto her plate.

"Well," Caroline said, clearly eager to change the subject, "Given the circumstances, I'm really glad I picked this up for you, Adam." She slid a slim white box onto the table.

"What's that?"

"A cell phone. Welcome to the twenty-first century."

Adam looked down at the box with surprise, as if the simple gift touched him profoundly.

"I set it up for you already. I've put everybody you know in the contacts." Caroline pulled out the phone, opened an app, and swiped the screen. "There's Elizabeth's number."

"Is he on Insta yet?" Tony asked, his mouth full of frittata. "He can check out my food porn."

"I think we might wait on social media for a bit," Caroline said. "We don't want to scare him away from the internet."

Elizabeth watched Caroline guiding Adam through his new

phone, listened as Tony cracked a joke. The three of them, seated side by side across the farmhouse table, looked like a unit. They were firmly rooted in this place, together, and she could see that gave them a deeper foundation, deeper relationships. They were proof that having someone by your side, facing the darkness, made it easier to bear.

The longing that shot through her heralded a truth she'd been denying: she did want those things—a place to belong to, people to love. A family. She wanted that closeness, she craved it. And not with just anyone, she wanted it here with these people, in this place.

But it would never work. She'd known since childhood there was something lacking within her, some failing that kept her in the foster system, some reason families never seemed to want her. Maybe she'd been broken by the death of her mother, or maybe she'd been born with something inside her profoundly lacking. The result was the same—nobody wanted her. She was exempt, somehow, from the dynamics of loving relationships. It was a tough lesson to learn, that she wasn't enough.

And suddenly the need to leave the kitchen, to run away from these impossible desires, overwhelmed her. She leapt from her seat, spilling coffee onto the table, onto her shirt. Three faces looked up at her in surprise.

"God, I'm sorry."

"Let me help." Caroline grabbed a dishtowel, cleaned up the coffee, and dabbed at her shirt. "If you're determined to stay at Cliffhaven, we'll just have to make sure it's safe. In the meantime, we'll all be watching out for you, right guys?"

"Absolutely." Tony lifted his fork in salute.

Adam nodded, his eyes dark and dangerous.

Elizabeth leaned back, blinking in surprise. "Thanks. That means a lot."

Tony shrugged. "That's what friends do, isn't it?"

She sank into her chair, picked up her fork, took another bite of frittata, enjoying its flavor for the first time.

Her friends were going to look out for her. Her lips curved into a smile even as her eyes grew misty.

At that kitchen table, even if it was only for a moment, she'd found a place she did belong.

CHAPTER 22

*S*he was in the grand foyer when the lights came on, bent over the sculptural newel post at the bottom of the double staircase, restoring the wood. The electric light in the chandelier above flickered to life, and the air filled with music that echoed across the vaulted ceiling. The music was scratchy, full of the crackles and pops of vinyl records. It was an old song she recognized—a woman's voice, delicate and haunting, singing about seeing her lost loved one in all the old, familiar places. She followed the sound to the corner of the great hall, where an old gramophone spun.

Adam stood next to the revolving record, the ghost of a smile on his lips. "Let there be light."

"Hallelujah."

Days had passed since the discovery of the dead animal had overshadowed the illicit kiss they'd shared. If she closed her eyes, she could still feel his lips on hers. But then the echo of his apology rang in her ears, opening a pit in her stomach. She shook her head firmly and clenched her fists at her side. It was foolish to care so much about one man's rejection.

"The electrician's in the basement," Adam said, oblivious to her internal turmoil. "It should help with your work, I hope."

"Definitely. I'm almost done with this sculpture." She gestured to the newel post, and Adam followed her to the foot of the grand staircase.

The sculpture was a monolith at odds with the rest of the house—straight, clean lines forming a three-dimensional triangle capped with a wicked point. The wooden pyramid had been dusty, the finish scratched and nicked, but now it gleamed.

"I know this isn't in my job description," she said, "but it was calling to me, and it didn't take long. Amazing, isn't it?"

"Other than those broken parts, you mean?" Adam bent toward the woodwork, inspecting it. "I cracked the wood when I was a boy, playing catch with Christopher. My mother tried to glue it back together, but she did a terrible job."

She ran her finger lovingly over the flaw in the wood. "Have you heard of *kintsugi*, the Japanese art of repairing broken pottery? They don't try to hide the fact that the pottery was broken. They use gold on the cracks, highlighting the damaged places. It adds character to the piece, so it's valued more for being scarred."

"I suppose there's a lesson in there, somewhere, for me?"

"Only if you want there to be." She smiled and began packing her tools into a small kit. "If it were my sculpture, I'd inlay those cracks with turquoise, or maybe copper, since it's part of your family's history."

"That would be . . . beautiful."

Suddenly, his eyes sparked. "Would you like to see one of Cliffhaven's secrets?" He didn't wait for her to answer, just grasped her hand, pulling her toward a large landscape mounted on the wall. His fingers reached behind the ornate picture frame, something clicked, and the painting opened to reveal a dark hole in the wall.

Her pulse quickened. "Is that a secret passageway?" She

peered into the dark corridor, where cobwebs hung from dusty stone walls.

"Want to go in?"

"Absolutely."

She scrambled through the portrait hole, turning back to clasp his hand and draw him in. He closed the portrait door, and the passageway plunged into perfect darkness. It smelled of damp, dusty stone.

They moved slowly, her feet searching in the darkness for each step. She slipped, and his arm came around her waist.

"I've got you."

He held her there, pressed against his chest, for one moment longer than necessary. "Thanks."

At the end of the passageway, Adam groped in the darkness until his finger found the mechanism that opened the secret door, and light flooded the corridor.

"Where are we?"

"The library." He helped her through the awkward doorway built into one wall of bookshelves.

"That was incredible! I feel like Nancy Drew." Suddenly the house seemed ripe with mysteries, possibilities. "I want to know all Cliffhaven's secrets."

His smile faded. "If you knew all Cliffhaven's secrets, you'd leave and never return." And, just like that, his guard went up and the haunted look returned to his green eyes. What had made him turn so morose and withdrawn?

"That's the thing about secrets," she said. "We hold them and hide them without realizing they're poison, infecting us, weighing us down."

She approached him tentatively. "People tend to tell me their secrets. Maybe because they know I move a lot and won't be around to tell anyone. You can tell me anything, Adam."

"Someone like you can't even imagine the darkness that exists in the world."

"Really?" Her blood heated. "Someone who watched her mother die? Who got passed around like an unwanted heirloom, who survived an orphanage full of rapists and abusers? Why do you imagine I'm unfamiliar with the dark?"

He reached for her, as if he might caress her cheek, then his hand fell to his side. "Because you're so full of light."

She rested her hand on his forearm. "Does this have something to do with why you live in these ruined rooms? Why you feel you don't deserve anything better?"

"Isn't it obvious? All this," he waved his hand, gesturing to the house around him, "is because of *me*. My parents should be here right now, living their lives! But they're not, because of me."

"Adam, the fire wasn't your fault."

His eyes turned dark, his mouth a thin line. And she suddenly knew she shouldn't offer more words of comfort, words denying the guilt he carried. Because maybe there was a reason he carried it. He obviously held some dark secret close to his heart—one that left him torn apart by guilt. Were there things she couldn't imagine?

She reached out, her hand brushing his shoulder, and he recoiled like it was a branding iron. "You should leave me alone."

It stung. She couldn't deny that it did.

It's all right, she assured herself as she let the door shut behind her. *I'm an expert at leaving.*

Outside the leaded windows of the grand foyer, snow began to fall. Light, delicate flakes danced in the air as if to Chopin. She watched them, awed by their beauty and grace. But the flurry was over as quickly as it started, as if it were only a herald of the cold weather to come—a warning to prepare for the bitter northern winter.

CHAPTER 23

"*T*here you are, Miss Watson!" Jack Arrington's voice boomed across the parlor in that particular tone common to lawyers, actors, or anyone else craving attention.

Elizabeth froze, bent double over her restoration tools. She'd been laying them out neatly under the fresco in the parlor when the unwanted voice interrupted her.

"Good afternoon, Mr. Arrington. What brings you to Cliffhaven?"

"Actually, I was hoping to have a word with you." He shut the parlor door, and she tamped down on impatience.

Jack set his Gucci briefcase on a side table, and his burly frame dwarfed the delicate queen Anne antiques, making them look like doll furniture. "How do you like working at Cliffhaven?"

Well, the mansion full of art is my dream come true, my employer is the closest friend I've ever had, and there's a handsome, mysterious man who I feel like I've known all my life. And I'm becoming too attached to all of it.

"I love it."

Jack raised his eyebrows, shooting her a pointed look. "But I heard you've had some unpleasantness. It's all over the island. Something about a dead animal in your room?"

Images flashed through her mind—the wire hanger wrapped around the rat's neck, blood matting its fur. "The police are handling it."

"I'm sure they are." He folded his burly body into a covered wing-back chair. "I imagine you're finding life at Cliffhaven quite uncomfortable."

"I don't require a great deal of comforts."

"And we aren't even deep into winter yet. The storms up here can be dangerous, particularly for southerners who don't know how to handle the conditions."

She stepped behind a powder-blue settee as if it might shield her. "I'm a quick learner."

"No doubt. But many before you have come up here seeking adventure only to find they couldn't cope with the brutal winter. There's no shame in it."

"Not until I finish my work."

"Your work." He wrinkled his nose like he'd smelled something rotten. "So what happens after you've restored these frescoes? They'll be removed, yes? And sold?"

She bit her lip. "That depends on whether Adam and Caroline decide to restore the house."

The lawyer leaned back in his chair and tapped his fingertips together. His eyes, as they roved over her, were shrewd. "I'm here because I'm hoping you can help me with a matter of great importance to the Arrington family." Jack leaned toward her, and the scent of his expensive aftershave enveloped her. "A development company has made an offer of purchase for Cliffhaven and the entire estate. Quite frankly, it's an incredible offer. Caroline and Adam would make a great deal of money."

"What does that have to do with me?" Her stomach twisted, an uneasy feeling growing within her.

"You want what's best for Caroline and Adam. We all do.

And it's my firm opinion that any money sunk into this house would be a huge loss with no return on the investment."

"You must know it isn't my decision to make."

"Of course not." Jack smiled. "But you seem to have some influence over Caroline and Adam. If you told them that, in your expert opinion, the restoration of Cliffhaven is too expensive and difficult, it might convince them to abandon the project."

"You truly believe the Arringtons would be better off if they sold the land?"

"Without a doubt." Jack pounded one fist on the arm of his chair. "I care about Adam and Caroline. They're more important to me than anything. I realize that, to you, they're just clients, but—"

"They aren't just clients." The words escaped her before she could reel them back. "I mean, I'm fond of Caroline and Adam."

"Then you must see that staying here isn't good for Adam. He needs a new environment, to get out of this place that's haunted by his past." Jack's gray eyes were almost pleading. "Help me, Elizabeth. Help me do what's best for him."

She looked down at her fingers, which picked at the settee's upholstery. Would it truly be best for Adam to leave this place?

"I realize not everyone is motivated by altruism," Jack said, leaning closer. "So if you can convince them to sell, there would be a large commission for you. Perhaps one year's salary in exchange for your expert opinion. Does that sound fair?"

Her mouth dropped open, and she sank onto the covered couch. A year's salary would pay off all her student loans, releasing her from crippling debt. Not to mention someone had vandalized her car and left a dead animal in her closet. And she was living in a haunted house.

But the real problem was that she cared about all of it too much—Caroline and Tony, the house . . . Adam. And the more she cared, the more painful it would be when she had to leave.

The longer she stayed, the more her problems would multiply, and those things she cared about would become roots, binding her, fixing her in place. Trapping her. *Take the money,* a dark voice inside her whispered. *Pay off your student loans and go somewhere safe and warm where there are no complications.*

Jack's conspiratorial smile snapped her out of her reverie. He was asking her to lie, to abandon Cliffhaven to the wrecking ball. Impossible.

"I'm sorry, Mr. Arrington, I can't recommend giving up on Cliffhaven. It will be difficult, and it will take a great deal of money, but the house can be saved. It would be unethical to imply otherwise."

"If it's a matter of more money, I'm sure we could arrange—"

"Let me be clear. There is no amount of money that would persuade me to lie to Adam and Caroline."

The smile disappeared from Jack's face. "I'm sorry to hear that." He shook his head sorrowfully. "I suppose I shouldn't have expected someone like you to understand the complexities of finance."

"It's true, money has never been my area of expertise. But since Caroline hasn't hired me to advise her on those matters, it's of little consequence." She rose from her chair. "I need to get back to work."

Visibly saddened, Jack gathered his coat and briefcase. "I'm sorry we don't see eye to eye, Miss Watson."

After he'd gone, Elizabeth was left alone with the seeds of doubt he'd sown.

A FEW HOURS LATER, Elizabeth put down her tools and stretched. She'd finished the inspection of the fresco, and, fortunately, it hadn't suffered much degradation. Her next step would be to clean the fresco, then protect it against the humidity and bacteria that would slowly degrade the plaster and paint.

She rifled through her kit with worried fingers. She had everything she needed to begin cleaning—the organic solvent she would mix with water, the sponges she would use to apply the microemulsion. She was ready to begin, so what made her back away from the work of art as if it had claws and teeth?

She left the parlor like a soldier deserting the field of battle— scurrying through the hall, cursing herself for her cowardice.

Her phone chirped in her pocket, a welcome sound after days of sporadic service. It was a new message, from Adam. A thrill shot through her.

> Elizabeth,
>
> Meet me where we had our picnic. I have something to show you.
>
> Adam

She smiled as she read the formal message. He clearly hadn't gotten the hang of texting.

What did he want to show her? Probably something to do with work, with the restorations.

Sure, he probably found a fresco in the forest. Right.

The jittery thrill of expectation lifted her spirits. She could keep it professional. Forget the kiss she could still feel, could still taste.

She shot off a quick text telling him she was on her way, dressed in her new winter gear—a heavy parka, hat, mittens, and boots she'd purchased in the village—then burst out the back door.

The grounds were blanketed with newly fallen snow. It sat, thick and fluffy, on every branch and twig, transforming the grounds into a fairyland. The snow continued to fall in fat flakes, and she laughed, delighted, as they floated through the air around her. It felt cool on her cheeks—like tiny, sweet kisses. Imagining Adam waiting for her, she made her way cheerfully through ankle-deep snow towards the forest.

Outside the stables, Meeks stood squinting at the flint-colored clouds on the horizon. "We're in for a blizzard, I reckon," he said, gesturing toward the horses. "They're real jumpy. Sure sign bad weather's coming."

His arthritic hands secured the lock on the paddock gate. Were those hands strong enough to wrap a wire hanger around an animal's neck? Was there anger or hatred bubbling inside this man, capable of bursting out in violence and vandalism?

Meeks eyed her from under his woolen cap. "I'll bet this snow changes your mind about staying through the winter."

Individual snowflakes landed on her mitten, each a distinct geometric pattern against the green wool. "Not really. It's beautiful."

"You won't say that in March, after we've had three hundred inches of it," he grumbled.

She shrugged as she walked by him. "Honestly, I don't think I'd mind."

"Hey, where're you going?" He called out after her. "It's going to be dark soon."

She turned back to the frowning man. "Don't say you're worried about me." He snorted derisively and returned to his work.

As she neared the trail that led into the forest, she glanced to the west, where dark clouds billowed and grew over the roiling lake. The tops of the cedars and maples crashed against each other as wind gusted. All reminding her this was a place where nature ruled, where winter was a force. She shrank into her coat, hesitating at the edge of the tree line.

Then she thought of Adam waiting for her. Wanting her. And she stepped into the dark forest.

~

ADAM GAZED out the window of his library. Though it was already dark, he could see the snow no longer fell in delicate, dancing flakes. It was coming down hard from the sky in vast amounts, and the wind made a roaring sound as it tore around the house, rattling the shutters.

He'd always enjoyed a violent snowstorm, but tonight he couldn't shake an unsettled feeling. So he paced in his study, waiting impatiently for dinnertime.

When the appointed hour arrived, he burst from the library like a caged animal set free. He was eager to see Elizabeth, ready to share a fine meal with her and hear how she'd spent her day. Her company was sure to banish his unease.

But when he arrived in the dining room, the table wasn't laid for dinner. His anxiety grew, a pit in his stomach that widened with every passing moment. He pushed open the kitchen door with more strength than necessary, paying no attention to the loud crash that resulted as it slammed against the wall.

The noise startled Tony, who dropped a paring knife onto the floor. "Damn. What's eating you?"

"Where's Elizabeth?"

"I haven't seen her for hours. Did you try calling her?"

Adam pulled his phone from his pocket. There was a new message, from Elizabeth. *On my way.* What the hell did that mean? He scanned the messages before her most recent one, then fixated on the message sent from his phone. His confusion lasted only a moment before yielding to burning anger, then cold dread.

Tony wiped his hands on his apron. "Something's wrong, isn't it?"

Adam touched his phone and held it to his ear. After a moment, the cheerful chirp that was Elizabeth's ringtone rang through the air. He followed the sound to her office, where her phone vibrated uselessly on her desk.

"Would you tell me what's going on?" Tony asked, concern coloring his voice.

"Did you send a text from my phone?" His voice was savage, ragged, as he thrust the cell between them. "Some kind of joke?"

"What? Of course not."

Tony's baffled, honest face was all he needed to see. He turned away without another word and stormed into the dining room.

Caroline stood next to the dining table, peering out the windows. "This should be quite a storm."

"Have you seen Elizabeth?"

She blinked. "I just got here. The roads are terrible. Is something wrong?"

Tony swung through the kitchen door. "Can someone please tell me what the hell is going on?"

"Look at this text to Elizabeth." He slammed the cell onto the dining table, and Caroline and Tony bent over the screen. "I didn't write it."

Silence filled the room.

"How is that possible?" Tony asked.

"I left it on my desk in the library all day."

Caroline raised her head to meet his gaze, her face reflecting a horrifying realization. "Are you saying she's out there, in the blizzard, alone?"

"I'm calling the police," Tony said, reaching for his phone.

Adam shook his head. "Even if Ogie could get that ancient squad car up the hill through the snow, we can't waste time waiting for them. I'm going to look for her."

Leaving Caroline and Tony to gape after him, he ran to the hall, opened the closet, and yanked out his winter gear.

Following closely on his heels, Tony held his phone to his ear. "Damn! Now I'm not getting a signal. It must be the storm."

"Adam, this makes no sense," Caroline said when she'd caught up to them, her voice wavering. "You could get lost in the snow just as easily as she could!"

"I know the forest better than she does." He jumped into snow pants then threw on his parka.

"You know that doesn't matter!" Caroline raked her fingers through her hair in frustration. "The temperature's dropping. You could freeze out there."

"So could she." He yanked on heavy gloves and reached for the door.

"Then I'm going with you," Caroline said firmly.

"No!"

Caroline blanched at the heat in his voice, and he closed his eyes, fighting for calm. "Please, stay here in case Elizabeth comes back. Keep trying to call the police. Tony, find Meeks and have him plow the drive so emergency vehicles can make it to the house."

"Sure thing," Tony said.

Caroline's eyes filled with tears, and Adam looked at her, willing her to understand. "I have to go," he whispered urgently.

"I know." She wrapped her arms around him. He stiffened in surprise, then hugged her back fiercely.

Then he left the comfort of Caroline's arms, stepping into a tempest of tearing wind and blinding snow, going willingly into the heart of the storm.

CHAPTER 24

*E*lizabeth trudged through the deep snow, pausing to rest between each labored step. She was lost in the forest, the path buried by three feet of fresh snow that had fallen in a matter of hours. Nothing looked familiar in the alien, white landscape.

When she'd entered the forest hours ago, she followed familiar landmarks along the path. But the snow fell heavily, obscuring the trail. She'd gotten turned around and continued to blunder deeper into the woods, refusing to believe she could be lost. It was only when night fell that she realized she'd made a deadly mistake.

Now the snow was past her knees, making every step difficult. The exertion caused small beads of sweat to appear on her skin, but the moisture only made her colder. Her exhausted limbs were failing, but she gritted her teeth and kept going one grueling step at a time.

Night had descended long ago, and the storm continued to worsen. The snow blew sideways, blinding her and stinging her exposed flesh. The woolen scarf wrapped around her cheeks did little to protect her skin from the biting snow and wind.

The wind roared, filling her ears, making a mockery of her cries for help. She'd stopped shouting long ago, and the wind had turned into white noise, filling her head with fear and doubt.

You're going to die out here. She squeezed her eyes shut against the dark voice in her head. *Be honest with yourself. How much farther can you walk?* She wrenched her leg from the snow and took another step.

Would anyone at Cliffhaven miss her? Send help?

Nobody will even notice you're gone.

She tried to ignore the voice of fear, reminding herself there was reason to hope. She'd been through these woods before. Surely her survival instincts could take her back to Cliffhaven.

Survival instincts? You don't have what it takes to make it through this wilderness. Adam told you once, but you didn't listen—you don't belong here.

Exhaustion weighed on her limbs. The cold seeped through her parka, sapping her strength. But she had to keep going— back to Cliffhaven, back to Adam.

Why bother? You're fooling yourself if you think Adam would ever want someone like you. Nobody wants you.

Her heart wrenched. Tears beaded in the corners of her eyes, though she couldn't tell if they were from the wind or her despair. She paused in her struggle to walk, breathing heavily.

You're going to die out here, in the snow. Just like your mother.

Memories flashed through her mind—the car crash, the twisted metal, the scent of gasoline. The familiar urge to run strangled up her spine, but she couldn't. Just couldn't.

Sometimes it felt like she'd started running after the accident, away from the stench of death and violence, and had never stopped. She'd run through her life, refusing to stop moving, stubbornly insisting she didn't need anyone. And look where it got her—alone in the northern wilderness. Dying in the snow.

And suddenly, there was no fight left in her, no reason to

keep going. Her legs buckled, and she fell back into the soft snow. It molded to her body, forming a cocoon around her. It was a relief to stop moving, stop struggling.

All at once, the wind died down. The roaring in her ears subsided, and the snow began to drift down lazily, no longer biting into her skin. She tilted her head up, finding herself in a clearing circled by evergreens blanketed with pure white snow. The surrounding forest was still and peaceful.

Would it be painful to freeze to death? Maybe she would just slip away, become one with the frozen landscape. And there would be nobody, really, to grieve when she was gone. Somehow, that bothered her more than anything, more than the cold invading her limbs, more than the thought of imminent death.

She closed her eyes, wishing she'd done things differently. She'd been a fool, a wounded child masquerading as an adult.

And then a roar, primitive and primal, tore through the night. "Elizabeth!" The voice was desperate, pleading.

"Adam?" she croaked, her voice no more than a whisper.

"Elizabeth!" The voice grew nearer, filling her with strength.

She willed herself to sit up and yelled, "Adam!" Then she saw him—a shadow between the trees, moving toward her.

"Adam." Now her voice was a whisper, filled with wonder and gratitude. He was there, charging through the snow, sliding onto his knees before her and wrapping her in his arms.

Emotion engulfed her, and it was more than relief, more than gratitude. More, even, than hope. She hugged him fiercely, wanting time to stop, to mark the moment something profound shifted inside her.

"Thank God I found you." His voice was tattered. "Are you hurt?"

"I . . . I don't think so. I can walk."

He pulled back, examining her limbs, his face creased with worry. "Then why weren't you?"

Because I gave up. Because I was overwhelmed with grief and sorrow and hopelessness—lost in more than just the forest.

She turned her face into his chest, and he gathered her into her arms, lifting her into his lap.

"Thank heaven," he whispered as he pressed her tightly to his chest. "We have to go. The storm will worsen any minute now." Without hesitation, he swept her into his arms and stood.

"I can walk," she said, even as the wind began to roar, and the snow became a wall encircling them.

"But you don't have to." He clutched her closer to his chest.

"You can't carry me all the way to Cliffhaven."

"Yes, I can." And the fierce determination in his voice left no room for doubt.

"But there's no trail to follow. Look, you can barely see your footprints."

"I know these woods, every inch of them."

His arms locked around her protectively as he took the first step, and she had no choice but to trust him, to let go of the control she constantly exercised. She lay her face against his coat, shielded from the blowing snow, and closed her eyes.

She'd needed him, and he'd been there. As he carried her through the woods, strength returned to her—to her limbs, to her heart.

True to Adam's words, the storm worsened. The wind howled around them, the snow blinded, and the cold assaulted her. His legs sank into the drifts, and every step seemed like a struggle. Then a dark shadow emerged from the swirling snow and slowly took shape.

"It's one of the staff cottages!" He shouted over the roaring wind.

It was a small log cabin with snow piling around the base, drifting from the roof.

"The snow's blocking the door. I'll have to dig it out."

"You can put me down." When he hesitated, she said, "I'll be fine."

He put her down slowly, holding her until she was steady on her feet, and she sunk into snow up to her thigh. He dug with gloved hands until the door opened enough for them to squeeze inside. They stepped into the dark cabin, and he slammed the door shut against the wind and snow.

She sagged against the wooden door, relief flooding her. The cabin was just one room, housing a rustic table with two chairs, a tiny kitchenette, and a brass bed decorated with a patchwork quilt. But it was a welcome refuge, a haven from the storm that raged outside its walls.

Adam pulled the gloves from his hands and flicked the light switch, but the room remained dark. "Electric's out."

He pulled out his phone and checked the screen. "I'm not getting a signal."

She sank into one of the rustic dining chairs and eyed the stone fireplace. "What are the odds there's any firewood?"

"There's some in that box by the hearth." Adam moved toward the kitchen by the dim light of his phone.

She heard rustling, then the strike of a match, and golden light illuminated his face. He'd found a lantern.

His eyes were serious as he appraised her. "You're shivering."

"I can't seem to stop." Her entire body was quivering, struggling to warm itself. And exhaustion was seeping into her limbs, weighing them down. Still, she could smile, because something inside her glowed with so much warmth, it banished all fear.

She'd needed him, and he'd been there.

"I'll be all right."

"Shivering's good, actually." His eyes, so heavy with concern as they roved over her, belied his words. "Your body's trying to warm itself."

He kneeled next to her, and his fingers were warm on her wrist as he felt her pulse. "Your heartbeat's strong. I don't think you're hypothermic, but we need to warm you as quickly as we can."

She met his gaze, and suddenly the room seemed too small, too intimate. "Should we try to get back to Cliffhaven? Caroline will be worried."

"That blizzard could be raging for a while. If you go back out there, you could get hypothermia." He ducked his head. "But I understand if you don't want to stay here with me."

She listened to the wind howling around the cottage. "I don't want to go back out there."

"Then let's light a fire."

She stood, crossed the room with stumbling steps, and sat heavily by the fireplace. When she tried to remove her mittens, her stiff fingers wouldn't cooperate. "My hands are frozen."

"You might have frostbite. Keep your mittens on until I get the fire going."

He knelt next to her, arranging the wood and tinder. The kindling was dry and caught quickly, flashing soft light on his face. They watched as the flames travelled across the wood and grew.

She took off her gloves, revealing skin that had an odd, yellowish tint. She stretched her hands toward the flames.

"Ouch!" She pulled her hands away from the fire. "It stings."

"That can happen during the early stages of frostbite. It might hurt a little, but keep your hands near the fire."

It did hurt, like pins and needles poking at her sensitive skin, but it wasn't long before normal feeling returned.

"May I see?" Adam cradled her hands, inspecting them. "There aren't any blisters forming. How do they feel now?"

"Much better."

He kept her hands within his own, sharing his warmth. "How are your toes?"

"I think they're okay." She tried to unlace her boots, but her fingers fumbled, and she slumped back in the chair. "I can't do it."

"Let me." He kneeled in front of her, untying her boot and sliding it from her foot. "It's okay to need someone else, now and then."

"I don't need anyone." The words spilled out of her mouth by rote, memorized long ago and repeated often. But this time, the sound of them was hollow, the truth of them belied by his nimble fingers untying her other boot, accomplishing a task she could not. His lips turned up in amusement and he caught her gaze, one eyebrow raised as he pulled off her other boot.

The fire blazed, casting off heat that quickly filled the small cabin. He rose gracefully, uncurling his massive body until he towered over her. He stripped off his parka and snow pants, revealing a thermal base layer of fabric that clung to his muscular form.

"We need to raise your core temperature." He ran his fingers through his coal-black hair, his eyes catching hers then darting away. "You have to . . . take off any clothes that are wet."

She looked down at her soaked parka, where melted snow dripped from her clothing onto the bare wood floor. "Will you help me?"

Her heart thudded in her chest as he pulled her damp woolen socks down her ankle and over her foot, his hands warm on her chilled skin. Then he peeled the wet clothing from her skin layer by layer—first the wet parka, then her sweater and fleece-lined pants. He moved efficiently, seeming to make every effort to touch her skin as little as possible. Within minutes, she was stripped down to her long sleeve t-shirt and underwear.

"Now we need to get you warm."

Cold seeped into her very bones, and her limbs were heavy. She eyed the brass bed. "I'd love to lie down."

She slipped under the heavy quilt, between the sheets, and recoiled. "It's freezing!"

The bed was an icy nest, and her body was incapable of warming even that small space. Her muscles began to shake violently, her entire body tight and tense as her teeth clattered together. She closed her eyes, overcome by her body's fight for survival.

Adam paced next to the bed, raking a hand through his hair. Then he stopped, his forehead furrowed, hands clenched into fists, looking down at her as if the sight was killing him. "This isn't working."

"Don't they s-s-say something about skin-to-skin contact?"

He stilled. "I don't want to make you uncomfortable."

She groaned. "You would be making me *more* comfortable. Please, give me your heat."

He climbed into bed beside her carefully, as if she were something delicate. Then he lay on his side facing her and opened his arms, his face unsure. Heat radiated from him, and her limbs sought his of their own volition—her hands searching out the warmth of his firm stomach, her chest pressing against his torso, her cheek nuzzling his neck.

She moaned. She actually moaned. "You're a furnace."

"Is it all right if I . . ." His arms went around her, two bands of warmth over her icy skin. He rubbed his hands across her back, and his touch was tender. Gentle.

Her body relaxed into him, and his intoxicating scent—leather and cedar—enveloped her. He pressed his cheek to the top of her head.

It should have felt strange to be held. Her past experiences with intimacy had always ended after the last orgasm, when she would pat her lover on the shoulder, thank him, and awkwardly gather her clothes from the floor before dressing in the bathroom. Not once had she let a man sleep in her bed, and she'd never fallen asleep in a man's arms.

But now there was a new feeling blazing in her chest, as warming as any fire. She didn't want to give that feeling a name, didn't want to identify or quantify or question. She just held tight to it, embracing it, treasuring it, until it rocked her gently into the sweet oblivion of sleep.

CHAPTER 25

*W*hen she woke, the brass bed was empty. She was blissfully warm and comfortable nestled under the thick patchwork quilt, but the space next to her was cold. The window above the bed was dark, and wind still howled outside.

She sat up, blinking in the dim light. Adam was there, sitting on a rustic wooden chair next to the fire, staring into the flames. The firelight danced across his marble features, across the wine-colored markings on his cheek. He looked pensive, somber—like a man grappling for answers.

"How long did I sleep?"

"A few hours. The snow's still coming down." He moved to her side, kneeled next to her. "How do you feel?"

She took stock of her body, marveled that she felt so strong, so alive. Every breath was like a gift. "It's crazy, but I'm perfectly fine. Thanks to you."

He stood abruptly and walked back to the fireplace. "Don't look at me like that. Like I'm some kind of hero."

She blinked, baffled by his words. He'd searched the wilderness for her in a storm, found her, and *carried* her to safety. What, in his mind, would it take to be a hero?

There was pain, there, in his face. Was he thinking of the family he'd lost, the parents he hadn't been able to save?

"You saved my life. I needed you, and you were there." She stood and walked to him, still wrapped in the quilt that trailed behind her. "You can't imagine what that means to me. There is literally nobody else in the world who cares about me enough to risk their life in a blizzard."

He shook his head, staring down at his dinner-plate sized hands. "There was nothing brave about what I did. I had to go, had to find you."

"Why?"

He looked at her, capturing her with his emerald gaze. "You really don't know?"

Her breath quickened, and her throat went dry. "I don't think I do."

He just looked at her, his eyes burning with intensity, and her heart began to pound.

"I know you don't belong here," he whispered. "I know I don't belong with you. But that doesn't stop me from wanting you, and I'm consumed by it."

His voice was low and intense, his eyes earnest. "You've taken over my mind. You're all I think about. I want you, more than I've ever wanted anything."

She froze, his words echoing through her mind. *He wants me.*

He dragged his hand through his unruly hair and turned away. "I know it's impossible. No woman wants a beast of a man —someone scarred, repulsive."

"Stop." She touched his arm, turning him back to face her.

She reached toward his cheek, and he watched her, tense and wary. She trailed her fingers over his eyebrow, down the textured, discolored skin. He closed his eyes, completely still, as if he focused entirely on the sensation, the feel of her.

When he opened his eyes, they were inches away from one another, eyes and lips aligned. Waiting. Wanting.

The air itself seemed to crackle, charged with the electricity between them. Her breath quickened, her pulse hammering a primitive beat.

She wanted to touch his body, wanted to feel his strong muscles beneath her fingers. She'd known lust before, had burned for other men, but new to her, now, were the crazy impulses to run her hands through his dark hair, caress his face, kiss his scars.

At any other time in her life, she would have run from those feelings. But now her fear was gone. Lost. It had fled in the face of a much greater truth—people need each other. *She* needed.

It was probably a bad idea. It would almost definitely lead to heartbreak. But for this one night, she didn't have to be alone.

Urgency pounded through her, the feeling that if she moved quickly enough, she could take everything she needed so desperately, fulfill every desire, and still outrun the consequences.

It had to be now. And it had to be fast.

She clutched his shirt in her hands, yanked him toward her, and pressed her lips to his. He froze for a moment, as if in shock, then his lips were searching hers.

The kiss burned. It scorched. It was fierce and fast, demanding everything with an urgency that couldn't be denied. But she had to have more—he might stop at any moment, might apologize and reject her again.

As if he could read her mind, he hesitated, pulled back. "Are you sure you're all right? I don't want to take advantage—"

She drowned out whatever objection he might have by claiming his mouth with her own, then said, "I'm fine. Better than fine."

"You're not cold?"

"I'm on fire, Adam." She pressed his palm to her neck, where heat blossomed. "Can't you feel it?"

His fingers flexed convulsively, pulling her toward him, even as his emerald eyes betrayed his doubt.

"I want this, Adam. God, I *need* it."

His eyes roved over her face, her hair. He reached out tentatively and touched her cheek with his fingertips, looked at her as if he couldn't believe she was real. And she saw the moment he decided—when she won whatever war battled within him.

They moved for each other at the same moment, with the same urgency, lips crashing together. And if she thought he'd kissed her before, it was nothing to this—he devoured her. He was a man unleashed.

She let the quilt fall to her feet. He lifted her off the ground, pressing her against the cabin wall as their tongues twined. His lips broke away from her mouth to trail down her neck, and she arched back to give him better access, making a small sound of pleasure deep in her throat. Wanting his mouth, she twisted her hands into his hair and pulled him back to her lips.

They broke apart, taking ragged breaths as they gazed at each other. Firelight danced across his face, and in that moment, like the eye of a hurricane, something tender entered his eyes. And she knew that he *saw* her, that he wanted her. For a woman who'd been a girl no one ever wanted, it was everything.

She tugged the hem of his shirt up, pulling it over his head and dropping it to the floor. She placed her hands on the hot skin of his chest, and they roved down, over his stomach, skimming the clearly defined muscles.

He slipped his hands under her t-shirt and pulled it over her head to reveal her breasts, spilling out of the confines of her bra. He inhaled a sharp breath. "My God, you're beautiful."

While the compliment warmed her, she had no patience for niceties. Any minute he might come to his senses, stop this madness. She fumbled with his belt until he undid the fastening, allowing the rest of his clothing to fall to the floor. Then she stepped back, taking in the sight of his powerful, naked body in the firelight. Her hands ached with the need to touch, to explore him.

He reached for her, and they embraced, skin to skin. Heat flooded her body, consuming her. "The bed," she gasped.

He swept her into his arms, kissed her deeply, and laid her on the small brass bed. He pushed her bra over her head and cast it aside. The lace landed on the floor by the crackling fire, then his mouth found her nipple and she lost all coherent thought.

He sucked and nipped her, and the pleasure washed over her in waves. But she wanted more, more of him.

"Adam." His head came up, his green eyes questioning. "Adam, please, I want you inside me."

His eyes smoldered, but he shook his head. "Not yet."

She moaned in impatience. His mouth found her other nipple, and her moan turned to a cry. She reveled in the pleasure, then reached down and wrapped one hand around him.

Urgency pounded through her, an insistent heartbeat. "Now, it has to be now," she demanded breathlessly. "Please."

"I think all you'd have to say is 'please', and I'd do anything you asked."

He moved over her, bringing his head to her level, and kissed her. The hard length of him pressed into her thighs, and she opened them greedily. He broke the kiss and held her gaze as he slowly entered her. He groaned—a sound of both relief and torture.

Finally, she was joined to him, forming the connection she'd wanted for so long. For someone who kept people at arm's length, this act—letting him inside the heart of her—was precious.

She'd known sex with Adam would be everything she needed, months' worth of touch and pleasure in one explosive moment. But she hadn't known that he would overwhelm her, that it would mean more than she could comprehend.

"Adam," she moaned, and it was a plea.

He continued to move inside her, slowly. Inexorably. And it was as close to rapture as she'd ever been.

The pace gradually increased, the pulsing waves of pleasure threatening to overwhelm her. She quivered, close to the brink.

"Elizabeth," he whispered.

The sound of her name uttered with such reverence caused her to fall apart, her orgasm rushing over her like a tidal wave. With a deep sound of triumph, Adam thrust into her one final time, finding his release as the blizzard raged around them.

ELIZABETH WOKE to sunlight streaming through the windows of the cozy cabin, illuminating Adam next to her on the bed, still asleep.

The sky was blue and sunny outside the cabin window, and the wind no longer roared through the cabin's eaves. The storm was over, and the world was blanketed in white—it hung from the evergreens, buffering every sound.

Adam stirred, simultaneously opening his green eyes and reaching for her.

She pulled the patchwork quilt over her breasts and smiled shyly. "The snow stopped. We can go back to Cliffhaven."

Adam groaned into his pillow. "What if I don't want to?"

Delighted, she burrowed back under the covers and rested her head against his chest. He made a small sound of pleasure and kissed her hair.

"So we're just going to stay here all day?" she asked, smothering her grin against his skin.

"Sounds perfect."

Adam lay on his side, his elbow cocked beneath him, resting

his head on his hand, gazing at her. He ran the tip of his finger across the skin of her cheek, and she made a purring sound deep in her throat.

"So beautiful," he whispered. "When I first saw you in my library, I knew I'd never seen anything as beautiful as you in candlelight. Like an exotic bird appearing suddenly in my back-yard—more precious for being out of place, making me hold my breath so as not to frighten you away."

"I thought you couldn't stand me. You said you wanted me to leave!"

"I'm ashamed of how I acted then." He rolled onto his back, staring at the ceiling, one bare arm resting on his forehead. "Your arrival disturbed my routine, mocked the shabbiness of my existence, exposed my loneliness. But that's no excuse for my behavior."

His ebony hair was tousled even more than usual, his eyes repentant and admiring. She wanted him again, and her body stirred in response, but something held her back.

She'd had mind-blowing sex before, but this was something else. It had been infused with something more, something bigger. And now, rather than being physically sated, she was left wanting more of him, craving their connection, wanting it to be deeper. She wanted to know all the secret parts of him, and felt a deep, desperate yearning for him to see the secret parts of her.

He reached for her hand, pulling it up to kiss her palm. "Thank you for last night. I hope it was all right. For you, I mean. It's just been a while, and I guess I was pretty starved for touch."

A tightness gripped her chest. *Am I just the first girl who happened to come along?*

She pulled her hand from his. "I'm glad we could . . . service one another."

He drew back, eyes searching her face. "Is that what this was? Scratching an itch?"

"It can't be anything . . . more. You know I'm leaving when the job's finished."

"But you're here now. And I won't ask for more." But there was something in his eyes that told her he would demand more, that he would take it. "I just want to know you. All of you."

Fear and desire warred within her. "I don't know if I know how to do that."

"Neither do I." A tentative smile warmed his face. "Just look at me when I touch you." His fingers trailed down her chest, and his hand cupped her breast, lighting a fire within her. "Let me see what you're feeling. Don't hide from me."

He slid his body down the length of her, kissing first her neck, then the side of her breast. "I want to explore every part of you."

She wrapped her arms around him, reveling in his strength. He hardened against her thigh, filling her with sweet antic-ipation.

It was at that moment that the door to the cabin burst open, revealing a tall, hooded figure standing in the doorway.

CHAPTER 26

*E*lizabeth stifled a scream. Snow swirled into the room, and frigid air swept over her exposed skin.

Vanessa stood in the doorway of the cabin, covered with snow, her mouth hanging open in surprise. Elizabeth gasped and pulled the quilt up to her chin, struggling to cover her breasts.

Vanessa stepped through the threshold, closing the door behind her and removing her hood. She looked perfect in her bright blue ski suit and matching cashmere hat, blonde hair trailing in a braid over her shoulder. She could have just stepped off a gondola in a luxurious Swiss ski resort.

As she brushed snow off her coat, her eyes skimmed over Elizabeth. Was that surprise she read in them? Contempt? Elizabeth stuck her chin in the air and sat straighter, striving to look dignified.

Then Vanessa's gaze shifted to Adam, and there was no surprise. Only anger.

Adam seemed to take the situation in stride, saying calmly, "Close the door, would you? You're letting in the cold."

He retrieved his shirt from the bedpost and pulled it over his head. "Are more people looking for us?"

"Of course." Vanessa's voice was cold and accusatory. "Caroline's beside herself."

Guilt washed over her. "We should have gone back to Cliffhaven as soon as the snow stopped."

"We just woke up," Adam clarified.

"Really?" Vanessa snapped. "Then you slept through most of the morning. The snow stopped hours ago, and we've been looking for you since then."

Vanessa's eyes roved over her, cold with contempt. "You surprise me, Adam. Though I expect nothing less from other men, so why should you be different?"

"Vanessa—"

"I'm just glad I was the one to find you, and not someone from the village." Vanessa placed her hand on her hip, and her lips curled with disgust. "You've put me in a very awkward, embarrassing position. It won't happen again."

The focus of Vanessa's scorn shifted to her. "And you. Have some respect for yourself."

"*Excuse* me?"

"Vanessa, that's enough." Adam gestured to the door. "Go tell everyone we're all right. We'll be right behind you. Give us some privacy to get dressed, for God's sake."

Vanessa stuck her nose in the air, looking coldly dignified, and disappeared into the snow without looking back.

After the door shut behind her, Elizabeth turned to Adam. Surely he would have some explanation for Vanessa's outrageous behavior. But he simply threw the blankets aside and stepped out of bed.

The sunlight streaming through the window cast golden light on his naked body as he retrieved his pants from the bedpost. Everything about him was large and powerfully built, from his broad shoulders to his muscular legs. Still, he moved with surprising grace. He looked completely unperturbed, and for some unfathomable reason, his nonchalance heated her blood.

"That was embarrassing, don't you think?" she said.

"Not particularly." He turned back to her with a frown, as if something had just occurred to him. "Does it bother you that Vanessa knows about us?"

She bit her lip. Caroline might not love the idea of her brother sleeping with her employee. "Do you think she'll tell anyone?"

"I can ask her not to mention it, if you like." Adam's voice was tight, and he didn't look at her as he stepped into his pants.

He gathered her clothes, placed them on the bed, and crossed the room to the kitchenette. With a quick glance to ensure his back was turned, she climbed out of bed and slipped into her clothes.

"Ready to go?"

She didn't want to abandon the cozy cabin where they'd spent such a wonderful night together. But Vanessa's presence had been a sharp reminder of the world that waited outside, full of obligations and other people's expectations. She wanted to live in their own world, the one she and Adam created, a few moments longer. So she walked to him, put her arms around his waist, and laid her head on his chest.

He stiffened, but then his arms went around her, and he laid his cheek on her hair. After a moment, he whispered, "We should go."

"I know."

As she pulled on her parka, an empty, aching feeling started in the pit of her stomach. Now it would be even harder to leave Adam when her work at Cliffhaven was complete.

But it was for the best. She wasn't looking for a serious relationship—she didn't want anything that would leave her hurting and wanting when it inevitably ended.

As they walked back to Cliffhaven through the snow-covered cedars and Adam reached for her hand, happiness spread through her. It was a joy so peaceful, so profound, that she wondered if it might be worth the pain.

～

WHEN THEY ENTERED Cliffhaven's great hall, Caroline fell on them tearfully, pulling them both into a shared embrace. Adam assured her they were both perfectly fine, but she kept touching each of them as if to make sure. Then she dragged them both to the kitchen, where Tony stirred something on the stove.

He dropped the spoon and pulled Elizabeth into a hug. "It's a relief to have you home."

Caroline ushered her into a chair at the farmhouse table. "We were so frightened."

Tony set a mug of steaming tea before her, and Elizabeth inhaled its flowery aroma.

"Is Vanessa here?" Adam asked, taking the seat next to her.

"She left as soon as she gave us word you were okay," Caroline said. "I've never seen her so upset. I guess we were all worried."

Caroline took two bowls to the stove, and Tony filled them with soup. They moved together cooperatively, seamlessly, as if they didn't need words to communicate.

"You must be exhausted," Caroline said as she slid the bowls of soup onto the table and sat on her other side.

"I'm all right. We managed to get some sleep last night." When they weren't making mad, passionate love. The infuriating heat returned to her cheeks, and she buried her face in her mug of tea.

Caroline's brow furrowed. "Frankly, you don't look like you just escaped death."

"After I found her," Adam said, stirring his soup, "we stumbled onto one of the staff cabins and slept there."

"Once we lit the fire, it was pretty warm," she said, avoiding Adam's gaze. "We didn't think it would be safe to come back to Cliffhaven in the blizzard, but I'm sorry you were worried."

Caroline looked back and forth between Elizabeth and Adam, then leaned back with a satisfied smile. "I'm just glad you're back and safe."

"What were you thinking, going off on your own like that?" Tony asked gently as he sat down at the table.

"Adam sent me a text saying I should meet him at the dunes. I got lost, and I wasn't prepared for the blizzard. I had no idea it could be so dangerous."

Caroline shook her head. "But Adam didn't send that text."

"What do you mean?"

Adam's jaw hardened. "I didn't write it."

"Then who did?"

Silence filled the room, then the realization hit her like a slap. Someone had forged the text. Leading her into a blizzard, into danger.

Cold invaded her again, freezing her blood, but this was a chill no fire could warm. Her muscles tensed, wanting to jump out of her seat, but she tamped down on the urge to run.

She rounded on Adam. "Why didn't you tell me earlier?"

"Things have been a little intense since I found you last night."

"Still, that's an important piece of information you deliberately kept from me."

"I just wanted to get you home, make sure you were all right, before I told you something that would make you worry." She raised both eyebrows, and he let out a breath. "But I see now that I shouldn't have kept it from you. I'm sorry."

"Either way," Tony said, "we need to figure out who sent that text."

The four of them looked at each other, and unease creeped up her spine.

"Do you keep your phone locked?" Tony asked, and Adam shook his head. "Come on, man. It's the default setting for a reason."

"Lesson learned." Adam's mouth was a grim line. "I left it sitting on my desk in the library."

Caroline's eyebrows raised, her face hopeful. "Maybe it was just some kind of prank."

"It doesn't feel like a prank," Elizabeth said. "Not after what happened to my car. And that poor animal left in my room." *And the hauntings, the message written in fire.*

"But to send you into danger like that?" Caroline's sweet, green eyes were shocked. "Who would do such a thing?"

"Maybe they didn't mean for her to be harmed," Tony suggested. "Maybe it was just meant to scare her into leaving."

"But why would anybody want Elizabeth to leave?" Caroline said.

She toyed with her soup. "Meeks doesn't want me here. And I found red spray paint in his shed."

"What? Why didn't you tell me?"

"Come on," Adam said. "Meeks isn't running around the estate, vandalizing your car and leaving dead animals in your room. And I'm sure he's never sent a text in his life."

"What about Christopher?" Tony asked.

Caroline stirred her tea absently. "He definitely doesn't want us spending money fixing up the house."

"Why would he possibly care how I spend my money?"

Tony ran his fingers through his red hair and frowned. "Maybe he thinks you won't have enough left to invest in his schemes."

"The text mentioned our picnic," Adam said. "I didn't tell anyone about it. Did you?"

She shook her head. "Maybe someone was watching us. Like that day I was swimming and saw someone on the cliffs."

The thought of unseen eyes watching, plotting, sending her into danger was overwhelming. Inconceivable. The kind of thing you only heard about in the news or true crime podcasts.

She deflated, placing her elbows on the table and resting her chin in her hands. None of this made any sense.

Adam's eyes, as they swept over her, were turbulent. In them she could see, so clearly, the danger she was in.

ELIZABETH SANK into the bathtub until bubbles reached her chin. After dinner, where Caroline had fussed, Tony entertained, and Adam sent her intense, pensive looks, she'd excused herself early. The electric charge between them was too intense, her need too strong.

She'd drawn a scalding bath in the claw-foot tub, determined to banish the chill that invaded her. Had it only been a few hours ago that she'd lain in the cozy cottage bed with Adam's strong arms around her?

She floated in the blissful, bubbly water, recalling their night together—the feel of his hands on her skin, the strength of his body pressed against hers, his gentle lips trailing a path across her breasts. Lying in bed, Adam gazing at her as if she were a goddess.

But after Vanessa had arrived, he'd seemed withdrawn. What had made him pull away? Her brows drew together in consternation, and she sank further until the bubbles reached her lips. He was probably embarrassed to be caught in bed with the help.

When she rose from the bath, the cold room chilled her, raising goosebumps on her pale skin. She stared at the tiny bumps on her arms, the vulnerable flesh that had been exposed to the elements last night. It was crazy to think that she'd almost died, frozen to death in a blizzard. And someone had sent her into danger deliberately.

Something was wrong at Cliffhaven. First there'd been the hauntings—fires that started themselves, the message written on the damask wallpaper, and strange sounds slithering behind the walls. Warnings, all of them. Warnings that someone meant her harm, and who could doubt it? Her car had been mutilated, a dead rat left dangling in her armoire, and now this forged text sent her into danger. Someone was messing with her, trying to manipulate her. Trying to hurt her, even. But why?

She stepped out of the bathroom into the dark, silent corridor. It seemed to stretch out infinitely, with closed doors on either side offering so many places to hide.

She scampered down the hall, into her room, and closed the door firmly behind her. Pressing her ear against the heavy wood, she strained to hear any sound. All was silent.

She jumped into bed and pulled the covers up to her chin. As the wind wailed outside her window, she felt quite alone in the cold, cavernous house.

In the darkness beyond her window, a sound pierced the night—the sound of a woman screaming.

She jolted upright, her heart pounding in her ears. But as the howl receded, another barking sound filled the air, and it evolved into the long, mournful cry of a wolf. More canine voices joined together, howling, and she was stabbed by a visceral, primal fear.

She told herself she was safe, surrounded by the walls and doors that separated her from the wilderness. But the hairs standing up on the back of her neck spoke of an instinctual knowledge—that predators prowl the darkness, and she, like any other creature, might be prey.

CHAPTER 27

*E*arly the next morning, when the sun's first rays shone on the newly fallen snow, Elizabeth stood in front of the fresco in the parlor, her tool belt slung across her hips.

She bit her lip as she contemplated the fresco. She'd taken samples of the pigments and had them tested, confirming her hunch that the mural had been painted during the Renaissance period, probably in Italy. That meant the fresco was centuries old—a priceless work of art and more important than anything she'd ever worked on.

She'd prepared the microemulsion that would clean the fresco, and there was nothing left to do except begin. But she stood in front of the wall, frozen, as self-doubt rose within her.

She took a deep breath, slipped earbuds in, and turned the volume up. Then she moved quickly, afraid she might lose her nerve. As she applied the microemulsion, joy spread through her. It was satisfying work, watching the dull pigments come to life before her eyes, restoring the beautiful matte finish with her own hands.

As she dabbed and scrubbed, her mind drifted to thoughts of Adam. He hadn't come to her room last night, so maybe their newfound intimacy was already at an end. She told herself it was for the best—the passion they shared was more intense than she'd ever experienced, and it worried her that they connected so quickly and completely.

She looked up to find Adam standing in the doorway, watching her. With his black hair artfully tousled and his muscular body leaning against the doorframe, he looked wildly handsome. Her blood heated under the intensity of his emerald-eyed gaze.

He crossed the room like a panther, graceful and ready to strike, and lifted her as if she weighed nothing. She laughed and instinctively twined her arms around his neck as he braced her against the wall next to the fresco.

He drowned her laugh with his lips, and the intensity of the kiss surprised her. His passion aroused her own, and just when she was ready to abandon all decorum, the kiss changed, became tender. His lips gave one final, reverent caress, and when she opened her eyes, he was smiling at her.

"Good morning," he whispered.

"It sure is turning out that way."

He still braced her against the wall, distracting her with the proximity of his hard, lean body. They stood there, smiling at each other in silence, for a long moment.

"You look surprised," he said.

"I guess I wasn't sure where we stood, after yesterday. I thought you might have regretted what we'd done."

"My only regret is that we didn't stay at the cabin another day or two." His lips skimmed over her mouth. "But I guess it bothered me that you didn't want anyone to know about us. I thought you might be embarrassed about being with me."

Her mouth fell open. "That's not it at all! I was worried Caroline might not approve. But she needs to know, even if there's nothing serious going on between us."

Adam tilted his head, and his brows snapped together. "You

can tell her today. The roads were too bad for her to drive home, so she spent the night. Tony, too."

He lowered her slowly to the floor, and her curves slid down his body. She stepped back and looked down at their hands, which remained entwined.

"So you've started on this fresco." Adam surveyed the painted plaster, shaking his head at the neoclassical scene. "I've never liked this. Let's paint over it."

"Are you crazy? This fresco is a masterpiece! It's an important piece of historical art, absolutely priceless."

"It's well done, but I've never liked the subject." He pointed to the fresco's center. "That woman lying on the rock is so vulnerable. She's half-naked, surrounded by centaurs—danger is literally closing in around her, and she's just lying there waiting for them to attack her."

"You've missed a few important details." She pulled him closer to the picture. "Look. She's not defenseless."

He peered at the fresco and made a small sound of surprise. "She's hiding a knife under her hair."

"Look in the trees behind her, there's a group of Amazon warriors waiting to strike. She's not a defenseless victim—she's the bait for the trap."

"Incredible." He turned back to her, his gaze warm and appreciative.

She leaned back, tilting her head as she appraised the fresco. "Sometimes I feel like that woman—surrounded by danger. Someone's been lurking around Cliffhaven, trying to intimidate me, maybe even cause me harm. And I've mostly ignored it, tried to pretend it wasn't happening. But I don't want to be vulnerable and defenseless. I want to be that woman with the knife."

His eyebrows drew together in concern. "You want to be bait for a trap?"

"I don't know, exactly. It just makes me want to be

proactive."

"There are ways to be proactive that don't put you in danger. Let's make the house secure and do our own investigation into who could be responsible for these acts."

Footsteps drew their attention to the doorway, where Caroline appeared. Though she wore the same pale pink blouse and wool trousers from the day before, she was beaming with unbridled happiness.

"You look very well, Caroline." Adam smiled at his sister. "Coming home seems to have agreed with you."

"Thanks. It makes me happy to see everything coming together so nicely." Caroline gestured to the fresco, but her eyes were on Adam and Elizabeth.

"Well, I'll be in the library if anyone needs me," he said. "There are some security matters I need to address."

After Adam left the room, Caroline walked to the large windows of the parlor and gazed out at the grounds. The sun shone brightly on the newly fallen snow, making it sparkle as if it were coated with millions of diamonds.

"It will take me an hour to dig my car out." Caroline sighed. "I think I'll just stay a while. Tony's offered to teach me how to bake biscuits. Should I tell him I'm hopeless in the kitchen?"

"He's bound to find out sooner or later," Elizabeth laughed. "The two of you seem to be getting close."

"It's all moving so fast. On the surface, I'm scared Tony and I are rushing things, but deep down, I just know it's right."

"That's wonderful. You seem so good together." She cleared her throat nervously. "Caroline, there's something I'd like to discuss with you."

Caroline sat on a dusty velvet settee and patted the cushion beside her. "Sure. What's up?"

"It's a personal matter." She sat next to Caroline and took a deep breath. "It's Adam and I. We've started a . . . well, I'm not sure what it is." Heat flooded her cheeks. Why did she keep clasping and unclasping her hands? "I guess I'm trying to say I'm interested in Adam."

"Elizabeth, I know that."

"Am I that transparent?"

"Maybe not to everyone else, but I could tell."

Her hands clenched, and her fingernails dug into her palms. "Do you mind?"

"Of course not! He's obviously interested in you, too, and it makes me happy to think of the two of you together."

Something inside Elizabeth relaxed, making her realize how important Caroline's good opinion was to her.

Caroline took her hand. "Almost from the first day I met you, you've been much more than just an employee. You're my friend, and if you and Adam are happy together, I think that's wonderful. It's almost like you belong at Cliffhaven, like you're meant to be here."

She felt her smile melt away, and she pulled her hand from Caroline's. "I wish that were true. I love my work here, and I'm glad we're friends. It will be harder to leave Cliffhaven than I ever imagined."

"You still plan to leave in the spring?"

"As soon as the frescoes are restored."

"You know," Caroline began, speaking slowly. "There's so much art in this house that needs restoring. There would be enough to keep you busy for years, I would think. You could stay."

"Stay?" Her fingers fluttered to her throat. How could one word hold so much longing, so much hope? "That's impossible."

"Why?"

"I just can't." She caught herself about to bite her fingernails, a nervous habit she thought she'd left behind in childhood. She redirected her fingers to the arm of the settee, where they tapped a nervous beat.

She might fantasize about a life with Adam, here at

Cliffhaven. But a lifetime's experience had taught her that fantasy was impossible. There was no place she belonged, no relationship that lasted. It had been foolish of her to get caught up in the moments of pleasure with Adam, forgetting that they must eventually end.

"What about Adam?" Caroline asked. "What happens to him when you leave?"

"What do you mean?"

"I mean, what happens if he falls in love with you, and then you leave?"

Elizabeth smiled wryly and shook her head. "He's not going to fall in love with me."

"How do you know?"

She shrugged and turned to face the window, clamping down on the sorrow that washed over her. "Nobody ever has."

Caroline reached for her hand again and said gently, "Maybe that's because you don't stay in one place long enough. Maybe you don't let anyone love you."

"It's not that. Moving around helps me keep relationships casual. It's better this way." She rose and stepped toward the fresco, reaching for her magnifiers. "I should get back to work. I'm charging you for today, you know."

After a moment of silence, Caroline sighed. "I guess I'll go back to the kitchen and ruin Tony's biscuits. See you at lunch?"

"Maybe." She didn't turn away from the fresco as Caroline left the room.

As she pulled the magnifiers over her eyes, Caroline's words circled her mind, refusing to be ignored. *Maybe you don't let anyone love you.*

It was true she'd deliberately kept her relationships with men superficial. But if she had built walls around her heart, it was only to protect it.

Relationships end. People leave. Shielding oneself from the pain of loss was just common sense . . . wasn't it?

She ripped the magnifiers off her head and cocked her arm back, ready to throw them across the room. She paused, the expensive tool still in her hand, surprised by the anger coursing through her. Then she set the magnifiers onto a table carefully, as if they might explode.

Being alone—truly alone, with no close friends, family, or people to love—caused its own pain. And didn't she want to love someone and be loved in return?

She pressed her hand to her heart. Of course she wanted love. Once she acknowledged this truth—that the desire for love, for family and a home, was all she'd ever really wanted—her spirit lifted.

She glanced at the doorway where Caroline had disappeared and knew the blossoming in her chest for what it was—hope.

"Do we have the house to ourselves tonight?"

Elizabeth and Adam sat close together at one end of the mammoth dining table. The dining room was lit only by candlelight, making the cavernous room intimate. Their meal sat before them, untouched.

Adam nodded. "Caroline and Tony went back to his house. Are they . . . together?"

"Yes. Does that bother you?"

"No. It's not my business, anyway. I just want Caroline to be happy."

"Tony seems to make her happy."

They ate together, talking and laughing. She could hear herself dominating the conversation. But he listened so completely, giving her all his attention as if her words captivated him.

His leg pressed against hers, spreading warmth through her body. "I love how you talk," he said. "You're so expressive, especially when you talk about art." His finger traced a lazy trail down her neck. "And when your mouth curls up in a secret smile like that, God, it makes my heart beat faster."

He leaned down, and she tilted her head up to his. Their lips met softly, hesitantly.

The tender kiss deepened. His hands reached for her waist and pulled her closer, while her arms wound around his neck. He touched her, and she moaned into his mouth.

Voracious need surged through her. "Take me right here, on the table."

He shook his head and brushed one chestnut curl away from her face. "Tonight, I want to take my time." As if to prove his point, he brushed his lips down her neck slowly. "I want to touch every part of you. I want to hear you sigh with pleasure."

His words made her tremble. "I want that, too."

She led him to her room, where they reveled in touches, kisses, and sighs. They learned each other's bodies, drawing out the pleasure until neither of them could wait any longer. When they finally came together, it was like something from a dream.

Afterward, she laid her head on his chest, inhaling his scent of leather and cedar. His warm arms surrounded her, making her feel safe and desired.

"We should have done this weeks ago," Adam murmured. "We've wasted so much time."

"Actually, I thought you and Vanessa might have something going on." She lifted her head, observing his reaction.

"Vanessa?" Adam raised his eyebrows in surprise. "No, there's nothing between us."

"She definitely shows interest in you."

"She shows interest in every man. That's just the way she moves through the world."

"So, you've never been interested in her? Romantically?"

Adam paused, as if unsure he should speak, then sighed. "When we were teenagers, we went out a few times."

"Did you sleep with her?"

He lowered his head, then looked up at her through his dark eyelashes. "Do you really want to know?"

She groaned and pressed her face into his shoulder.

"It was a lifetime ago," he said.

Elizabeth grunted. She couldn't help but envy Vanessa, who seemed to embody everything she wasn't. Her slim figure, the self-confidence that commanded respect, the certain knowledge that she had a place in the world where she belonged were all things Elizabeth desired but had never possessed.

"Are you jealous?" he asked, a surprised smile curling his lips.

"No!" She picked at her pillow. "Maybe a little."

"How could you possibly be jealous of Vanessa?"

"You can't deny she's gorgeous."

"Vanessa's beautiful." He shrugged. "But it's a cold type of beauty. The kind you admire from a distance but don't want to curl up next to. You, on the other hand," he murmured, pulling her close, "are soft and warm and welcoming. Your body is perfect for making love."

"Say that again."

"Your body is perfect."

She pressed her curves against his muscular torso, enjoying the electricity that ignited between them. He dipped his head low, kissing her gently. He touched his forehead to hers and left it there for a moment, his eyes closed.

"I don't want anyone but you," he whispered.

His words sent a shiver through her body. She pulled his mouth to hers and kissed him fiercely, desire flaring between them like a flame.

After they'd made love again, Adam fell asleep with his arms around her. But the groans and creaks of the old house invaded the sanctity of her dreams, and even in sleep she felt the weight of unseen eyes upon her.

CHAPTER 28

When Elizabeth opened her eyes the next morning, the first thing she saw was Adam. He lay on his side facing her, bare-chested, his dark hair tousled from sleep, looking more handsome than any man had a right to be. He was propped up on one elbow, his face serious as he studied her. When she smiled sleepily, his lips curved up in answer.

"Good morning."

She wanted to reach for him, pull him closer, but shyness prevailed. "What time is it?"

"Just after nine."

Her eyes widened. She gasped and threw back the covers.

"What's wrong? Where are you going?"

"I slept in. I never sleep in."

She balked in front of the cedar armoire, the frigid air raising goosebumps on her naked skin. *Don't think about it.* She reached for her clothes, imagining her hand brushing against cold fur, slick with blood.

Adam yawned and stretched. "It's freezing in here. Come back and I'll keep you warm."

"That's very tempting." She slid into an amethyst-colored

tunic and returned to the bedside for a lazy kiss. "But the contractor Caroline hired set up scaffolding for me in the ballroom, before the blizzard. I can't wait to get up there and check it out, but I have a few other things to do first."

As she pulled on leggings, Adam reclined against her headboard with both hands behind his head, looking relaxed and pleased with himself as he watched her dress. "Don't you have something to do today?"

"I think I'll paint for a while," he said. "Then I have a security specialist arriving this afternoon."

"We could meet for lunch."

"All right." He drew her close for an unhurried embrace that left her wanting more.

She left him lying naked in her bed, an image she enjoyed as she travelled through the house. Then she retreated to her tiny office and stocked her toolkit with the day's restoration supplies. She consulted a battered textbook, dog-eared and highlighted, on restoration techniques for Renaissance-era frescos, though she practically had the text memorized.

A sharp rapping at the door to her office jerked her out of her single-minded study. Probably Adam, come for a quick kiss. "You're early," she called out, swiveling her desk chair toward the door with a smile.

"That's funny." The soprano voice took Elizabeth by surprise. "My timing is usually perfect."

At her office door stood Vanessa, looking beautiful and self-assured. Her clinging, scarlet dress seemed out of place in the tiny office.

"I'm just paying a visit to the Arringtons and thought I'd see how your work is coming along." Condescension dripped from Vanessa's words.

"There have been some setbacks, but we've made decent progress."

Vanessa brushed off the corner of Elizabeth's desk and sat

on it. "Setbacks. Is that what you call getting lost in the woods and almost dying in a blizzard?" The amused glint in Vanessa's eye was mocking.

She leaned back in her chair, meeting Vanessa's gaze. "I underestimated this place. I won't do it again."

Vanessa's eyes hardened. "You have accomplished more than I thought possible. I never would have guessed you and Adam would become . . . involved." She said the word as if it left a nasty taste in her mouth.

A frown settled onto Vanessa's perfect, pouting lips. "Frankly, I don't care one way or the other. It's unpleasant to think about you and Adam together, but nothing I can't handle. I just want to make sure you don't have the wrong idea about the future."

An angry pulse began to hammer in her throat. "What kind of wrong idea could I have?"

"The idea that Adam could ever be serious about you." Vanessa's tone conveyed a maddening blend of contempt and pity. "I've seen other women like you."

Elizabeth's hands clenched into fists. "Women like me?"

"You know—working girls that fall for someone way above their station. It always ends badly."

Elizabeth's skin felt tight and hot as an angry blush bloomed on her cheeks. "Working girls? *Above my station?* This isn't the nineteenth century, Vanessa, and none of this is any of your business."

"None of my business?" Vanessa spat, her eyes narrowed. "Adam and I are practically engaged. You have no chance with him. So if you're trying to catch a wealthy husband, you should leave before it gets unpleasant."

Elizabeth rose, her fists clenched, so furious she couldn't speak.

"Be realistic," Vanessa said, her face scrunched up in distaste. "Adam's rich. And you're not the type of girl a rich man wants for forever. He's fucking you because you're convenient. That's all."

Her words were like a punch to the gut, knocking the breath out of her. Vanessa took in Elizabeth's white-knuckled hands, looking immensely pleased with herself as she rose from her chair.

"You shouldn't need me to tell you this. You don't belong here. You don't belong with him." For a moment, Vanessa looked as if she truly felt sorry for Elizabeth, then she slipped out the door and was gone.

Her legs weakened, and she sank back into her chair. Could Vanessa and Adam really be engaged? Was it possible he was stringing her along?

You're convenient, that's all.

Hadn't she had the same thought—that Adam would have been drawn to the first woman to walk through Cliffhaven's doors?

She knew it would be wiser to wait, to let her temper cool before approaching Adam. But even as she told herself to sit back down at her desk, she threw open her office door and marched across the house in search of him, hoping there was an explanation for Vanessa's words that wouldn't wound her.

When she opened the art studio's French doors, the soft sounds of a violin concerto greeted her. Adam was painting, and he seemed lost in the work, eyes shining as his hand moved in quick, bold strokes. His dark hair was disheveled, as if he'd just rolled out of her bed and picked up a paintbrush. He looked so content, so appealing and seductive, that her temper fell a few degrees. She had plenty to spare, though, and crossed her arms at her chest as Adam glanced up from his canvas.

His welcoming smile dazzled, but she was determined to discover the truth. "Why does Vanessa think the two of you are practically engaged?"

"What?" Adam's smile faded. "She said that?"

"Come on, Adam. She didn't just pull that idea out of nowhere. How long ago was it, exactly, that you two were together?"

"We were teenagers." He laid down his paintbrush and opened his hands wide in a gesture of innocence. "We went out on a few dates, but it didn't take me long to realize we didn't suit each other. We broke up before . . . before the fire." His face fell. "Don't you believe me?"

She paused, examined his earnest expression, and blew out a breath. "Yes, I believe you. But why would she say those things to me?"

"Maybe she was playing with you, trying to get you to react. Vanessa can be like that. Do you want me to talk to her?"

"No!" Her voice was too loud, too hot with anger, so she took a breath. "That would make things worse, let her know she got a reaction out of me. Let's just forget her."

He closed the distance between them and wrapped his arms around her waist, pulling her closer. "Forgotten," he said, lowering his lips to hers.

Look how convenient you are.

The unwanted thought made her pull away, scowling.

Her eyes fell on the row of canvases with their faces leaning against the wall, and she recalled the macabre images of fire and torture. "Why do you hide your work?"

"I don't hide it." Adam followed her gaze to the row of canvases. "You've seen those?" He shrugged. "I was going through a dark period when I painted them. Painting helped me get through it, like therapy. But not all of my work depicts darkness and pain." He crossed the room and turned a large canvas to face her.

The painting shimmered with light he'd created, swam with hues of blue. "It's the lake," she murmured, transfixed. She stepped closer, fighting the urge to reach out and touch the textured oils. It made her feel as if she were swimming in the sea—primal, invigorated. It evoked such a visceral response that, for the briefest moment, she could smell the lake's wild scent.

"You're incredibly talented. Have you ever shown your work?"

"Publicly? No, that doesn't interest me."

He set down the canvas and glanced at her before looking at the floor. "I was wondering if you'd like to go to dinner tonight."

"Sure. It's Tony's night off, but he'll leave us something cold."

"I want to take you out to dinner in the village." When she raised her eyebrows at him, he said, "Is that so shocking?"

"A little. I'm not sure you've left Cliffhaven since I arrived."

"I'm not a complete hermit." Adam looked down at his hands, then stuffed them in the pockets of his black slacks. "We could go to Christopher's new restaurant. Check out my investment."

"I can't imagine it will be nicer than our dinners here, with candlelight and Tony's cooking. But I'd love to go out with you." Their eyes locked, and all the insecurities Vanessa had uncovered were banished. Her insides went all dreamy and soft, like she was melting into a pleasurable puddle.

Adam's eyes burned with sudden inspiration. "Let me paint you."

"What? Like this?" She laughed, gesturing to her casual tunic and leggings.

"No." His voice lowered. "I want to paint all of you."

"All of me?" She tilted her head to one side, her eyebrows scrunched together in confusion. Then her eyes widened. "Naked? Sorry, that is not happening."

"Why?" He looked genuinely surprised.

"Surely there must be more beautiful and stimulating subjects for you to paint."

"There isn't. Truly." He ran the back of one hand across her cheek, then lifted her chin, so their lips met. The kiss was gentle, reverent, and left her shaken.

She put both hands on his chest and pushed him away gently. "Thanks, but I'm still not posing nude."

"One day, you'll let me paint you. I can wait."

She arched one eyebrow. "You seem awfully sure of yourself."

"I'm a patient man, and we have all the time in the world." His words were said lightly, so why did they disturb her?

She pulled away without meeting his eyes. "I'm leaving when the frescoes are done. I think I can hold out that long." But the thought of leaving left a lump in her throat, an emptiness in her chest.

Adam froze, his face impassive. Only the tightness of his jaw indicated he was fighting to suppress emotion.

There was a heavy silence, then his gaze locked onto hers. "I know you're going to leave. I know it's inevitable." He stalked toward her, and she retreated, her eyes widening, until her back pressed against the wall. "So I'm going to take everything you offer, soak up every ounce of pleasure while it lasts."

He kissed her greedily, like a man drinking water before journeying through the desert. When she returned his kiss with hungry desperation, he made a small sound of surprise.

They took each other against the wall as if it might be their last time together. And when they were finished, wrung out by pleasure and emotion, he pressed his cheek to hers.

"God, this pull toward you is relentless." His voice was a whisper in her ear, almost too low to be heard. "Where will it end, Lizzie?"

ELIZABETH STOOD in the gilded light of the ballroom, gazing up at the fresco on the domed ceiling. The Greek goddesses smiled down at her, cavorting on clouds, dancing together under the languid gaze of brawny gods. Awe burned through her, ballooning inside her until she thought her heart might burst. Here was evidence of the best of humanity, the beauty we're capable of when truly inspired. In one corner, rain damage had eaten away at a cherub's face, distorting its features into a gruesome grimace. Elizabeth glared at the spot as she buckled her tool belt around her waist. She could make it right.

She had to make it right.

The roofing crew Adam had hired was assembling in the west wing, filing past the glass wall of the ballroom, equipment in hand. Bob Whitewater, the contractor leading the laborers, spotted her, raised his hand in greeting, and slipped through the French doors into the ballroom.

He was middle-aged with a face that was tanned and deeply lined, and he had an easy, professional manner. He stuck his thumb in the belt loop of his faded jeans and said, "You sure you don't want us to start on the roof here?"

"Definitely. I need to secure the fresco before you do any work on the roof, or it could cause even more damage."

"Well, my crew's ready to start on this wing as soon as you're finished." He reached out a calloused hand and gave the metal scaffolding a firm shake. "We set this up before the blizzard. You know how to climb it?"

"I've used them lots of times."

"Then I'll leave you to it."

She gathered her tools into her belt, humming a happy song under her breath, tingling with anticipation. She appraised the sturdy-looking structure of wood and metal and began climbing.

She was ten feet up when the scaffolding beneath her feet gave a violent jerk. She clutched the metal rung, her heart lurching in her chest.

"Stop!" Bob yelled from below her. "The safety pins!"

But she had no time. The structure was falling away, collapsing around her, and she was falling. It was like something from a nightmare—the frantic feeling of spinning out of control, clutching at air; the thunderous sound of wood and metal collapsing around her as she hurtled toward the stone floor.

Pain shot through her, a lightning bolt of agony. Then everything went black.

CHAPTER 29

*W*orried voices floated above Elizabeth. She struggled to reach them, as if she were fighting to wake from a nightmare that wouldn't release its grip.

"She's breathing normally, and her heart rate is fine." Caroline's voice was calm, reassuring.

"Then why isn't she waking up?" The anxiety in Adam's voice called out to her, and she fought through the fog to reach him.

"Elizabeth? Can you hear me?"

She tried to nod, but the movement set off a piercing pain in her head. "I'm awake."

"Lie still a moment," Caroline said. "Do you remember what happened?"

With effort, she opened her eyes, and the bright light of the ballroom made her wince. "The scaffolding collapsed."

"Does anything hurt?"

"Just my head."

Caroline's competent hands applied gentle pressure to her arms and torso. "Is there ringing in your ears? Are you seeing stars?"

"I'm fine. Just a headache and wounded pride."

She tried to sit up, but Adam stopped her with a hand on her arm. "Lie there for a minute. We've called an ambulance."

She groaned. "No ambulance, please."

"I want you to come to the clinic for tests," Caroline said in a tone that brooked no argument. "You probably have a concussion, and I want to make sure there isn't a more serious injury."

She closed her eyes. "I should have inspected the scaffolding before I started the climb."

"It wasn't your fault." Caroline took her hand, and there was worry in her green eyes.

"She doesn't need to know now." Adam swiped a hand through his black hair. "Get her to the clinic. Make sure she's safe before you worry her."

"What is it?" she asked, pushing herself up on her elbows. "Tell me."

But Adam's features hardened, the worry in his eyes transforming into fierce anger, and she knew. A tremor passed through her, as if the blood in her veins had turned to ice.

"Bob says someone removed the safety pins on the scaffolding," Caroline said. "It was sabotage."

THEIR DINNER DATE WAS CANCELLED. Instead of flirting over French cuisine, Elizabeth lay in bed, surrounded by a mountain of down blankets and every other comfort Adam could provide.

"Lie back." The gentle appeal in his voice was persuasive. "You're supposed to rest."

"Caroline said it was a *mild* concussion," she reminded him. "I hate lying here when there's so much to be done."

"You still look so pale." He sat on the edge of her bed, looking disturbed. "I can't stand the thought that someone did this to you."

"Officer Ogie said it's possible Bob's crew forgot to put in the safety pins," she reminded him. "It wasn't necessarily sabotage."

"I talked to Bob. He swore he put those pins in himself. He doesn't strike me as the kind of person who makes mistakes or covers them up when they happen."

She sighed and leaned her head against the pillow. "You're right about that. If Bob says he put the pins in, they were in." She shook her head, then winced at the pain. "But why would someone deliberately sabotage the scaffolding?"

"You were the only one meant to use that scaffolding."

After a pause, she sighed with resignation. "I know. And I know what it means." Someone meant for her to fall.

The thought sent a chill across her skin, and she shivered. "I just don't understand why anyone would target me this way. First my car, then the dead rat in my closet, the text sending me into the blizzard. Now this."

And the hauntings. Hadn't something in this house been warning her, ever since she arrived, of danger?

Adam paced over the Savonnerie carpet. "If Bob put the pins in at the end of the day, when were they removed?"

"Maybe last night. The house was empty except for you and I."

"So someone's been creeping around Cliffhaven at night." His voice was a growl.

Then he sat on the edge of her bed, took her hand, caressed it. "Have you considered it might be safest if you left Cliffhaven?"

Everything inside her froze. "You want me to leave?"

"No, I want you to be safe. Right now, it might be safest for you somewhere else, at least until we figure out who's behind this."

She leaned against the pillow, squeezing her eyes shut. He was right. She would be safer if she left Cliffhaven. It made sense to leave while she still could, and if this had been any other job, she would have packed her bags and been on the road weeks ago.

She struggled to sit up, but the pounding in her head forced her back onto the pillow. She couldn't run away. The idea was laughable. She was helpless—stuck here, reliant on the people around her in a way she'd never been before.

Adam stroked her hand, warming her skin, and she remembered her revelation from being lost in the woods—*people need each other.* Maybe it was time to ignore her old instincts to run. Time to make herself live a new way.

Her life at Cliffhaven, the relationships she'd built with Adam, Caroline, and Tony, had sparked so much joy. A slow, cautious hope had been building inside her. Maybe she could have everything she'd ever dreamed of—a house, a family, a love that lasts. Maybe she did belong somewhere—to this place, to these people.

She rolled over, ignoring the pain in her head and the worry gnawing at her belly. Ties were binding her to this place, these people. Ties she'd avoided as long as she could remember, because she'd thought they'd be ropes binding her in place, leaving her helpless and vulnerable.

But now those ties didn't feel like bindings. They felt more like roots, giving her stability, helping her grow.

"Please don't ask me to leave."

"What if something more serious had happened?" Adam's voice was bleak, his face haunted. "I can't protect you."

"I'm not asking you to protect me."

"You should. What good am I if I can't keep you safe?"

"Don't say that. You're important to me." She wanted to say more, to tell him how her heart leapt when she watched him paint, how she felt more for him than she ever had for anyone.

"Someone did this to you." He closed his eyes, jaw tightening, looking like a man fighting for control. Something passed over his face—was it fury, carefully contained? Her eyes travelled over his powerful body, wondering what his anger would look like when unleashed. "And there's nothing I can do about it." His hands fisted around the duvet. "It's just like before."

She reached for him. "Do you mean . . . the fire?"

His face shuttered, and he turned away. "No. Not then."

After a moment in which he seemed to war with himself, he reached for her, pulling her to his chest with arms like steel. "I know it's wrong for me to be with you. You're so full of light, and I'm dragging you into the dark."

Even as he held her, frustration beat at her contentment. Why wouldn't he confide in her? Was there a part of him, still, that didn't trust her? She pulled away, leaving him holding just her hand.

He looked down at her fingers. "And still I want more, more of you. I want to wake up next to you, want to know the hidden parts of your heart. You're holding a part of yourself back, where I can't reach, and it's driving me crazy."

She pulled her hand from his and crossed her arms over her chest. "But you're holding something back, too, aren't you? You have secrets."

There was silence, then he shook his head with a pained expression. "Don't ask me, Lizzie. I can't lie to you, any more than I could bear to see you looking at me with disgust and contempt."

"How can this work between us if there are secrets?"

"You're leaving, anyway, aren't you?" He shook his head. "I have no illusions that you'll stay. Everyone I've ever loved has left. You should go now, before something terrible happens."

She swallowed the lump in her throat. How was she supposed to shore up the walls around her heart when he talked like that? "You don't deserve to be alone."

His mouth twisted. "You don't know anything about what I deserve."

She reached for him, pulling his head to her chest, and he didn't resist. When she ran her fingers through his hair, he sighed.

He needed to unburden himself. Whatever secrets he kept were eating away at him. How could she let him know that she wouldn't judge him, wouldn't turn away with disgust?

On the other hand, could she make that promise? Not every action was forgivable. What, exactly, had he done?

CHAPTER 30

"*L*et's have a party!" Caroline said, her eyes bright with inspiration.

The four of them sat at the farmhouse table in the kitchen, enjoying breakfast together. With Tony cracking jokes, coaxing laughter out of Adam between bites of quiche, Elizabeth reveled in the camaraderie.

"A party?" she said, spreading cherry jam on toast. "That's a fabulous idea."

It would be a perfect first step to opening the house up to visitors. It would ease Adam into the idea, show him it wouldn't be as hard as he thought to let the outside world in.

But Adam looked dubious. "You want to open Cliffhaven to all those people? I don't think the house is ready to entertain."

"If we focus on the rooms we'll use for the party," Elizabeth said, "we could do it."

Caroline tucked her strawberry-blonde hair behind one ear. "If I hired a cleaning crew, this place would look great."

"I don't know why we would clean up the house when we haven't even decided what to do with it," Adam grumbled. "And

I'm still not sure a party is a great idea. With everything that's been going on."

"I'm with you," Tony said as he bit off a bite of toast. "Formal parties make my palms itch."

"Just think of the food you could create if we brought in more staff to help." Caroline raised her eyebrows at Tony.

"Don't try to bribe him onto your side," Adam said, pointing a pastry accusingly at Caroline, though he softened the gesture with a smile.

Tony looked intrigued. "How many more staff?"

"The sky's the limit, my love," Caroline said, smiling over her coffee.

Tony's eyes got a faraway look. "We could make some real showstoppers. Something sculptural for dessert, a miniature Cliffhaven out of gingerbread, maybe."

"Traitor." Adam tore a bite from his pastry. "I guess if that's what you all want, I'm not going to object."

As the rest of them chattered about party preparations, Elizabeth was lost in talk of invitations, decorations, and food. She smiled as she sipped her coffee, enjoying the buzz of conversation that floated around her, making her feel like they were all a single unit—something like a family.

After breakfast, Elizabeth pulled Adam into the dining room. He looked down at her as she leaned her forearms on his chest and said, "I'm sorry if you felt pressured to say yes to the party. If you don't want to see people yet, I'll convince Caroline to have it somewhere else."

"It's not that I don't want to see people."

"Then what's bothering you?"

He turned her toward the antique mirror that decorated the wall of the dining room. The morning light shone harshly on the textured skin of his face, highlighting the damage done by the fire. "People don't want to see me."

She reached up to caress his cheek. "Adam, your scars aren't that bad. I hardly notice them anymore."

"It's more than the scars. When people look at me, I feel like they're wishing my parents had survived, or that they're blaming me for their death."

She shook her head. "How could anyone blame you?"

His lips pressed into a thin line, and his eyebrows came together before he turned his face away.

"There are people on this island who care about you, who want to see you. Wouldn't it be nice to be part of the community again?"

"I suppose it would." For a moment, he looked wistful. "Has it occurred to you that having a party now, when we still don't know who sabotaged the scaffolding, could be dangerous?"

Fear pricked the edges of her. Of course it had occurred to her. An unknown enemy wished her harm, someone willing to kill an animal. And *something*, some benevolent spirit, had been warning her for weeks to take care, to leave this place. She knew, deep in her bones, that she was in danger.

Run, Lizzie.

Something fierce took hold of her. "We can't hide away, waiting for something else to happen." Not when so many things were turning out right—her work, her relationships. Not when she finally felt like her life was on the right path. "We have to live our lives. Nobody is taking that away from me."

He looked skeptical, so she threaded her hands into his hair, bringing him close for a kiss—a kiss woven through with the ferocity and desperation pumping through her blood. His hands wrapped around her waist, pulling her closer.

"So I'm going to keep working. We're going to keep living." She pulled him by the hand into the ballroom and gestured to the magnificent fresco on the ceiling. "Cliffhaven's beauty has been hidden away for so long. I want it to shine as brightly as it did before the fire."

She placed her hand on his cheek, capturing his green-eyed gaze. "I can restore the art, we can fix the broken pipes and crumbling stone, but Cliffhaven needs more than that. It needs people who care for it to bring back what was lost in the fire—it needs heart."

His eyes roved over the magnificent fresco, and, for the first time, they held a sliver of doubt. "If I did agree to restore the house, what then? I can't picture it."

She fought the urge to pounce, to wrestle his objections to the ground, to make him understand that restoring Cliffhaven was *right*. "It's your estate. What would you want to do with it?"

With a faraway look in his eyes and his lips curving up ever so slightly, he said, "I want it to be a home again, for a family." His eyes darted to hers before looking away. "If it can't be my family, maybe Caroline's. I want this house to be full of life again."

She could picture it. Lights burning in the stained-glass windows, laughter floating out through the ballroom's open doors, kisses stolen on the terrace on dark summer nights. "That's exactly what I want for this place. What it deserves."

She grabbed his hand, searching his eyes. "But it could be so much more. You could open Cliffhaven to the world."

He leaned away from her, his eyes widening. "Open Cliffhaven? To the public?"

"All of humanity should be able to see this beauty." She squeezed his hand reassuringly. "You could still live here. Open the showpiece rooms on the weekends, block off the parts of the house that are just for family."

He cocked his head and raised one eyebrow. "We don't need the money."

"It's not about money, and you know it." She gestured to the fresco, to the paintings decorating the wall above the priceless gilded paneling. "This art represents the best of humanity. It should be shared."

"I don't know." His forehead wrinkled, and he rubbed the back of his neck. "Uncle Jack thinks we should sell. So does Christopher. And Vanessa."

"Just think about it."

His eyes lit. "If I did agree to restore the house, we would need an art expert, wouldn't we? Someone to oversee the restorations."

Though her heart beat faster, she shook her head. "Don't make any decisions based on me."

A sad smile passed over his face. "No, of course not. But wouldn't you want to stay, to see Cliffhaven come back to life?"

Oh, God. She wanted that more than anything. "Is that . . . something you would want?"

His lips curved up, then. "Yes, Lizzie. I'd want that very much." He took her hand and gently kissed her fingertips, but his eyes burned as he held her gaze. "Let me come to your room. I'll show you how much I want you to stay."

Her heart began to pound. It was disturbing how much she wanted that future—to stay and make Cliffhaven her home, to be with Adam, to finally have a place she belonged.

"As tempting as that is, it's back to work for me."

"Didn't Caroline tell you to take it easy today?"

"She did, and I will. But that ceiling fresco needs to be stabilized. I lost time recovering from that concussion, and I need to make up for it."

He frowned. "How did the scaffolding get back up, anyway?"

"Bob's crew set it up yesterday. We'll give it a thorough safety check; I don't make the same mistake twice."

His jaw was tight with tension, and he looked as if he wanted to object, so she stretched on her toes to kiss him. "I'll be fine. It's sweet of you to care, but please don't worry."

"Someone hurt you." He closed his eyes, took a deep breath,

looking as if he were fighting to remain calm. "I don't know who, and I don't know how to stop them from doing it again. How am I supposed to not worry?"

"We have to keep going, Adam. Nothing is going to stop me from finishing my work at Cliffhaven."

"I suppose I should admire your tenacity. At least the security system is being installed today."

When the time came to climb the scaffolding, she took two steps then froze, her heart thudding in her ears. Memories washed over her—the panicked feeling of falling, the thunderous crash, the clawing fear of an unknown enemy.

She shook her head, as if that could rid her of the unwanted fear. Then she looked up at the fresco, the swirling colors, the gods and goddesses looking down at her, and climbed determinedly.

CHAPTER 31

Snow fell for weeks, blanketing the cedars and lawn until the world was white. It piled up past the dining room windows, drifting against the lead panes. It made the world softer, more peaceful, and Cliffhaven was a cozy refuge from the winter landscape. Mornings found Elizabeth walking the grounds, watching ice spread across the lake's edge, feeling like part of the wilderness around her. Afternoons, she was snuggled inside the house, lost in restorations, coming to love Cliffhaven more than she ever thought possible. Evenings were spent at the dining table with Caroline, Tony, and Adam, drinking wine and laughing. And her nights were spent in Adam's arms, forging a deeper connection as the snow piled higher around the house.

The northern wilderness was a different world. And it suited her. She felt like a sled dog who'd spent its life in the desert, finally seeing the snow, knowing she was born to be a part of it. Even the memories of her mother, the ones that came sharp and fast, were welcome.

Though she loved the winter, she was equally eager to see Cliffhaven in spring. Adam said that when the mountains of snow melted, they created rivulets of water cascading over the cliffs, forming scores of waterfalls. She wanted to see them, wanted to see flowers bloom, see Cliffhaven's grounds bursting with new life.

Now she stood in the ballroom, gazing at the ceiling fresco with Caroline by her side. She'd finished it just yesterday, and the neoclassical scene added a dreamy quality to the ballroom's ambiance. Her stomach clenched as she waited for Caroline's opinion, so she turned to the wall of windows, where the sun was a ball of orange fire sinking into the dark blue waters.

"Elizabeth," Caroline murmured, her mouth hanging open as she turned in a circle. "It's incredible."

Something loosened inside her. She stared up at the ceiling, at the perfectly repaired plaster, the flawless faces of *putti* capering among the clouds, and pride swelled in her chest.

She'd been so afraid to make a mistake, so afraid she didn't have the skills to do the restoration properly. But she'd done it. She'd taken something the world had broken, something neglected and damaged, and made it right. It was her best work, her career's crowning achievement. And in the battle for the soul of Cliffhaven, it was a resounding victory.

"Has Adam seen it?" Caroline asked.

"Not yet."

She struggled to swallow the lump in her throat. The world was full of chaos and degradation, but she wasn't helpless. She had the power to restore some things. Protect them.

Caroline clasped her hand. "You're crying."

"It's a good kind of cry." She wiped at the tear and laughed self-consciously. "This work has meant more to me than anything I've ever done. Thank you for bringing me here."

Caroline wrapped an arm around her shoulders and squeezed. "I should be thanking you. You've done so much for me, for my family. You've given us the courage to change, to bring Cliffhaven back to life. And you know I just adore you."

Elizabeth took a deep breath, gathering her courage. "You're the best friend I've ever had."

Tears pooled in Caroline's green eyes, then she swept her into a tight hug. "That means so much to me."

"I can't believe the party is tomorrow," Elizabeth said, shaking her head. "These last weeks have passed so quickly."

The ballroom door opened, and Adam appeared, directing a team of a half-dozen security guards, all clad in black, who looked capable of putting down a small uprising.

"It seems like overkill," Elizabeth said, "considering that expensive security system he installed."

Adam spoke to his team briefly, pointing to the windows and exits, then directed them back into the great hall. Before he left the ballroom, he cast one smoldering look at Elizabeth, and her breath caught. His gaze was full of promise, and she thought of the night to come, when she would again find herself in his arms.

When Adam slipped out the ballroom door, she turned back to Caroline, pressing the back of one hand to her heated cheek. "I'm sorry, where were we?"

Caroline raised one eyebrow in amusement. "That look Adam sent you was scorching."

"Sorry. That's so unprofessional."

"Well, you weren't rolling around on the floor. Honestly, I love seeing the two of you together." Caroline's brow furrowed as she considered her. "But what's bothering you?"

She lifted her hand to her mouth, as if that might stop the words, but they spilled out, anyway. "What I feel for Adam—I've never felt anything like it. It's kind of scary."

"What are you afraid of?"

She bit her lip. The fear that remained, underneath all the joy, was the fear of what would happen if she fell into the relationship without holding anything back. When her time with Adam ended, as it surely must, what would be left of her? She'd be broken into a thousand pieces, like shattered crystal—something that could never be put back together. And she couldn't shake the feeling that there would come a day when he would see the truth of her, find the part of her that was lacking, unlovable. And he would shake her hand, let her down gently, and set her adrift.

"It is scary, isn't it?" Caroline said, patting her hand. "Because we know pain is part of it. Your partner will hurt you, and you'll hurt them, even if only by accident. I'm just hoping there's something you gain from knowing someone so well, sharing your life with them. That there's a deeper love, a stronger bond that grows over time. But I know that to have it, we have to be strong enough not to run when it's painful, and brave enough to be vulnerable. To open your heart and say, 'here I am, love me the way I am.'"

"But you know what it's like to lose someone you love."

Caroline nodded. "It's heartbreaking. But it's worth it, isn't it? Because what's the alternative—never loving someone? Running away because we're afraid to be hurt? That's a lonely road to take."

Her words settled on Elizabeth with the weight of truth—a truth she was living out. Her life of travel and shallow relationships had left her lonely and brittle. She wanted more, but was she brave enough, strong enough, to have a lasting relationship?

She wanted to seize this new life with both hands and refuse to let go. She could imagine what it would be like to stay—for Adam to be her man, Cliffhaven her home, Caroline and Tony her family. She wanted it all, and the depth of her desire overwhelmed her. It was everything she'd ever longed for, and having it now was like having every wish fulfilled.

She looked up at the stabilized fresco, the plaster and paint she'd lovingly restored with her own hands. Since arriving at Cliffhaven, she'd done things she hadn't known she was capable of. Maybe she was capable of even more. And if anyone did let her down, if everything did fall apart and she was set adrift, maybe she was strong enough to save herself.

~

FOR ONE TERRIFYING MOMENT, Elizabeth thought the scream that echoed through the second-floor gallery had come from one of the portraits. She froze on the grand staircase, one hand on the dusty banister, staring at the painting of a particularly grim looking ancestor in amazement.

But then the sound of weeping filled the air, and she ran up the remaining steps. "Who's there?"

It was Meeks, standing next to the fireplace on the second-floor gallery. His grizzled face was pale and bloodless, his lips quivering. A man on the verge of collapse.

She stepped toward him tentatively. "Are you all right?" In answer, his legs buckled, and she caught him under the arms. "Here, sit down."

She led him to the armchair next to the hearth, under Audrey's portrait. His entire body trembled.

She knelt before him and whispered, "What was it?"

He pulled the cap from his head and wiped the back of one shaking hand across his brow. "It was . . . Audrey."

"Here?" A thrill sang through her blood. "Did she speak to you? Call your name?"

"I saw her." His mouth was slack with shock and disbelief. "Audrey Arrington, walking through the gallery, just as sure as you're standing here."

She drew in a quick breath. Was it possible?

Meeks placed his hand over his heart. "She let me see her. Finally." Then the man broke, and tears streamed through the gray whiskers on his hollow cheeks.

Elizabeth clutched at his thick flannel shirt, caught his arm. "Where? Where did you see her?"

"There. Just under her picture." He pointed to the life-size painting of Adam's parents in its thick, gilded frame.

"I called her name," he said, his voice shaking. "Then she just disappeared."

The man crumpled, as if crushed by an invisible weight. He curled into his chair, his red-rimmed eyes swimming. "She's still here. Because of me." His breath hitched. "She'll never forgive me."

A chill tore through her, and her hands tightened around Meeks's bony arm. "Forgive you for what?"

He looked at her then, as if he'd forgotten she was there. Then his eyes darted away. "I promised her I'd protect them. Her and the children." His voice broke, and he looked down at his empty, arthritic hands.

"Protect them? Why would Audrey and the children need protecting?"

"From him." Meeks's face twisted with hate. "Stephen Arrington."

A sick twisting lanced through her gut, and she placed one hand on her stomach. "Adam's father?"

"He . . . he hurt them." Meeks's hands shook, as if they couldn't contain his rage and wanted to strike out. "Used to hit them something awful. It got worse as his money ran out."

Meeks's eyes took on a faraway look, lost in memory. "That last day was the worst. When he found out there was no copper at Cliffhaven. Jack, that *lawyer*," he spat the word as if it left a foul taste in his mouth, "brought the survey saying the mine was no good. Stephen gambled everything on that mine, and he lost. And he took it out on Audrey."

A chill expanded in her chest, cold as the grave. Adam's father had beaten Audrey. And his children, if Meeks could be believed. Sorrow took hold of her, a profound sadness for Adam and Caroline, for childhoods ruined by violence and trauma.

"Arrington left her bruised and bloody. She could barely

walk." Meeks's jaw clenched, and his teeth scraped together. "I told her to go to the hospital. She wouldn't."

A vein throbbed in his temple, purple and pulsing in the dim light, and he growled, "I could've killed him."

With rage in his eyes, Meeks looked, for the first time, like a man capable of violence. She glanced at his hands, twisting around the hat in his lap as if he might tear it apart. They were strong hands, now bent and twisted with age, but still evidence of the vitality that must have been his in younger days. How much strength remained in those hands?

"Then Cliffhaven burned," he whispered. "And they were both dead."

His head fell into his hands. "I promised I'd protect her. And that man was the death of her, in the end."

"Meeks," she said, locking eyes with him. "Did someone start that fire? Maybe it was an accident, or . . ."

His face closed off, and he drew back, eyes narrowed. He shoved his cap back on the wisps of gray hair clinging to his skull, pulling it low over his eyes. "All I know is the bastard's dead."

His eyes lifted to Audrey's portrait, as if afraid of what they might see there. "And she's still here. Always here."

And she knew, then, that he'd loved Audrey. His grief was all-consuming, the kind that swallowed you whole. It was a grief she recognized, the kind that only came from losing someone you loved with all your heart.

Hope consumed her. If Audrey could return, that meant others could. "Did you see anyone else?"

Giving no sign that he'd heard her, Meeks rose from the chair on shaky legs and stepped to the damask wallpaper. He ran his fingers over the blackened paper, the remnant of the message written in fire. "Run," he whispered.

Then he looked at her, his eyes burning. "She's warning you. I hope to God you listen."

As Meeks limped down the grand staircase, she continued to kneel by the fire, both her mind and body frozen. Meeks's footsteps were the only sound until the front door closed, reverberating through the house like distant thunder.

She stared into the cold fireplace, thinking of fingers striking a match, of Cliffhaven engulfed in flames. Of rage and guilt, and the dark emotions that drove people to violence.

CHAPTER 32

*a*t dinner, Tony seemed particularly nervous. His toe tapped a swift beat on the kitchen floor, and his eyes darted between Caroline and Adam.

But Caroline's face was shining with joy, and as Tony laid dinner on the table, she burst out, "We have an announcement."

"Caroline!" Tony said, casting a nervous glance at Adam. "Are you sure this is the best time?"

"I can't wait." Caroline bounced on the seat of her chair. "We're pregnant."

Elizabeth leaned back in her chair, eyes wide, and clapped her hands with delight. "That's wonderful!"

Adam's face was inscrutable. "Is this what you want?"

Caroline's eyes filled with unshed tears, though she was smiling. "I thought my chance for that life was over and now, suddenly, I'm standing on the brink of everything I've ever wanted." A laugh bubbled out of her. "Maybe I should be scared, but I'm not. I'm ridiculously happy."

Adam's face softened. "Then I'm happy for you. And you should have Cliffhaven. Raise your family here."

Caroline shook her head. "I couldn't leave Tony's house on the river. It's my home now. Is that all right?"

"Of course. I only want you to be happy."

"You, too." Caroline wiped at her eyes, laughing. "Everything is so perfect!" She reached across the table and clasped Adam's hand. "I have my brother back. And I didn't realize how much I missed him."

"Show him the ring," Tony urged.

Caroline obliged, extending her left hand, where a diamond sparkled. "He thought you might be mad that we weren't married."

Tony leaned back in his chair, grinning. "That was just an excuse to get you to say yes."

"We want to get married here, at Cliffhaven, in the spring." Caroline turned to her. "Elizabeth, will you be my maid of honor?"

Warmth radiated through her body, and she placed her hand on her heart. She glanced at Adam, and he seemed to be waiting for her response. "Of course. I wouldn't miss your wedding."

Something about Caroline's unbridled joy sparked hope inside her. As they ate and laughed, Elizabeth was struck by the ease with which she slid into this group, this little family. And something in her chest expanded, filled with awe at the absolute perfection of it.

After dinner, Adam and Tony headed to the kitchen to do the dishes, leaving Caroline and Elizabeth to lounge at the table with an extra glass of wine. But the wine made Elizabeth maudlin, and Meeks's words reverberated through her. His dark accusations hung in the air, floating between her and Caroline.

Elizabeth ran her finger around the rim of her wineglass. "I'm really pleased with the progress of my work here. But I haven't been able to convince Adam to restore the entire house."

Caroline leaned back in her chair and blew out a breath. "Me either."

"I wish I understood more about what's holding him back, why he's so resistant to the idea. I get the strangest feeling he thinks he deserves to live like this, in a ruined house. That he doesn't deserve to be happy."

"That makes sense." Caroline's eyes hardened. "My father drilled it into his head that he was never good enough."

Elizabeth recalled Meeks's shaking hands, evidence of both the love he'd had for Audrey Arrington and the hatred he felt for her husband.

"Caroline," she said slowly, her stomach clenching with nerves, "what was your father like?"

Caroline turned her head toward the wall of windows, her face deadened by pain. "Why do you ask?"

"Meeks mentioned some things. That your family had . . . secrets."

Caroline flinched, and Elizabeth took her hand. "I know this must be painful, and I wouldn't ask, except I think it might be the key to helping Adam. I just want to help."

"I know. And you are helping, more than you realize." Caroline bit her lower lip, staring past the endless lake. "Secrets are strange. You start keeping them because you think you have to. So you hold them close, burying them inside you, carrying them for years until you can't remember why you thought you had to keep them in the first place.

"But burying secrets only gives them power, makes them stronger, somehow. And I'm tired of secrets." Caroline looked at her, and her green eyes were sharper, full of strength Elizabeth hadn't known she possessed. "My father was abusive."

Elizabeth's heart squeezed, filled with sorrow for her friend.

Caroline inhaled a shaky breath. "Adam took the brunt of it. And not just because Dad seemed to hate him the most. Adam would deliberately get in between my father and I, or my mom, and make sure he was the one who got hurt. To protect us."

Caroline's chin trembled. "I was so little, having to hide bruises, make excuses for black eyes."

Revulsion snaked through her, winding its way through her stomach and chest, and she shook her head. "I don't understand what kind of man can hurt people smaller, weaker than himself. Did no one ever tell the police? Try to get help?"

"For a long time, it was a secret—just the way we lived life. But it got worse, and eventually Adam went to the police." Caroline made a bitter sound. "That was useless. Ogie was willing to look the other way."

"What about your uncle Jack?" With his linebacker's body, he could have protected them.

"He didn't approve, but he didn't help, either. Maybe that's the way it had always been in their family, women subjected to men's violence."

Filled with sorrow, she took Caroline's hand and squeezed. "I'm so sorry you went through that."

"It's all right now. After I left Cliffhaven, I went to therapy, which helped. I learned it wasn't my fault, or my mother's. My dad was a monster, one who felt most powerful when he was terrorizing someone else."

Caroline's delicate hands balled into fists. "I can know all that, and still hate him. And even though I know it's wrong, a part of me still hates myself, a little, for letting him hurt my mother.

"So maybe that's why Adam feels like he doesn't deserve to be happy. Maybe he still blames himself." A sad smile haunted Caroline's face. "But he's healing. I can see it. And you're such a big part of that."

Her head spun, trying to make sense of it all. What must life have been like for Adam? Terrorized by a violent father, protecting his mother and sister, keeping family secrets safe? Her heart twisted, hurting for the boy he'd been.

But he was a man now. And he needed to abandon the guilt

and self-loathing heaped upon him by a father who hadn't deserved him. He deserved to be happy, to live in a place of light and love.

But as she drained her wineglass, something niggled at her— a tiny seed of doubt. Did this really explain all of Adam's guilt, his shame? Was there more to the story? And if there was, would she really want to know?

~

LATER THAT NIGHT, Elizabeth took off her robe, exposing her naked skin to the cold night air, and slid into bed beside Adam. He opened his arms, and she fit snugly next to him, resting her head on his shoulder. He'd slept in her four-poster bed every night that week.

"You make me so happy," Adam whispered, and he kissed her hair.

"Really?"

"Truly. I haven't been this happy since . . . before the fire."

She thought of Cliffhaven as it had been when she first arrived—dark, desolate, and neglected, with an aura of loneliness heavy in the air. She kissed his shoulder. How could she make him open up, to reveal the secret pain he'd kept locked inside himself for so long?

"I can't imagine how strange it must have been for you here, after the fire."

Adam was quiet for a moment, stroking her hair. "It felt like I lost my entire world. My parents were gone. Then Caroline left, and I had nothing."

She rubbed her cheek against his chest, nerves jangling through her. "I know why you think you don't deserve Cliffhaven. And you're wrong."

The muscles in his chest tightened, froze. "What are you talking about?"

She sat up, held his gaze. "I know your father was abusive." Adam's mouth slackened in surprise. "I know he hurt your mother and Caroline, and you might blame yourself for it. But it wasn't your fault."

"I know that."

She leaned back, letting her fingers trail off his chest.

"I'm a lot of things, Lizzie, but I'm not an idiot. I know it wasn't my fault that my father was scum. That as a skinny kid, I was no match for him. That it wasn't my job to protect my mother."

"Then . . . why do you think you don't deserve Cliffhaven?"

He sat up, swinging his legs over the side of the bed. His back was to her, and her fingers itched to grab his shoulder, spin him around, and make him confide in her.

He doesn't trust you.

Then his head fell into his hands, and he said, "You deserve the truth. Before we make any plans for the future."

He jumped from the bed to pace across the Savonnerie carpet, under the leering faces hidden in the damask wallpaper. His face was full of doubt, lips pressed against words he clearly didn't want to say.

Her heart plunged into her stomach. *He doesn't want you. And he's finally going to say it.* She fought to keep her breath slow and even. "Whatever you're going to say, it doesn't make you a bad person."

Something about her words triggered him, because he whirled around, and his shoulder slammed against a mirror hung on the wall. It fell to the floor, shattering.

"Damn." He bent to retrieve the broken glass, and a sharp shard sliced his finger. Blood appeared, a fine red line on his flesh.

"Adam!" She flew to his side, still wrapped in the bed sheet. Blood pooled in his hand, dripping onto the priceless carpet, but he made no move to stop the flow. "You're bleeding!"

She tried to take his hand, but he yanked it away. "I should bleed, should give more than blood."

"Adam, it wasn't your fault. None of it—not the fire, not your father. You can't carry this guilt forever."

"You don't know anything about my guilt." His voice was ragged.

"I know you tried to save your parents. You did save Caroline."

"That isn't enough, not after what I did."

Silence filled the room.

"What did you do?" she whispered, hardly knowing if she wanted the answer.

Adam finally looked at her, and his eyes were full of anguish. "I killed my parents, Elizabeth. I killed them. And that changes everything, doesn't it?"

CHAPTER 33

"On the night of the fire, he'd hurt us all. He'd left my mother broken and bleeding."

Candlelight flickered across Adam's sculpted face as he spoke, casting shadows over his wine-colored scars. When his eyes darted to Elizabeth's, they were full of miserable resignation, as if he expected her to bolt from the room at any moment.

"We were supposed to have left for vacation that day, but he cancelled it. Jack had brought him that survey, the one saying Cliffhaven had no copper. My father was furious, desperate, and he . . ." His throat worked with emotion.

She laid a hand on his forearm, caressing. "You don't have to talk about it."

"Yes, I do." He sank onto the velvet chaise, his eyes fixed on the bookcase. "My mother was in bed, broken. I'd begged her to go to the hospital. He'd locked Caroline in her room. Maybe he was scared someone would see her black eye.

"And I hated him." He closed his eyes and shook his head in self-disgust. "Do you know what it's like, wanting someone to die?"

Her heart ached, and emotion tightened her throat. She took his hand and squeezed, but he was lost in memory.

"I woke up to smoke choking me. I had to break down Caroline's door to get her out. Then I went looking for my mother." He took a shaky breath.

"I heard screams coming from my parents' room. There were flames everywhere. It was hell, come to life." For a moment, she thought she could see flames burning in his eyes. "My father was trapped under a fallen beam. He yelled at me to help, to pull him out. I just stood there, staring at him. Hating him for all the times he'd hurt my mother or Caroline, all the times he'd hurt me."

He shuddered, as if pain shook his body. "And I left him there."

She lifted one hand to her mouth, unable to hide her shock.

"I wish to God I hadn't. Then my mother ran into the room, saw my father trapped. She tried to save him." He looked tormented, his eyes swimming with tears. "Why did she do that? Why would she try to save her abuser?"

"I don't know. She must have been very kind, forgiving."

He nodded then took another deep breath. "She was trying to lift the beam, but she wasn't strong enough. She looked up at me, begged me to help. And I just stood there. Then the ceiling came down on us all."

He ran both hands through his hair in anguish. "It's my fault she died. If I'd pulled him out when there was time, we would have made it out of that room. She would still be alive."

Her cheeks were wet with tears, and she swallowed thickly. Adam's confession explained so much—why he'd hidden himself away at Cliffhaven, why he'd let the house fall to ruin around him.

"It was just one second," he whispered. "One moment of my life when my hate for that man rose up in me. I made the wrong decision. And I can never take it back."

Adam looked at his hands as if they were useless, despite their size and strength. "I would give my life to take it back."

She sat next to him on the chaise, ran her hand down his back. "You were a child tormented by an abusive father. What you did was understandable. And if you had pulled your father out of that fire, he might have killed you all, in the end."

She leaned back on the chaise, pulling him down to press his head against her chest. Then she whispered soothing words and ran her fingers through his ebony hair.

When his ragged breathing slowed, she said, "Adam, how did the fire start?"

"We don't know." He sighed, a whisper of breath on her breast. "It doesn't matter."

Didn't it? She thought of Meeks, of his love and his rage.

"Now you know everything," he said. "It's better that you know, so you understand why my life will never be more than it is now—a penance for my sins."

"We all make mistakes," she said. "Sometimes terrible mistakes. Your mother wouldn't want your mistake to ruin your life."

"We'll never know, will we?" he said harshly, rising and pacing across the floor. "She's gone. So I understand why you're leaving when the work is done, why it's right that you should. You're in danger here, and you don't belong in a place as dark as Cliffhaven."

She went to him, feeling his anguish like it was her own. She hated the haunted look in his eyes, the defeated hunch in his shoulders. And she didn't want to hear him echo her thoughts that she didn't belong there, that the time was near when she would leave.

She let go of the bed sheet, and it fell to the floor, revealing her naked body. "Paint me."

He blinked, cocking his head to one side. "What?"

"Paint me, like this." She gestured to her bare breasts.

He shook his head as if to clear it. "Why are you offering this to me now?"

She couldn't tell him that she wanted a part of herself to stay at Cliffhaven forever. She didn't know how to say that leaving her portrait would be like leaving a part of her with him. "I want to do this for you. For us."

Warring emotions flashed across his face—disbelief, hope, and longing. Then he scooped her into his arms, ignoring her gasp of pleasure. "Let's do it now, before you change your mind."

She clung to his neck as he crossed the room and laid her onto the chaise. He positioned her in a pool of moonlight streaming through beveled windows. Then he draped the ivory silk sheet around her.

"I can't believe you're still here, after everything I told you."

"What you did was understandable, Adam. It may have been wrong, but it was forgivable."

He closed his eyes, his face relaxing, as if she'd poured a soothing balm over an angry wound. Then he pulled a notebook and pencil from his nightstand, sat before her, and began sketching.

She lifted a hand to the unruly curls cascading over her shoulders. "I should brush my hair or something."

"No, this is exactly right. I want you to look like we just made love. Put your hand in your hair—yes, just like that."

She reclined against the chaise, and his hands flew across the page as he studied her. As she'd hoped, the haunted look was gone from his eyes, and he was lost in the work. His heated gaze roved over her flushed skin, examining the curve of her belly, the roundness of her hips. For the first time, she welcomed the intimacy. She longed to strip away the barriers between them, was burning for him to really see her, all of her.

And when he stopped in his work for a moment and gazed at her, he seemed to be filled with quiet joy.

With one final stroke of his pencil, he finished the sketch and examined it. "It's perfect," he whispered. "Elizabeth, illuminated from within. Surrounded by darkness but still smiling at me, like all is forgiven."

He laid down the pencil, walked to the edge of the chaise, and kneeled before her. "I love you. No, don't turn away. Let me tell you." He ran his fingertips gently down her cheek. "I'm grateful for this love, humbled by it."

Her breath caught in her throat. "Adam, I—"

"You don't have to say anything. But there's something I have to ask. Will you stay? When you finish the frescoes, will you stay at Cliffhaven?"

She pulled the sheet over her breasts, wrapping it around her skin as if it might shield her.

"There are enough frescoes and paintings at Cliffhaven to keep you busy for years," he said, smiling. "I'm not asking you to commit to a lifetime. Just stay, at least for a while, so we can see what this is. What this could be. Because I think we could have something incredible, something that comes along once in a lifetime."

He was right, she knew he was right. But he could never understand her fear—that if she stayed too long in one place, she'd be trapped. He couldn't understand her self-doubt—that someone like her would never belong in this incredible place. But most of all, he could never understand that if she stayed, he would discover there was something profoundly lacking in her, something that made her unlovable.

Still, underneath all her doubts and fears was a small spark of something bright, something hopeful.

"All I'm asking is for you to give us a chance." Adam's face shifted, uncertainty furrowing his brow. "Or is it that you don't want to be with me? If that's it, tell me. I'd rather know."

"Oh, Adam." She caressed his cheek, running her fingers over the rough, textured skin. He closed his eyes and leaned into her hand. "I want you more than I've ever wanted anything. I'm just so afraid."

"You? Afraid?" His lips curved into a smile, and he whispered, "Be brave, Lizzie."

He was everything she wanted, everything that tethered her to this place. He was more than her best friend, as much a part of her as her very limbs. And he was offering everything she'd ever wanted—love, a family, a home. But to have it, she would have to live differently, take down the barriers she'd built to protect her heart.

Be brave, Lizzie.

Something wild and bright pierced her heart. "Yes, Adam. I'll stay." She began to tremble—her fear and hope colliding, fighting it out inside her skin.

He swept her into his arms, letting out a cry of raw emotion as he kissed her face, her hair. And joy spread through her as if it had entered her bloodstream.

Then he was kissing her as if he would devour her, his lips trembling, hands searching her body. She wrapped her arms around him, pulling him over her as she leaned back on the velvet chaise.

The muscles of his chest pressed against the silk sheet over her breasts, and a pleasurable ache spread through her body. Her hands throbbed with the need to explore him.

"Take this off," she whispered, tugging at the hem of his shirt. He lifted it over his head, letting it fall to the floor, and firelight danced across his golden skin.

He sat back on his knees, watching her with hungry eyes. "I know it's hard for you to stay, to take a chance on me. And I swear, I will never give you cause to regret it."

He pulled on the silk sheet, and it slid across her breasts, baring her. His fingers traced her skin, heating her blood. "You're so beautiful," he murmured.

"So are you." He raised his eyebrows doubtfully, so she said, "Really, you're . . . magnificent."

She grasped the waistband of his flannel pants and pushed the material down, freeing the hard length of him. She stroked him, and his eyes burned with passion, setting her aflame.

He lifted her from the chaise, carrying her as if she weighed nothing, and laid her gently on the bed. The dark scent of him enveloped her.

His face glowed with some kind of triumph. "To know that you trust me, that you want me, makes me feel like a god."

Emotion rose within her, threatening to overwhelm. He made her believe in herself, made her believe in *them*. Every touch, every caress, was full of the possibility of what might be, of what they could have together. And the promise of this new life, the perfection of it, was intoxicating.

He kissed a line of fire down her neck, onto her breasts, across her stomach. His lips against her skin made her feel as if she were turning to shining, liquid gold. She wanted to urge him on, but he moved languidly, drawing out every moment until her pleasure felt endless. Until every bolt of pleasure pierced her heart.

"How can I show you how happy you make me?" he said. His lips travelled lower, his nose skimming her most sensitive part. "I'm outrageously happy. Deliriously happy."

He inhaled the scent of her with greed, and she gasped. Then he spread her thighs, kissing and biting them until the delicious torment was unbearable. Then his mouth was on her, rocketing her up to a place of pure ecstasy, a place where she shattered and came together again. She cried out, fisting her fingers in his hair.

Her mind was a jumble of feelings, a whirling maelstrom of emotion.

She was going to stay. To open her heart to this man, this place.

She'd never felt so completely exposed. So raw. So vulnerable. But that only intensified the feel of his teeth on her skin, his fingers inside her. Was this her reward for being brave—all her emotions so heightened, all the pleasure more exquisite?

She opened her eyes, finding him balanced above her with a satisfied smile on his lips. He hovered over her, motionless, joy and awe shining in his eyes.

"Adam." Her voice broke, and tears stung the corners of her eyes. "Please, Adam." God, she was begging, and it was for something more than pleasure, more than his touch.

"Tell me what you want."

Don't ever hurt me. Don't leave me broken at the end of this.

She pulled his mouth to hers and poured everything into a desperate kiss. "Make love to me."

Then he was there, between her legs, the weight of him teasing her thighs, and she writhed with need.

"I told you my deepest secret, and you stayed." He held her gaze as he entered her slowly, gradually, making her fight for breath. "I'm so grateful. So full of love for you."

They moved together, and it felt as if her heart were growing too large for her chest, like it might burst with euphoria and passion and joy. The barriers she'd erected to protect her heart fell away, leaving her unguarded. And in that empty space where walls had been, love was free to occupy.

When they came, it was together. The moment stretched out, endless and full of indescribable beauty, until she thought it might echo through her heart forever.

Finally, they stilled, each of them panting, still joined. Then they simply gazed at each other.

He placed a kiss, soft and delicate as a butterfly's wing, on her lips. "Elizabeth. You're the light inside all this darkness."

Then he gathered her close, kissing her lips, her forehead, her hair. She melted into him, feeling . . . cherished. This was what it felt like to be treasured.

To belong.

"I want to restore Cliffhaven."

She froze. "What?"

He looked at her with eyes that were hopeful and reckless. "Let's do it. The entire house."

Her heart jerked and skipped. "Don't do it because I want you to. Or even because Caroline does."

He let out a breath. "This is what I want. What I've wanted so badly, for so long." He brushed a curl from her forehead. "Now it finally feels possible."

Joy suffused her entire body, and she blinked back tears. Cliffhaven, and all it contained, would finally be restored. Protected.

His thumb brushed a tear from her cheek. "I didn't realize it meant so much to you."

"It's . . . everything."

Then he kissed her, and she realized she was wrong. *He* was everything. What they had together was everything.

She lay in his arms, practically vibrating with excitement, when he kissed her forehead and said, "I'm going for a quick shower. Get some sleep. We are hosting a party tomorrow, after all."

After he disappeared into the corridor, she leaned against the down pillows with a sigh.

Her heart glowed, as if lit from within. She'd let him in, let herself be vulnerable, and now she felt different. Stronger. Like she'd unearthed something that had been buried within herself. It was a treasure, this strength. And now that she knew it was there, she hugged it tightly to herself.

Joy suffused her very skin. She was going to stay. Unpack her belongings, finally try to make a home for herself. Cliffhaven would be restored. And the strongest, kindest man she'd ever known was by her side.

She burrowed into the softness of her four-poster bed,

watching the fire dying in the hearth, casting flickering light across the bookshelf.

One moment her cheek rested on her pillow, the next she was floating through Cliffhaven's halls. But the corridor wasn't silent and empty, as it should have been. It was crowded with spectral spirits. Gruesome faces stared at her, their twisted faces mocking, scornful, jeering. She twisted around, desperation rising within her. She was looking for something, she *needed* it, but the spirits blocked her way, reaching for her with pallid, decaying skin.

"Adam!" she gasped, just before hands closed across her mouth, cutting off her words, choking her. Spectral, ghostly hands, cold and full of death, squeezing the life out of her, dragging her down.

Lightning bolts of fear electrified her body, and a scream tore through her throat even as her eyes burst open, bulging with fear. Deep breaths wracked her body as she struggled to orient herself in the darkness. She was in her own bed, the duvet clutched in her fingers, fighting for breath in the dim light of her chamber.

Just a dream. Everything's all right.

But her pulse hammered at her throat, and her muscles tensed, ready to run.

"Adam?" she croaked, her palm sliding across the mattress where his body should have been. The sheets were cold.

He's still in the shower. She'd slept only a few minutes.

But hadn't the lamp on the nightstand been lit? Now it was extinguished, and in its absence, the darkness was impenetrable.

She fought to calm her breathing, but her body was still poised for flight, her ears still straining to catch every sound— the sighs of the house settling around her, the creaking and shifting, the wind whistling through the eaves.

Get a grip, Elizabeth.

And then she heard it—a small sound in the silence. The slithering, scraping sound that was all too familiar.

She froze, breath catching in her chest. There it was again, the scratching behind the walls.

And she knew she wasn't alone, that unseen eyes watched her from the darkness. The room *felt* occupied—the very air was charged, heavy with the weight of another presence.

Then the smell hit her, that scent that had nausea roiling through her guts—sulfur. The scent of Hell.

Her skin prickled as the tiny hairs on the back of her neck stood on end, and she slipped one leg out of bed, ready to run.

"Elizabeth."

Her heart thudded to a stop, she swore it did. The sound had been so quiet, it might have been wind whispering through the eaves.

"*Elizabeth.*" A woman's voice, whispering. Pleading. Calling out but distant, as if travelling through barriers of time and space.

Her eyes jerked to the corner of the room between the book-shelf and the fireplace, and she squinted into the darkness. Something was *moving*. Her eyes bulged as the shadows coalesced.

A woman. Dear God, it was a woman, materializing out of thin air. She was faceless, made mostly of shadow, wearing a long gown.

A ghost. Standing in her room, silent as death.

Emotions whipped through her like lightning cracks—fear, awe, hope.

Her heart leaped to her throat. "Mother?" she whispered, and it was a pained, hopeful cry wrenched from deep within her.

The figure glided forward, into a patch of moonlight streaming through the leaded windows. And her heart sunk, because this dark-haired figure bore no resemblance to her fair mother.

Raven-black curls cascaded over the figure's shoulders, falling to her waist. A bridal veil obscured her face, and the lush material of her gown was pearl-colored, luminescent in the moonlight.

Electric adrenalin rushed up her spine. She knew that gown. She'd seen it in the portrait gallery, worn by a doomed woman who smiled with maternal grace.

It was Audrey Arrington. The ghost of Adam's mother, come to haunt her.

CHAPTER 34

*S**he shouldn't be here.*

A bone-deep fear accompanied the knowledge that this was impossible, that this spirit should have departed long ago. But, somehow, it had remained. The impossibility of it! Splintering the orderly laws that govern our reality, throwing Elizabeth into a realm ruled by nothing but chaos.

But underneath her fear and confusion, something like triumph surged through her blood—it *was* possible! Our loved ones *could* return! And longing—so childlike, so desperate—overwhelmed her.

Then the figure moved. It beckoned. With long, feminine fingers.

"Audrey?" she whispered, her heart racing.

"Danger." The figure's voice was a harsh whisper, and it shot a thrill across her skin.

Audrey gestured wildly, and sparks shot from her hand, arcing through the air, landing on the carpet. Impossibly, the sparks ignited, and flames leapt into the air. Then the fire was spreading across the Savonnerie carpet, devouring everything in its path.

"Run, Lizzie!" the figure begged, her voice urgent and terrified.

Her eyes bulging in horror, Elizabeth jumped out of bed, dragging her duvet with her and diving at the flames. Fear lodged in her throat as she threw the duvet over the blaze, pounding it with her hands. The hungry flames ate through the material, licking the flesh of her palms, but she kept smothering the fire until every spark was extinguished. When there was no trace of flame, she sat back on her knees, panting.

The room was empty. Audrey's ghost had disappeared. Vanished into the darkness, leaving no trace except the scorched rug and smoke lingering in the air.

She looked down at her shaking hands. Her palms were burned, bright red and throbbing, her face wet with tears.

The chamber door creaked open, and she whirled, muscles stiff with fear. Adam stepped into the room, his ebony hair dripping wet, naked but for a towel wrapped around his waist.

"Sorry that took so long. I had to go downstairs, and . . ." He stiffened, lifting his nose, scenting the air. "Smoke!"

He rushed to her side and crouched before her, running his hands over her limbs. "Are you hurt?" She shook her head, and he pulled her to her feet, eyes scanning the room.

"There was a fire, but I put it out." She clutched his hand. "It was the ghost, Adam. The ghost of your mother."

"What?" He recoiled, leaning away from her as if she'd just said something repugnant.

She knew her words wounded him, but her skin was too hot, her mind spinning too crazily to be calm. And she suddenly burned with desire to see the portrait, to confirm that her eyes hadn't deceived her. She snatched her phone from the night-stand and charged into the hallway, down the corridor, stopping only when she'd reached the painting of Audrey and Stephen. There she was, looking tragic and beautiful, her luminescent gown shining with impossible brilliance.

"Elizabeth, this is insane." Adam's voice sounded behind her. "It was your mother. She was wearing that gown, had those long dark curls."

She turned back to him, and he was all pain—forehead furrowed, eyes wounded, scars standing out red against skin that had gone pale. He tilted his head, looking at her as if trying to discern why she would wound him this way.

"You don't believe me. How do you explain the fire, then? You think I started it?" Her voice rose in pitch, reflecting the panic that danced around the edges of her. "She was wearing that *exact* dress, Adam! It was unmistakable. I saw it as clearly as I see you standing there."

He looked back to the portrait, seeming to hold his breath, then shook his head. "That was my mother's wedding gown. It was made for her."

She paced, gnawing her fingernails. "She's warning me, telling me there's danger. Telling me to leave."

He looked at her with something too close to pity, and she planted her feet. "You think I'm crazy."

"No. If you say you saw someone, they were here." He grasped her shoulders. "But it wasn't my mother, Lizzie. There's no such thing as ghosts."

"Say that when there's one in your room, shooting sparks from her fingers."

His eyes fell to her hands, still red and throbbing. "My God, Lizzie. You're burned." He turned her hands over, revealing skin that was bright red.

"I'm fine," she said, snatching her hands away. "Adam, where's your mother's gown? Did it burn in the fire?"

"It's preserved in the attic."

She pulled on his hand, taking one step across the gallery floor. "Let's see if it's still there."

"*No.*"

She turned back, surprised by the steel in his voice. He

pulled her close, eyes sweeping the dark corners of the corridor, muscles tense and ready to do battle. "Whoever was here could be hiding somewhere in the house. We should be searching for them, not my mother's dress."

"That's pointless, Adam. You can't search for a ghost."

"It isn't a ghost." His voice was taut with frustration. Then he looked at her, and his eyes softened. He looked at her as if he knew her profound loneliness, as if he understood all her secret hopes and fears, and his voice gentled. "It isn't your mother."

She crossed her arms over her chest, looking down at her bare feet. "I know."

"It isn't mine, either." He held up his hand when she started to object. "And I can prove it to you."

His green-eyed gaze was so steady, so understanding, that she let him lead her down the grand staircase, through the great hall. His eyes scanned the darkness like a wolf's, predatory and protective, as if part of him wanted an enemy to appear so he could rip it to shreds.

When he pulled her into his art studio, her impatience boiled over. "Do we have to do this now?"

He stopped in front of the sink, where several objects lay on the countertop—a matchbook, a paintbrush, and a small glass filled with clear liquid. He held up a blank piece of white paper. "Watch."

He selected a match, struck a flame, and held it under the corner of the paper. There was a faint crackling sound, and after a moment, the paper under the match turned black. When he pulled the match away, a black line slithered across the pristine paper. It snaked its way to the right, burning the paper, curving, leaving holes with blackened edges in its wake. Forming letters.

She drew in an awed breath. "A message written in fire."

When the black line stopped slithering across the paper, the blackened edges of the holes spelled the word "Elizabeth".

She grabbed the paper and turned it over in her hands. "That's exactly what it looked like when the letters burned into the wallpaper upstairs. How did you do that?"

He picked up a paintbrush and dipped it into a small glass jar filled with liquid. "It's a simple mixture of sugar, water, and potassium nitrate." He brushed the liquid onto a new sheet of paper, and it was barely visible.

"You have potassium nitrate sitting around?"

"It's only saltpeter. Meeks keeps a bag in his shed to remove tree stumps."

"And it just occurred to you to put tree stump remover on a piece of paper and light it on fire?"

"I googled it. It was the first result when I searched for fire writing."

He laid the paper on the counter and placed his hand over hers. "Do you see what this means? Someone used this mixture, or something like it, on the wallpaper upstairs. A person did this. Not a ghost."

She froze, rooted to the ground as the knowledge reverberated through her like a shockwave. Ghosts don't haunt houses with potassium nitrate. The fire, the message, the warnings . . . were human. Had been human all along.

"So someone came into the house," Adam said, "wrote on the wallpaper with potassium nitrate. Then, when the fire started in the grate, the flames spread along the floor on a predetermined path, leading to the wallpaper."

Run, Lizzie.

She shook her head. "But how could anyone know the significance of those words to me?"

"Have you told anyone else?"

"Not a single person in my life. Only you." When his eyes lit with something like pride, she turned away. "I don't see how anyone else could know."

She placed a hand over her heart. Realizations shot through

her mind one by one, each leading to the next, like dominoes falling. "But I *saw* a woman in my room tonight. She was there. Are you saying someone . . . dressed up like your mother in the portrait? And started a fire in my bedroom?"

"It's the only thing that makes sense. Maybe someone's playing some sick game. Like dress-up or cosplay—pretending to be the prophetic ghost, haunting the halls of Cliffhaven, painting the walls with potassium nitrate."

"In someone else's house?" she said. "That's . . . crazy."

"So is leaving a dead rat in your closet. Or sabotaging scaffolding, or forging a text that sends you into a blizzard." Concern flashed across his face. "Are you all right?"

Definitely not.

Cold and heartless truths fell upon her. There was nothing special about Cliffhaven, making it a place spirits could inhabit. There were no ghosts. Her mother wasn't watching her from the spirit realm, guiding her, silently supporting her.

Grief sunk into her, heavy and consuming. She felt hollow, as if the hope that had lived inside her had been evicted, and now there was too much empty space. She'd wanted to believe in ghosts, wanted to believe her mother was still here, that she might still feel the touch of her hand in that time when the veil was thin. She'd been so eager to believe.

She'd been a fool. It had all been fake, an illusion, a desperate fantasy invented by her lonely mind. It was pathetic, actually.

Her gaze skittered to Adam. Were there other things she was blind to? Other things she wanted to believe in so badly that she ignored the truth?

"Whoever did this could still be here," Adam said. Emotions warred on his face, and when he spoke, his voice was tight. "You need to leave Cliffhaven. Just for now, until it's safe."

Pain knifed through her, and she crossed her arms over her chest. "I won't leave Cliffhaven to the mercy of whatever psycho is prowling around. What if they want to damage the house?"

"Damn the house. It means nothing compared to your safety."

"Caroline's party is tomorrow."

"Damn that, too!" He raked a hand through his hair. "I would sacrifice anything to keep you safe. And you're talking about a party?"

She wiped her hand across her face, rubbing her forehead. "I've been running away my whole life," she whispered. "Please don't ask me to do it now."

His face was bleak, as if he were caught in the grip of fear and hopelessness, and he whispered, "This place is death."

"No, Adam." Her voice trembled. "Cliffhaven is filled with beauty and light and love. It's a place for your family and friends —a home. And that's everything." She dashed at the traitorous tear trickling down her cheek. "Take it from someone who's never had one—a home like this is worth fighting for."

"The people I love are more important than bricks or walls or art. You're my home now, and I don't care if Cliffhaven tumbles into the sea." He closed the distance between them, engulfing her in his arms and leaning his cheek against her hair. "The idea of you in danger drives me mad."

She could feel herself leaning into his strength, needing it. So she pulled back, building a wall between them, just for now, brick by brick.

CHAPTER 35

*O*n the night of the party, Elizabeth paced in front of the fireplace in her room. The cavernous fireplace crackled, but its warmth didn't penetrate the chill that lanced through her. Her chamber felt foreign, alien—a malevolent space watching her fall apart.

Guests would arrive within the hour, and she couldn't shake the nervous energy that plagued her. Her eyes kept returning to the charred remains of the Savonnaire carpet. Something so precious, so fragile, destroyed so callously. So easily.

She slipped on the emerald-green cocktail dress she'd purchased at a boutique in the village. Was it her imagination, or did the smell of sulfur and smoke cling to the dress, a sick reminder of last night's events?

She shuddered, and anxiety swept over her. For years, she'd clung to the idea that her mother's spirit was still with her, still watching over her. After coming to Cliffhaven, seeing evidence of spectral warnings, her belief in the afterlife had cemented, and for the first time in years, she'd felt hope. Hope that maybe she didn't have to be alone, that she was capable of giving love, worthy of receiving it.

But it had all been an illusion. And the grief and loss that consumed her was suffocating. Isolating. The worst of it, though, was the crushing weight of a brutal reality: in this life, she could only count on herself.

A soft knock sounded at her chamber door. Adam entered, wearing a perfectly tailored black tuxedo. He was clean-shaven, but his hair was artfully disheveled, his eyes intense, giving him the look of a wild animal recently tamed. He paused at the doorway, gazing at her as if drinking her in, capturing every detail of her and storing it in his memory forever. "You look amazing."

"Thanks. I wasn't sure about the dress."

"It's perfect."

He crossed the room, then stopped one step away, looking hesitant. He shifted his weight from foot to foot, then pulled a small box out of his pocket. "I have something for you."

She bit her lip as she contemplated the vintage velvet jewelry box. "You don't have to buy me gifts."

"I didn't buy it." He handed her the box with a shy smile.

She opened the gift, her eyes still on his nervous face. Nestled inside was a necklace—beautiful and delicate, with rows of emeralds that reflected the firelight brilliantly.

"It belonged to my mother." His eyes shifted to her face, and his smile faltered.

She pushed the velvet box into his hands, shaking her head as she backed away from him. "I can't accept this."

"What do you mean?"

"It's priceless. Caroline should have it."

"Caroline has tons of my mother's jewelry, and she never wears any." He watched her carefully. "You don't like it?"

"It's not that. It's gorgeous." A lump formed in her throat. "But it's a family heirloom. You should hold on to it for a while, just in case."

"In case what?" His fingers tightened around the velvet box.

"In case you decide to leave next month? Next week? Tomorrow?"

"I told you I would try to stay for a while, and I will." She swallowed thickly. "But I don't want you to give me heirlooms or buy me expensive gifts. That's not what this relationship is about."

He looked at her then, piercing her with the intensity of his gaze. "What is this relationship about, Elizabeth?"

"Please don't make it complicated. Everything between us has been moving really fast. Maybe we should slow it down a little, at least until we figure out what's been going on around here."

Adam's face was impassive, but his fingers jerked reflexively. "It seems I'm unfamiliar with your arbitrary rules of what defines a complicated relationship. But now I know we aren't close enough to give each other gifts."

"You're making me sound ridiculous."

"Thinking a relationship is defined by jewelry is ridiculous!"

They stood facing each other, his hands clenched into fists around the velvet box, her chin jutting out in defiance, both breathing fast. As they looked at each other, his eyes lost their anger and grew soft, and she could see his pain.

Seeing his expression, something inside her ached. She wanted to fall into his arms, thank him for the gift, and be his. But instead of reaching for him, her arms folded across her chest.

"Please don't go to all this trouble," she said, her voice tiny, insignificant. "I'm not worth it."

"What?"

He was going to find out, anyway, and maybe it would be better if he knew now. She looked down at her bare feet, twisting her fingers together. "There's something broken in me, something lacking."

"How on earth could you say that?"

"Plenty of families could have adopted me, and they didn't." Her lips trembled, and she swiped at the single tear trickling down her cheek. "There has to be a reason, something wrong with me."

"That's a child's reasoning." His thumb skimmed her cheek, wiping away her tears. "Maybe it wasn't that they didn't want you. Maybe you didn't want them."

She blinked. She thought of the ways she'd sabotaged the relationships with her foster families. How she'd only wanted her mother. How she'd been afraid loving a new family would just cause pain when they left, too.

She'd thought there was something wrong with her. Was it possible that the only thing holding her back had been her own fear?

He embraced her. "Poor, sweet Elizabeth. God, what I would give to go back in time, change things for you."

With a sigh, he removed the necklace from its velvet confines. "It's already yours. It was always going to be, from the moment you came to Cliffhaven. And it always will be."

As he gently placed it around her neck, she trembled. He fastened the clasp, kissed her neck lightly where it lay, then stepped back and appraised her.

"I love you, Lizzie." He whispered it, the words full of raw emotion.

And suddenly, her heart was so full, she thought it might engulf her. Full of desire, of yearning, fear, and some other emotion—bigger and stronger than them all, so all-consuming and foreign that it terrified her. She lowered her gaze to the floor, her lips quivering.

Adam shook his head. "You don't have to answer. Loving you is an honor, a gift you've given me. I won't ask you for anything more."

"You deserve more."

He ran a fingertip down her cheek. "Before you came, I'd

given up hope of experiencing love like this. If you leave tomor-row, loving you for even this brief time would still be worth the pain of your absence."

She leaned her head against his chest and whispered, "It scares me."

"Why?"

She let out a shuddering sigh. "Because it can't last. It never lasts. And the more I feel for you, the worse it will be when it falls apart."

His arms wrapped around her, drawing her closer. "It doesn't always fall apart."

"Doesn't it?" She shook her head. "I'm scared, Adam. I'm scared I'll make a mistake and destroy some precious part of Cliffhaven. I'm scared of whoever is putting me through this nightmare. But mostly I'm afraid of loving you." He started to speak, but she put one finger over his lips. "Let's not talk about it, please. I don't want to talk."

She grasped the lapels of his jacket and pulled him close until their lips met. Desperation clawed at her, the feeling that if she kissed him fiercely enough, if she took enough, she could cement the two of them together. His hands went around her hips, pulling her closer, and the kiss deepened.

Then the door to her room opened. Adam whirled around, stepping in front of her like a shield. But it was only Caroline, looking chic and elegant in a pale blue gown, her hair artfully arranged.

Caroline's green eyes widened as she took in Adam's protec-tive stance. "Is everything all right?"

"Yes," Elizabeth said, stepping out from behind him. "We're just a little tense tonight."

"Is that mother's necklace? Oh, Elizabeth, it was made for you!" Caroline beamed as she looked between them. "The guests will arrive soon. You should go to the hall to greet them."

She wanted to argue, to stay locked in Adam's arms and let

him convince her they could make a life together. But Caroline looked at her expectantly, and she knew it wasn't the right moment. As Adam took her hand, smiling tentatively at her, she thought the conversation could wait.

She thought they had plenty of time.

CHAPTER 36

*H*undreds of candles lit the ballroom, casting their golden glow on the gilded paneling. Haunting music echoed across the domed ceiling, played by a string quartet seated on the dais. Scores of guests milled around the ballroom, eating Tony's luxurious food, dancing to the mournful music.

"This is your idea of a casual party?" Elizabeth said, nudging Caroline.

Caroline shrugged, and the cap sleeves of her ice-blue dress slipped down her porcelain shoulders. "This room turns any party into a ball."

Elizabeth wiped her damp palms on her cocktail dress. Worry gnawed at her like a parasite. Her eyes kept flicking to the ceiling fresco, but her pleasure at its restoration was elusive. The faces of the gods and goddesses no longer looked benevolent; they were impossibly distant, unreachable. Despite the crowded room, she felt profoundly alone.

Vanessa sidled up to them, looking stunning in a strapless scarlet gown that could only be couture. She was ironed, coiffed, and made up so that every detail of her appearance was perfect. "Caroline!" she said, leaning close and kissing the air above her cheek. Her eyes skimmed over Elizabeth dismissively.

Vanessa waved her manicured hand around the ballroom. "This party will be the talk of the island for years. Except for the decorations. No offense, darling, but they are *très gauche.* It's just so *dismal.*"

Caroline rolled her eyes to the ceiling, as if she might find patience there. "Thanks for coming, Vanessa. Your dress is beautiful."

Vanessa looked gratified, as if Caroline's casual comment had communicated a deep envy she'd always suspected. "It is divine, isn't it? I brought it back with me from Paris. It does look incredible on me."

Her gaze shifted to Elizabeth, and her eyes roved up and down her body with contempt and pity. "But I've always found that if a woman stays slim, she can look great in just about anything."

Elizabeth's hands curled into fists at her side.

"Beauty comes in all shapes and sizes, Vanessa," Caroline said sharply. "Elizabeth, you look amazing tonight. I wish I could fill out a dress like that."

Vanessa raised her eyebrows, which were perfectly plucked into a graceful arch, and looked as if she'd tasted something foul. "You must be joking. You wouldn't want to be overweight, Caroline—it's what happens when a woman doesn't respect herself."

"I couldn't disagree with you more." Caroline folded her arms across her chest. "And if you're implying that Elizabeth is overweight because she doesn't have the figure of an anorexic fashion model, you're not only rude but also ignorant. In any case, Adam seems to enjoy her body a great deal, which couldn't make me happier."

As Vanessa's perfect features contorted with anger, Caroline took Elizabeth's arm firmly and led her away, whispering, "That was more satisfying than you can imagine."

Tony appeared, his navy suit wrinkled, his copper hair standing on end, and led Caroline onto the dance floor. Even his normally wide, infectious grin seemed subdued.

Alone again, her gaze found Adam in the center of the ballroom, towering over his friends and neighbors. Even as he laughed at something Christopher said, he looked alert, ready to detect the slightest signs of danger. By the tense set of his jaw and the way his eyes flickered around the room, she knew he was as wary as she felt.

Adam saw her watching, excused himself from the group of people, and came to her side. Tension rested between them, thick and palpable. If only she knew how to dispel it. She ached for him, for the comfort of his touch, but the strength of her need only added to the anxiety building within her.

He reached toward her, as if he would put his arm around her waist, then he pulled his hand back and shoved it in his pocket.

She gulped champagne, hoping it would cool the heat in her cheeks. "You okay?"

"Surprisingly, yes." The corner of his mouth turned up. "No one gasped when they saw me. No one recoiled in disgust."

"You thought they might?"

He half-shrugged, then his gaze scanned the crowded ballroom. "But I keep looking at my neighbors, wondering which of them likes to dress in women's clothing and haunt my house."

"Me, too." Her gaze shifted from face to face. "Where's Meeks? Didn't you invite him?"

"Of course. But I wouldn't be surprised if he didn't come. He doesn't like crowds."

Adam lifted his head, spotting something across the room. "Uncle Jack's waving me over."

"Go ahead."

She watched him cross the room, wondering why his departure felt like some kind of abandonment. What was wrong with her tonight? She gulped the last of her champagne and set it on the tray of a passing waiter. She brushed at her polyester dress, which felt out of place in the elegant ballroom, cheaper than the crisp uniforms of the servers.

"Dance with me." The voice, so close to her ear, startled her. It was Christopher, wearing his characteristic megawatt smile. He wore a winter white jacket and exuded bonhomie—aided, perhaps, by the excellent champagne.

She hesitated before placing her hand in his outstretched palm, and he led her to the edge of the group of dancers. He held her close, surprising her with a tight grip on her waist.

"Have you finally had enough of this gloomy place?" he asked.

"I don't think that's possible."

"I would have thought you'd be done with your work by now. So, will you recommend restoring Cliffhaven?" He sounded nonchalant, but his eyes were sharp and serious.

"Actually, yes. I think Cliffhaven should be restored."

His hand tightened on her wrist. "Honestly, that doesn't seem like the best use of Adam's money."

Her blood heated. "And how do you think Adam's money should be spent?"

His eyes narrowed, but only for a moment, then his face broke into a relaxed smirk. "I have some ideas. I'm a bit of a venture capitalist, myself. Adam and I've been investing together for years."

"And have your investments been successful?" If he noticed the sharp tone of her voice, he ignored it.

"You win some, you lose some." He smiled flirtatiously and pulled her closer, clearly a man used to charming women into doing whatever he wanted. "But if Adam's money is all tied up in this money-pit of a house, he'll miss out on some good investments. You'd be doing him a favor, actually, if you recommended that Cliffhaven not be restored."

Elizabeth pulled back, her feet frozen to the floor, and let her arms fall to her sides. She stared at Christopher, suspicion welling up inside her.

Then the music stopped, and the delicate sound of a spoon tapping crystal filled the air. They turned to the center of the dance floor, where Adam stood.

"Thank you, everyone, for coming. We're blessed to have such wonderful friends and neighbors." Adam gestured expansively, beaming at the crowd. If he was nervous being the center of attention, he hid it well. "We'd also like to announce that Caroline and I have decided to restore Cliffhaven. It's time for this estate to be returned to its former glory."

Elizabeth expected applause. She expected handshakes and enthusiasm. But the guests looked stunned, murmuring amongst themselves. Jack shook his head, his thin lips pursed in disapproval. Vanessa folded her arms across her chest, looking murderous. Christopher slumped against the gilded wood paneling, mostly in shadow.

Only Caroline appeared content, fairly glowing with happiness as friends and neighbors approached her. She raised her eyebrows at Elizabeth, gesturing for her to join them, and she crossed the room to stand by her side.

Jack joined the small group, the eyes of several women travelling over him appreciatively. The disapproval that had been so apparent on his face was gone. He clapped his hands together, the muscles of his arms straining his suit jacket. "This is welcome news, isn't it?"

"Absolutely," Tony said, pulling Caroline closer. "Restoring Cliffhaven can only be good for the family, don't you think, Jack?"

"Without a doubt." Jack nodded. "I've always thought Cliffhaven should be restored. Adam has made the right decision. He knows who to listen to for advice." He winked at the ladies, as if gratified that Adam had listened to his good advice all along.

Jack smiled, looking wistful. "It's just a shame his father can't be here to see it. Stephen would be proud of the man Adam's become."

Caroline stiffened. Her smile faded, and pain pinched the corners of her mouth. "Excuse me," she murmured, backing away.

Jack snagged a glass of champagne from a passing waiter and nodded sagely. "It's no secret that family always came first for my brother."

Anger welled inside Elizabeth, and her hands turned to fists. Jack said Stephen's family—the children he'd hit, the wife he'd abused—had come first? Jack *knew* about the violence, and he'd stood by and let it happen. If anyone could have stopped Stephen from hurting his family, this man, so full of strength and obvious power, could have.

"Secrets," Elizabeth said, unable to keep the fire from her voice. "You're good at keeping secrets, aren't you, Jack?"

He tilted his head, and his gray eyes focused on her, bemused. Assessing. "A good attorney has to be," he said smoothly.

THE PARTY WANED, the swell of guests diminishing until Adam found he could finally relax. He retreated to a hidden corner of the ballroom and leaned against the wall, half-hidden by a potted fern. He'd thought himself alone until Christopher stumbled into him, grabbing his sleeve for balance.

He looked up at him with bleary eyes and said, "What are you doing, bro? Sinking money into this pit of a house." He shook his head. "Mistake, bro."

Adam placed a supporting arm around Christopher's shoulder. "Let's get you some coffee."

"I'm fine," he slurred, pushing at Adam's hand like a cranky toddler. "It's about that girl, isn't it? You're going to lose your shirt over some piece of ass?"

Adam froze, then looked at his friend like he was seeing him clearly for the first time. "You're worried about my money? I've been funneling cash into your so-called investments for years. *Years,* dammit. I never expect a return, and I do it for you, you asshole. Because you mean more to me than money."

"Some of my investments made money. Anyway, you've got enough to go around."

"Is that what I am to you? An ATM?" Adam's shoulders stiffened, and he shook his head angrily. "I'm happier than I've been in years. Does that even matter to you?"

Chris shook his head, looking sheepish. "Man, that's not what I—"

"Go home," Adam said, his voice filled with disgust. "You're drunk."

Christopher staggered away, and Adam's eyes followed him across the ballroom.

Somebody needs to take his keys. He let out a breath and took two steps toward Chris.

Vanessa appeared out of nowhere, sidling close to his side. "Hello, Adam." She placed her palm on his chest.

"Thanks for coming, Vanessa." He stepped back, so that her hand fell away from his jacket. "You look nice tonight."

"Thanks. I know you men enjoy having something beautiful to look at." Her smile was secretive, her eyes satisfied. She closed the distance between them, pressing her chest against his. "Adam, we've danced around each other long enough. I want you. I know you want me." She leaned close and whispered in his ear, "Take me to your room."

"Vanessa, I'm flattered. But you and I wouldn't be good

together."

"Of course we would. We were born to be together, here at Cliffhaven." With complete self-assurance, Vanessa stood on her tiptoes and pressed her lips to his.

He gripped her arms and pushed her away gently. "No, Vanessa. I'm in love with Elizabeth."

She stepped back, appraising him with calculating eyes. "That's impossible. She's a servant. Just look at her!"

Adam's jaw clenched, and he started to speak, but she covered his mouth with one finger. "I know you think you love her, but you must see she doesn't belong here. You can't expect someone from her class to fit into our society. It's just lust, and I don't blame you—the way she parades her whore's body in front of you."

Fury ripped through him. "You don't care about me, Vanessa. Stop pretending you do. You only want what I can give you—money. I've tolerated your flirtations, the fake affection you heap on me, for the sake of our friendship. For our families. But insulting Elizabeth is the final straw.

"Get out of my house. I don't want to look at you." Vanessa's mouth dropped open in shock. "And don't ever come back, unless you can treat the woman I love with the respect she deserves."

ELIZABETH WATCHED from a distance as Vanessa touched Adam, kissed him. Her stomach churned, her mind swimming with champagne and betrayal. Part of her wanted to fight for her man, to rip Vanessa off him and claim Adam as her own.

Instead of fighting, she fled. As she scurried to the parlor and slammed the door behind her, the feeling of running away was painfully familiar.

In the empty room, her legs buckled, and she slid down the

wall to the floor. *Alone again.*

The emerald necklace around her neck suddenly felt heavy —a burden too great to bear. Her shaking fingers fought with the clasp until it opened, and she looked down at the jewels cupped in her hands. How could she ever have thought something so beautiful, so valuable, could be hers?

The necklace needed to go back where it belonged. Feeling numb, she slunk through Cliffhaven's dark corridors until she approached the servants' staircase that led to the second floor.

She inhaled the smell of cold, damp stone, remembering the last time she'd been on the stone spiral staircase. It had been with Adam, the moment she'd decided to restore the frescoes, to take the next small step toward the future she wanted so desperately. Choking on the memory that seemed to lodge in her throat, she started up the narrow steps.

Then a sound broke the silence—footsteps on the stairs below. She drew in a startled breath, turning toward the steps that wound their way toward the basement. A beam of light, cold and white, pierced the darkness there, and footfalls echoed up the spiral staircase.

"Adam?" she said. "I thought you were in the ballroom."

The footsteps stopped. The twisting staircase hid the figure from view, but a large shadow was now visible painted against the stone wall—the dark outline of a person.

"Adam?" Her voice faltered. "Is that you?"

The shadow was silent. In that silence, it was as if she could feel malice emanating from the person like dark waves, a hatred she couldn't fathom. Her blood turned to ice in her veins.

Then, all at once, she knew—the dark shadow on the stone wall belonged to the person who'd plagued her since her arrival at Cliffhaven. The one who'd vandalized her car, killed the rat, sabotaged the scaffolding, and led her into the blizzard. They were here.

And she was alone.

CHAPTER 37

"I'm calling the police!" Elizabeth's voice cracked, belying her show of courage. The dark shadow on the stone wall of the staircase didn't move.

She took one step up, her feet making no sound on the stone stairs. But her next step was panicked, and in her distress, she tripped over her dress and crashed to the floor.

Footsteps filled the darkness—the unmistakable sound of the person on the stairs moving toward her, their footfalls quick and sure on the stone steps. Terror gripped her, nightmarish and suffocating. She scrambled to her feet and ran up the stairs, taking them two at a time as she cast a panicked look behind her.

A strangled scream tore from her throat. She leaped off the last step and sailed into the second-floor corridor. She pumped her legs hard now, running for her life through the darkened hallway, then skittered into her room.

She shut the door softly and backed away. Her eyes darted around her bedchamber, frantically searching for a place to hide. Her gaze fell on the bookcase, and her eyes narrowed. It was . . . open. One side of the bookcase jutted out from the wall, revealing a dark space that led *into* the walls.

Another secret passageway. Here, in her room.

Her heart thumping with fear, she opened the bookcase wide and scrambled inside, into the space behind the walls. Scraping her fingers against the rough wood, she pulled the bookcase closed behind her and was engulfed in darkness.

She froze, silent and still. Listening.

Something scurried over her foot, alive and unafraid. She clapped her hands over her mouth, forcing back a scream. The high-pitched squeal of a rat echoed against the stone walls, and she flinched away. How many vermin lived behind Cliffhaven's walls?

Her breath came in shallow gasps. For a few tense moments, all was silent, but her heart refused to stop its hammering. Whoever chased her could be out there, waiting.

Her eyes swept the darkness of the secret passageway, drawn to twin pinpoints of light streaming through the wall. She crept toward the lights, careful that her feet made no noise on the stone floor. The murky light shone through two holes in the wall at the level of her face, perfect circles carved into the wood and plaster. She stepped close to the stone wall, lining up her eyes with the holes, and peered through them.

It was a perfect view of her bedroom, with a direct eyeline to her four-poster bed.

A peephole.

An icy shiver danced down her back. An image sprang, unbidden, into her mind—a faceless figure pressed against the peepholes, watching her and Adam writhe together in the dark, their naked limbs glowing in firelight.

Revulsion churned her stomach, and she backed away from the peepholes. She pulled her phone from her pocket with shaking fingers and cast its light around the passageway.

There were things there, lying on the stone floor. A tattered woolen blanket, crumpled on top of a sleeping pad, the type one would take camping. Plastic food wrappers littered the floor, crumbs still clinging to the cellophane. And next to the makeshift mattress was a half-full chamber pot. Only then did she notice the rank smell, putrid and suffocating.

Dawning horror infected her. Someone was sleeping here. *Living* here, just behind the walls to her room. Spying on her from the darkness, watching her sleep.

The hair on the nape of her neck lifted. Suddenly the passage was too tight, the walls closing in on her. She had to get out of there.

Just then, footsteps reverberated through the walls. Someone was coming.

She fumbled her phone, almost dropping it before she could turn off its light. Then, her breath coming in shallow spurts, she inched her way to the peepholes. Wiping her clammy hands on her jeans, she pressed her eyes to the tiny circles of light. The door to her room creaked open.

Then the light went out.

She blinked, her eyes fighting to adjust to the sudden darkness. The muscles in her legs quivered, ready to flee. Then the dark outline of a figure creeped past her bed, disappearing into shadow, and soft footsteps approached the bookcase.

A bolt of fear struck her, sharp and cold. *They know about the passageway. They're coming.*

She clutched her throat, desperation clawing at her. Then she bolted, stumbling forward through the dark passage, scraping against the stone wall as she ran. After a few steps, the floor disappeared beneath her feet, and she pitched forward, almost falling down a tight spiral staircase. Regaining her balance, she scurried down the treacherous steps, descending into darkness. Then she ran, face first, into the end of the passageway, crushing her nose against wood.

Blood trickled over her lips as she ran her hands frantically over the wood that made up the wall in front of her. Her fingers slammed against a lever protruding from the wall, and she yanked. The wall swung open, letting in bright light, and a tiny moan of relief escaped her lips.

She staggered into the golden light of the great hall. The entry to the secret passageway was a false wall hidden in the paneling behind the double staircase.

She slammed the door of the passageway shut and backed away, staring at the false paneling as if a monster might leap from it. Her back came against something solid, and she whirled.

It was only the newel post, the sculptural pyramid at the bottom of the grand staircase she'd restored. The tip of the pyramid, that wicked point, gleamed in the light.

Then footsteps sounded on the gallery above her, accompanied by the rustle of fabric.

"Elizabeth."

Panic electrified her body as she recognized that voice, that harsh whisper, calling her name. Heart pounding, she raised her eyes to the gallery above.

There was a grunt, the broken sound of wood splintering, and a startled scream. Then it was as if everything happened in slow motion, like time slowed for the sole purpose of showing her the events in graphic, agonizing detail. A body dropped from the gallery above, trailing white, diaphanous material—a gown that caught the light and sparkled as it plummeted. The dark-haired figure screamed as it fell, clutching at air, before hitting the banister with a sickening thud.

Elizabeth gasped, and she stood, frozen in horror.

It was Audrey Arrington, fallen from the second-floor gallery. She'd landed on the sharp point of the sculptural newel post, and now lay upon it, impaled. The wood Elizabeth had restored with her own hands jutted obscenely from her chest. The satin-clad figure was draped over the banister like Fuseli's

Nightmare Painting, blood blossoming on the snow-white wedding gown like a grotesque work of art.

Elizabeth opened her mouth, but the scream was trapped in her throat.

Audrey's long, dark curls hung askew. It was a wig, hanging from her skull haphazardly, as if it might abandon the wounded woman. The figure groaned into the sickening silence.

She was still alive! Her mouth still moving under the bridal veil that covered her face.

Help her! A voice inside her screamed, and Elizabeth rushed to her side. Holding her breath, she picked up the veil between her thumb and forefinger and moved it aside. The skin under the veil was pale and sallow, pockmarked with old acne scars, the hair gray and frizzy.

It was Hodges. The housekeeper who'd given her notice that first day at Cliffhaven. Dressed as Audrey Arrington, impaled by the sharply pointed newel post. Blood trickling from the corner of her mouth that was pinched in agony.

Hodges's shoulders twitched, and she lifted her head, hands clenching at the wood piercing her chest. Her gray eyes were wide with terror.

Elizabeth clasped her trembling hand. "It's okay. You're going to be okay."

But she wasn't okay, would never again be okay. Blood flowed from the ivory satin onto the stone floor.

Hodges's mouth opened and closed soundlessly. Then her eyes met Elizabeth's. A pained, urgent look fixed on Hodges's face as she struggled to speak, her voice hardly a whisper. "Run."

Elizabeth tried to back away, but Hodges's hand held her in a death grip. Her eyes burned with urgency. "Run, Lizzie!" she croaked, and it was a pained, wrenching plea that stole her breath.

Then her head lolled back, and her hand went limp and lifeless over Elizabeth's. She was gone.

Blood pooled in the corner of Hodges's mouth, and the horror building inside Elizabeth demanded an outlet. She screamed, then, and the dreadful sound echoed off the cavernous walls of the grand foyer. Footsteps filled the air as guests rushed out of the ballroom to gawk, horrified by the gruesome scene.

Caroline pushed through the crowd and leaned over Hodges. Her hair fell onto the satin gown, and the strawberry-blonde strands were coated with blood when she lifted her shocked eyes to Elizabeth. "She's dead." Her voice was confused, incredulous, as if a grotesque prank were being played.

Elizabeth turned back to the crowd of guests gathering behind them, whispering among themselves. The faces of her friends and neighbors stared back at her, and for one terrible moment, they all looked malevolent.

CHAPTER 38

$\mathcal{T}$he party had fallen apart hours ago. Their guests had deserted them, scattering like frightened birds into the night. Elizabeth had finished a grueling interview with police, where Officer Ogie's eyes had been sharp and suspicious, but there was no evidence that Hodges's death was anything other than an accident. Now, finally, the police and paramedics were gone.

Hodges was gone. But the bloodstain on the floor remained, soaking into the pale stone.

Caroline sat on the grand staircase, crying soft, silent tears that dripped down her porcelain skin. Tony's arm was around her, his ginger head bent low over hers as he whispered words of support. Adam stood at the foot of the stairs, staring at the scarlet stain on the floor.

Elizabeth fought the urge to rush into his arms and bury her face in his chest. The shock of witnessing Hodges's violent death was wearing off, and in its place, she felt creeping dread. But she could handle it. Alone, if necessary.

"Hodges pretended to be the ghost of my mother?" Caroline said, looking as if the thought made her sick.

"She'd been living in the secret passageways. I found a camp bed, some food." Elizabeth heard the flatness of her voice, betraying the exhaustion that deflated her. "Maybe she never left."

"Why would anyone choose to live in those nasty secret passageways? In the dead of winter?"

There was one answer that made sense, that she understood far too well. "Maybe she had nowhere else to go."

"She was responsible for all of it, wasn't she?" Tony said, looking bewildered. "The fake hauntings, the messages written in fire, even the vandalism to your car."

"And the dead rat." Caroline shuddered.

Adam raked a hand through his jet-black hair. "Using the secret passageways, she had easy access to my phone in the library. It would have been simple to send the text that sent you into the blizzard."

"She would have had total access to Cliffhaven," Tony said, nodding. "Hey! She's the one who removed safety pins from the scaffolding!"

She shivered. "And those peepholes. She watched me for weeks."

"But *why?*" Caroline threw her hands into the air, her face twisted with grief and confusion. "Why would she want to hurt Elizabeth?"

"She was trying to frighten me away from Cliffhaven." She shook her head. "But that doesn't make sense. We didn't even know each other."

"Maybe she was just . . . crazy." Tony shrugged. "You know, living in secret passageways, wearing dead people's clothes, haunting Cliffhaven at night. It's nuts. Maybe there isn't any other reason."

Caroline shook her head, sorrowful. "If she was struggling with mental illness, I wish she'd confided in us. We could have helped."

Elizabeth ran her hands over her face. Something troubled her, like she was trying to make a puzzle piece fit, but the rounded edges just didn't mesh. "What would have happened if Hodges's plan had worked? If I'd been terrified by the fake hauntings and left?"

"Honestly," Caroline said, wiping at her eyes, "I probably would have given up on Cliffhaven. Figured it was a lost cause."

Adam cast an understanding glance at his sister. "Maybe then Hodges would have asked for her job back."

Elizabeth sank to the marble stairs and wrapped her arms around her legs. "That just doesn't make sense. And why would she chase me through the house?"

A muscle in Adam's jaw tightened. "I'm glad we'll never know. She might have hurt you, Elizabeth, or worse."

"But at the end, Hodges was still trying to warn me. She told me to run."

Tony massaged his neck, looking weary. "Who knows? Maybe she really believed she was Audrey Arrington, haunting her own house."

Caroline leaned her head on Tony's shoulder, looking sorrowful. "She's gone now, anyway."

"It's over now. All of it," Adam said, turning to face her. But there was still something troubling behind his eyes, a brooding fear he seemed to struggle to conceal. "You're safe."

A cold draft chilled her, raising goosebumps on her arms. She didn't feel safe.

But she could handle it.

Adam reached for her, and she skittered away. An awkward tension filled the air, a moment she could feel three stares dissecting her. "I . . . just need a minute."

Adam looked resigned, as if he'd expected her to pull away, then glared down at his empty hands.

"I'm going to make tea," Caroline said. "We could all use it." She gripped Tony's arm, pulling him toward the kitchen.

"Maybe I'll heat up some of those canapés," Tony said, stopping in the open doorway. "You know, eat my feelings." He gave them a sad smile and disappeared into the kitchen.

Elizabeth hugged her knees to her chest.

"She had my mother's dress on." Adam stared at the fire burning in the hearth, the flames alive in his eyes. Then he dragged his hands through his hair. "Will I never escape these memories? It's like I'm still running through smoke, trying to save the people I love but doomed to failure."

He looked at her, his eyes burning. Tortured. "What if you'd been hurt? Killed? I can't protect you."

The front door flew open, letting in a blast of snow and frigid air. Jack charged into the hall, shoulders thrown back, face set, ready to take command of the situation. "Everyone's gone—the police, the paramedics," he said, setting his briefcase on the stone floor.

Adam nodded. "Thanks for handling it. I think we're good for the night, if you want to go home."

"Nonsense. You need family at a time like this, not to mention your lawyer. What if the police charge you with a crime? Or, God forbid, a civil suit." His gray eyes settled upon the blood congealing on the stone floor. "Was the railing on the upstairs gallery broken? If you've been negligent in the upkeep of safety, you'll be liable for Hodges's injuries."

"The railing was fine," Adam said. "She must have just . . . fallen. Or jumped."

"She didn't jump." The words escaped Elizabeth's mouth before she contemplated them.

Jack turned to her, an impatient look flitting across his sharp features. "How could you possibly know that?"

Her eyes were drawn to the wicked point of the sculptural banister, where blood seeped into the wood. "There was terror on her face, at the end."

Jack raised one eyebrow, not bothering to hide his condescension. Then he rolled his eyes toward Adam. "Women. It's natural for them to be a bit . . . hysteric."

Annoyance pricked her, but she let it go. There were more important things now.

Jack clapped his strong hands together, as if the recent crisis had energized him. "It's been a long night." He crossed the hall and opened a small cabinet, pulling out a crystal decanter and glasses. "Are Caroline and Tony still here?"

"In the kitchen. They're spending the night."

"It's good to have family around." Jack handed Adam a crystal glass full of amber liquid. "Drink this. It'll help."

Adam drained the glass, and Jack offered one to her. She took the outstretched glass automatically, then stared into its depths.

Her pulse hammered at her throat as the familiar, impending anxiety rose within her. She couldn't banish the memory of Hodge's bloody, broken body. She'd watched someone die. Again.

Seeing someone die was a unique horror; knowing in gruesome detail how it happened—how much blood is spilled when a person is impaled through the chest, how Hodges's eyes looked when the lights left them. The smell of her mother's burning flesh.

Breathe, she told herself. *You've been triggered, that's all. Just do what you need to do to feel better. Cope.*

Adam placed his hand on her forearm, jolting her. "Are you all right?"

She stood, set the glass of liquor on a console table, then covered her eyes with shaking hands. "I . . . I don't think so."

"No, of course not. Let me—"

He reached for her, but she jerked away. One touch, and she might shatter.

His eyes searched hers, and whatever they saw seemed to darken his features even more. Did he blame her for this grim

turn of events? Did he finally see her for what she truly was
—inadequate?

She gestured frantically toward the staircase. "I need to . . ."
*Pack my stuff. Soothe myself, or I'm going to break into a thousand
pieces.* "Go upstairs. For a few minutes."

He watched her go with eyes full of doubt and accusation,
and she knew this long, gut-wrenching night was far from over.

CHAPTER 39

*I*n Elizabeth's room, the bookcase that led to the secret passage was still ajar, bringing it all flooding back—the vulnerability of being spied on, the frantic fear she'd felt running through the corridors, the horror of Hodges's violent death. Her eyes flitted to the peepholes, so well camouflaged by the intricate wallpaper.

Panic swelled within her. And she was a child again, needing to know she was ready to leave, if the need arose. Frantically gathering her belongings to make sure they weren't left behind. She yanked her suitcase from beneath her bed, and with every item she placed inside—clothes from the armoire, phone charger on the nightstand, toiletry kit from the dresser—the clawing anxiety abated.

When all her possessions were back in her suitcase, she knelt before it. *See? Everything's okay.* Her pulse slowed, and her breathing calmed.

Then Adam's voice sounded from the doorway. "Elizabeth?"

She turned in time to see his eyes travelling over the room that was now stripped of her belongings, his gaze freezing on her packed suitcase. "What are you doing?" His voice was thick with hurt and betrayal, but no part of him seemed surprised.

"It's not what it looks like." Her cheeks heated. "This is just something I do . . ."

How could she explain that it soothed her to have her belongings packed, ready to leave at a moment's notice? How it was easier knowing she was ready to leave, just in case? How before she came to Cliffhaven, leaving had always been inevitable, and it was better—so much better—if you were ready to go.

She pulled the suitcase closer to her body, lowering her head so her hair shielded her face. Adam would never understand.

He cocked his head, looked at her with a piercing gaze. "It looks like you're leaving."

He reached for her, but she shrugged away from his touch. At his pained expression, she blew out a jagged breath. "Just give me a minute. I'm still freaked out. Finding Hodges like that . . ."

But the fact that she didn't want his touch seemed to trigger something in him. His eyes darkened, and there was something broken in his expression, as if he'd given in to some profound sorrow that normally slept, dormant, within him.

"You're leaving."

"No, Adam, I—"

"Just be honest," he said roughly. "Say you don't want to be with me. Tell me you can't stand to be with someone who can't protect you, can't keep you safe. Tell me I'm fine to amuse you while you're stuck on an island in the middle of nowhere, but not good enough for forever."

Shock reverberated through her. "Adam, that is not how I feel."

He laid his hand over his heart, fingers spread wide, pressing down as if staunching a wound. "I knew you'd leave in the end."

His words sparked a fire of doubt inside her. *He never thought I'd stay?*

And suddenly there was so much space between them—a yawning chasm, impossible to traverse. "Did you never believe in us? In me?"

His eyes flashed. "It's you that doesn't believe. I've been pounding against that wall you built around your heart since you got here. I've told you over and over that I want to be with you more than anything."

"But how can you know what you want?" Her fingers clenched around her suitcase. "You've been hiding inside Cliffhaven for years. You would have fallen in love with the first woman to walk through that door."

"How can you say that?"

She pressed her lips together, biting back the truth—that there was something lacking inside her, something that made her unlovable. So she let the silence draw out, knowing her coldness hurt him and hating herself for it.

His face was haggard as he sagged against the wall. "Why did you have to come here? With your talk of restoring everything that's broken, your pretty lies about what Cliffhaven could be. I told you it was a mistake, that this place can never be restored."

And she knew that he was giving up—on Cliffhaven, on their relationship. And if he didn't believe, how in the world could she?

Her lips trembled. "Cliffhaven can be a home again. I know it can."

"Why do you even care?" he said savagely. "You have no intention of staying here, trying to make this work. You don't have a home, and you never will if you aren't willing to stay, to let someone in."

She froze, breath catching in her throat. Her chest suddenly felt hollow, as if some vital organ were missing.

She looked around the elegant chamber, the intricately carved furniture, the luxurious carpet, the priceless paintings on the wall. Her cheap, battered suitcase was the only object that didn't belong, that was so clearly out of place it pained her.

She'd been a fool to think she could ever belong here. How stupid she was, thinking this place, these people, were for her.

Something cracked inside her. And she knew the roots of her fears and doubts were still within her, like weeds one simply couldn't eradicate—a poisonous plant ready to bloom and infest.

You don't have a home, and you never will.

She'd forgotten the cold truths she'd learned as a child and was now paying the price of hope. And this pain she'd always feared, there was so much of it. Like a tidal wave, she saw it coming, knew it would break over her and suck her down.

Time to go. The familiar feeling crept up on her, seeping inside her soul like a miasma. All this pain could be left behind so easily, if she ran fast enough, far enough.

Her shoulders sagged, and she looked down at her suitcase. There wasn't even anything left to pack.

"You're right. I'll never have a home." She tightened her hold on the suitcase. *Never.*

It was frighteningly easy to revert to old habits—taking refuge in an icy numbness, handling the situation one movement at a time: zip the suitcase, slip her keys into the pocket of her dress, scan the room for anything she'd forgotten. Face blank, heart made of stone—heavy and cold. But underneath the numbness, she could feel the terrible shaking of her life, the foreshock that precedes a life-shattering earthquake. The kind that ruins lives, destroying everything.

"Elizabeth, no." Adam raked a hand through his hair, looking devastated. "God, I'm sorry. I didn't mean it." But his words sounded distant, as if filtered through noise-cancelling headphones, and they didn't penetrate her resolve.

She could barely grip the suitcase, her hands were shaking so badly. *Keep it together, at least until you're out of here.*

"Listen, we're both exhausted." Adam put his hand on her suitcase. "Don't go now. Not at night."

She jerked the suitcase away from his touch. "You're right. I was never going to stay. This was never going to work. And the longer we drag it out, the more it will hurt."

He recoiled as if she'd struck him. She pushed past him, marching down the hall and onto the grand staircase.

"Wait," he said. "Please, wait." But she kept moving down the stairs, refusing to look at him, and his words came out in a rush. "I used to believe I was better off alone, but now I know that isn't true. After living with you and Caroline, after having Tony here, I can see that people need each other. Why can't you see that?"

"Because I'm *broken*, Adam," she said, and the words were wrenched from somewhere deep inside her. Words that had burned a hole in a heart for decades. "Because there's something lacking in me. Because I don't know how to trust people, or how to maintain relationships."

Nobody's ever wanted me. Not for forever.

She stepped onto the stone floor of the hall, ignoring the scarlet stains. Then she stumbled to the closet, retrieved her coat, and pulled it on, hardly aware of what she was doing.

When she turned around, Adam was staring at her, looking anguished. "Don't go."

She brought a shaking hand to her forehead. "I don't belong here. You must see that."

He closed his eyes and nodded, looking pained. "But how am I supposed to let you go?"

A terrible ache formed within her as her hand closed around the doorknob, as if her heart were wrenching, ripping into pieces, left broken and bleeding. She opened the door, letting in the biting wind and snow, then turned back to him. "It'll be easier than you think."

It was only when the door shut behind her that she realized

she loved him. She loved him with all her soul, more than she'd ever loved anyone. Pain crushed her, agonizing and overwhelming.

Icy snow slapped at her face, and the wind shook the towering cedars, but she barely noticed the power of the gathering storm. Her heart felt as cold as the freezing lake, like ice had slipped into her bloodstream.

Blinded by tears that now flowed freely, she turned toward the dark, endless night, and was startled by a shadow. It was Jack, slamming the door of his car and jogging up the stone steps of the portico.

His eyes fixed first on her tear-streaked face, then on the suitcase she held. "You're leaving? In the middle of the night?" Jack opened the front door, his broad shoulders taking up the entire frame. "Stay, just a few minutes. Have a drink."

He gestured toward the door, and the corner of the leather briefcase he held banged into the doorframe. He fumbled the satchel, and it burst open. White paper fluttered out, floating to the ground like so many injured birds.

Numb and sick with heartache, she knelt, gathering the papers as Jack's thick fingers groped alongside hers. The word "Cliffhaven" caught her eye, printed boldly on heavy paper. She glanced at the document, then cocked her head in confusion. *Copper Assessment Report for Cliffhaven.* It was the old copper survey, the one Adam had framed on his wall, a souvenir of his father's mistakes. But there was something wrong, something different.

She scanned the document, then gripped the paper with too much force, her eyes widening as she read the words. She flipped a page, revealing a map showing copper directly beneath the mansion, branching off into the forest.

There's copper at Cliffhaven. Acres and acres of copper, running deep and wide across the estate.

But Adam said there were no viable mines on the island. And it was the same report, the same year.

She gripped the paper as if it might float away. Two surveys. Different results. Her eyes widened with dawning horror, and she looked up to find Jack's face inches from her own.

His gray eyes glinted with a predatory gleam. "Aren't you clever?"

Then he leapt for her, forcing his hand across her mouth, covering her scream. His heavy body crushed hers into the stone floor of the portico, and he lay atop her as she bucked and kicked.

Panic pumped through her blood, ripping at her throat as surely as the hand pressing against her windpipe.

"It's no use screaming," he whispered in her ear. "There's no one left to hear."

CHAPTER 40

*T*heir bodies lay near the crackling fire in the library. Caroline and Tony sprawled on the carpet, their limbs bent at odd angles, as if they just lay where they'd fallen. Next to them was Adam, silent and still as death.

Elizabeth drew back, terrified by the sight of his powerful body slumped on the carpet, defenseless. Her heart caught in her throat, then a moan escaped Adam's lips, and she breathed again.

"What did you do to them?"

Jack's fingers pulled on the plastic ties he'd used to bind her wrists, testing them, and the plastic bit into her flesh. She winced, and the corners of his mouth turned up in a reptilian smile.

"Antihistamine. In their brandy. I might have overdone it, but they're alive." His voice was as hard as his flinty, gray eyes.

Jack was different. It wasn't just that he'd thrown off his suit jacket and rolled the sleeves of his shirt over his muscular forearms, or even that he was towering over his niece's prone body. He was triumphant. Euphoric. Or perhaps it was only that he'd shed the mask he normally wore.

"The two surveys," she said. "You gave one to Adam's father, kept the other. You faked Adam's copy of the report, the one saying there's no copper. The Arringtons never knew."

His cold eyes lit. He *liked* that she knew. "You're smarter than I gave you credit for."

"There's only one reason you would hide this survey from the Arringtons, why you wouldn't want them to know about the copper. You wanted it for yourself."

With the confidence of a man who knew he was going to win, Jack smiled. "It's worth more than you could imagine, hundreds of millions. The most productive mine in the northern hemisphere."

Her mind raced, charged with adrenalin. "But the house is in the way."

"I needed the land, but Stephen loved this damn house, his precious art. He never would have left."

Elizabeth sat perfectly still as the truth, cold as the northern night, seeped into her bones. "You set the fire. The one that killed the Arringtons." Revulsion churned her stomach. "You murdered them."

Was that regret in his eyes? If so, it was only a flash before they hardened. "They were supposed to be out of town. It was meant to be a simple fire to take the house, then Stephen would sell me the land."

Jack gave a one-shouldered shrug. "But then they were dead. And with nobody taking care of Cliffhaven, it began to fall apart. And I realized I could have it all, if I'm willing to do what it takes."

He looked at her, then, and his lips curved into a satisfied smile. "I'm always willing to do what it takes."

The hairs on the nape of her neck lifted, and she began to pull at the plastic tie binding her wrists. "You didn't want Adam and Caroline to restore the house because you wanted them to sell it to you, cheap."

"Not me. A little company I founded offshore. I've taken great pains to distance myself from the purchase. Not that it matters now."

He jabbed his thick index finger toward her, frowning. "Because you showed up with your sentimental ideas about restoring this relic."

"So you decided to scare me off." Her mind scrambled to make sense of it all. The vandalism, the sabotage, the fake hauntings.

But Jack wasn't the one who'd dressed as a dead woman. "Hodges. How does she fit into all this?"

His lip curled with disgust. "You sleep with a woman one time, and she thinks she belongs to you. But she was convenient. And she jumped at the chance to help me get rid of you. It was her idea to convince you the house was haunted. She said you believed in ghosts, would scare easily."

She sucked in a breath. That staff meeting, when she'd first met Hodges, felt her sharp eyes watching her. Hodges had so quickly identified her weakness, then preyed on her vulnerability.

"I let her have her fun," Jack said, "starting fires and dressing in that moldy gown. Her plan was ridiculous, but I figured it might work on a woman." His cold eyes focused on her, dissecting her. "But it didn't. It didn't take me long to realize you wouldn't be driven away so easily. I thought the damage to your car might do it, maybe a dead animal in your closet, or getting stuck in a blizzard. But for someone who's always running away, you were difficult to get rid of."

"You sabotaged the scaffolding."

He tilted his head and smiled, as if she'd complimented him. "Hodges didn't like that. She didn't want to *hurt* anybody." He sneered. "She said if I didn't stop, she'd tell Adam everything."

"So you killed her. Pushed her off the gallery."

Jack squatted in front of the fire in the hearth. "When Adam announced the plan to restore Cliffhaven, I knew I couldn't fuck around anymore. This way is easier. Simpler."

He held a piece of kindling to the fire, then pulled it out and gazed at its flaming tip. Only then did she notice the haphazard pile of books and papers scattered around the base of long, velvet curtains.

She froze, breath catching in her chest. "That's your plan? Another fire?"

"Officer Ogie already told the whole island Adam's been starting fires. Everyone will think you tried to leave Adam, and he went crazy. Drugged his sister and her boyfriend, then burned the house down with everyone inside. Believable, don't you think?"

With a sick feeling in her stomach, she realized it was.

Jack poured liquid from a brown bottle across the books, and the familiar scent of sulfur filled the air. "A little accelerant should do the trick."

"All this . . . for copper?" she said bleakly.

"Money is everything." Jack leaned closer, and she could smell him—a sickening combination of fine cologne and acrid smoke. "And my brother got everything from my parents—the house, the land—because he's older. He wasn't better than me, he wasn't smarter or cleverer or more responsible. And I had to go to law school just to feed myself. Debasing myself in a shitty little office for the village idiots, writing their wills, suing their neighbors over fucking property lines, all just to scrape by. While Stephen had everything. Once this house is gone and I have the money from the copper, I'm going to live the life I deserve."

He towered over her, placing his hands on his hips, looking as if he enjoyed dominating her. "You should have run. You don't belong here."

Grief gripped her, washing over her like the black waves of the lake, dragging her down to the depths below. She squeezed her eyes shut against the images flashing through her mind—flames licking Cliffhaven's walls, engulfing her newfound family, destroying everything she loved.

She'd been searching her entire life for a home—a place she could feel safe and loved; a place to return to when she'd lost herself; a place to be found. After years of searching in vain, she'd told herself that place didn't exist. She'd resigned herself to living without it, without friends and loved ones and community—without roots. All because she'd believed she was broken, unwanted.

But how could anyone have a home if they never stopped running? How could anyone build deep relationships if they never let anyone get close? Why was it that now, with painful, perfect clarity, she could see that she'd been standing in her own way, preventing herself from having what she most wanted?

Outside the windows of the library, the snowstorm was building. Wind howled around the house, shaking the shutters.

Jack bent over Adam, examining the cable tie that enclosed his wrists. "I wish he'd wake up. I want him to know it was me." Then his foot shot out, connecting with Adam's hip. His limp body jerked in response, but he didn't wake.

"Don't!" Anger built inside her, a rising tide of crimson.

"You had *everything*," she spat. "Adam loved you! You had a family! And you lied to them. *Betrayed them.*"

Rage coursed through her, burning as hot and bright in her chest as the flame he held. As Jack bent over Adam, she twisted her hands until her wrists were wet with blood. In her struggles, her fingers brushed against something hard in her pocket, and she froze. Her keyring.

"You're wrong," she said, inching her fingers toward her pocket. "I *do* belong at Cliffhaven, with Adam. This place is my home, and these people are my family. I won't let you destroy it."

Jack lifted the flaming wood, and it burned brightly in his eyes. "Then you'll burn with the rest of them."

CHAPTER 41

*E*lizabeth's heart pounded fiercely in her chest, her eyes fixed on the flame Jack held. "I'm not going to let you do that."

He laughed, throwing his linebacker shoulders back. He was so confident, so sure she wasn't a threat, that he paid no attention to her fingers groping inside her pocket, struggling to grip her keyring with fingers wet with sweat and blood.

"How is someone like you going to stop me?"

Her fingers fought with the cap to her pepper spray. *Please, damn it!* Then the cap slid off with a satisfying click, and everything inside her stilled.

She looked up at Jack, determination pounding through her like a heartbeat. Strength flooded her limbs until she thought she could tear him apart, if given a chance. "I'm willing to die to save what I love. Are you?"

Uncertainty flickered in his eyes, and she charged at him, throwing all her weight against his massive chest. He grunted, but hardly moved, so unequal was their strength. The bastard was still smiling.

With a Viking battle cry charging from her throat, she aimed a jet of pepper spray toward his face. The cable tie around her wrist prevented a perfect shot, but still Jack screamed and threw his hands over his eyes, dropping his makeshift torch. His bulky body barreled into a cheval mirror, sending both the mirror and man crashing to the ground.

The sound of shattering glass filled her ears, and she dove for one of the sharp shards. On her knees, she frantically sawed through the cable tie around her wrists. When her hands were free, she lunged toward the flaming kindling Jack had dropped on the carpet.

But Jack, his red eyes watering, army-crawled toward her, a mirror fragment clutched in his meaty fist. He slashed wildly at her neck, and she threw up her hands. Glass sliced through her palm.

Pain shot through her like lightning, and she fell, her back crashing against the floor, grasping her hand that was now gushing blood. Jack climbed on top of her, straddling her like a deranged lover, and raised the shard of glass over his head.

Adrenalin raced in her blood, fueling a ferocity that seemed to electrify her. Her hands groped on the floor, then closed around broken glass. With a guttural roar, she swung the jagged shard, stabbing it deep into Jack's thigh. He screamed like a wild, wounded animal. She scrambled from beneath him and jumped to her feet.

Just then Adam, still sprawled on the floor next to the fire, groaned. Both she and Jack swiveled their heads toward him, but Adam lay unmoving, eyes closed. Jack's cold eyes flitted from her to Adam, as if unsure who to attack.

She had to get him away from Adam and Caroline, away from Cliffhaven.

"You'll never get away with this." She stepped back, toward the library door. "I'm going to the police, and you'll spend the rest of your life in a cage."

Then she bolted, and just as she'd hoped, Jack yanked the

glass from his thigh with a pained cry and gave chase. She ran through the darkened corridors with Jack only steps behind, knowing only that she had to keep him running. Away from her family, away from Cliffhaven.

She burst through the back door into the storm that raged outside, running for her life through the dark and blinding snow. The wind roared across Cliffhaven, bending trees until it looked like they would snap in two. The snow lashed sideways, stinging her face, blinding her.

A quick glance behind her revealed Jack, chasing her in a limping sprint, chin tucked, arms pumping, face coldly determined. And she saw her death in those cold, calculating eyes.

She jerked her head forward just in time, skidding to a stop as her feet found the cliff's edge. Before her was a great chasm, a gaping mouth—open and eager to swallow her. At the base of the cliff, hundreds of feet below, black waves crashed against icy rocks.

There was nowhere left to run.

The desire to live, to cling to her life that seemed more precious than ever before, was like a taste in her mouth—thick and desperate.

The rickety stairs to the beach were immediately to her left, treacherous with snow and ice. She stepped onto the rotten wood, clinging to the railing, as the platform beneath her feet groaned and swayed in the violent wind. Her heart pumped in her ears like a particularly fragile clock, ticking out the remaining seconds of her life.

Jack bore down upon her, eyes gleaming like a wolf's in the snowlight, terrifying in his determination. He was ferocious, relentless, a fate impossible to avoid.

He stopped at the cliff's edge, anger and excitement shining in his eyes. Blood seeped through his pant leg, but his face was triumphant. "It's over, Elizabeth."

She crouched, summoning all her strength. "Then come for me."

Jack leapt toward her, and she seized his outstretched arms, using his momentum to swing him toward the railing at the edge of the sea. He crashed against the rickety railing, and a violent splintering sound rent the air.

The stairs jerked, and the rotten wood gave way, pulling away from the metal securing it to the cliff even as Elizabeth leapt for the cliff's edge with all her strength. For a fraction of a second, she flew over the abyss, then the toes of her shoes dug into snow-covered earth, and she fell forward, scrambling across the ground.

She glanced back at the dangerously tilting staircase. With the reflexes of a jungle cat, Jack launched himself toward the cliff's edge just as the staircase fell from under his feet.

He isn't going to make it.

But Jack caught himself, both hands clutching a rocky outcropping at the cliff's edge, his legs dangling off the cliff. The wooden staircase crashed onto the rocks hundreds of feet below with a sickening sound. With a face like murder, Jack strained to pull himself onto solid ground, the monstrous muscles of his arms bulging. Then one hand slipped, and his torso disappeared into the black chasm. The only thing stopping him from plummeting into the abyss was one hand clutching a rock that was wet with snow and ice.

Then he lost his grip.

Jack plunged into the darkness, falling silently, his face a mask of surprised horror. There was no sound as his body hit the rocks below—no scream, no splash. It was as if Jack had just disappeared into the night.

Elizabeth collapsed onto the icy ground. Snow fell onto her upturned face, but she welcomed it. Her breath coming in tortured gasps, she turned her head toward Cliffhaven. A strange orange light flickered through the snowfall, illuminating the night. Even as she squinted, trying to make sense of the glowing orange light, flames burst through the windows of the library. Jack's fire had found fuel, after all.

Adam.

She jumped to her feet, pressing her blood-soaked, wounded hand to her chest. And ran toward the flames.

A man staggered from the back door, and the tall, muscular figure was unmistakable. "Elizabeth!" His roar pierced the night, and it was a desperate, primal cry.

"Adam!" A sob escaped her as she sprinted into his arms.

"Thank God." He held her for a moment, his breath fast and furious in her ear, then he pulled away, eyes raking over her body as if searching for any sign of harm. "You're bleeding!"

"I'm okay." She buried her face in his chest, inhaling the precious scent of him. "I thought you were dead."

"I think he drugged us. Jack." He sounded incredulous. Then his eyes narrowed, and he stepped in front of her, scanning the dark lawn. "Where is he?" His voice was low and predatory.

She tightened her hold on him. "He's gone, Adam—over the cliffs."

He continued to scan the darkness that surrounded them, as if he didn't believe the danger had passed.

"Caroline and Tony," she said, "are they all right?"

"They're fine. Outside, safe."

Flames burst through the library windows, and she moaned. "Cliffhaven! Adam, we have to do something." She moved toward the burning house, but he pulled her back.

"No!" His arms wrapped around her chest. "The library was an inferno by the time I got Caroline out."

Then sirens sang in the distance, and the sound filled her with relief.

"Jack did this?" Adam swept his hand toward the house, his face betraying his confusion. "Why?"

"Copper. There's lots of it, running through Cliffhaven,

across the island. Jack knew, and he gave your parents a fake survey so they wouldn't find out. But, Adam, there's more." Sadness filled her as she rested her hand on his cheek. "Jack started the fire that killed your parents."

"What? But . . . why?"

She shook her head sadly. "It doesn't matter now. What's important is that it wasn't your fault. You were never to blame for the death of your parents."

Adam's eyebrows drew together, as if he were struggling to comprehend this new reality. He looked back at Cliffhaven and sighed, then his face relaxed, like he'd finally set down a heavy burden he'd carried far too long.

He looked back at Elizabeth, then lifted her into his arms, burying his face in her hair. "You're here. That's all that matters."

He kissed her hungrily, even as her body slid down the length of his and her feet rested on the ground again. When their lips parted, he rested his forehead against hers and whispered, "You came back."

"I couldn't leave." He continued to look at her, and she knew he was waiting. "Because I love you, Adam. I love you with everything I have, more than I've ever loved anyone."

He closed his eyes, as if savoring her words like wine. "Then why did you leave?"

"I've always been afraid I would never find a place in the world where I belonged—a place that was home. When I came to Cliffhaven, fell in love with this place and you, it seemed too much to hope that I could ever belong here." She swept her gaze over the graceful lines of the stone mansion. "But that was because I didn't believe in myself. I didn't believe in us." She took his hand. "I do now. And nothing will ever make me doubt again."

"God, I love you," he whispered, his voice breaking. "You

know that everything I own is yours, that I would lay down my life for—"

She stopped his words with a kiss.

As they held each other and whispered words of love and promise, firefighters and the snow battled the flames together. And when the fire died and dawn broke, it was as if the last vestiges of all that had been wrong fell away.

CHAPTER 42

*C*aroline and Tony got everything one hopes for in a summer wedding—skies bluer than robins' eggs, flowers blooming across Cliffhaven in bright pinks and purples, and a balmy breeze wafting over the lake.

Elizabeth sighed with delight as she looked out over Cliffhaven's lawn, decorated for the occasion with rows of white chairs, tents for food and dancing, and canopies of white lace. She'd enjoyed playing hostess for Caroline, planning such a happy event.

"It looks incredible, doesn't it?" she asked, turning to gaze at Adam. He looked wildly handsome in a charcoal-gray linen suit that fit perfectly over his towering frame.

"It does," he said, wrapping one arm around her waist and pulling her close. "I like hosting parties at Cliffhaven, as long as you're by my side."

She tucked one strand of his ebony hair behind his ear as he smiled down at her. "You really don't mind all the people?"

"These are my friends and neighbors, and they're bringing Cliffhaven to life. I'm grateful for them." He arched one eyebrow playfully. "And I'd better get used to the crowds now, before they start flocking here in earnest."

She laughed. "You have months before we open up Cliffhaven to the public."

They stood on the terrace overlooking the lake, watching as a photographer snapped pictures of the newly married couple. Caroline wore summer flowers in her hair and a flowing white dress, while Tony looked slightly dazed and outrageously happy. With one hand, Caroline waved to Elizabeth and Adam; with the other, she cradled the baby bump that was just visible under white satin.

"I can't wait to be an aunt," Elizabeth said, watching Tony dip Caroline and plant a kiss squarely on her lips.

She followed Adam's gaze to her hand, where the elegant emerald ring he'd given her glittered. "You look incredibly happy, Mr. Arrington."

"Why shouldn't I be? All my dreams are coming true." He brought her fingers to his lips and kissed them.

But the sky, aflame with the setting sun, reminded her of other fires, and her face grew somber. "And to think that it was almost stolen from us. All of it."

Her eyes were drawn to the western wing, where the renovations to repair the damage done by the recent fire were well underway.

Adam's jaw tightened. "By people I trusted. Jack."

She sighed. "He's gone, now, anyway."

"And you're here to stay. Aren't you?"

"You doubt it? Even now that I'm wearing your ring?"

"Sometimes I wonder if you'll miss packing up and moving, if you'll get bored staying in one place."

She smiled and shook her head in disbelief. "How can you think that? Everything I've ever wanted is here."

When he still didn't look satisfied, she bit her lip. "And I know now running away won't solve my problems. I have to face them, or they follow me around, dogging my steps until I'm exhausted. And while I was so busy running from the past, there was no time to build the life I wanted. Because I'd been too busy looking over my shoulder, wondering when it would all catch up to me."

"Will you stay?" Adam asked, suddenly serious. He took her hands gently, pulled them to his mouth, and kissed each palm before pressing them to his heart. "I need to hear you say it. Will you stay, now and forever?"

"Yes." Elizabeth's gaze swept over Cliffhaven—the towering cedars, the sapphire sea that stretched past the horizon, and the magnificent house—and she knew she belonged. Smiling, she looked into Adam's emerald eyes. "It is my home, after all."

DEDICATION

For Jeremy, because he believed.

ACKNOWLEDGMENTS

So many people helped make this book the best it could be. Despite their best efforts, I'm sure I messed up somewhere. All mistakes are mine alone (and probably a result of ignoring their sound advice).

To my developmental editor Maria Tureaud, who knew where I'd gone wrong and how to make it right, thank you a thousand times.

For my gorgeous cover, I'd like to thank Maria Spada.

For everything artistic, thanks to Lisa S., who saved me from humiliation many times over. And for where I ignored your good advice to satisfy the whims of plot, please forgive me.

Thanks to everyone at Lilac Lake Press for taking a risk on an unknown author—you know who you are.

Thanks, also, to every beta reader who slogged through early versions of this book, particularly Sue T. and Linda E., who always served their criticism with healthy helpings of love.

And, finally, thanks to every reader, bookseller, librarian, BookTokker, and blogger who does what they do because they truly love books. May your lives be full of beautiful stories.

ABOUT THE AUTHOR

A. M. Grimm resides in Michigan, where she's living out her personal happily-ever-after with her husband and two children.

She writes thrilling stories filled with passion and suspense, but she's also backpacked across Europe, argued the law in front of a jury, hiked in the Alpine mountains, lived in a 16th century Italian villa, and sung opera in a crowded theater.

She adores writing and is most interested in stories about strong women, enlightened men, and the nefarious villains who stand in the way of love.

If you'd like to know more, sign up for her newsletter at AMGrimm.com.

Cliffhaven is her debut novel.

Made in United States
Orlando, FL
15 July 2024

48998690R00211